AFTER THE CRASH

AFTER THE CRASH SERIES BOOK 1

TARA ELLIS

MIKE KRAUS

Tara Ellis
2022

MUONIC
P R E S S

AFTER THE
CRASH
After The Crash Series
Book 1

By
Tara Ellis
Mike Kraus

© 2022 Muonic Press Inc
www.muonic.com

www.facebook.com/TaraEllisAuthor
www.taraellisbooks.com/

www.MikeKrausBooks.com
hello@mikeKrausBooks.com
www.facebook.com/MikeKrausBooks

CONTENTS

WANT MORE AWESOME BOOKS?

Find more fantastic tales right here, at books.to/readmorepa.

～

If you're new to reading Mike Kraus, consider visiting his website (www.mikekrausbooks.com) and signing up for his free newsletter. You'll receive several free books and a sample of his audiobooks, too, just for signing up, you can unsubscribe at any time and you will receive absolutely *no* spam.

～

You can also stay updated on Tara's books by following her Facebook (www.facebook.com/taraellisauthor).

SPECIAL THANKS

Special thanks to my awesome beta team, without whom this book wouldn't be nearly as great.

Thank you!

PROLOGUE

TIM
Yankee Stadium, New York City, NY
Saturday night
Nosebleed Section

THE ROAR of the crowd was deafening as thousands of feet stomped inside Yankee Stadium. It was a tradition so ingrained in New York baseball culture that it was as close to a tribal experience as most city dwellers would ever encounter, except for all of the banners, flashing signs and the blimp hovering over the stadium displaying the symbol of an atom incorporating the acronym "O.N.E."

Tim glanced over nervously at the woman seated beside him, who was shouting a string of insults at the home base ump to voice her displeasure at a call. According to Natia's online dating profile, she was a twenty-eight-year-old Pacific Islander with a biochem degree. She was beautiful - not in a cover-model sort of way, but the exotic stop-and-look kind – *and* intelligent. His favorite combination.

"Can you believe that?" Natia gasped, sitting back down. Her face was flushed and she had a small spot of mustard in the corner of her mouth. The half-eaten hot dog was clutched in her left hand; her cellphone in her right flashing the same symbol as the rest of the displays in the stadium. "And right before the countdown! What a way to go into the seventh inning, huh?"

"Uh, yeah," Tim stammered. It'd been two hours since they met out front, and he was still falling all over himself. In spite of his confidence issues, Tim knew he was a good-looking guy, but that knowledge did nothing for the internal battle that raged every time he got close to a woman he was attracted to.

Eating the last bite of nachos, he dropped the paper holder next to his feet and dug his own phone from the back pocket of his jeans. "How much time is left?" Tim asked, desperate to make some small talk, though as soon as the words left his mouth, he regretted them.

Natia laughed and pointed to the giant screen positioned above the outfield. It, like every other device in the stadium, had the flashing symbol along with a large countdown clock. The screen also showed the news coverage of a man on a stage next to a massive LED board emblazoned with the numbers: 1:58. The acronym O.N.E. was hovering above the time, pulsing with each second that ticked by as if it were a heartbeat. In a way, it was.

The launch of the Operational Networking Enterprise system had been decades in the making, meant to revolutionize computer system interconnectivity from the ground up. Fractured operating systems across public and private sectors would finally be replaced with a streamlined, secure, faster system that would be a boon to practically every industry.

Tim smiled back sheepishly at Natia as he held his own phone up. It displayed the same countdown as every other smart device on the planet. "There's supposed to be a huge firework show from behind the stadium, and the blimp—"

"Look!" Natia yelped, while pointing into the darkened night sky. Though it was less than an hour after sunset, it was dark enough for the advertisement – *Millions of Functions Reduced to O.N.E.* – on the blimp to be clearly seen in the distance. Tim figured they were timing its trajectory to be directly over the stadium when the switch was flipped.

Natia waved her phone while glancing around at the thousands of similar lights flickering throughout the audience. "This whole thing kinda freaks me out. Reminds me of the Matrix, or something."

Tim nodded, turning back to the screen above the field. Twenty seconds. The mastermind of the program, flanked by CEOs and government officials from across dozens of sectors was giving his final speech from Los Angeles.

"Tonight," the man bellowed, raising his hand above his head to the applause of the group of people in attendance at the observatory in California, *"we're turning a new page in the annals of history! An unprecedented era of productivity and security is upon us! Thank you all for joining us on this journey."* He made an exaggerated turn to the countdown clock behind him, then raised his other hand and looked back at the camera. *"Are you all ready for O.N.E.?"*

There was also a spattering of applause in the stadium that turned more enthusiastic as the crowd joined in, chanting the countdown out loud.

"Ten, nine, eight..."

Tim looked over at Natia and made a vow to himself to talk more during the course of the remaining innings. He'd start by telling her how his dad used to take him to the games while growing up.

"Three, two..."

"One!" Tim and Natia shouted with the throng and then smiled at each other. It was hard not to get caught up in some of the excitement.

The screen went dark and all of the lights went out. A hush fell over the crowd as the anticipation grew. The blimp had also blacked out and so when the word H.E.L.L.O. flashed onto the scrolling overhead banner, the billboard, and everyone's phones at the same time, the effect was complete.

Cheers erupted, though Tim and Natia leaned toward each

other instead. "I just want to get back to the game!" she shouted, and the warmth of her breath on his cheek made Tim nervous all over again.

A loud explosion drew more gasps and cheers as a burst of fireworks fanned out over the stadium, right on cue. A second and third round followed closely behind the first, creating a strobe-light effect through the bleachers. But instead of the expected "oohs" and ahhs", Tim heard a growing murmur of disdain and complaints.

"It isn't working!" a woman said from beside Tim. She touched impatiently at the frozen screen of her phone. He glanced upward, and saw that all of the displays looked the same. The symbol was back on them, but the countdown had stopped at 00:00:00 – and were they growing brighter?

"Figures," Natia grumbled, pulling his attention away from the signs. Pointing her cell at him, she confirmed what everyone else was experiencing. "Nothing will open," she explained. "None of the apps, or messenger." Jamming the device back in her pocket, she crossed her arms. "Maybe *now* can we turn the lights on and start the game."

An especially loud explosion made Tim wince, and he turned in time to see one of the industrial-sized firework mortars detonating prematurely. The percussion rocked his body as fire rained down onto the stands positioned under the giant videoboards, across from them in the outfield. People were falling over each other as they scattered away from it and the cheers turned to screams, spreading outward from the accident.

When the dual rows of hundreds of LED stadium floodlights and displays attached above the stands flickered on, the short reprieve from the dark turned to more confusion as they surged to a blinding brilliance before finally exploding into twin blankets of sparks, glass and plastic, arcing out over the stands and ballpark. Tim attempted to shield his eyes with his hands, disoriented by the sensory overload brought on by the lights and sounds. It blended with the fireworks so that it pulsed from all around them, and the smell of sulfur and burning electrical components replaced that of hotdogs and peanuts.

The power was pushed beyond their tolerance and the mechanisms combusted, plunging the stadium into an even more absolute dark. Small bits of glass showered the upper stands and smoke billowed, mixing with the bombardment from the mortars that continued to launch at too-low of an orbit.

The panic was immediate.

Tim reached out to grab at Natia's arm as people began to run into the strobing blackness surging around them. Ignoring the shrapnel from the lights that continued to fall, they jostled their way into the center aisle amid the grunts and cries of fear. Natia was several inches shorter than him, so Tim instinctively pulled her against his chest with one arm, while using the other to clear a path.

Long tongues of flame licked along the edge of the billboards, casting a new kind of light onto the field. It was growing at an alarming rate, twisting and morphing as if a living thing. The moving shapes it revealed looked more like faceless shadows than people.

Thrust against the guardrail by the mob at their backs, Tim's eyes were drawn to the center of the stadium. At first, he wasn't sure what he was seeing. A dark, billowing movement of a semi-solid structure was merging from above with the backlit shadows of the hundreds of people fleeing across the grass. Then the impact reverberated through the stands, and he felt the power transfer as the blimp collided with the ground of the infield, instantly combusting.

The ensuing wall of fire was so intense that Tim's skin was scorched by the heat from where they stood several-hundred feet away. Pain flared along his arms and face, and Natia pressed her own face to his chest in a vain attempt to escape it. Screams of agony and wails of terror also engulfed them, and Tim realized his voice was a part of it.

It was too much. He didn't know what to do. None of it made any sense.

"Run!" Natia shrieked, pulling at his shirt. Her eyes were wide and streaked with tears, highlighting the blisters that were already forming. "We have to run!"

Run

But everyone else was running, too. And with the force of thousands welling up like a wave, they had no choice in where it took them. Blind and gasping in pain, the two of them were dragged along the guardrail until the ground suddenly fell away into an exit aisle, but the cement stairs were unforgiving to anyone that got pushed down. Tim grimaced as he stepped on first a hand, a leg, and then something that might have been a head. His sense of direction became muddied. With Natia clasped to him, they were pushed along with the tide.

Screams, moans, and another explosion. Bodies slammed against them in the darkness, some of them falling as they cried out while fire flared from all around, moving closer. The air thickened as the atmosphere was sucked out to be replaced with toxins and a new sort of smell. That of burning flesh.

It was getting hot.

Which way was down?

Another platform.

They were beneath the grandstand seating. Aside from the bracing, the walls were open to the night, looking out over New York City. Free of the narrow aisle, Tim was finally able to maneuver them through the crowd and toward an exit, but the view made his legs go weak and forced him to stop.

"What's happening?" Natia sobbed, sagging against him.

The sky was on fire, the horizon lit from below by several skyscrapers burning in the distance. Transformers were exploding, sending up cascades of sparks in spectacular displays that fanned out from the parking lot. Smoke churned, mingling with various sources of fire and destruction.

Others in the crowd had slowed to take it in, and the surreal scene only added to the confusion. "Could O.N.E. have done all of this?" a woman gasped.

Tim felt like he'd been punched, and he looked at the woman as they were sucked back into the stream of people stumbling past them, their voices merging into a solid chorus inside his head. Was it possible? Did the catastrophic failures extend beyond the stadium and what they were seeing?

Glimpses of the cascading events flashed between the support columns, obscene images playing out like a stop-action movie as they continued to flee. Traffic had stopped along Interstate 87 and the Harlem River, as far as Tim could see, and what had to be dozens of car accidents dotted the ribbons of cement.

People running between the stalled vehicles in all directions, their cries for help going unanswered.

A train jumped the tracks, slamming into a parking garage that collapsed around it. Burning wreckage spread in its wake, the black billowing smoke engulfing the stadium parking lot like a tsunami, reaching out and threatening to overtake them.

Reaching up to touch his own burned skin, sobbing as he witnessed the death of countless others, Tim compelled his body to keep moving as large sections of lights began blinking out all over the city and into the distance.

Natia had gone silent, but didn't resist as the heat became unbearable ahead of the spreading flames at their backs. Tim coughed against the acrid smoke filling his lungs, and his eyes watered, blurring his vision.

"Mom!" a child shrieked from nearby, her cries blending into the cacophony of agony that was inexplicably growing.

Whatever was unfolding wasn't isolated to the stadium. In spite of his panicked mind, Tim grasped that something terrible had been unleashed upon the city. Perhaps the world.

They broke out into another open space on the ground floor. They were in the Great Hall, a massive entryway with a glass ceiling that was ablaze with the otherworldly light.

"This way," Tim grunted, coughing more aggressively as he pulled Natia through the people moving toward a row of exits.

Mechanized doors slammed down around them as they ran, covering vendor spaces and sealing off side passages. The hollow thuds resonated through the cement floor, like a gavel in a court-room where their fates were being sealed. The smoke continued to thicken in the dark, and the bizarre landscape morphed into a reprisal of hell. They all clamored blindly against each other, tearing at whatever they could grasp while making animal-like sounds in a feral display of desperation.

Nothing was working the way it should. No emergency lighting, alarms, or broadcasted directions on how to exit. Approaching the doors with the frenzied mob, Tim fell against the glass and sobbed in frustration. They weren't opening.

He slid his hands along the glass in the dark until he found the emergency release that pushed the doors partway out, pivoting in the tracks. While it created an opening, it was half of what it should be and he was on the wrong side of it, left pressed against the remaining glass as others plunged through like sand through an hourglass.

Bodies were already piling up and the growing pressure threatened to smother him. It was too late by the time Tim realized his mistake.

Holding onto Natia, the mystery date he'd been too nervous to talk to only minutes before, they fought together for their lives. To not be crushed against the glass by fifty-thousand people still trying to get out.

Another explosion from out in the parking lot shook the building as something of unfathomable size fell from the sky. The flare of super-heated light revealed what Tim already suspected.

Screaming at the vision, Natia thrashed and clawed at the fresh wave of people all headed to the same, inadequate openings. But even as they inched away from the glass, they were pushed back mercilessly into the growing mound of bodies.

Natia was torn away from him.

Tim's lungs spasmed and he struggled to breathe.

"No!" he moaned as he reached for any open space, his fingers splayed in a final plea for something solid. But there was nothing to save him, no one to hear his cries. Tim clasped at the empty air as pain merged with the compression of his chest, then his head. Shoved beneath the surface, his body was pummeled until he no longer knew where he began or the others started as he became a faceless part of the moving mass.

Drawing his last breath, Tim fell into the blessed darkness within his own mind, regretting that he'd never get to tell Natia about his dad.

About growing up in the ballpark.

About how he'd love to go on another date with her.

About a possible future forever changed for all of humanity.

PART I

SATURDAY

Day One

O.N.E.

"I think computer viruses should count as life. I think it says something about human nature that the only form of life we have created so far is purely destructive. We've created life in our own image."
-Stephen Hawking

1

S AGE
Redemption, South Dakota

THE BELL over the entrance to Olson's Diner rang especially loud as someone pushed their way inside with excessive force.

Sage looked up from where she was wiping down a table, already annoyed at whoever caused the old, wooden door to bang open. Her brows furrowed further when she saw the grey-haired man barreling his way toward her. He didn't even have the decency to wipe his muddy boots off.

"Sage!" he shouted, pointing first at her and then the big-screen TV mounted above the one and only pool table in a far corner. "Turn the news on. You'll wanna hear this!"

Sage dropped the bleach-soaked cloth and resisted the urge to brush back the loose strands of her long, black hair. She detested going home smelling like the day-old rag. "You hitting the sauce a little early at Mel's today?" she teased, but went behind the bar to retrieve the remote control.

"Haven't you been paying attention?" the older man snapped. He pulled a wooden chair away from a central table, the legs scraping across the weathered floorboards. "Don't you know what's happening?"

Two of the customers in the restaurant shared knowing looks with Sage as she scooted around their table. By seven in the evening, the Saturday night dinner "rush" was already ebbing, and the remaining locals were all familiar with each other.

Using the remote to flip through the stations, Sage made her way to the table and sat down next to the man. He was often flighty, but his current mood was unusual, even for him. "What's up, Dad?"

"O.N.E.," he lamented, waving a hand in her direction without looking. "Weren't you watching?"

Sage suppressed a sigh. Not *that* again. Her father was a retired computer engineer, and he'd been going on about the flaws in the new computer platform for months. If her mother had still been alive, she would have kicked him out of the house weeks ago. She'd been the mastermind behind the diner, and it was a legacy Sage was proud, if not weary, to carry on. "I was busy pouring coffee, Dad."

Pulling her smart phone from her back pocket, Sage frowned when the screen remained frozen after unlocking it. The home screen image, of the moose head located above the bar, stared mockingly at her. What had she been thinking when she chose that?

"Great," she said, tossing it onto the table next to the remote. "You were right. It's crashed the Internet of all that is, or whatever you call it, and turned our phones into doorstops. Can I get you a burger while the newest generation of computer gurus figure it out?"

A flash of light on the TV drew her attention, and the smile on Sage's face slowly faded as she saw what looked like a scene from a poorly made, under-budget war movie. Except, she was fairly certain she was looking at the LA skyline in the background. "What the—" scrambling for the remote, she turned up the volume while her father remained uncharacteristically silent.

An obviously distraught reporter sat behind a desk, watching the same imagery, supposedly happening in real-time. He pressed a hand to an earpiece and looked back at the camera. *"We just received some footage taken by our sister station, minutes after O.N.E. went live. I don't know what it is, but let's watch it together."*

More jostling camera footage settled on a face Sage didn't recognize, but it caused her father to sit up straight. "That's Michael Balinger," he spat. "The man who created it."

"...a result of a man-made worm being delivered and integrated into a one-hundred qubit, self-learning quantum computer," Balinger was saying.

The video blacked out, and the screen flashed back to the reporter still holding his earpiece, looking rather lost. *"We have growing reports of system-wide failures throughout most of the city, and we'll keep you—"*

The view cut away to yet another studio, apparently a national broadcast that had been picking up on the story out of Los Angeles. A woman and man were seated next to each other, attempting to look more professional, but clearly just as rattled. *"Unfortunately, it doesn't seem to be isolated to California,"* the woman said. *"We're less than ten-minutes now since O.N.E. went live, and already we're receiving reports out of Washington State, Montana, and now parts of New York of similar disturbances in devices and platforms unaffiliated with the...um, program."*

Blocks of color banded across the screen, distorting their features and breaking up the sound. The man looked off-set and back again, his eyes widening. *"We seem to be having some sort of technical problems with our satellite—"*

The image broke apart and then froze. Sage grabbed for the remote and tried changing stations, but found the same garbled view on every channel. Muting it, she met her father's gaze as he finally pivoted on the seat to face her. "Dad, what's going on?"

Ed Olson ran a gnarled hand stricken by arthritis along the edge of his jaw, a gesture he normally reserved for times worthy of serious contemplation. Sage didn't like it. She was much more comfortable when her father was his typical loud and energetic, opinionated self.

"It's a self-learning system," he muttered, staring off somewhere Sage never quite understood. Her father was brilliant, and while she would have likely also scored high on most IQ tests, she would never come close to the capacity he had for math and computational mechanics.

At thirty-eight, Sage had attended college and been married and divorced. No matter what she experienced, she always found herself drawn back to Redemption. After her mother succumbed to cancer four years ago, she was honored to have the diner willed to her. Sage was born and raised in Redemption, and while the tiny town nestled in the Black Hills National Forest of South Dakota had a smaller population than the university she went to, she was proud to call it home.

Finding the likes of Ed Olson there might have seemed an oddity, but the quaint storefronts and large estates surrounding main street housed a few secrets. An old mining town, the secluded and scenic location had slowly accumulated an interesting array of residents from various walks of life.

"Self-learning," Sage repeated. The door chimed, and she waved Mr. Johnson to his normal seat at the bar. "Be there in a minute!" she hollered. She turned her attention back to her father. "I'll admit that I wasn't paying a ton of attention before about all of this, but isn't that similar to the AI thing that was all over the Internet for a while, that you could have conversations with to make it learn?"

"This isn't an AI," Ed corrected. "But when you've got a quantum computer capable of processing and executing commands at a truly infinite rate...I honestly don't know what it could be doing. That has been my concern all along. One of our greatest flaws is having too much confidence in understanding that which we really don't comprehend."

Sage leaned back and mulled over the situation before standing. "Well, since I'm not going to solve this problem sitting here discussing it with you, I may as well go pour some coffee for Mr. Johnson."

The exasperated expression on her father's face shouldn't have made her feel better, but Sage couldn't help it. One of the key differences between her and her dad was the ability—or inability—to let things go. Sage liked living in Redemption because it reduced her world to something manageable. The isolation, limited expectations, and not having WiFi at her house located in the mountains above the town, were the main reasons she didn't suffer anymore from debilitating anxiety. And the irony of her father's career choice had never been lost on her. Or him.

Sage wasn't an advocate for ignoring problems, but she also accepted at a personal level that she couldn't worry about controlling things that were beyond her capability. That kind of mindset was typically shared amongst the residents of Redemption, and contributed to her feelings of belonging. They were her people.

Reaching for the coffee pot, she was trying not to consider the larger implications of the runaway program, when the lights flickered. Pausing, Sage looked outside the large front picture windows, still painted with an Easter mural from earlier in the month. It had been a clear, sunny day and although it only warmed up to a balmy fifty-five degrees, there wasn't anything weather-wise to cause a power issue.

Despite their remote location in the mountainous region, they were only twenty-five miles of maintained roads away from Deadwood. Though its population wasn't a whole lot more than Redemption's at less than two-thousand, the main power line came through there, and was typically pretty solid.

The power surged again, creating an odd brightening of the lights. Sage jumped as a few of the bulbs in the small table lamps burst with a loud popping sound, unable to handle the overload of electricity. Before she could think of how to react, the power cut out, in conjunction with an exploding transformer from outside, and the room was plummeted into a shadowy half-light from the windows.

In the few seconds it took for Sage to find her father in the semi-darkness, the generator kicked in. There was a collective sigh of relief from those inside the diner as the main lights came on, the pre-recorded country music started back up, and a semblance of normalcy returned. Sage was immediately thankful she'd splurged on the hardwired, propane generator the year before.

Her dad was already on the move, scrambling urgently toward the exit. Sage jogged around the bar to intercept him.

"You don't really think the power going out is connected to O.N.E., do you?" she asked as she followed him outside.

Ed hesitated, showing an unusual display of uncertainty for the second time that day. He looked up at the sky, perhaps to gather his thoughts before answering the seemingly innocent, but incredibly loaded question. Finally, he turned to his daughter and reached blindly for her hand, squeezing it tightly with his misshapen fingers when he found it. "We're under attack, Sagie."

Sage didn't try and follow him as he walked away. She knew he was likely headed for City Hall, to talk with his lifelong friend, the mayor. The use of her childhood name had the desired effect though, and she reentered the diner with a feeling of heightened awareness.

While she couldn't control it, Sage also knew that information was empowering, so she would try and collect as much as possible in order to understand whatever was happening, and how it might impact the town. Her phone and TV were useless, but she had a computer in her office. "Back in a minute, guys," she called to her remaining customers and friends. "I'll try and get us some more details on why we're in the dark."

As Sage passed through the bar area, she stopped by the hand-painted sign her mom had made years before, when she was still a child. It often helped to ground her, but that day the play on words didn't sit right and only added to her unease.

Welcome to Redemption...
The Best Place to Be This Side of Heaven.

2

KATHY
Near Las Vegas, Nevada

THE TRUCK HUMMED under and around Kathy Storm as she rolled along interstate 40 two hours southeast of Las Vegas, Nevada. Glancing at the clock on the dash, she gripped the steering wheel and refrained from cussing out loud. Six fifteen at night. There wasn't anything she could do about the time, or the flat tire on her travel trailer that caused her to get such a late start. She'd planned on having her rig tucked away at the campground and herself situated at a slot machine with a drink in hand by four, long before all of the ridiculous hype surrounding the software rollout came to a head. She already regretted her pig-headed decision not to spend another day in the Grand Canyon, which made the current situation all the more frustrating.

Colby moaned and perched his head on top of the center console from his spot in the passenger seat, staring up forlornly at Kathy. The black and white mutt was a rescue dog she'd adopted the year before, and whether it was the Aussie or Terrier in him, he was sometimes too smart for his own good. He was also a pro at picking up on her moods and often kept her in check.

Forcing a smile for the benefit of her co-pilot, Kathy relaxed her grip and eased back into her own seat. "No worries, Colby, my good man," she cooed. "I'm over it. See? I'm perfectly fine with being late and having some computer program crash my new phone." Widening her smile, she blew him a kiss, which he promptly chuffed at before lowering his head back down. There was no fooling the Colbster.

The classic eighties rock blaring from the speakers suddenly cut out, causing Kathy's frown to return. While she'd opted to put money into her older truck instead of buying a new one with all the bells and whistles, she'd broken down and subscribed to a streaming satellite radio service. Her wanderlust often took her through remote locations and having the uninterrupted, endless variety of music at her fingertips was worth the money. Her nose crinkling, Kathy glared at the assortment of tumbleweeds and scrub that filled the desert landscape spreading out to the horizon in every visible direction. They'd passed through Flagstaff, Arizona over a half-hour ago, so that there wasn't much more than dirt between them and Vegas. It was the kind of terrain where they buried the bodies in the crime shows. However, there shouldn't be any issue with the satellite coverage and she couldn't help but wonder if it overlapping with her dead phone was more than a coincidence.

Huffing in a way not dissimilar to Colby, she punched at a button to switch over to the AM/FM radio. It began scanning for stations, though she wasn't confident there was much out there to be found. To her surprise, it hit on one almost immediately.

"...*In addition to blown transformers, we're now getting multiple reports of other systems malfunctioning throughout the city, including traffic lights... appears that it isn't isolated to... and ... as far... ... Los Angeles—*"

"Blown transformers?" Kathy muttered. "What the—"

In the ensuing static, her scowl deepened as she glanced accusingly at the radio and then the ominous, frozen homescreen of her phone. Neither did anything to help lift her spirits. It had been impossible to ignore the malfunctioning phone when the update failed fifteen minutes earlier, as it was positioned prominently in its holder on the dash next to the radio and clock display. Kathy depended on her phone for GPS, but thanks to her somewhat neurotic need to intricately plan out her trips, she had the routes memorized and most of it was on main interstates and highways.

The reason behind the demise of the smartphone was quickly shifting from annoying to worrisome. She wasn't into social media and hadn't paid a whole lot of attention to the theatrics around the updates, but Kathy had heard the whispers of the naysayers and she was coming to understand that something had gone horribly awry with the... program, or whatever O.N.E. was supposed to be.

"I told you months ago that it was a bad idea," she said to Colby, without looking away from the scattered traffic. "And it isn't just because I don't like change. It's about the power and manipulation involved with it. You put too much of it in one place, and you're asking for trouble."

She figured the reporter on the broadcast had to be talking about stuff happening in Los Angeles, as that was where the launch and headquarters for the company heading it up was located. Hopefully Vegas was far enough away so that it wasn't impacted by whatever mayhem had been unleashed.

Kathy eyed the barren hills that surrounded the interstate and then shifted her scrutiny to the large mirror outside her window. As far as foothills went, they didn't amount to much, but it was still enough to block her view of the city of Flagstaff that lay miles behind them, and she suddenly found herself feeling very isolated. Blind. Out of control. And Kathy didn't like being out of control. It was the main reason why, at forty-five, she'd sold her successful veterinary practice in northern California and reduced her world to things that were easily manipulated. Five years later, she had a little cabin tucked away off the grid in a small community, and worked weekends at a very uncomplicated local animal clinic. Kathy reveled in having the ability to follow her wanderlust and travel whenever she wanted with a home on wheels, where everything was literally within arm's reach. She didn't like unknowns.

Leaning over, Kathy ran her fingers soothingly over Colby's head and gave his neck a reassuring scratch. "We'll get to the campground before dark and find out what this mess is all about," she said with more assuredness than she felt. Funny, how having a dog to care for could make you put on a brave face. She'd encountered the phenomenon numerous times with clients during her years of practice, but the knowledge didn't diminish the compulsion for her. Instead, Kathy leaned into the feeling of obligation to her furry friend and used it to help steady her nerves.

They were headed for a truck stop outside Vegas, which was massive and had all the amenities, including a casino, so she wouldn't even have to go into town. She could fuel up, shower, eat, and play some slots before turning in for the night. It was an overnight stop along the way to her next real destination: Zion National Park. After a week of exploring, she would then move on to Yellowstone before heading home. At least, that had been her plan only twenty minutes before. Now, she was just hoping to get information, and the rising pull to be back home where she felt safe was overwhelming. The broken static hissed through the speakers, ebbing and flowing like the rush of the ocean, with indiscernible voices sporadically breaking through.

Settling back into her seat, Kathy pushed her short, strawberry blonde hair away from her face. She was suddenly feeling warm as beads of nervous sweat gathered along her forehead, and her heart beat out a rapid tempo like she'd just finished her morning run. Colby whined and lifted his head, once again picking up on her shift in mood.

A small car flew past, weaving erratically in its lane as it disappeared over the next rise. It reminded Kathy that she wasn't alone out there on the road, but also added to the surreal feeling that was growing and spreading from the pit of her stomach. Things were...

off. Uncharacteristically ignoring Colby, she punched a button to scan for another station.

Nothing but static until the fifth hit.

"*... the only thing clear at this point... O.N.E. creator Michael denies—*"

More static. The scanning resumed. Kathy glanced up from the glowing screen and then gasped in shock as she was forced to brake and swerve around a semi stopped in the middle of the interstate.

"What the—" throwing out a hand to brace Colby like she would for a child, Kathy kept a firm grip on the wheel and resisted the urge to overcompensate and cause her trailer to fishtail. The anti-skid breaks kicked in and the whole vehicle shuddered before she moved her foot to the accelerator and pulled them out of the slide.

Allowing the vehicle and trailer to slow under its own inertia, Kathy controlled her breathing through the adrenaline rush and quickly assessed the road around her. The two lanes were empty of vehicles ahead of her and up to the rise, but there was another truck hauling a boat close on her tail. Her hands shaking, she returned her foot to the gas and cautiously moved back into the right lane. There was a wide shoulder that would allow her to safely pull over and give herself a few minutes to recover. Maybe she'd go throw some flares out for the semi. While she was still contemplating what the right move was, the scanner hit on another transmission. One that overrode any other thoughts she might have had, and made her listen.

Beep...beep...beep...

The three short bursts were followed by one long tone and it was enough to make Kathy forget about everything else for the moment as the truck rolled along a good twenty miles under the speed limit. During her fifty years on the planet, she'd heard the emergency alert enough times to have it elicit the desired response.

"*This is the Emergency Broadcast System, stand by for... not... test... ... warning... shelter in place. Repeat. There has been... ... ... in place immediately and wait for furth—*"

The cold sweat spread to the base of her neck and Kathy reached to rub nervously at the muscles there. She was approaching the crest in the small rise of the road and a green sign announced that the town of Seligman, Arizona was ten miles away. Her eyes shifted to the intense blue sky beyond the sign, and the rising smoke. Seligman had to be where it was coming from.

Her hand froze, pressed into her neck like the claw of a raven clasped desperately on a branch. She was afraid to let go. Her own touch was the only thing keeping her grounded to a thin veil of reality.

Colby barked.

Blinking rapidly, Kathy yanked her hand away and slapped it back onto the steering wheel. "You're right, Colbs," she said, her eyes flicking over to the dog's earnest face and back again to the road. "Freaking out isn't going to help anything."

What in the world was happening? Was that a local or national alert broadcast?

"Transformers," Kathy whispered, leaning forward over the steering wheel while squinting to study the small black plumes rising in the distance. "The guy on the radio said that transformers were blowing." While it was a small relief to figure out what she was likely seeing, it also meant that whatever was causing it went well beyond the borders of Los Angeles.

"That was a shelter in place alert," she said to Colby. Speaking to the dog would help calm them both, and Kathy didn't feel at all funny doing it. She had conversations with her best friend on a regular basis, so it was nothing new. "It's normally issued for some-thing really bad on a big scale, like a hazardous spill, weather event, or attack."

Attack.

Was it possible? If Kathy were a gambling woman, and she was, she'd wager there was more askew than frozen apps and blown power grids. And it was hard to believe a computer program to help organize the internet was to blame.

Where she'd normally feel a certain sense of freedom in the

wide-open space of the desert, Kathy was instead feeling vulnerable. Except at the moment, it appeared even the smallest of towns were susceptible and so maybe stopping right where she was would be the best option. At least until she could get more information.

Aiming for a broader span of shoulder that was quickly approaching, Kathy began to slow as the glaring sun was momentarily blocked and a large shadow drifted over them and across the two lanes of highway. Easing to a stop, her mouth hung open when she craned her neck to look out the windshield and she spotted the source: A fireball was streaking across the sky, heading west toward Vegas.

Throwing her weight into the door, Kathy dropped down from the pickup, ignoring the other two vehicles stopping in the middle of the road nearby. The heat of the day engulfed her, adding to the intensity of the dramatic scene playing out overhead.

It wasn't a meteor or a missile. The wings of an airplane were clearly visible as it tumbled in the midst of an eerie silence. There should have been a horrendous roar: a sound appropriately suitable for the catastrophe and loss of life she was witnessing. Instead, there was a silence that was so much worse, and the wretched sob that escaped around Kathy's fingers as she threw her hands over her mouth did nothing to ease the horror of it.

3

Wes

Baker House, MIT Campus
Cambridge, Massachusetts

WES DUNCAN SAT with his head in his hands. He was utterly, completely and thoroughly screwed.

"What have you done?" Carrie screeched from across the small dorm room, her wail a perfect reflection of Wes's inner voice slamming around inside his head.

"This wasn't Helix," Wes mumbled. His words were muffled by his fingers but he didn't care if Carrie or Steve could understand him. He shouldn't have to say it. They helped create the coding for the worm, so they knew it wasn't capable of causing *any* of the things happening outside their window.

"Facebook and Twitter," Steve croaked. He was openly crying and didn't even bother to wipe the snot from his face since he was too distraught to notice.

Wes peered up at his best friend, his view reduced by his hands to slivers of their shared room and the part of Steve's upper lip that was glistening. Their world was literally falling apart, but all he could seem to focus on was how his buddy needed to blow his nose.

I'm in shock.

Wes lowered his weak attempt at a shield and shook his head, trying to stave off the very real possibility of a mental breakdown.

"Facebook and Twitter," Steve repeated, finally dragging his sleeved arm over his nose and mouth. "It was supposed to freeze the platforms for two hours, just long enough to expose O.N.E.'s vulnerability and crash its stocks, then everything would go back to normal. No harm no foul. That's what you said, Wes. That's what you said!"

Wes flinched at the accusatory tone and struggled to form a cohesive sentence. "This can't be Helix," was the only response he could muster. Standing, he began to pace, which in their shared dormitory amounted to ten steps in either direction. Though one of the nicer buildings at the impressive MIT campus, the room was still small.

A brilliant flash of light pulled his attention to the window, and he paused in mid-stride, mouth open. They were on the third floor of the old six-story brick building, facing the Charles River. It was a magnificent view day or night, except that at the moment it was providing a first-row seat to a level of destruction his brain couldn't wrap itself around. Scattered power poles were burning in the aftermath of the blown transformers, and were easily discernable. But as the cascading infrastructure failure spilled over the river and into the meat of downtown Cambridge, it became one big blur of chaos in the gathering darkness.

Wes swallowed around the growing lump in his throat. The blossoming flames from across the water, based on the location and line-of-site, had to be the Museum of Fine Arts. He wasn't sure why that knowledge suddenly made it all feel more real. Maybe because it was such an iconic building that shared a green space with the legendary Fenway Park. Accepting that it was in the process of being destroyed meant he couldn't deny the unfolding series of events. Or that they were connected, and coordinated, and...*deliberate.*

"No." Wes stumbled backwards until he butted up against the central couch that divided the room. Collapsing onto it, he pointed a hand blindly at the dark laptops sitting on the desk opposite him, under the window. "No!" His voice was edged with hysteria, but the cogs inside his brain were finally settling into a solid pattern of thought. "We all know this can't be Helix. I wrote it. You both helped with the coding. It has to be something else, like a flaw in the original system. Shit," Wes stammered, running a hand over his shaggy brown hair, his eyes wide. "No one really knew *what* would happen when a one-hundred qubit self-learning quantum computer was turned on and given a set of algorithms to follow. It's the whole reason Entangled wanted it shut down!"

"Yeah, well maybe we should ask Mystery Dude for some answers," Steve retorted, his attitude of blame unwavering.

Wes rolled his eyes but let the use of the ridiculous name go. It was an old argument that he didn't have the energy for. Dude was an online name used by the leader of a hacker group called Entangled. They'd first contacted Wes covertly in a chat room the year before, and after feeling him out for several months, finally offered Wes twenty grand to create a worm he later named Helix.

The idea was simple: rebel against the tightening matrix of information control and stick it to the man by disrupting what some were calling the next step in a One World Order. The easiest way to weaken power was by cutting off its flow of money. A quick hack and breach, immediately at the launch of O.N.E., was aimed to decimate its stocks and likely sink the company behind it. Entangled had fed Wes information to help with the creation of Helix that only someone on the inside could have gotten, and then they took care of the "delivery".

Wes had been happy to go along with the propaganda, but the reality was that he could care less about politics or conspiracy theories. His only interest had been in taking out the competition. Himself, Steve, and Carrie had already been working on a similar program before the announcement of O.N.E.'s release. So when the opportunity to knock them out of the game presented itself, in addition to the irony of using the money as a start-up fund for his own tech company, it not only sounded beneficial but... fun.

Fun.

Bile burned the back of his throat. Coughing once, Wes glanced at the frozen, pixelated image on the small TV screen mounted on the wall. The last broadcast had been of a local reporter running through the streets of downtown Cambridge amongst countless car accidents, fires, and people in general freaking out. It was clear enough that several levels of infrastructure were being targeted, but he had no idea of the scope of it. He needed more information, and everything in their room was digital and ran off Wi-Fi, which of course was down, just like their phones. "We need a radio."

"A radio?" Carrie countered. Anger was replacing the fear and her nostrils flared as she pointed a long, narrow finger at him. "What we need is a plan. Because if it *was* Helix, or something that piggy-backed on it, whether it was intentional or not we're in way over our heads." The terror slammed solidly back into place as Carrie realized the ramifications of what she'd said. "Oh—" A hand fluttered to her mouth and she pulled at one of her black braids with the other while pivoting to face Steve. "I can't go to jail. What are we going to do? We have to get out of here!" The two of them had started dating recently, which added a whole other layer to the dynamics of their group friendship, let-alone navigating through their present predicament.

The three of them were all working towards a master's in computer science, though Wes was a couple of years younger than his friends. At twenty, he'd already completed his bachelor's and was being actively recruited by several large tech firms. He'd been called a prodigy by enough professors so that he was coming around to believing them, though he clearly lacked enough common sense to keep him from doing stupid things. This time, it was on a whole other level from the hack he pulled on the FBI fingerprint database his freshman year in high school.

Steve reached for Carrie. "We're not going to jail."

Wes's face involuntarily contorted, his lips twisting as his brows drew together.

Oh, my friend, we are absolutely going to jail.

But Wes's thoughts were sidelined by what Carrie had said, before he spoke the words aloud.

Something piggy-backing on it.

"Of course," Wes muttered. His revelation did nothing to make him feel any better. As he went to retrieve "the" thumb drive from the hiding place behind his bed, his understanding of the potential for an escalating mountain of devastation made it feel like he was walking through wet sand. They'd all seen the same news feed. People were dying. If he was right, a whole lot more people were going to die, and no matter how hard he tried to turn and shift the perspective, he was still responsible.

His face burned and sweat began dripping from his forehead as he bent over and reached behind the headboard. Wes's whole body felt cold...numb, and he fumbled with the simple latch that held the door of the metal case glued to the underside of the wood.

I'm a murderer.

The latch pivoted and the flash drive fell into his hand. A wave of dizziness forced Wes to drop to his butt and then lean against the wall as the edges of his vision greyed. The bile rose with more force, and he lunged forward onto his hands and knees before vomiting onto the hardwood floor.

"Wes?" Carrie squatted down beside him.

"You were right," he sputtered, not bothering to try and convince her that he was okay. Because he wasn't. Hanging his head, he shifted back onto his heels to avoid the mess he'd created. "Entangled. They were using us all along. And I thought I was so clever." Cackling in a way that caused Carrie and Steve to exchange a worried look, he then held the small drive up that contained the original program. "Helix was their trojan horse. I designed it specifically to breach O.N.E.'s system. That was the whole purpose in recruiting me. It was never their goal to just freeze a couple of apps and make a statement. That—" he pointed at the window and the flickering light beyond it, "was what they'd planned to do all along."

Steve jumped to his feet as the implications drove home. "If they created a feed-back loop in a quantum computer of that size with the right execution codes..."

Carrie paled and looked like her dinner might join Wes's on the floor. "They could target pretty much whatever they wanted. Anything that was connected to the internet. They—they're terror- ists. We helped terrorists!"

With the words said out loud, all the cards were on the table and there was no taking it back. Wes didn't know what to do. He didn't know how to fix it. How could he possibly atone for what he'd unwittingly been a part of?

The lights flickered and then went out, plunging them into a darkness that was fitting. And while it should have made Wes feel even more helpless, in a way, he welcomed it. He could hide in the dark. Maybe he could stay there, cowering forever, and no one else would ever know what he'd done and look at him with the hate and loathing he deserved.

"Doesn't the building have a generator?" Steve said as he fumbled around in the dark.

Wes listened to him open and close a couple of drawers before a light clicked on. Wincing, he resisted the urge to demand he turn it off. Wrapping his hand more tightly around the flash drive, Wes knew what the right thing to do was, and it was going to be a lot harder than sitting there in the dark.

Heavy footfalls suddenly hammered down the hallway, echoing through the long corridor as someone started yelling while they ran. "Everyone get to the basement!" a man screamed. He repeated the same message several times as he approached and then passed their closed door. "The basement! There's a shelter in place order and we all need to go to the basement!"

Carrie stood, her fair skin glowing stark in the harsh glare of the flashlight. Pulling again at her braid in a nervous habit, she turned from Wes and took a step toward Steve. "What should we do?"

Steve lowered the light, and his silhouette was highlighted by the orange glow filtering in through the window he was standing in front of. He looked at Wes, his face a camouflage of shadows. "We don't have a—"

Steve's words were abruptly cut off as an odd popping noise coincided with a small hole being punched through the glass of the window. Steve's head snapped sideways and Carrie grunted.

Wes watched in horror as his best friend crumpled silently to the ground, his misshapen head slamming into the wood with a hollow thud. Carrie landed next to him, blocking Wes's view, so that all he could see as the flashlight spun on the floor was the patch of blood spreading out across her chest.

4

DAKOTA
Redemption, South Dakota

"I CAN'T FIX IT, SAM." Seventeen-year-old Dakota Adams leaned against the doorframe and stared into the murky bedroom at her little brother. "Turning your PlayStation on and off isn't going to change the fact that the Wi-Fi is out. The generator is the only reason the lights came back on, so you and your buddies are going to have to wait until later to destroy the alien colonization of Mars."

Making a classic Sam grunt, he dramatically dropped the controller and rolled his eyes with an impressive expression of exasperation for a nine-year-old. "It's not Mars, and they aren't aliens. They're cyborgs, and you used to know that kind of stuff back when you were still cool."

Dakota blinked, uncertain as to whether she should focus on the slam or the backhanded compliment. Deciding neither was important at the moment, she instead pushed away from the wall and motioned for Sam to follow her. "C'mon. I'll get you some dinner. It's already late and you know Dad will give me a hard time if he finds out I didn't feed you, power outage or not."

While she was playing things down for her little brother, Dakota was trying hard not to freak out. It was more than the power. She'd been on a Zoom chat with Becky when it all started. Becky was the best friend she'd been forced to leave behind in San Francisco the year before, when her dad had dragged them all across the country to "start over". Dakota was determined to celebrate O.N.E.'s big debut with Becky, since it had promised to make their late-night talks and constant life updates seamless for the rest of the schoolyear, until they could finally graduate and go to college together.

Dakota replayed the snippets of video in her head as she pulled a pot from the cupboard and began filling it with water. The transformers outside Becky's apartment window had begun exploding right away, but it took several minutes before the single one down at the end of Dakota's rural street blew. Both of their phones froze immediately, and just before the live feed on her laptop cut out, Becky had run back from her window and leaned in close to the camera. She'd never seen her friend so terrified, and her last words hung like some ominous prediction that Dakota couldn't shake.

"Something bad is happening out there, Dax!"

"Mac and cheese *again*?" Sam whined. Dragging one of the tall wooden stools away from the counter, he hopped onto it and slammed his Nintendo Switch down harder than necessary.

Ignoring his complaint, Dakota set the pot on the stove and got the milk and butter from the fridge while eying the handheld device. She hadn't seen the Switch since Sam burned out on it a month after getting it for Christmas. It made her think of the long-running rule of two hours of screen time a day, set by her mom back when Dakota had been thirteen and still really into gaming. The emotions drudged up by the memory temporarily overrode her fear and blindsided Dakota with an intense flash of grief.

Gritting her teeth, her nostrils flared as she breathed through the physical pain in her chest and focused on closing the refrigerator without dropping the gallon of milk. Two years. Two years after the knock at the front door and visit from the police that had changed her life, and she was still a prisoner to the sorrow and raw feelings it evoked.

"Dax?" Sam was sounding more concerned than accusatory, and the nickname used by only the closest people in Dakota's life pulled her back from the brink.

"Are you really going to turn down this cheesy masterpiece?" Shaking the remnants of the past off, Dakota did her best to smile as she faced Sam. "Because I was thinking of adding at least two extra kinds of cheese to it, and maybe even a couple of hot dogs."

"And beans," Sam added, scooting forward eagerly on the stool.

Dakota grimaced while digging around for a can of pork-n-beans, and then added it to the growing pile of goods on the counter. Sometimes her brother was just really weird. He was big for his age, loud, charismatic, and already a ring-leader among his friends in the third grade. Pretty much all the predominant personality traits of their dad.

Dakota, on the other hand, not only got her mother's darker complexion from their distant African heritage, but also her quiet demeanor and inquisitive nature. Where Dakota thought of herself as nerdy and "just average", her mom had always called her extraordinary. She missed that.

Dakota loved her dad, but he was a career military guy who was forced to retire early from the Air Force to take care of them. She got that, and so hadn't fought him about the move to Redemption, where he surprised everyone by taking a job as a county deputy.

It wasn't that Redemption was a bad place, because any other time Dakota would have thought the rugged mountains and small-town life was kinda cool. But going into her senior year, it wasn't even worth the effort to try and fit in there. At least back home she'd already been established as a nobody on the teen food chain. She'd worked hard to create and nurture a small tribe of friends while avoiding the rest. Socializing took way too much effort and a certain amount of role-playing that Dakota simply didn't have in her. She didn't care enough about what the other teens thought, and that was a character trait frowned upon in the current social media-driven world.

Social media.

The irony wasn't lost on Dakota. The same thing she despised in so many ways was also what she relied upon to keep her connected with the friends she'd left behind. Which was why her anxiety was at an all-time high, as thoughts of potential causes for the sudden and abrupt loss of the power and tech tumbled around in her head.

It wasn't isolated to the phones. She'd managed to navigate a few other sites on the internet with her laptop while Becky stepped away from their video chat to see what was going on. Nothing would open. It was like every major platform, or their servers, had crashed. When the failure spread to the power grid, that was when Dakota got scared. It sure seemed like it was all part of the same thing. What that was, she didn't have a clue, and the feeling of help-lessness was growing with each minute. She had to do something. She couldn't just wait and see what happened next.

"We'll have dinner and then ride our bikes to the police station," Dakota announced, having made up her mind.

Sam paused and looked up from the game he'd just started play-ing, his brows furrowed. "Why? I thought you said the power was out 'cause of the transformer that exploded. What's dad gonna do about it?" He shrugged and went back to rapidly pumping the buttons with his thumbs while sticking his tongue out between his lips in earnest concentration. "I don't care, as long as the generator's running."

Wishing she were young again and free from responsibility, Dakota stirred the boiling noodles and tried to come up with a believable reason. Sam didn't have a smart phone and wasn't paying attention to the program launch that day, so as far as he knew it was just a normal power outage. "I ... ah, just want to check in," she fumbled. "You know. Let him know we're okay and ... stuff." Dakota bit her lip. She'd never been good at making stuff up on the fly.

The boiling water became louder in the absence of Sam's

clicking and Dakota turned to find him staring at her. "Why are you acting so weird?"

"I'm not," she countered, stirring more aggressively. She'd have to try and explain it to him, or else he'd become an even bigger pain. "Look, it's not just—" before Dakota could finish the sentence, a familiar chime rang from the back pocket of her jeans, where her phone was tucked away. Relief flooded her as she reached eagerly for it.

Maybe it was all a coincidence after all, and everything would be back to normal. Her wild imagination got her into trouble sometimes, and she was prone to jumping to conclusions. As a smile spread across Dakota's face, a small part of her also worried about how something as simple as a text message notification could wield so much power over her, and elicit such an immediate, emotional reaction. "Pavlov's dog," she muttered, referencing the famous conditioning experiment.

But as she turned the phone over in her hand, her stomach tightened in an even stronger response. She didn't see the expected text message from either her dad or Becky. It wasn't even open to her normal home screen, but was instead cycling through data so fast that Dakota hardly recognized some of it. Pictures, apps, icons, various platforms and snippets of messages, all interspersed with lines of code that were gibberish to her. The phone was getting warm in her hand.

Another familiar tone echoed down the hall from Sam's room. "Yes!" he shouted, jumping down from the stool.

Dakota watched him scurry down the hallway before reaching behind her to turn off the stove. The phone was continuing to heat up. Clenching her jaw, she slowly placed it on the counter next to the Switch, as if it were an unstable stick of dynamite.

The imagery on the screen paused for a moment, just long enough for Dakota to see the familiar hot spot notification before it turned back into a blur of data.

The Switch chimed.

Its paused game disappeared to be replaced by a similar jumble of random pictures and strings of code.

Dakota began to reach for the game, but jumped at the unexpected two-tone motion alert from the doorbell camera. Spinning around, she sought out the display screen that was mounted in a far corner of the kitchen. It was on, though there wasn't anyone at the door. The screen blinked out, then came back on, replaying video from earlier in the day when their dad had left for work. It went dark again, and then flashed on to show footage from the day before. Dakota watched herself walking down the steps before it started rewinding.

Swallowing around a rising lump in her throat, she backed away and then ran from the kitchen. She'd left her laptop on, so Dakota wasn't surprised to find that it was also in a state of what appeared to be some sort of info-dump. Standing at the entrance to her room, she was afraid to go in. She didn't understand the visceral reaction. It was stupid; there was no physical threat. Yet...she couldn't stop the shaking in her hands and the sweat that was working its way through her shirt. It was hard to breathe, and her legs suddenly felt very heavy.

She was afraid.

Pictures, hundreds of them, were scrolling across the screen of the laptop so fast that it was like watching a stop-action movie. It was much faster than her two-year old computer was capable of. Dakota took a step back, her eyes flitting to the window and the gathering dusk beyond it. It felt like she was being watched...like, someone or *something* was erasing everything after learning all it could about her. About them.

"Dax!" Sam shouted, the whine back at full-force. "Something's wrong with my PlayStation!"

Dakota took another step back so that she was in the middle of the hallway. She looked first toward the kitchen, and then back to where her little brother was waiting to have his demands met. She didn't know what to do.

Her left wrist was burning.

"Oh!" she gasped, while throwing her arm out in front of herself and clawing at the Fitbit that was attached there. The small screen was glowing a solid green. Whimpering as she pulled at the strap and let the device fall to the floor, she then rubbed at the skin on the back of her wrist that was already blistering.

As the pain registered, it broke through her paralysis. Dakota ran to her brother's room.

"Come on!" she shouted, ignoring the bursts of info on her brother's TV. "We're going to find Dad."

Sam's face was bunched up, ready for an argument, but when he saw his sister, his whole demeanor changed. His eyes dropped to where she was holding her wrist. "What happened?"

Loud static began hissing from the family room. The giant sixty-five-inch smart TV was also Wi-Fi connected. Dakota couldn't ignore the obvious conclusion.

"My phone..." she muttered, spinning away from her brother.

It was being used as a hot-spot to connect everything through the 5G. She didn't even think it would normally be able to handle that much data all at once, but nothing was making sense at the moment.

Running back to the kitchen, Dakota dove for the junk drawer and pulled out a small hammer normally used for hanging pictures.

"Killing me softly, with your love..."

The music streamed from the Alexa speaker in the family room, which was open to the kitchen. Dakota approached the phone with the hammer as Sam scooted into the room, his mouth hanging open in a surprised O. He turned in a circle, taking in the various sounds from all of the activated devices that were merging together into a loud cacophony, and the sickly artificial light being cast throughout the house from the various screens.

Raising the hammer, Dakota noticed a thin wisp of smoke coiling out from the television, and there was a hot electrical smell that was getting stronger. "It can't hurt us," she whispered, and swung the hammer down.

5

JAMIE
Marsh Fracking Site
Near Redemption, South Dakota

JAMIE PRATT JUMPED down from his 5th wheel as he flung the smoldering phone to the ground. Shaking his hand, he cursed under his breath before kicking the thing once for good measure.

In the gathering darkness, he could see that the screen was still glowing and felt more annoyance. He'd already tried to turn the damn thing off without any luck, and that was before it started back up on its own. Rubbing at the back of his neck as he considered kicking it again, Jamie decided a beer sounded like a better idea. Bringing his hand around to scratch at his beard, his irritation didn't dissipate. It'd been years since he'd let his dark hair get so overgrown, or suffered through an itchy face. He couldn't wait to shave it off in a few weeks. Maybe two beers were in order before turning in for the night.

Mounting the stairs to the spacious trailer, Jamie paused at the top and squinted back at the phone. He assumed it all had something to do with the upgrade, but he'd been so secluded at the remote fracking site for the past month that he'd been totally out of touch with what was happening in the rest of the world. But the countdown on the screen had made it impossible for him not to know when it initiated, and being without cell service for any amount of time made the isolation feel that much more complete.

Going to the fridge, he grabbed the first beer and then glanced at the battery level indicator on the wall. The power went out shortly after the phone froze, though he didn't have a reason to assume the two events were connected. Their power was always sketchy, which was why the main site had a couple of redundancies to prevent a total loss from ever occurring. That would result in catastrophic failures no one ever wanted to experience.

Feeling restless, Jamie went back outside into the refreshing, pine-laden air. It was around seven-thirty and the sun was just starting to set, causing an alpenglow along the crest of craggy mountains jutting up immediately to the west of the clearing. The Black Hills was a beautiful, rugged country where a person could feel the power of nature emanating. A twinge of regret over his occupation crept into his attempt at a Zen moment, and Jamie closed his eyes.

It was relatively quiet, though he could hear some music and a loud conversation from one of the other trailers nestled among the trees, over the constant hum of the nearest wellhead. The operation was privately owned so wasn't nearly as big as most of the ones controlled by the major oil and gas players in the state, but Jamie had to give credit to Bucky Marsh for having a good set-up.

The guy owned several-hundred acres of land, handed down through his family for close to a hundred-and-fifty years. It included the mineral rights, so when he discovered the rich oil field he decided to get in on the fracking boom and put together his own operation.

There were more than a dozen working wellheads, and Jamie was an operator on the newest one going in. They were moving into day three of transporting a million gallons of slick water to pressurize the hole, so the end was in sight. A month of twelve-hour shifts with only a few days off was enough to challenge his stamina. At forty, Jamie wasn't able to pull off as much as he had in his younger years, growing up on the family farm in Wyoming. It'd been a while since he'd had such large callouses on his hands and although he enjoyed working outdoors again, it wasn't the environment he'd normally choose.

While most of the operators lived in trailers housed on the cleared area close to the wells, some of the guys with more permanent positions rented houses in town, or lived in company-owned bungalows. Redemption was only ten miles away and since they relied on tourist income for most of the year, they had some great restaurants.

Jamie would have preferred a small cabin on the outskirts, but being on the site was all a part of the required set-up for his... goals.

The sound of a large truck speeding up the gravel road interrupted his thoughts, and Jamie turned to face the pickup being driven by his friend and co-worker. Carter was a good ten years younger than Jamie, and made a habit of taking trips into town for various reasons. He was never short of an excuse, and that night it had been to pick up some burgers for the two of them.

Jamie was ready to give him a hard time for taking so long, but when he saw how erratically Carter was driving, he took a long pull from the bottle as he frowned. They were on the backside of the oil well platforms, so all other associated traffic used a different road, but they were still mindful and didn't usually act like idiots. Gravel and dirt kicked out and peppered the trailer as Carter slid to a stop, his door opening before he even had the vehicle fully in park.

Carter leaned back inside the truck as Jamie approached, and when he spun around, his smoking cellphone flew from his hand and landed near Jamie's feet. Hopping back a step, he felt a sharp pang of apprehension. He'd assumed the malfunction was isolated to his own phone.

"Things are getting strange, man," Carter snapped. Rubbing his hands together, he then pointed at the road that led to Redemption. "After the phones locked up, all the transformers in town started popping off. Power's out everywhere, and when I say everywhere, I mean *everywhere*."

"That doesn't make any sense," Jamie countered. He shifted his focus to the smoldering phone, his mind spinning. He had a decent understanding of modern technology and even some basic programming, but he couldn't see how it was connected.

"I know it doesn't!" Carter reached into the truck and pulled out a paper bag with grease spots on the bottom. Tossing the food at Jamie, he then grabbed his cowboy hat off the seat and pressed it onto his mop of brown hair. Giving the brim a tug, Carter pointed accusingly at his phone. "Locals at the restaurant said before the satellite feed cut out, news stations were saying all kinds of crazy stuff. Showed video footage of power failures in major cities, traffic systems going down and even what looked like a plane crash! Then my truck started—"

"The satellite feed stopped?" Jamie interrupted. It was a major leap in reason, but there was no denying that the quantum computer was the first of its kind. The opponents to the technology had warned the computer could quickly outsmart the people running it, but how could that translate to blown power grids and failing satellites?

Loud music suddenly blared from inside his trailer, making both men jump. They stared at each other for a moment, and Jamie was the first to move. As he rounded the 5th wheel, the music changed from country to hard rock, and his step faltered. Feeling like a kid entering a funhouse, he peered into the trailer and at the entertainment center. The tuner had been turned off, but was now glowing as the digital display scrolled through various stations and functions. It stopped on another one of the saved selections from his personal playlist. From the bedroom at the front of the trailer, his tablet chimed. He'd been reading something the night before and left it on the stand next to the bed.

He moved back outside without going all the way in and turned to face Carter, who was lingering nervously behind him. "Anything with Wi-Fi capability is being activated," he muttered.

"Yeah," Carter agreed. "I was trying to tell ya that my truck's GPS was wigging out, and was engaging the lane control. Almost forced me off the road a few times."

"Is this someone's idea of a joke?" someone yelled from one of the closest trailers, visible through the scattered trees on the next site over.

"If it is, I wanna have a conversation with 'em!" a man yelled back as other operators began emerging and gathering in the gravel road.

"The well!" Carter grabbed at Jamie's arm and gave it a shake, his eyes wide. "They'll be good for power, but the software that controls the pressure is uplinked for GPS and updates."

They both ran for the truck. It was a short drive to the pad and Jamie braced his hand against the dash as Carter took the narrow road at a dangerous speed. "Kacey's working tonight," Jamie said as they approached the assortment of trucks and water tanks.

"That's good." Carter maneuvered between two tankers and slid to a stop as he kept talking. "He would have immediately cut back production with the power issues per protocol, but he wouldn't have a reason to try and shut down the monitoring system."

The area near the pad was jammed with machinery, semi-trucks, waste-water storage pools, and various equipment trailers. It appeared chaotic but was strictly organized and everything had a purpose. Carter left his door open as he rushed straight for the main platform positioned over the well.

Jamie leapt from the truck and ran after Carter, pushing himself to keep up with the smaller, faster man. Kacey was the Fracmaster and in charge of the site, but Carter was hired specifically to oversee the state-of-the-art downhole communication system comprised of both specialized equipment and software that allowed for minimal downtime and greater safety.

As they approached the wellhead, there was no doubt Carter had been right to be concerned. Operators were bailing from their rigs and running past them as the roar from inside the main pipe reached a deafening pitch. Jamie could feel the ominous vibration moving through the ground under their feet as the pressure built, and he knew a catastrophic failure was imminent.

He grabbed at Carter and pulled them both to a stop. "It's too late!"

Carter tried to shrug him off just as the first explosion ripped through the air and a stream of slickwater erupted like a geyser from a ruptured high-pressure valve less than fifty feet away. Jamie staggered backwards, dragging Carter with him. A second, much larger explosion knocked them to their knees, and Jamie watched with a feeling of helplessness as the five-story high steel-framed platform disappeared inside a massive plume of pressurized water.

6

M*ICHAEL*
Griffith Observatory, Los Angeles, California

"THIRTY-THREE MINUTES!"

Squinting against both the glare of the lowering sun and the mayor's grating voice, Michael Balinger looked up at the woman hovering over him. "What?"

Her eyes darted nervously away from his face and over at his business partner, Alex, before focusing back on Michael again. Her once perfectly styled grey hair and make-up was in disarray and she wiped at her face, further smearing a black streak of mascara. "It's been thirty-three minutes since O.N.E. went live, and I think it's safe to say that in that amount of time, your program has caused more damage than any other recorded natural disaster in LA County." When he only shook his head and went back to typing furiously at his laptop, she grabbed his arm and nearly hauled him off the chair he was on. "You have to stop this!"

"What do you think I'm trying to do?" he yelled back, yanking his arm away. "It's a computer program. It's not like I can shoot it. The phones—"

The sound of a heavy cement brick smashing into the ground from a few feet away cut him off, and Michael looked over to where a large security guard stood. He'd pulled one of the stones from a nearby retaining wall and used it to destroy all of the gathered cellphones.

"That was the last one," the man barked. Gesturing over his shoulder at the chaotic landscape behind him, he then wiped his hands on his jeans while shaking his head. "Though I don't see how it's going to make a difference with what's going on down there."

The view of the LA basin from the cliffside setting of the Griffith Observatory was something Michael normally enjoyed. He'd been driving up to the iconic spot to look at the stars since he was a boy. It held a special meaning for him, which was one of the key reasons he'd chosen the location for the televised launch party.

It was a grand event, even by Hollywood standards. To close the observatory to outside visitors for a whole Saturday afternoon was something only the mayor could accomplish, and the irony was enough to make him grimace.

They'd taken the slight risk of an outdoor venue and it turned out to be a typical late April day in California, with nothing but sun and a comfortable seventy-four degrees. A monstrous ten-by-twenty-foot LED display board that had been erected alongside a stage now sat dark, transformed from an exciting element in the countdown to an ominous reflection of what it had turned into. What exactly that was, Michael could only speculate, but it was enough to break his normally iron clad nerves.

The frozen electronics followed by the escalating infrastructure failures was bad enough, but when the smart devices reactivated and O.N.E. started matrixing, that was when Michael knew they were in even more trouble than anyone could fathom. It was the closest word he could think of to describe the collection, processing, and destruction of data that was happening so fast that it was almost simultaneous.

"Michael…" Alex muttered, squatting down in front of him. He was Michael's best friend, business partner, and co-founder of BalexTech Corp. — in that order. They'd both regretted the awful company name they'd come up with all those years ago, over a half-rack of cheap beer and even cheaper cigars. At the time, the witty combination of their names had made perfect sense.

Ignoring his friend, Michael continued to frantically search for a way to make his own coding work. It was impossible. It shouldn't… *couldn't* be happening. Yet somehow, the isolated and firewalled backdoor system to O.N.E. he'd created was locking him out.

The launch of the much-anticipated Operational Networking Enterprise system was the birth of Michael's brainchild. In the modern world, information and the control of it was equal to power. And although there'd been attempts to prevent his company from holding so much power, there wasn't any precedent by which to fight it. His quantum, self-learning algorithm was the first of its kind.

The source code he wrote for the Natural Language Progression (NLP) software was an upgrade to Microsoft's much-touted GPT-3 self-learning interface and it was supposed to change the world. Only, not in the way that was unfolding.

Alex leaned closer, his face a mix of fear and terror. "What am I going to tell them?"

Michael slammed the top of the useless laptop and looked beyond Alex at the people he was referring to. Most of the two-hundred guests had already left, including the Governor of California and his entourage. That left some other state officials and the media. He'd already told them what he knew, and from what he could see, the reporters had shifted their focus onto the much more dramatic footage of carnage raging across the LA basin.

Like something ripped from an action movie, the city of Los Angeles glowed from countless points of fire, and columns of black smoke were already streaking the sky. From their vantage point of more than a thousand feet, it looked like a miniature live-action set, and was hard to accept as real.

Ignoring Alex's continued pleas, Michael jogged over to the nearest telescope mounted along the edge of the broad observatory platform. He'd used that particular one on many occasions, though rarely in the daylight. Focusing in on the nearest of the fires, Michael confirmed it was a burning power pole that had spread to some nearby trees. Panning out, he then re-centered on downtown LA, where traffic was at a standstill and backing up onto the intersecting highways leading to and away from it. Shifting to the north, he confirmed the road he needed was still clear. It was time to go.

A large explosion suddenly blossomed a couple of miles down the valley, and the percussion reverberated through the hillside. "Oh!" the mayor cried, pointing at the rising mushroom cloud of roiling flames. "That's a transfer station. I'm sure of it! How—" She turned to look at Michael with an incredulous expression. "We *trusted* you." She pointed a finger accusingly at Michael. "It's become aware! You said this couldn't happen. When opponents of this warned of a singularity event, you said it wasn't possible!"

"It's not." Michael motioned for Alex to follow him as he attempted to walk away, but the mayor blocked him. Gritting his teeth, he barely held in a scream. He didn't have time to explain things. *No one* had the time. He had to get to where they housed the computer.

"I already told you and the reporters that this was caused by a highly sophisticated worm. O.N.E. is not an Artificial Intelligence, and this has nothing to do with self-awareness. This isn't about an AI going after us, but our own wanton desire to destroy things. Now, get out of my way so I can shut it down!"

Michael and Alex were supposed to be celebrating as they made the long, solitary drive back down the cliff and to a remote location just outside of town. Not to the large office complex in downtown LA, which everyone assumed was the hub of O.N.E.

There was a case of beer and some very expensive cigars waiting at the site: a small house that sat on top of a large basement, which contained the world's fastest quantum computer. It was roughly the size of two bedrooms, and no one else knew of its undisclosed location. No one.

Alex was jogging to keep up, and he tripped on the edge of the lawn as they entered the large parking area. "What about the kill switch? Why didn't it work?"

"There's foreign coding present." Michael reached the car first, ignoring the Mayor who was still yelling something at him. "It's somehow locked me out. It was probably intended to shut down some functions, like Facebook and Instagram. At worst, it was a sort of self-destruct sequence for O.N.E., but the quantum system has entered into a spiraling feedback-loop. O.N.E. is still doing what it's programmed to do, but under a new directive. It's making computations and executing at an astronomical rate. Completing in minutes what would take an average computer over a thousand years to accomplish."

"It's destroying itself," Alex said, turning back to look up at the sky.

Michael nodded, pulling the drivers-side door open. "Yes. And unfortunately, it considers any technology...anything connected to the internet, as part of that which needs to be destroyed." Looking back at Alex, he motioned for his friend to get in. "We have to go."

The black Tesla Model S was one of the few purchases Michael had made with his substantial earnings, and he was thankful for the speed and maneuverability as they flew along the cliffside road.

It was impossible to ignore the multitude of growing fires that dotted the valley, and the unimaginable loss of life that would be the result if O.N.E. wasn't shut down. With well over a thousand planes coming and going in a day from the international hubs, flying blind through that sort of traffic would inevitably result in a series of wrecks.

"This could be playing out on a multitude of platforms," Alex moaned, his hands pressed to his face in the passenger seat. "The infrastructures of most cities are reliant on networking. Everything from 911 dispatch, to traffic lights, the power grid, subways, water treatment plants. Ahhh..."

Michael glanced over at Alex, alarmed by his breakdown. Everything he said was true, but they had to keep it together until they got to the house and did whatever was necessary to turn the machine off. It could already be too late to stop what it had put into motion.

Alex lowered his hands, revealing a pale complexion and red-rimmed eyes. "If O.N.E. really is in a loop, like you say, and she looks beyond the obvious and targets *everything*?"

"We'll stop it," Michael said simply. That was all they could do.

"Autopilot now engaged."

"What the—" Michael pulled his hands back as the steering wheel began to move on its own, and the gas pedal fell away from his foot as it pressed to the floor. The car sped up.

"Autopilot disengage!" Michael shouted into the air.

No response.

Alex started touching buttons on the intricate screen located on the dash between them. It didn't respond.

"Autopilot disengage!" Michael tried again as new beads of sweat broke out on his forehead.

"Unable to comply," the singsong voice replied.

While the car was capable of some seriously impressive auto-driving abilities, that wasn't how it worked. It couldn't just start—

The console blinked, and the shutdown message Michael came up with himself flashed on: G.O.O.D.B.Y.E.

"It's connected," Michael said, turning to Alex with a look that must have reflected his rapidly growing horror, because Alex immediately started slamming a fist at the car's controls.

As they approached one of the many hairpin curves on Western Canyon Road with damaged guard rails, and marked by a 15-mph sign, the car continued to speed up. Michael tromped his foot on the brake, but it didn't respond.

The view was spectacular as the narrow road dropped away to the canyon floor several hundred feet below. The car wasn't turning.

"It's going to kill us!" Alex wailed as he clawed ineffectively at the locked door.

"No," Michael said. "It's not killing *us*." He felt a strange calmness as he watched the approaching guardrail, marked by the tips of evergreens growing on the side of the cliff. In the last moments he yanked at the emergency brake, but as expected, the powerful engine continued to rev and threw them into an uncontrollable spin.

The Tesla slammed through the railing and, grunting from the impact, Michael then felt a moment of weightlessness. He thought of the computer, humming softly in a basement no one else knew about, working to erase what mankind had been obsessed with since the discovery of electricity.

"It's destroying the technology in the car," he whispered, drawing his final breath.

"It's destroying it all."

7

S AGE
Redemption, South Dakota

SAGE YANKED the electrical cord from the wall, and then took a step back while looking up cautiously at the TV. This was usually the part in the movie where it would keep acting possessed even without the power supply, and given the current situation, she wouldn't have been surprised if that was exactly what happened.

There was a collective sigh of relief from the townspeople gathered behind her as the screen went black, and Sage realized they must have all had similar visions. But the relief didn't last long when the noise of the TV static was replaced by a random rock song, as the restaurants hard-wired stereo system maxed out its volume. Wincing, Sage dropped the cord and spun back around, trying to remember where the stereo was plugged in. Maybe it'd be better to run outside and just shut down the generator.

Sage took a few steps toward the front door, still looking so innocent with its painted Easter bunnies on the glass, but her step faltered when she saw one of the smoking phones scattered on the wooden floor. Killing the generator wouldn't do anything about the battery-powered devices, and the thought of being left in the dark made the whole bizarre situation feel that much worse.

"It's affecting everything with Bluetooth or Wi-Fi capability," Mr. Johnson yelled over the music. The older man was what locals called a "lifer" of Redemption, and although he was well into his eighties, people listened when he talked.

Several of the other residents scattered around the diner nodded in agreement, and Sage could clearly see their expressions of fear rachet up another notch. They'd started showing up within minutes of the blackout, drawn like moths to the light spilling out into the early twilight. Coming together to talk over food and drink during an emergency wasn't something new. It was a long-standing tradition in Redemption, though it was usually during storms, and Olson's Diner had been the hub for over thirty years, long before Sage's mom owned it.

Feeling a certain sense of responsibility for the people staring expectantly at her, she was struggling to find the right words of encouragement when suddenly, everything stopped at once. The music cut out, the phones fell silent, the register stopped chiming, and an assortment of other unknown electronics all went dark.

In the vacuum the noise left behind, there was a moment of expectant tension as everyone froze. Sage held her breath, certain the crescendo-like apprehension she was experiencing meant something greater and more menacing was about to implode.

When nothing happened, everyone started talking at once.

"Maybe it's an EMP—"

"Like from a solar flare?"

"All of these phones are fried." A woman squatted and touched one of the black screens, dropped only minutes before with the others. "It's hot."

"My wife said this is all being caused by the computers. They said so on the news, before it stopped," a man Sage didn't know sputtered. Probably a vacationer.

"Then how do we really know? Maybe it's a cyber-attack," Mr. Johnson said with certainty, nodding.

"Nah," Old Gus countered. He was Johnson's best friend and used to be the town's constable, back in the day. They were both permanent features at the bar top. "It's gotta be one of those EMP's from a nuclear detonation. Probably the Russians."

"Hey!" Sage shouted over the din while waving both of her hands in the air. The door chimed as the small crowd shifted its attention to her, and Sage saw yet another family was entering hesitantly, like refugees from an unknown battle. "Why don't you all find somewhere to sit and I'll put on some fresh coffee. My dad's out gathering information right now, so I'm sure we'll have some answers soon."

Mr. Johnson leaned back on a bar stool and wiped at his nose. "You got any more of those stuffed tator skins left? Those could take a man's mind off of things for a while." He shared a wink with Gus who grudgingly complied and sat back down beside him.

Appreciating the laughter and break in tension his comment caused, Sage smiled and reached out to pat his arm as she passed. "I think I can manage that."

Glancing up at the old-style clock over the bar as she passed under it, she was shocked to see that it was only seven forty. Less than an hour since the power went out, and only a half-hour or so since her dad ran out. It felt like a whole day had passed, and Sage was already emotionally exhausted. Her laptop had been as useless as her phone, so other than the obvious and daunting connection between the failed apps and possessed electronics, she was in the dark just like everyone else.

A fresh rush of anxiety compelled her to take a detour to her office and confirm that nothing was burning. The laptop on her desk was warm under her hands when Sage lifted it up, and as she turned it over, she saw where the plastic was charred. Something in its guts had gone critical, but whatever process caused it appeared to be done. Crossing with it to a back door, Sage stepped outside and placed it several feet away from the building in the graveled parking area behind the restaurant. She'd collect all the cell phones, too. No point in taking any chances.

The fresh air helped to clear her head, and looking up, Sage saw the first stars of the night winking to life. The dark-colored pines that gave the hills their name covered the mountain range that rose steeply to the west. Letting her gaze drop down to them, Sage pictured herself home and safe in her cabin where she didn't have to worry about anyone else.

Let the world fall apart. Up there, it didn't matter. Nothing else did.

The lure was so strong that Sage closed her eyes and had to take several deep breaths before stepping back inside. That kind of mindset was what led her down a dark path before, and she knew that the next step would be finding a bottle to take with her. Because the only way to *really* numb her feelings to the point of not caring was with a little help from an old, wicked friend she'd left behind before returning home.

"Sage?" a woman said softly.

Jumping at the familiar voice, Sage spun around, her face red with shame from even entertaining the idea. She thought she was stronger than that, and the realization she wasn't, scared Sage more than anything some rampant computer program could throw at her.

Lisa stood holding two large cups of coffee, the sleeves bearing the cute moose-head design they'd come up with together. Her best friend owned the solitary coffee stand in town and while Lisa and her husband had only moved there a couple years ago, it was like they'd always been friends. They'd met over coffee in Sage's restaurant while Lisa had been in Redemption on vacation, and it was what started the conversation about needing decent coffee in the active tourist area. The rest was history.

"You okay?" Lisa asked, holding the latte out.

Thankfully taking the drink, Sage averted her eyes while nodding. Caffeine was her vice of choice nowadays. "You close early?" Once spring hit, between the tourists and oil workers, there were enough customers for Lisa to stay open until eight on the weekends.

"Yeah," Lisa said absently, taking a step closer. "Generator ran out of gas and then the electronics started freaking out. But forget about coffee, Sage. What the hell is going on? I saw your dad running down the street twenty-some minutes ago. *Running.* Cam stopped by with the kids and said things are shutting down everywhere. That we're like...totally cut off right now."

Sage took a long sip and closed her eyes. "Um-hmm."

"Did I mention your dad was *running*?"

Sage opened her eyes and studied the deep creases of worry on her friend's younger face. She was normally an annoyingly upbeat person.

Yup. Not a dream.

Taking a steadying breath, Sage steeled herself to face reality and be the voice of reason. "Dad's been going on about O.N.E. for the past few months, so now he's convinced this is all somehow a result of the program flipping out. Honestly, I don't know what's worse: his being right or wrong. Where's Cam now?" Sage pressed, referring to Lisa's husband.

"I told him to meet me here after he stopped to check on the house," Lisa said, waving a hand like she was swatting at a fly. "Don't change the subject. What does your dad think?"

Shrugging, Sage maneuvered her way around Lisa and headed into the kitchen. She'd sent the cook and only waitress home when the power failed, and she had a feeling she was going to soon regret it. The sound of people talking animatedly from the dining area was getting louder, and she was afraid to look and see how many townspeople were there.

Opening the walk-in freezer, she spoke over her shoulder to Lisa as she reached in for the tray of homemade stuffed potato skins. "We saw a news report before everything shut down, and the guy who created the program was saying something about a worm, or a virus, or whatever— and Dad was...pretty worried."

Sage stepped out and slammed the freezer shut, but found Lisa blocking her way to the deep fryers. "So, we're talking something like the whole Y2K debacle, only a couple of decades late?" Lisa speculated.

"Maybe..." Sage frowned, thinking back over how her dad said they were under attack. It hadn't been until her phone reactivated and started accessing everything around her that she'd gotten scared. Scared that her dad was right.

In her restaurant, a fried television set and laptop wasn't a big deal. But in a large city where pretty much everything was online and dependent on it to function, the scope of what that could lead to was something she couldn't even fathom.

Setting the coffee down, she surprised Lisa by taking her free hand and giving it a squeeze. "If we're lucky, that's all it is."

The front door chimed again, and several voices called out greetings to the new arrivals. Lisa glanced through the small opening between the kitchen and bar and gasped when she saw the size of the crowd. Shaking her head, she gave Sage's hand a quick squeeze back before setting her own cup down and reaching for an apron. "I can't in good conscience allow you to make the coffee."

Thankful she wasn't alone, Sage paused for a moment, watching Lisa move about the kitchen with purpose. The contrast to her thoughts from only moments earlier was striking, and a firm reminder as to why she'd returned to Redemption.

It was easy to be alone. It was easy to get drunk and pretend life didn't hurt. To get to a point where you'd forget you were afraid. But it was also a lie and a miserable way to exist.

To really live, you had to *feel*. To let your guard down and allow people in. In Redemption, Sage had family. She had friends and a community that came together when things got rough, like they were this night. The town had its fair share of trouble and even some secrets, but like with any family you had to sometimes over-look the bad to get to the good.

The door chimed again, and someone called out her name.

It was going to be a long night.

8

KATHY
Near Las Vegas, Nevada

KATHY CLIMBED up into her idling truck and slammed the door. The cool air blowing from the vents was a blessed relief against her burning skin and she closed her eyes for a minute. She had to think. To collect her thoughts and attempt to make any kind of sense out of what was coming down around her.

Colby licked her hand as soon as she set it on the center console. The gentle touch was almost enough to unnerve her, and Kathy responded by opening her eyes and moving her hand to place it on his head. Wiping at her eyes with the other hand, she leaned over and kissed the dog's face. She refused to cry again. She had to keep it together and get them home where they'd be safe.

Safe.

Kathy chortled, and Colby raised his ears and cocked his head questioningly at her. "I'm good," she said to the dog with little conviction. "Just a little shook up. It's not every day you see a plane crash and have your own technology turn on you."

She'd never experienced such a feeling of helplessness as when she'd watched the airplane fall to the Earth, though there was nothing to be done about it. It went down at least fifty miles away, and there wouldn't be anything left to save, anyway. Reaching up to nervously tuck some stray hair behind her ear, Kathy glanced outside at the other observers still milling about.

They were all likely in a state of shock, but some had certainly taken the whole situation better than others. The truck hauling the boat had left in a hurry before the mushroom-shaped plume of smoke and fire had even begun to dissipate. It had taken several minutes of stunned horror before those remaining in the other two vehicles began talking to Kathy, and she learned more from them about what had been transpiring while being removed from it all on an isolated desert highway.

Kathy compared her own experience with that of a husband and wife traveling to the coast, and a lone man also going to Vegas. It didn't take long to determine a few critical pieces of information.

"Everything stopped, Colbs," Kathy said, scratching the dog's neck. "It wasn't just my phone. It happened to everyone. Well, all the people out there, anyway." She gestured out the window to the three people who'd been joined by a group in another car and a truck that was pulling up. "One of 'em heard on the radio before it cut out that power grids are down all over the country. And that—" she pointed to the windshield and the dark smoke spreading out along the horizon from both the fires in the distant town and the plane crash. "I'm thinking that has something to do with what caused our electronics to suddenly wig out."

Her phone lay in the dirt on the shoulder of the road, where she'd thrown it after it started smoking. The truck's radio wasn't far from it, smashed against some rocks. Kathy had spent enough on it that she'd opted to get a stereo system that was removable to prevent theft, so it'd been easy enough to pull it out.

While watching the plane crash, the shorting-out electronics didn't seem that important. But as she sat there staring at the hole in her dash, Kathy's confusion was snowballing.

Setting her elbows on the steering wheel, she clasped her head in her hands before rubbing roughly at her face. "I'm not going to figure anything out sitting here," she mumbled through her fingers.

Making up her mind, Kathy twisted in her seat and reached into the back of the quad cab. Grunting with satisfaction, she hauled a large road atlas up into her lap. While the GPS on the phone was a no-brainer, she was still old school enough that she liked to look at a physical map while plotting her trips. Kathy had always kept a current atlas in her vehicle since she'd been a teen and her dad had required it before letting her go on any trips. More than once, it had helped her with some of the more obscure roads and sections of state and federal parks.

"Here," she said aloud after studying it briefly. Turning the soft-covered book to show Colby, she tapped her finger at the page. "There's a big rest area that I'd guess is about five miles away, before the next town. We can stop there and figure out what the hell is going on, and the best way to get us home."

Shifting in his dog bed on the passenger seat, Colby chuffed with apparent approval and smacked his jowls. His haunches were quivering and he moved his front paws in an alternating pattern of what Kathy knew was a display of angst.

"Don't worry, bud," she cooed. The empathetic dog was going to need a lot more attention and reassurance than she could give him at the moment, and she couldn't wait until they could curl up together on the small bed in the trailer once they got settled somewhere. They both needed it.

A sudden banging at her window made Kathy jump, and she turned to find the husband and wife huddled next to her truck. She didn't like their expressions. With growing apprehension, she rolled the window down.

"That last truck that stopped has a CB," he rushed without any preamble. "Guy says that plane went down outside of Vegas, and... that it's not the only one."

"Define, 'not the only one'," Kathy said, resisting the urge to look again at the black smoke.

The man glanced anxiously at his wife while shifting back and forth on the balls of his feet. "He said the reports are coming from all over. Could be every major airport, but it's impossible to know for sure because it's all just a jumble of word-of-mouth since basically every other form of communication is out."

"This all has to be connected," Kathy said hollowly, unable to process the information and come up with the appropriate emotional response. It was too much.

The man took a step back as he nodded in agreement. Pulling at his wife's hand, he was clearly eager to leave. "Power grids, communication, satellites and planes. It's coordinated. It has to be."

Kathy mulled the information over and couldn't find a reason to disagree. "And the electronics? Is this some sort of cyber-attack? I mean, I don't even know how something like that would work. Maybe it's one of those electronic pulse things from the sun. A massive power-surge might do it; don't you think?"

The man shook his head. "No. It's coordinated. It's happening in steps, so this isn't a random act of nature. I'm sorry, we wish you well but we've gotta go. I have to try and get our car started so we can get home to our kids."

The couple scurried away toward their vehicle, left in the far lane of the highway.

Kathy wasn't sure why she found herself looking for ways to convince herself it was a natural disaster. It wouldn't make it all any less dangerous, though it would definitely feel less...sinister.

How could a stupid internet platform be responsible for taking out satellites? For taking over her phone and radio, and—

Her eyes narrowed as she thought about the stopped semi, erratic drivers, and the newer model BMW owned by the couple, that acted up at the same time as the rest of the electronics. If airplanes could be knocked from the sky, then what else was 'it' capable of?

As Kathy stared out her open window, the sound of an

approaching vehicle drew her attention back down the long stretch of highway. It was a semi, and it was approaching much faster than it should have been.

"Get out of the road!" Kathy shouted, scrambling to open her door. As her feet hit the ground and the distant rumble grew louder, she yelled back into the truck. "Come, Colby!"

Blindly reaching to scoop Colby up as he landed near her feet, Kathy quickly assessed the roadway. There were the three smaller cars and one pickup, and all but the BMW with the couple already inside were near her, in the right lane. The other man she'd spoken to earlier was leaning in through an open driver's-side window of the truck. He was chatting with someone, and he stopped to look up at her before startling, and then searching around to find the source of the revving engine. It was going to be too late.

"Run!" Kathy screamed, as she stumbled around the front of her truck. Colby wasn't a large dog, but it was still a struggle to navigate while carrying his forty-five pounds. Her foot slipped on the loose gravel of the steep embankment beyond the shoulder, and she sat down hard. Letting out a grunt of pain and frustration, Kathy slid the five feet to the bottom while hugging Colby against her chest protectively.

Throwing her back against the opposing hillside, she spun around to face the highway just as the first collision shook the ground.

There was no sound of braking, or any sign of an attempt to stop. Just the roar of the eighteen-wheeler as it bore down on them.

It plowed into the BMW first, and Kathy was far enough away so that she saw the carnage from her lowered viewpoint. Time slowed down, and she heard her own ragged breaths mixed with feral-like sounds as the scene played out in agonizing detail that would forever haunt her dreams.

A disfigured clump of metal cleaved away from the semi, and what was left of the BMW slammed into the truck where the man had been standing only a moment before. The semi continued on to strike the other car at the front of those stopped in the right lane, shearing off the front of the sedan before flying over and off the shoulder, landing in the ditch on its side.

Someone was yelling as they ran toward her. Kathy could see and hear the man, but in her hyper-focused state was having a hard time discerning the different sounds as they merged together, much like the vehicles. They'd become malleable; everything. Time, sound, her surroundings, and the metal that was claiming the lives of those it once protected.

His silhouette grew as the man leapt down the embankment, and Kathy understood his terror when she saw the road behind him. The truck hit by the BMW was still moving, spewing sparks while emitting a high-pitched scream of tormented steel as it barreled down on them.

Her trailer stopped it. The implosion was catastrophic and shoved her truck forward several feet, stopping just short of the edge. Below it, Kathy sat huddled with Colby and a stranger whose face she'd never forget.

And in that single point in time, beyond anything else that had happened, Kathy knew her life was forever changed.

9

W^{ES}

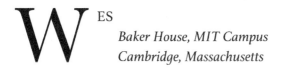

Baker House, MIT Campus
Cambridge, Massachusetts

"I'M SORRY, I'm sorry, I'm sorry," Wes muttered like he was chanting some distorted mantra meant to bring back the dead. Because Carrie was dead. Carrie and Steve were both dead and it was his fault.

Moaning, Wes rocked in rhythm with the words while keeping his hands pressed against the wound on Carrie's chest. It had only bled for a few minutes. Her head lay limply in his lap, her lifeless and accusing eyes staring up at him. "I... I'm—" The words hissed through his clenched teeth as he grappled with his raging emotions.

He'd lost track of time. Had he been blabbering, incapacitated by shock and fear for minutes? An hour? It was most likely somewhere in between, since the blood on his hands was congealed but not yet dry.

Wes jerked upright and yanked his hands away as if he'd realized for the first time what he was doing. What he was touching...*who* he was touching. Blinking rapidly, he held his hands out in the shadowy light cast by the single flashlight on the floor. Fingers splayed, he forced himself to look at the evidence. The pressure against his thigh became unbearable and he scooted backwards awkwardly, shuffling frantically until Carrie's head slid free to smack onto the wooden floor.

The sound made him freeze, and Wes's face twisted in a grimace full of shame and horror. Flexing his fingers, he slowly reached down and touched the pallid skin of her cheek. It had grown cold.

It became hard to breathe.

They're dead!

The thought caused a spastic reaction, and Wes balled his hands into fists and rocked back onto his heels, squeezing his eyes shut. He couldn't bring himself to look at Steve. The memory of his distorted head snapping back paralyzed Wes, but it also gave him a thin strand of something else to focus his thoughts on.

He'd been shot. Steve was shot in the head, and Carrie in the chest. Possibly by the same bullet. Was that even possible? Would it have to be two separate shots? Wes didn't remember hearing anything other than a single popping sound.

Wes's analytical mind clung to the lifeline of critical thinking, tossed into the dark pit of his panic.

He forced himself to open his eyes and look up at the window. An orange glow still flicked beyond it against the night sky, and he could clearly see a single, small hole silhouetted there.

They were on the third floor, facing a river with nothing between them but a couple of roads and grass. Confused, Wes's breathing leveled out as he worked the problem.

No way it was a random act of violence. They were targeted; being eliminated. It had to be Entangled. Were they covering their tracks? No. They were making sure the one person who could stop the process was out of the equation.

The cafeteria.

Wes considered the outcropping that housed it. The old, artistically designed dormitory was famous for its architecture. The main structure itself was shaped like a wave so that all of the rooms faced the river, but there was a two-story cafeteria nestled in the middle. If someone were to say... go onto the *roof* of that building, they might have the right view and angle to make the shot. At least, in a spy-movie with professional hitmen, they would.

Wes surprised himself with a hysterical-sounding burst of laughter, and he slapped a hand over his mouth. He had to keep it together, otherwise he was as good as dead.

If the shot came from someone on top of the cafeteria, that meant they were inside the dorm. They had access. Wes pivoted to look at the door as a fresh burst of adrenaline dumped into his veins. It caused a new level of fear to course through his body. A primal response reserved only for the hunted.

His senses sharpened, and his pupils must have dilated because the outline of the door grew sharper as the coppery stench of blood became overwhelming. He had to get away.

Coward!

Flinching at his own recrimination, Wes carefully picked up the flash drive he'd dropped near his feet. It contained Helix, and was the only possible reason he and his friends would be targeted for assassination. Clasping it tightly, he then jammed it deep into his jeans pocket. He couldn't let them catch him.

Coward! You didn't even try to help Carrie!

"I couldn't," Wes gasped, turning away from the bodies of his friends. "There was nothing I could do." Touching the thin outline in his pocket, he clenched his teeth together. It wasn't about saving himself, but getting the information to the right place to try and stop Entangled. That was the only form of atonement he could ever hope for.

He had to get out of the building.

Why hadn't they come to finish him off yet?

Staring again at the door, Wes envisioned it bursting open any moment, and his heart slammed in his chest hard enough to hurt.

Why were they waiting? Did they think he'd been the one shot and the job was already done?

They want to make it clean.

Wes nodded in agreement with himself. The whole point would be to make him disappear and not give anyone a reason to suspect his involvement and go digging through his work. Drawing attention to Wes by a full-out assault on a college dorm was the last thing Entangled would want. He imagined there'd be a clean-up crew standing by to make things look kosher when they were...done.

Wes couldn't believe what he was imagining. Was he being ridiculous? Paranoid?

His eyes flickered over to where Carrie and Steve lay. He swallowed painfully. No. He wasn't overreacting.

Crawling across the floor to avoid the window, Wes stopped at his closet to pull on his tennis shoes and felt around until he found his backpack. It wasn't the one he took to classes, but wore when he went home. It had his hiking essentials in it and a change of clothes he'd failed to wash since the last trip. Unzipping an outside pocket, he removed his smaller utility knife. The blade seemed heavily inadequate, but it was easy to handle, and clipped quickly to one of the belt loops on his jeans. While Wes had a slight build and excelled in math instead of football, he'd always had a natural athleticism and was known to fight back when pushed into a corner. And he was currently in the biggest corner of his life.

Shrugging awkwardly into the pack while crouched on the floor, he then cautiously reached up to scoop his keycard off an end table. It was the only way to move around the building, although he didn't know if the doors would still work with the electricity being out. He imagined they were magnetized mechanisms with their own internal batteries that would still operate without an external power source.

Huddled by the door, Wes gripped the card with both hands and tapped it against his forehead. He was on the third floor, without a balcony, and only one door in or out of the room. There was a good chance someone would be waiting somewhere to pick him off...possibly in the hallway, but it was only a matter of time before they came for him. Even if he was the only target and they thought they'd already shot him, someone would come to confirm it and look for any trace of Helix. They couldn't risk the original worm getting away from them.

His plan was simple: get down to the sublevel. His bike was stored there, and it would be a good way to navigate the blocked roads and slip out under the cover of night.

He had to move.

Taking three rapid, deep breaths, Wes wrapped his hand around the doorknob and yanked it open. He was so intent on getting through the opening as fast as possible, that he slammed his hip into the frame as he sprang up into a crouch and lunged forward.

Cursing as he fell sideways, a bullet punched into the wood where his head had just been, and then another thunked into the heavy door as it swung shut behind him.

Stunned, Wes whimpered as he pushed up off the floor and staggered to his feet. Even though there were two cooling bodies lying in his dorm, having the whole diabolical plot in his head confirmed was a lot to take in.

The stairwell. He had to get to the stairwell.

It was darker in the hallway, with only a few emergency lights scattered along the narrow corridor to mark the way. Combined with the heavy silence, it was like walking through a catacomb deep underground, and Wes couldn't shake off the feeling as he lurched to his right.

There was a stairway located at either end and he chose the one that would let out closest to where the bikes were kept. Flinching at the loud noise his feet made as he ran, Wes expected a bullet to hit him in the back and was surprised when it didn't immediately happen.

Gaining speed, empty dorm rooms slipped by, the occupants having evacuated to the basement as ordered. Wes concentrated on the door at the end of the hall. He could see it. He was going to make it.

He was less than ten feet away when it began to open.

It swung inward with enough force to make it bounce off the

wall, and a dark figure lunged through, silhouetted by a red exit sign behind him. As Wes went into a feet-first slide, he heard a similar sound from the other end of the hall.

There were two of them.

Hands flailing, Wes grunted as he slammed into the man's legs and he fell on top of him. The guy was big, dressed in black, and cursed with a very New York accent as Wes's momentum carried them into the wall and a gun clattered as it spun across the floor.

The first punch was near his right kidney.

Fight back!

Hot breath near his face. Wes struggled under the weight of his attacker to free his arms.

The second punch caught his lower jaw and veered off into his throat, the pain blossoming through his Adam's apple and making him gag.

Rapid footfalls from the far end of the hall.

The weight on his chest shifted as his attacker pushed away. He was going for the gun that lay nearby.

Fight!

Wes sucked in air around his throbbing throat and frantically grabbed for the man's leg as he twisted his body. He was too big. He wasn't going to be able to stop him.

The door swung back and hit against Wes's back.

He was so close. He clung frantically to the assassin's foot.

The knife.

Making small guttural sounds, Wes grasped the knife at his waist and released the four-inch blade. Rolling toward the man's outstretched leg, he lashed out and cut through the tendon at the lower back of his exposed calf. As the hitman roared in pain and floundered around to reach for the wound, Wes slapped his hand over the pistol.

It all happened in a matter of seconds, slowed down by his state of terror. So when Wes dove backward into the stairwell amid the scream of pain from his hobbled assailant, he was surprised to see the other man was only halfway down the hallway.

A buzzing sound was punctuated by shards of concrete exploding off the wall behind him before the door shut. Ducking instinctively, Wes ignored the fresh sting as a piece of cement cut his cheek. He cradled the gun, made heavier by a bulky silencer attached to it.

Without slowing, Wes leapt onto the stairs and went up instead of down. It wasn't a conscious decision, but an action spurred by pure intuition.

They'll be waiting for me at the bottom.

Of course they would. If they'd gone to this much trouble, someone would be watching the exits. He'd have to outsmart them if he was going to live.

He was going to the roof.

It would be unexpected, and he would have the advantage. Gripping the weapon, he could hope that being armed might make them more hesitant, and it was unlikely they knew he was an avid hunter back home.

Thoughts of the late-night parties spent under the stars on the roof helped distract him from the burning in his legs as Wes climbed through the darkness.

The sound of the door opening from below him spurred him on. Pounding feet echoed. He focused instead on the layout of the roof, and his destination at the south end: beyond the card tables and tiki candles that Carrie insisted on having. He could still hear her laughter.

Wes's step faltered. Carrie was gone, Steve was gone, but his family wasn't. Wes could still help his parents and younger brothers. He slid his free hand to pat at his pocket as he shouldered the roof door open and stepped out into the cool night air.

The only way to protect his family was to stay alive. To get the Helix code to the right person.

The expansive roof lay before Wes like an oversized football field, and he sprinted onto it in a way he'd never thought he was capable of.

Eighty yards.

Sirens rang in the distance, punctuated by numerous car horns and people yelling. Flames rose from the museum across the river, adding to the surreal landscape that looked as if he'd already been thrown into hell to suffer for his part in it.

Sixty yards.

There was a metallic clang as the rooftop door opened.

Wes didn't look back.

The roof was dotted with various vents, piping, and massive air conditioning units that he dodged between while plunging ahead.

Forty yards.

A bullet sparked off a pipe near his head. Wes veered the other way, knowing it was only a matter of timing and luck that the next one wouldn't be in the back of his skull.

They had to be using silencers, because all he heard was a muffled crack as the shot struck the ground near his feet. Wes tripped, and fell headlong into the card table. It didn't collapse, but slid forward several feet and he rode it like a surfboard on a bad wave. As he rolled off the other side, he shot blindly behind him, and a tiki torch leaning in a sand bucket next to him exploded at the same time. Scented oil splattered his back as he took off running again.

Twenty yards.

He was going to make it. Wes could see the metal rails from the fire escape where they rose up above the edge of the building. They'd always dared each other to go down it, but none of them had ever been stupid or drunk enough to attempt it.

Running in a crouch, Wes prayed that the darkness and his parting shot would buy him the time he needed. He slid into the top of the ladder like he was crossing home plate, risking death by dropping over the edge as he grabbed at one of the railings with his free hand while rolling onto his stomach.

His feet flailed in midair for a nauseating moment before finding purchase on a rung. Steadying himself, Wes finally looked behind him and leveled the weapon.

There were two people chasing him. One had just reached the

roof, while the other was jumping over the remnants of the tiki torch and table. Wes shot twice, and felt a sickening satisfaction when the nearest man grunted and fell to a knee.

He started climbing down.

Six stories were all that separated Wes from what had seemed impossible only a few minutes earlier.

His heartbeat pounded in his head and his breath came in short gasps as he clambered down the rungs. Forced to tuck the pistol into the waist of his jeans, Wes felt more vulnerable, but without both hands he would have fallen.

Two floors.

"I'm going to make it," he whispered, staring down at his feet and the final platform he had to pass through.

Snap!

A shot grazed the rail just above his hand.

His head jerking up, Wes could see the outline of a man leaning over the roof, looking down at him.

One floor.

Clinging to the ladder, he pulled his feet out and began a loosely controlled slide the rest of the way to the ground.

Ten feet.

A bullet slammed into his backpack, catapulting him off the ladder to land in a heap at the bottom.

He should have been dead, but instead the wind was simply knocked from his lungs. Dragging himself onto his hands and knees, Wes fought through the pressure and deep ache in his ribs to suck in the precious air. Something in his backpack must have stopped the bullet.

Moaning with the effort it took to stand, he didn't look back. Or up. From that moment on, he could only look forward.

Wes ran into the night.

10

DAKOTA
Redemption, South Dakota

THE CHAIN on her mountain bike rattled in protest as Dakota peddled with a ferocity it was unaccustomed to.

"Dax, wait for me!" Sam shouted.

Glancing over her shoulder, Dakota felt a pang of guilt at the sight of her little brother desperately trying to keep up. Forcing her legs to stop, she stood on the pedals and allowed the bike to coast and slow down on its own. Adjusting the wide headband buried in her frizzy hair with one hand while waiting for him to catch up, she impatiently tucked some stray black strands under it. On a good day, the soft spirals were easily her best feature, but when it wasn't, the strongest of headbands weren't enough to tame the natural curls.

"Geeze," Sam howled as he came alongside her. "We're not even supposed to be riding this late. It's already dark, and Dad's gonna be mad!"

He was right about the time. It had to be close to eight, and twilight was rapidly progressing into full-on night. Their bikes weren't equipped with lights, but Dakota figured that given the circumstances, their dad would understand and agree with them going to the police station. She'd tried starting their new truck parked in the garage, but it wouldn't turn over.

They lived on a long rural block of nice houses with huge lawns and lots of trees, right at the edge of town. The center of Redemption was less than a mile away, and the national forest began across the street from their house. Their dad called it the best of both worlds, but Dakota instead chose words like 'isolated' and "backwoods".

An owl hooted from somewhere deep in the forest, and another answered from even further away, adding weight to Sam's complaint. The moon hadn't yet crested the mountains, and without any of the yard lights in the neighborhood working it was darker than normal.

Unable to shake her fear from the whacked-out electronics, Dakota's resolve waivered. Since she had no idea what was causing it, her little brother might be right and it could be more dangerous outside than in. But looking at the dark windows of another house they were passing, she couldn't stand the thought of going back to their own. It was eerily quiet, so that it felt like they were on a forbidden trek in the middle of the night.

There were only five other houses on the block, and two of the driveways were empty so Dakota suspected they weren't even home. The police station was arguably the safest place in town, which was exactly the reasoning she planned to use with her dad.

"Come on," Dakota urged, starting to pedal again. "It'll only take us ten minutes to get there."

Sam huffed but kept pace while resting a hand on a ridiculous fanny pack around his waist. "Doom is cold."

Dakota couldn't stop herself from looking at the pouch, and bit back a smart retort when she saw the white, whiskered nose poking out of the opening in the zipper. Dr. Doom was Sam's pet rat and he'd refused to leave the rodent behind.

It was silly. Dakota knew that, but she also understood that her little brother's irrational behavior when she told him they were leaving the house was because of fear. As hard as it was for her to try and think clearly, it was even more difficult for his young brain to cope with what they'd experienced. The rat was his constant. It was a term Dakota's grief counselor had used two years earlier while explaining his trauma to her, and the coping mechanisms of a then seven-year-old.

Because, Sam had been in the car. In the accident that killed their mother. Dakota still didn't know what he'd seen, but he hadn't spoken for more than a month afterward. Back then, his constant had been an absurd toy that changed from a pig to a robot. Dakota couldn't remember where he'd even gotten it, but he'd had it with him in the car that day. It somehow made it into the ambulance, and by the time she'd seen Sam for the first time in the hospital, he refused to let go of it.

It went everywhere with him for months afterward, until one day he simply left it behind in his room. The counselor had explained it like a lighthouse in a storm: when your brain can't process the chaos in your reality, and so you gravitate toward the one thing you recognize and cling to it. Something like that. It was a type of coping mechanism for extreme trauma.

A new sort of fear caused Dakota to stop peddling and she stared at her brother's back as his bike slipped past her. She couldn't lose him again. Not like that.

"We can go back, Sam." She tried to sound normal, but was failing. Failing to protect her little brother from being scared and afraid his life was going to get flipped upside down again.

Stopping, Sam dropped his feet down to brace himself while looking back over his shoulder at her. "You said it wasn't safe."

Cringing inwardly, Dakota decided the best thing to do was to be honest with him. Clearly, the whole 'don't worry about it' route wasn't working out. "I don't know. Maybe that was just some freaky electrical feedback stuff that's done now, and it'll be fine. But since I don't know for sure, I thought it'd be better to go be with dad since I can't call him."

Sam's face bunched up as he thought about it, but before he could voice his opinion, a flash of headlights flared behind Dakota. Twisting on her seat, she saw a pickup had pulled out of one of the driveways and was slowly approaching them.

The driver leaned out their window as they pulled to a stop, and Dakota recognized Mr. Cartwright. He was an older man that played cards with her dad on the weekends. "You kids okay? Your dad at work?"

"We're on our way to see him now!" Sam said enthusiastically, apparently having made up his mind. He likely felt the same sense of relief that Dakota did at seeing another person.

Mr. Cartwright shifted his focus to Dakota. "Need a lift?"

She almost said yes, but then thought about the real potential of passing her dad on the road at some point, without a way of letting him know where they were. "It's only a few blocks," Dakota answered after a brief hesitation. "Do you know what happened?"

Shaking his head, the older man glanced over nervously at his wife in the passenger seat. "Not a clue. That's why we're headed into town. Your phone not working?"

"No," Dakota confirmed, trying not to feel defeated by the confirmation that it was widespread.

Mrs. Cartwright leaned forward to call out the window. "If your dad isn't at the office, leave him a message and come to Olson's. The diner is on a generator so I'm sure they'll be open. We'll buy you both a hot chocolate."

That put a smile on Sam's face as he nodded vigorously, and Dakota wished she could hug the woman. "Thank you!" she said instead, before the truck drove away.

"Come on, Dax!" Sam called as he sped after the Cartwrights, apparently in a race to the end of the road.

Feeling much lighter, Dakota followed her little brother. Being given the choice, as well as seeing someone else who was familiar and unchanged, was the boost he needed. And the simple use of her nickname also helped to keep her grounded.

The evolution of the nickname wasn't totally clear, except that Sam was the first to use it after watching a favorite Star Trek episode with her one day. Over the years it had stuck and she'd even dressed up as the character the previous year for Halloween. Unfortunately, the older series from the Trek franchise wasn't popular among her peers at the prep school, so it upped her nerd rating, but that wasn't necessarily a bad thing. It made it easier to remain in the background.

As another block of houses flew by, Dakota saw more people out milling about in their yards, talking to each other. One car passed them, and then a second, and although the power was out everywhere it still helped to feel a certain level of normalcy. They weren't alone.

Redemption was small, even by small town standards. Downtown consisted of an organized grid of streets. The ones running north and south were all named after trees, while the other direction was numbered. They stopped at ten.

Other roads had been added over the years, fanning out from the main grid, but those were mostly houses, bed and breakfasts, and other touristy shops. Before they'd moved there, Dakota had been shocked when she Googled it and saw the population was barely over six-hundred. She'd expected a ghost town, so even though it was a culture shock, she was still relieved to find the streets relatively busy during the Spring and Summer months.

As they approached Pine Street, Dakota had mixed feelings. Scattered western-themed store fronts had a few working lights inside, but the rest of the town was in the dark. She could smell smoke, and it wasn't the sweet applewood kind, but thick and acrid. While there were several cars parked a few blocks away at the diner, most of the streets were vacant and she imagined people were treating it like a storm and hunkering down, hoping that whatever it was would pass by morning. Maybe they had the right idea.

They were only one block away from the station when a car

turned a corner and sped toward them. Dakota recognized the old-style police car right away and stopped, waving her hands over her head, though she was sure he'd already seen them.

"Dakota!" her dad shouted out his open window, before he'd even come to a complete stop. Derrik Adams jumped from his car and reached for Dakota as she stumbled off her bike, letting it fall to the ground.

As her father wrapped his arms around her, she pressed her face into his vest, even though all the things attached to him poked her ribs. As hard as she tried to hold it in, Dakota felt the tears slip out, and she sagged against him.

"Are you okay?" he demanded, holding her back out at arms-length so he could study her face. "Sam?" he said when she nodded. Shifting his attention to his son, he removed one hand from Dakota's shoulder and pulled him in. "You good?"

"I'm good!" Sam proclaimed, suddenly the stronger one. "You should have seen it. My PlayStation started freaking out, and the TV smoked, and the radio was going all crazy, and oh! Dakota's Fit thingy burned her wrist! She smashed her phone. Is she gonna get in trouble for smashing it? I told her she would."

Derrik hung his head for a moment before taking an audible breath and releasing them. "No, she's not in trouble. I'm sorry it took me so long, guys. I was stuck on the other side of town at a fire. This weird electrical stuff is happening all over the place."

"What is it?" Dakota asked. Though she wasn't as transformed as her brother, her relief at being with her dad made it possible to think clearly again.

Shaking his head, Derrik hooked his thumbs in his vest and looked up at the sky. "Other than it's some sort of critical failure that's somehow translated into what seems like attacks against our infrastructure, no one is sure."

The radio clipped at his shoulder crackled and he tipped his head toward it as he keyed it up. "Romeo twenty-two to base, I'm clear of the call and out with family. Status four, no checks necessary."

"Your radio works?" Dakota asked, encouraged that not everything was down.

"Not with central dispatch in Deadwood," her dad explained. "Only our local handhelds are operational, so we're having to dispatch our own calls out of the station through word-of-mouth as they come in. I figure the large repeater used to relay over the greater distance has suffered the same fate as everything else. Thankfully, our office manager, Ellen, is a retired dispatcher or we'd be struggling even more than we already are."

"Are you coming home?" Sam asked. He was holding Doom, and looking hopeful.

Petting the rat, Derrik smiled at Sam. "Sure, bud. I'll get you guys back home and make sure you're safe, but then I have to go do a few things." Turning to Dakota, he grew more serious. "I need to coordinate with the mayor and determine what our course of action is. There's only one other deputy in town right now and..." he glanced at Sam and shifted his feet nervously before looking at the sky again. "There's a lot of unknowns."

What small wisp of optimism Dakota had been nursing suddenly vanished. The only other time she could remember seeing her father act like that was after closing the door on the man who'd told him his wife was dead.

It was brief, but the break was there and it was enough to convince Dakota that things were worse than she'd thought.

Her dad was afraid.

11

J AMIE
Marsh Fracking Site
Near Redemption, South Dakota

THERE WAS nothing they could do for Kacey. The Fracmaster's body still lay where it'd been thrown, twisted into angles not compatible with life.

Jamie could barely see him under the glare of the floodlights being reflected off the water that was showering him, as he struggled to turn the valve wheel clenched in his hands. He was two pipe-sections back from the rupture, which was closer than he should have been. But someone had to shut off the flow of slick water, because as bad as things were, they could get a whole lot worse.

His eyes stung, and he kept his mouth clenched shut, trying to blow the water from his nose in between breaths. The slick water was ninety-nine percent water, but the rest was a proprietary formula of chemicals and sand specially designed to increase the water flow and pressure in the well. Though Marsh claimed his site used mostly biodegradable materials, it wasn't something Jamie would ever voluntarily have on his skin.

If the balance of pressure tipped and they had an uncontrolled reversed spill of the produced wastewater from deep inside the well, it would be an entirely different story. The compounds leeched from the ground during the fracking process ranged from highly toxic to radioactive, which was why there were several massive, lined pits nearby ready to have the wastewater pumped into them once they reached that step in the production. From there, it was another process to safely remove and dispose of it.

By the time the initial water plume had receded enough so that Carter could reach the platform, the drilling computer system was already completely unresponsive, so it became a matter of manually shutting down the well. It was taking a coordinated effort that Jamie was just one part of.

Shaking the soaked hair from his face, he leaned into the wheel and grunted as he strained to slowly inch it around. Jamie could hear the heavy machinery cutting out and men yelling back and forth as the other operators raced to get things under control. While he wasn't as experienced as most of the men at the site, his other training had kicked in and compelled him to take action where he saw that it was needed. After barking orders to anyone close enough to hear him, Jamie then took on the most dangerous task himself.

Without either the intake or outflow being regulated, the pressure would continue to increase and another blowout was imminent, making the piping he was standing over as dangerous as any bomb. Shutting down the pumps improved their odds, but Carter would have to act fast to manually counter it and incrementally bring the production to a full-stop. It was something that aside from the Fracmaster, no one other than Carter had the knowledge to even contemplate trying.

His knuckles white, Jamie turned the valve the last few inches and hung his head in relief when the flow of water finally slowed. Staggering away from the frac pumps, he ran the short distance to a required exposure station and stripped off his shirt before activating the outdoor shower.

Opening his mouth, he swished the plastic-smelling water around before spitting it out. Forcing his eyes to remain open as he looked up, Jamie hissed in response to the intense sting and tried not to think about any possible permanent damage to his sight. He could see stars dotting the night sky beyond the showerhead, and he tried to focus on them while he counted to thirty. As the initial pain ebbed, he ran his hands aggressively over his head before stepping out from under the spray.

The danger wasn't over, and he needed to go check in with Carter and see if there was anything else he could do to speed up the shutdown. As he took a step toward the oil platform, Jamie experienced an overwhelming sense of déjà vu. In the brief time it took to place one foot in front of the other, he was back on the farm where he grew up.

It had been around the same time of year, early Spring, and Jamie was thirteen. He was finally old enough to help bring the crop in, so he'd been out in the field when it happened. The sound of his father's screams was something he'd never forget, and seeing his arm stuck in the machinery caused an instant, guttural response similar to the one currently raging through his body.

The flashback faded to be replaced by the continuing sounds of the straining wellhead and harsh glow of artificial lights, but Jamie still blinked and took a shuddering breath to shake off the remnants. His father had healed and lived to continue working the farm for another twenty years before selling, but it was the most traumatic memory from his childhood.

"Get a grip, Pratt," Jamie muttered, concerned with his break from reality, however brief. He normally thrived in chaotic situations, and his ability to compartmentalize and perform was what made him successful in his career choice. He couldn't afford to make any mistakes.

He was ten feet away from the tower when the lights flickered.

When a well was going in, it was a twenty-four-hour operation, so industrial flood lights were erected around the perimeter and came on automatically at dusk. The majority of them were tied into their own portable power distribution center that was a remote, central power hub. They shouldn't be faltering.

Jamie approached the base of the five-story, steel tower and craned his neck to look up at Carter, where he was perched on the third tier. As he raised a hand to get his friend's attention, they were plunged into darkness.

"Carter!" Jamie shouted above the remaining pumps and hiss of water still spilling over the lip of the well pad.

Carter's silhouette appeared at the railing above him, and then solidified as a few scattered lights came back to life. Jamie saw that they were the cheaper, solitary flood lights not tied into the fancy distribution unit, and had their own battery packs as back-up. Frowning, he was frustrated with his lack of understanding. Maybe it was because of the adrenaline still clouding his thoughts, but he was having a hard time connecting the dots. Any of the dots, for that matter, and Jamie's greatest short-coming was his need to be in control. When he wasn't, he tended to act aggressively to regain it any way necessary.

"It's all part of the cyber-attack!" Carter shouted.

Jamie's gut clenched at the choice of words. "Attack?" But he knew Carter was right. It was the only explanation that properly translated into everything he was seeing, and he got a fresh surge of adrenaline as he began taking the steps two-at-a-time.

"I think we're good here," Carter said without preamble as soon as Jamie reached him. Gesturing to the manual controls he then pointed out to the trucks still idling near the pad. "It's going to take the rest of the night to bring it all the way down, but it's manageable. You get washed off?"

"Yeah," Jamie said, waving off his concern. "I'm fine. But what the *hell* could cause all this? I thought that downhole communication program was state of the art. How'd it have such a catastrophic failure just because the satellites went down? It doesn't translate, man," he added, rubbing at his jaw. "None of this does."

"Because this attack—it did a lot more than taking out communications." Carter crossed the platform to stand in front of the dead computer station. "The program wasn't just fried. It was *taken over*, Jamie. It's almost as if... like, the system sabotaged itself before going dark. The new pressure settings and parameters were set to make this well fail. Looking at the numbers, I would have guessed it was intentional."

"Intentional?" Jamie pressed a finger to his temple, where a headache was brewing. "How's that possible?"

Carter stared back at him. "It isn't. Or, it shouldn't be. Except that we know that as soon as that quantum computer went live, all our smart devices were essentially taken off-line. Power grids went down."

"And then anything with WiFi capability was...*infiltrated*," Jamie finished, feeling some small relief with the logical deduction while his anxiety rose at the same time.

"Those lights?" Carter pointed at the portable power center over by the storage sheds, which included a large generator and panel, housed in a steel frame. "It has Bluetooth tech that allows it to be remotely monitored for fuel and power usage, among other things."

Jamie thought about all of the implications behind the revelation. He couldn't even fathom how many systems and forms of infrastructure could be impacted. From something as simple as his trailer stereo, to nuclear power plants. His gut clenched again, and he felt slightly nauseous. Who would do such a thing?

"It might not even be deliberate," Carter said, seeming to read Jamie's thoughts.

Jamie understood where his friend was going, but he'd never believe a computer program could act totally independent of human input.

Carter jerked away from the dark control panel, and his eyes widened. "We have to initiate a shut-in on the other wells!"

While the current well was the only one that was being actively fracked, there were a dozen other working oil wells spread out across the Marsh Oil Fields. Each and every one of them had the potential for some sort of failure if any number of elements involved in the production was interrupted or altered. A shut-in was a term used to describe reducing or shutting down production. Oil wells weren't like a switch that could be flipped. It was a lengthy and tricky process that had the potential of never being reversed.

"I'll check the radios in the trailer." Jamie was already running for the stairs. "I don't think they're digital, and they run off an analog repeater on the property."

The "trailer" was the only permanent structure erected at the site, and included an office and bedroom for the Fracmaster, an aid station, and communications room. Without working phones, it was the only way to reach the operators out in the field.

While the other wells didn't require twenty-four-seven oversight, there were enough of them in various stages that there was always a crew or two out working them. Jamie assumed the guys would have already taken some precautions after the power fluctuations, but unless something was going critical, only the Fracmaster or owner could order a shut-in, and they'd need help.

As Jamie approached the trailer, a large 350 dually pickup came tearing up the road and slid to a stop only a few feet away. The bright-red vehicle belonged to the owner, Bucky Marsh, and he was known for peacocking around town in it every chance he got.

Jamie waited as the large man dropped down to the ground, tugging at his leather duster and adjusting his matching cowboy hat. His greying hair lent his jowly face an air of prestige, though his beady eyes portrayed more of a weasel than a true cowboy. While the lighting was too poor to reveal his features, Jamie had met the man before on three other occasions. He was impressed with the size of the private operation, but wasn't as equally impressed with its owner.

"Why is production stopped?" Bucky bellowed. "Whoever's responsible is going to wish he'd never set foot on this site!"

Fracking was an inherently dangerous job—that was why it paid so much. Accidents happened, and between the satellite failure and tech going rogue, he'd be hard-pressed to blame anyone for Kacey's death. But Jamie needed a target for his anger, and the obnoxious man made it easy to give into his rage.

"Production wasn't *stopped* by anyone!" Jamie yelled back, taking a step forward so that his finger was pointed just shy of a foot away from Bucky's face. "We've suffered a catastrophic failure, and if you took a moment to pull your head out of your ass before looking for someone to blame, you'd see that the man you want to crucify is already dead!"

Bucky's features first contorted in fury as his cheeks went crimson. But in the face of Jamie's anger and formidable size, emphasized by his shirtless chest, fear flickered in his dull eyes and he took a hesitant step backward, bumping into the open door of his monster-truck.

What have I done?

Jamie dropped his hand and moved away from the owner, but he knew it was already too late. The damage had been done, and he'd likely destroyed weeks of planning, and more than a month's work of laying the proper foundation.

With one wrong move, he'd just destroyed his cover and the chance of successfully carrying out his mission.

12

B UCKY
Marsh Fracking Site
Near Redemption, South Dakota

BUCKY DIDN'T REMEMBER the guy's name, not that it mattered who the half-naked neanderthal was. He would destroy him for daring to drum up the long-buried shame he kept safely packed away.

It was the closest Bucky had come to cowering in years. He'd grown up afraid; bullied and ridiculed for most of his life by people like him for his name, size, and the stutter he'd eventually learned to control. He'd shown all of them, and risen higher than anyone else in Redemption could ever dream of. Not only was he now the richest man in town, but the whole freaking county. He'd never be made to grovel or get belittled by anyone ever again. By the time he was done with the—

*Wait. Did he say someone was **dead**?*

Bucky stepped away from the truck and toward the irate operator, his fear of the man overridden by thoughts of lawsuits and investigations. As he did so, Bucky noticed for the first time how dark the site was, as his tunnel-vision receded. He'd been so blinded by his fury over the thought that someone had inexcusably shut down his operation that he'd failed to notice how *wrong* everything else was.

"What's happened?" he demanded, turning to stare at the idling pump-trucks, the men running between the piping, and then finally up at Carter who was climbing down the tower. "What kind of failure? Why wasn't I immediately notified?" Bucky twisted around to look back down the gravel road, his anxiety mounting. "Why isn't there an emergency response if someone is dead!"

The operator appeared exasperated, and wagged his finger again to encompass the building and equipment around them. "What, have you been in a cave for the past hour? We've been experiencing some sort of cyber-attack, or technological crash on a catastrophic scale."

Bucky's head spun. Sure, his phone had crapped out, but they could have raised him on the radio he carried with him at all times. He knew there was a power outage. He'd noticed it as soon as he left his brother's property, where he'd been out helping him price his cattle for auction. The electrical issue was why he'd come to the site, but that didn't account for what he was seeing. "An outage hardly qualifies as an *attack*," Bucky spat. "We have contingencies in place to prevent this from happening!" He turned his fervor on Carter as he approached. "Two things, Carter. Find Kacey for me and get this ass out of my face!"

Carter was already pale, making his noticeable blanching even more remarkable. He glanced nervously at the other man and then back at Bucky. "Mr. Marsh, I can only assume you're unaware of what's transpired, but—"

"How can cellular interruption cause my well to *explode*? Who's dead?" Bucky interrupted, his confusion growing. He struggled to focus on which questions he needed answered first. "He said someone was dead!"

"If it weren't for Jamie, several more people might have died," Carter said, his voice rising. "We had a rupture in the main line and it was due to the downhole communication system being...reset from an outside influence. It isn't just here, Mr. Marsh. The whole country was experiencing infrastructure failures prior to the satellites cutting out, after the new system went live.

"Satellites," Bucky repeated, dumbstruck. As he grappled to make sense of the information, someone snapped on additional portable lighting they'd set up, revealing more of the well pad. That was when he saw the body.

Carter saw where he was looking, and hung his head. "It's Kacey, sir. He was trying to stop it."

"Of course he was," Bucky whispered. He would have expected nothing less from the man. Kacey was a friend. He'd been his one true friend for the past five years, ever since he'd hired him to organize and run the site. Their daughters were the same age and Bucky had his whole family out to his ranch on several occasions.

Even though he was only a few years younger than Bucky, Kacey could still hang in there with the youngest of the operators, when he had to. It was because of his expertise and... loyalty, that the whole operation had ever made it off the ground as a private endeavor, let alone made him rich. His death was both a huge personal and professional loss and Bucky didn't know how he'd recover from it.

"I need to get to the communication room and try to reach the other operators still out in the fields," Jamie said. "I think our handhelds might still work, and we've got to start shut-ins on the rest of the wells."

Carter took a cautious step toward him. He knew Bucky well enough to understand he was unpredictable emotionally. He'd been known to have some major blowouts with operators during some of his regular visits. "If I'm right, and this is happening with all of the equipment, this is all about to get a lot worse if we don't act now."

Bucky continued to stare at Kacey's still, mutilated form, and his body sagged as the fight left him. He took an unsteady step backward and leaned against his truck. "Yes. Do whatever you have to. No one else gets hurt."

As Jamie jogged past him, toward the trailer, Bucky thought of his family and suddenly wanted nothing more than to go home. To make sure his wife and three kids were safe.

It's Saturday night.

His memory was muddied by the fear, but Bucky didn't think they had any plans. He'd phoned his wife earlier to let her know he'd be late for dinner. His brother was ill-prepared for the upcoming auction, as usual, and he'd offered to stay and help him. His children ranged from ten to fifteen-years-old. His only daughter was twelve and had a big 4-H show the next day that they were all going to. Would that be cancelled?

Bucky blinked, trying to focus on the present. But he was having a hard time accepting Kacey's death, or that it was up to him to call the shots and determine what needed to be done next.

Did Conner have a baseball game today? No, I would have been there. Wouldn't I?

He should know if he had a game, but they'd grown apart lately and butted heads. What if he'd been out when...whatever this was, happened. He'd have no way of reaching him.

"Mr. Marsh?" Carter was shifting from foot-to-foot, clearly wanting to be back in motion. "I still need to coordinate some things with the other operators."

It felt like a dream. Bucky shook his head and wiped roughly at his mouth. His lips were numb.

"Mr. Marsh?" Carter moved in close and placed a hand on his shoulder. "Are you okay? I know this is a lot to take in, but we need to get some things done. Now."

Nodding, Bucky concentrated on the pressure from Carter's hand to ground him. Jamie was handling the active wells, and he'd rely on Carter to finish shutting things down. He'd look at damage control later, in the light, when they had more information. "Yeah, do whatever's necessary. You—you can handle that?"

Although Bucky had studied every aspect of the operation, he'd never gotten his hands dirty. At least, not in a physical sense. That wasn't what an owner did. It'd been up to Kacey to oversee the site, and he had an office back in town for the engineer and secretary, as needed. There were several other senior operators, of course, but he didn't see any of them at the moment, and Carter had worked closely with Kacey for the year he'd been with the company.

"We'll need all hands-on deck," Carter replied. "But we're cut off, and I can't spare anyone to leave the site."

When Bucky realized what he was asking, he jumped at the opportunity to do something, as well as having an excuse to leave. "I'll drive back to the campground," he offered, which was what they called the field where all the trailers were set up. "I'll make sure there isn't anyone that hasn't already responded. Then I'll head into town and do a door-to-door to get all the senior operators up here." Bucky was nodding decisively as he spoke, already feeling better with a plan in place and taking control of the situation.

"Don't let anyone touch him," he added as an afterthought, pointing at Kacey. "But cover him up. I'll stop at the police station and notify them about the...death. They'll need to do an investigation, so we'll want to cooperate fully. Is anyone else hurt? Do I need to get the fire department out here?"

Carter turned to look at the wellhead and then the trucks, barely visible in the dim lighting, before squinting back at Bucky. "I don't think there's anything our fire department is going to be able to do out here, and I'm sure they're needed in town. As bizarre as this situation is, a valve rupture in itself isn't unheard of, so I wouldn't expect too much interest from the police. If this is as widespread as I think it is, I doubt the spill will even get investigated."

He shouldn't have felt relief, but Bucky still let out a sigh as he climbed into his truck. In all of the possible scenarios of how his life and strategies could go wrong, a grid failure, or whatever the hell it was, hadn't come up. Work delays, supplier issues, market fluctuations, and nosey local politicians he could handle.

The keyless startup on his truck failed to turn over, so he was forced to remove the physical key from the FOB and do it manually. Frowning, Bucky's eyes flitted from his useless phone on the floor to the dark digital display on the dash. The camera system should have automatically engaged when he put it in reverse, but it appeared disabled just like the stereo and GPS. Grunting, he swung the vehicle around and headed back down the gravel road. So long as it still ran, he could live without all the bells and whistles. He'd grown up driving an old farm truck held together with rusty wire and bolts, before his dad turned from scratching a living from the land and into his hardware business. That was when nobody knew about the goldmine of oil resting right under their feet for all those years.

Darkened woods flew by as he drove the short distance to the campground—woods that had been in his family for going on a hundred-and-fifty-years. His great-great-grandfather had founded Redemption, led there by his gold lust when the US government took the Black Hills from the Lakota Indians in 1877 and sold it to miners after a large find of placer gold. Turned out the rumors of gold were vastly overstated.

Redemption was the perfect trap back then: a raw, beautiful setting a man could lose his soul in. Lulled there by dreams of fortune, only to get stuck and slowly rot. Winters were bad, and people died, but the pioneers were determined and they found a way to etch out just enough refectory gold ore to keep themselves fed while constructing the first buildings of Redemption. From there, they turned to farming, and eventually when that began to fail them, the remainder climbed on the tourism train.

Bucky refused to get stuck in the same trap as his dad and siblings. He'd escaped to college where he earned a business degree that took him to Wall Street. He'd been determined to earn his fortune as a stock broker and return the hero. He almost made it. Almost. Instead, he was forced home with his tail between his legs, penniless after losing it all in a market crash.

In an act of rebellion, he'd moved to sell off his chunk of land, which he inherited when he turned thirty, the same age Charles Marsh had been when he first settled Redemption. With it, his plan had been to start over someplace else far away from judging eyes and preconceived impressions. It was the day he was talked into adding a mineral survey into the series of steps to determine the land value, that forever changed his life.

Slamming to a stop near the scattered trailers, Bucky laid on the horn, and the noise yanked him back from his thoughts of the past and into the painful present. A domino effect had started. One that threatened to upset everything he'd set in place. Without Kacey there to right things, it would be up to Bucky to take care of it himself.

As much as he wanted to check in on his family, he had some other stops he'd have to make first, after carrying out the tasks discussed with Carter. Then, he needed to have a conversation with the mayor.

Bucky had a lot of work to do.

13

S AGE
Redemption, South Dakota

FALLING into the rhythm of taking orders, making distracting small talk with customers, and wiping down tables was a great way for Sage to keep her mind off the most pressing of questions. It was easy to allow the companionship and feeling of facing the adversity together lessen the severity and turn it into something almost... festive. There was nothing like an emergency to bring people together, and shared fear forged a strong bond.

Pouring another cup of coffee for Mr. Johnson, Sage kept expecting the power to kick on, the generator to cut out, and for things to go back to normal. That someone would simply reboot whatever had failed in the mega computer located God-only-knew where, and make it all right again. She could *almost* pretend it was possible, which made it easier to breathe.

Realistically, if that reboot were to happen, the power company would then have to make their way around to repair all of the fried transformers and power stations. Even then, there were increasing reports of internal damage to wiring inside houses and businesses. Because it wasn't a storm, and no matter how much Sage tried to simplify it in her head, there was no getting around how complicated just that one aspect would be to rectify on a country-wide scale. And the phones? Well, if the millions of other phones and electronics across the United States suffered the same fate as those right there in good ol' Olson's Diner, nothing would be coming back "on" any time soon.

A bony hand rested gently on top of hers, causing Sage to jerk back to attention. She was standing frozen, her arm outstretched with the coffee pot hanging over Mr. Johnson's very full cup. "I think that'll do," he said with a small squeeze and a look of understanding.

Embarrassed, Sage's attempt at a smile was more of a grimace as she stepped back from the tall counter, where she'd been navigating her way expertly between Mr. Johnson and Old Gus. It was something so normal, so ordinary, that it suddenly felt incredibly wrong. How could she be waiting on customers as if nothing had happened?

Looking out at the bustling dining room housing thirty or so people, most of them familiar faces, Sage suppressed a moan that threatened to work its way up from deep in her gut.

Because it wasn't a storm.

There was no wind, or hail, or snow, or lighting to pass over so that they could then go about their easy, unburdened lives the next morning.

It was the fear of not knowing that made it so much worse. Being completely cut-off could be both a blessing and a curse, and at the moment she wasn't sure which one was winning out. They'd have to send someone to Deadwood, if her father came up empty-handed.

"It's been two hours, Sage," Old Gus said when she failed to move away from them right away, thinking she was looking for conversation or support. "Give it time."

Time.

Time for what? She'd never been good at sitting around and simply allowing life to happen. From a young age, Sage had needed to *know*. Always asking questions, to the point of being reprimanded at school for it, she'd sought out the whys and hows of the world around her.

It got her out of Redemption, while most of her friends stayed behind, and through graduate school in record time, but it had also been at the root of a lot of her problems. From taking her dad's computer apart when she was twelve to find out how it 'worked', to the debilitating anxiety and dependency issues later on, it was the one aspect of her personality she'd never mastered. Shrinking her world had helped, which was ironic, since as a teen she wanted nothing more than to move beyond the borders of Redemption and expand it. But in the face of such a big unknown, it was threatening to shut her down, so Sage's only option was to attack it.

"We saw what was on the news," she whispered, not wanting the other townspeople to overhear. "Even if this is limited to the power grid and our electronics, how long do you think it'll be before things are restored here? What other sort of cascading effects will it have on the rest of the country? On the things we rely on beyond electricity, like food supplies, gas, and medicine?"

Gus and Mr. Johnson exchanged a worried look. Old Gus had a bad heart and Sage had to assume he was on an assortment of medications. Did the small local pharmacy keep what he needed in stock, or was it a special order? Redemption had a fairly large retirement community. That one implication alone could pose some major issues.

"The people of Redemption have always looked out for each other," Mr. Johnson said. "These mountains never change, no matter what man throws at them, and this will be no different. That's what we can rely on."

Sage ran her free hand through her hair as she took a step back, and shifted her focus to the coffee pot gripped in the other. She wanted to believe that. She wanted to believe that simply having faith would be enough, but an important step in faith was also acting on it.

The supply truck came every Thursday, so she was fairly well stocked. Pivoting, she studied the crowd again, but in a different way. Several tables had plates of the limited appetizers Lisa was cooking up for her back in the kitchen, and most of them had drinks.

She went over a mental checklist of the walk-in freezer. What if that was it, for... what—several weeks, or even months?

Her heartrate accelerating, Sage knew she was working herself up, perhaps unnecessarily, but avoiding such a harsh truth could prove very detrimental later on. If there was even a chance she was right, acting immediately to conserve supplies was essential.

"Sage, do you think we could get a basket of tater tots with our beers?" Mr. Cartwright asked while waving to get her attention. He and his wife had arrived about an hour earlier, along with a few other families. Her dad played cards at their house every Friday night and she'd known them for most of her life.

Sage started to say no, but found she couldn't do it. Not yet. It was ridiculous, but denying Mr. Cartwright his taters would make it all too real. "Sure, I'll have Lisa drop some for you."

Raising her voice, she moved over to the small step up that led behind the bar so she was slightly elevated. "I'll keep the restaurant open past our normal closing time and provide drinks, but the kitchen will be closing!"

"I told you I don't mind staying to cook," Lisa said as Sage moved into the prep area. "So long as I know Cam and the kids are safe." Her husband and two young children were part of the crowd in the diner. The seven and nine-year-old girls were excited to be out past their bedtimes and were chowing down on fries and hot chocolate.

Barely acknowledging her friend, Sage moved to the freezer and opening it, pulled out the stock notebook she kept inside on a shelf. Setting it on an open space on the counter, she flipped to the first page and slid her finger over the columns of numbers.

"What are you doing?" Lisa asked, an edge of concern creeping into her voice. "Why are you acting so weird?"

Sage glanced up, her brows drawing together at the observation. "*I'm* acting weird? No, I'm not acting weird, I'm just not in denial. Look," she added when Lisa flinched at her accusatory tone. "I'm sorry, maybe you're right and it seems like I'm overreacting, but I'm beginning to think we have to prepare for the very real possibility that we're in this for the long-haul."

Lisa glanced at the bubbling deep fryers and other food that was scattered around them. "You're worried about supplies?" Her face screwing up as she thought about what that implied, she readjusted her blonde ponytail before chewing nervously on a nail. "Now you're freaking me out. I know you like living somewhat off the grid, but I never took you for a serious prepper."

Chortling, Sage braced her arms on either side of the notebook and gave her head a shake. "It's called disaster-preparedness. Something anyone living essentially out in the middle of nowhere should at least have a basic plan for. I know this situation is a lot harder to wrap our heads around, because it isn't something we've ever mentally prepared for. But Lisa...my dad was *running*."

Swallowing audibly, Lisa reached out and deliberately flipped the power switch controlling the vats. "Right."

Relieved she'd gotten through to her friend, Sage moved to lift the last three baskets of fries and tater tots out of the cooling oil and started preparing the baskets while she spoke. "A bunch of the lights already blew when the whole power surge happened, but I'd like to go around and shut down everything that isn't essential. We'll leave a few lights on out front, but let's get some candles out to offset the ones we turn off."

Lisa looked toward the back of the building. "The generator," she said quietly as she began grasping the bigger picture. "Oh, man. My little one at the stand already ran out of gas. We've got a couple of five-gallon containers at our house for the one we have there, but I have no clue how long that'll last."

"Let's hope this won't even end up being an issue," Sage said quickly, feeling guilty for being the one to cause her friend so much worry. "But just in case it is, if we start conserving now, it'll be better for everyone. The city has an emergency supply of both gasoline and natural gas. Enough to keep essentials running for a couple of weeks, so we don't need to start panicking yet."

"Yet," Lisa repeated, not sounding all that encouraged.

The front door chimed, and when several people called out a greeting to her dad, Sage left the open notebook to run out and meet him.

He looked harried, with his bushy grey hair in disarray and his glasses slid down his nose. He was holding a flashlight, which he switched off as Sage approached. "What's all of this?" he said disapprovingly while gesturing to the tables. "This isn't the right time to be throwing a party."

"I know," Sage barked as she stepped forward and took him by the arm. Leaning in close she spoke to him with a hushed urgency. "I've already shut things down and we're taking steps to conserve power. People needed...*something*, Dad. Just a little something."

Patting her hand, he nodded, seemingly satisfied with the answer and that she'd already grasped the seriousness of the situation. "That's good. That's what we all need to do. The outage and subsequent electronics failure amounts to what I'd term as a cyber-attack of catastrophic proportions. Everything is down, Sagie, and I mean everything." Shifting slightly so he could address the crowd of mostly friends mixed in with a few tourists who were already listening, he put it bluntly. "I'm afraid we're going to be on our own for an unknown amount of time, and it's impossible to say at this point what sort of other impacts this disaster might be having in the bigger cities, on a larger scale. For those of you not from Redemption, it might be safer to stay put for the time being."

"Did you find Mayor Irv?" Trent asked, standing up from the table he'd occupied in the corner while Sage had been in the back. Trent was a forty-something year-old local farmer and a member of the city council. "I tried getting to Deadwood before stopping here, Ed. There was a downed power-pole across the road about five miles out, so I turned back since it was dark. I don't feel comfortable cutting on a connected pole, burned up or not, without first knowing something more about what's happening down the line."

Ed scratched at his mane of grey hair and harrumphed at the news. "I'm sure those wires are dead, but you're right that it wouldn't be a good idea to go about it in the dark. We'll wait until morning and send out a crew to clear a path. Until then, I think we all need to just do our best to conserve what resources we have. We'll learn more tomorrow and come up with a plan."

"The mayor?" Sage pressed.

"Not home." Ed moved to the bar and sat down next to Old Gus.

Shuffling around to the other side, Sage got a clean mug and poured him the last of her coffee. "He was supposed to be back from his trip to Yellowstone last night or this morning. Before the council meeting Monday night, anyway."

Ed shared a look with both Old Gus and Johnson before glancing over at Trent. "I drove out there and used my key to let myself in. Doesn't look like he and Annie made it back. Trucks gone, and I'd say that no one has been there recently."

"You know what that means," Gus said with a hint of amusement, tapping his cup to Sage's empty coffee carafe.

The significance of his comment hit Sage like a punch to the gut. The clatter of the metal pot dropping down on the bar top was loud enough to draw several curious stares, and she threw a hand to her mouth to try and hide her shock. Or terror, or pure and unadulterated rejection at the idea of her being in charge.

Earlier that year, Sage had begrudgingly accepted the appointed position of Deputy Mayor. After being elected to fill the long-held city council position vacated by her mother, she'd simply gone through the motions of attending the meetings and putting in an occasional appearance at the appropriate town gatherings. While passionate to fight for some issues on behalf of her mom, politics wasn't her thing; it never had been.

When Irv approached her about being deputy mayor, her old English teacher had pulled out every stop and wouldn't relent until she'd said yes. "It's just a title," he'd said. "You'll never have to act in any official capacity," he'd promised. "Do it for me," he'd begged.

"I'm the acting mayor," Sage muttered, looking out at her crowded diner with a new perspective. With Irv away in another state and no way to contact him, it fell on her to organize and run Redemption in his absence. Those people were now her responsibility.

It should have been enough to cause her anxiety to rise to an incapacitating level. Instead, in a strange twist of fate, it provided the perfect outlet for her abhorrent need for knowledge and action.

While Sage's degree in geology might not be beneficial in running a city, her years of experience managing the restaurant would be. And with her father, other council members, and town elders to help guide her, she was sure they'd pull together and get through whatever was coming at them.

14

K ATHY
Near Las Vegas, Nevada

KATHY HAD NEVER BEEN SO relieved to reach a rest stop. It was one of the nice ones, funded by the state and well maintained with green grass butted up against the dirt and tumbleweeds. It had separate parking areas based on what you were driving, to make pulling in and out easier. The first lot was for regular passenger vehicles, while beyond it had pull-throughs for travel trailers, and then finally the big rigs. The set-up was completed with a grassy, covered picnic area to make an overnight stay more accommodating.

Twilight was settling over the desert, so the large halogen lamps should have been flickering to life, but instead stood as dark sentinels to a world gone awry. Under their worthless guard, it looked as if several other travelers had the same idea as Kathy. Where she normally would have expected two or three cars on the lone stretch of highway, there had to be close to a dozen scattered throughout the large swath of cement. A glow from somewhere beyond the building might have been a campfire, which felt misplaced, given the circumstances.

Begrudgingly pulling into the smallest of the three parking areas, Kathy was painfully reminded of the trailer she was forced to leave behind. She'd been lucky to escape the mess with her life, but the loss of her trailer was still hard to accept. It had taken close to an hour just to free the hitch of the wreckage, and she wasn't convinced her truck had escaped unscathed. She would have to get it looked over after she got home to make sure the frame wasn't jacked.

Home.

Kathy's breath hitched, causing Colby to look up at her as she turned the truck off. "We'll get there soon enough," she said as much to herself as her furry companion. "We'll drive all night, Colbster. I'll get a nap in the morning and you'll be eating kibbles out of your favorite bowl before midnight, tomorrow."

She suspected the route home would be faster if she were to turn around and head back through Flagstaff, since her plans to go to the other national parks were now kiboshed. It would also allow her to avoid the crowded area of Vegas. "That might not be a bad idea," she muttered while pulling the road atlas off the floor and onto her lap. As Kathy did so, she noticed her hands.

It was a full thirty seconds before she moved. Slowly and deliberately, she slid the large paperback onto the center console and opened her door without turning her head. "I'll be back in a minute, Colby. You're in charge."

Making sure the windows were cracked, she then mechanically got out of the vehicle and headed for the restroom. It wasn't dark enough to need a flashlight, but it would be soon. Something about that made Kathy feel slightly better. That under the cover of night she wasn't as vulnerable.

As she approached the small square building, Kathy got a view of the semi lot on the far side. She was slow to process the scene, and her step faltered twice before she put a hand out to steady herself against the building while continuing to stare. There was a small crowd gathered, and beyond them, a eighteen-wheeler was burning.

How did I not notice that?

Her reaction was minimal. Like the people milling about, silently watching, there wasn't anything to be done. It was impossible to call for help, unless another trucker was able to get through to a dispatch center via their CB's.

Will the 911 centers be working?

It was a disturbing thought, and Kathy shook her head to get rid of it.

There was nothing she could do.

Just like...

"No," she whispered, the air hissing through her clenched teeth.

Turning abruptly, she grabbed at the bathroom door and yanked it open. Thankfully, there was some sort of emergency lighting in the sink area, because she'd failed to consider how dark it would be inside. It cast an orangish-red glow onto the white ceramic and lent a sort of funhouse feel to the room.

Kathy ignored the stalls and hurried to the stained basins, turning the water on as her breathing sped up until she was panting. Her chest hurt, and her eyes stung with unshed tears while she watched, unblinking, as the water gathering in the bottom of the sink turned crimson.

It wasn't because of the lights.

"Oh, God..." she moaned, scrubbing frantically at her fingers under the weak stream of water.

...the torn flesh and coppery smell of fresh blood.

...her inability to even get inside the mangled BMW, let alone do anything to help the already deceased couple.

Kathy closed her eyes and leaned against the sink, breathing in through her nose and out through her mouth. "Stop." Her voice echoed in the small space and surprisingly, had the desired effect.

She moved to the other sink and started over, using the small dispenser of soap above it first. Lathering up her hands, she thought instead of her trailer, and what she had been able to salvage. It'd been impossible to get to everything she wanted, but at least between herself and the guy who's name she never got, they recovered most of her camping gear and clothes.

...the smear of blood along the pavement, leading to—

"Stop!" Kathy's head jerked up, the fury in her own voice scaring her. What she saw in the mirror frightened her even more.

SHE TOOK A STEP BACK, and then another, until her features faded enough into the shadows that they were indiscernible. Kathy had seen that woman only one other time in her life. With wild eyes like a dog backed into a corner, mouth open in a desperate attempt to suck air into lungs that were being crushed by a despair so deep, and so brutal that it hurt.

Slapping a hand to her chest, she balled the t-shirt in her hand and ran the other over her face. She couldn't blink. If she did, the images of the accident might be replaced with those of her own nightmare from five years earlier.

The door opened behind her.

An older woman walked in hesitantly, eyeing Kathy suspiciously at first, and then empathetically after seeing something she must have recognized. Raising a hand like she was trying to approach a wounded animal, the woman tilted her head and smiled warmly. "Are you okay?"

Unable to force the automatic response past her lips, Kathy instead focused on the lady's hand, glowing orange under the light. It was clean, with polished nails and a large, glittering diamond on her ring finger. Her eyes drifted to the woman's face, lined from years of laughter and living under a scorching sun. She looked kind, concerned...and very much alive.

Kathy cleared her throat. Her breathing slowed, and once she'd stopped hyper-ventilating, her thoughts sharpened and she could think again.

What am I doing?

She hadn't had a flashback for years.

"I'm fine," she croaked, and cleared her throat again. "Really. I'm okay, now. Thank you for asking. Are you..."

"My husband and I are almost home," the woman said, when Kathy's voice trailed off. "Are you by yourself?"

Kathy thought of Colby waiting for her in the truck, and she was suddenly eager to get back to him. "No. I'm not alone. I need to go." Turning to the door, she paused and looked back again. "I hope you get home safely."

Not waiting for an answer, Kathy nearly ran outside and partway down the cobbled sidewalk. She could see her truck and just make out Colby sitting in the window, his nose stuck partway out, waiting patiently for her.

The semi in the other lot was burning brighter, and the wind must have shifted because she could smell it, too. The sound of people talking caused her to change directions, and she hurried across the parking lot toward where they were all gathered. It wouldn't hurt to try and gather more information. That was originally her reason for stopping in the first place.

It was an odd situation. Approaching them, Kathy was reminded of a juvenile, late-night bonfire in the woods. Like they were all somewhere they shouldn't be, doing something daring and wrong, but not caring if they got caught.

Maybe it was because it felt wrong and out of place to simply be standing there chatting while the truck burned. Everyone should have been on their phones, either calling for help or recording it. Someone should have been yelling. It should have been a big deal.

Except that it wasn't. Not in the scope of everything else that had and was still happening. It was disturbing how quickly social norms shifted in the face of overwhelming adversity.

A man who Kathy guessed was the driver, was standing the closest to the front of the truck, holding a spent fire extinguisher. Two other men stood alongside him, and one patted him on the back. There were two other rigs parked a safe distance away, still idling, and there were two other extinguishers lying on the ground. At least *someone* had tried to do something.

"It's a singularity, man!" a young woman was saying to an older man. "This is it. The machines are coming for us."

The man shook his head emphatically. "No! It's an outside attack by something very human. I was listening to the radio after this all started, and the guy who *created* the program said it was a virus."

"What, you think he's going to admit he caused it?" the woman yelled back, waving her arms. "It's the computers!"

"I want my movie!" a young boy around six years old hollered. He was standing in between another man and woman, and was pulling incessantly on his mother's shirt.

Batting his hand away, the woman then squatted down so they were at eye-level. "I told you, it's broken. You'll have to wait until we get home."

His face puckered and he stomped his foot. "Then gimmie your phone!"

Glancing up at the man for help that wasn't coming, the woman took the boy's hand and stood. "It's broken, too."

Dropping all of his weight, the little boy hung from his mother's grasp and started kicking at the ground. "Gimmie your phone! Gimmie your phone!"

Ignoring who Kathy assumed was his son, the father stepped far enough away to avoid being kicked. "Did you hear anything else?" he asked the other man. "Did they say how long it was going to take to fix?"

"Fix?" the girl chortled, looking at the on-going tantrum with disdain. "I'm telling ya, this is just the beginning. You better teach your kid to like books."

Backing away, Kathy decided she didn't need any further human interaction. She'd heard enough.

It was dark by the time she reached her truck, and Colby whined when she opened the door and the dome light came on. Ignoring the bloody fingerprints on the road atlas, she grabbed for it as she settled into the driver's seat. "We need to get out of here," she said to Colby as he closely watched her movements.

Hearing confirmation that the computer was responsible wasn't a surprise, but it still bolstered her desire to get home as fast as possible. The more she thought about the possible ramifications, the more daunting the outlook was, and seeing the kid having a meltdown exposed another aspect she'd yet to consider.

People standing silently around a burning vehicle would be nothing compared to the social breakdown about to occur. Their society was one that had become dependent on its technology. More than that, they'd become emotionally dependent on it, too. It wouldn't be long before it wasn't only little kids having meltdowns, and that was when things would get really ugly.

Kathy had personal reasons for choosing to live a secluded life off the grid, but she also had practical ones.

She needed to get home.

Dropping the map, she started the truck and headed toward the exit. The rest stop was the only one for fifty miles, so there was an overpass to the eastbound lanes, and that was where they were headed. Away from the larger cities and more populated areas, and where she would feel more at peace.

But as they entered the long stretch of highway, Kathy had a heavy, pressing feeling deep in her gut that she was chasing something that was now impossible to find.

15

Wes

Cambridge, Massachusetts

WES SAT HUDDLED at the base of the monument, clutching a large knife in his hands. He couldn't stop shaking and wasn't sure if it was from the cold, or shock. Probably both.

His head throbbed. Reaching up tentatively, he poked at the largest of the wounds on his face. The cut across his forehead was likely from the chunk of cement in the stairwell.

From when he was almost shot.

Shot.

Wes dropped his hand back to the sizable knife and wrapped it around the blade hard enough to be painful. It wasn't the smaller one he'd used to save his life earlier. That was lying back on the roof of the dorm somewhere.

The leather sheathing he'd pulled off the one he currently held lay at his feet, the unimpressive indentation in the pelt the only proof of how it had saved his life. The knife was handmade by his grandfather, and passed down to Wes from his father. *Duncan,* their family name, was chiseled into the bone handle that was carved from an antler. It was one of the few treasured items he always carried in his go-bag, the backpack he'd been wearing. It fit perfectly in the interior pocket, which was how the six-inch steel blade had stopped the bullet from going into his back.

Leaning his head against the cold cement at his back, Wes stared up at a star-filled sky. It was incredibly misleading. It looked the same as any other night he'd come out to the John F. Kennedy park to stargaze. He was less than three miles away from the dormitory, and it had taken him over an hour to get there, due to all of the accidents and having to hide in the shadows.

Even on a chilly night in April, Wes would have normally ridden his bike. It was easy enough to get around that area of Cambridge without his car, which he reserved for his thirty-hour drive home. He made that pilgrimage at least four times a year, because aside from not being able to afford the plane ticket, he was terrified to fly.

Wes grunted in frustration and ran a hand over his face, trying to focus. He was sweating in spite of the cold, and it was only adding to his distress.

He couldn't think straight. Why was he sitting in the park?

The random thoughts of home and stargazing flitting through his head scared him. In his shock, everything was too jumbled together. The harder he tried to make the pieces fit, the harder it was for him to see the bigger picture.

Why didn't I just get in my car and drive home?

"Because they're trying to kill you!" Wes hissed, slamming the knife down onto the cement platform, the metallic clang reverberating through the space.

The sound was like a slap to the face, and Wes jolted to attention.

They were trying to kill him.

Entangled.

"Steve...Carrie."

Speaking their names out loud, it felt like he'd plunged the knife into his own chest. Gasping, Wes released the blade and pushed at the ground with his heels until he was several feet away from it and the evidence it held that he couldn't deny.

It was all real: Helix going rogue, the destruction, Steve and Carrie being killed— the attack, and his race through the burning city. He hadn't risked going for either his bike or his car, not that he could have driven on the blocked roads.

As his awareness sharpened and his senses returned, Wes understood why he'd chosen to hide behind the dry water fountain. Part of the Harvard campus was in the distance, at his back, and he could still hear people yelling. He'd passed some of the historic buildings on his way into the park, several of them with dark smoke pouring from windows, and others with visible flames licking the night sky from their roofs. Water flowed down the streets from broken water mains, and it was hard to tell which way was safe to go.

Sirens wailed in the distance, their route likely blocked by one of the countless accidents. Accidents that were caused by the traffic system failure, and based on what people were saying in the streets, also by the self-drive systems in vehicles taking over.

As Wes sat there, recalling his trek through the city, he could smell smoke and natural gas, and something like...sewage.

"All of the infrastructure," he muttered.

Everything was computerized. In addition to the obvious power grid, there were also the water, sewage, and gas lines. All of it was regulated at some point by a system that was connected to the internet. Wes's head pounded with more intensity as he thought of the scale of the attack.

A terrorist group could wreak havoc by simply focusing on a single point. By messing with the intake, outflow, or pressurization of the sewage and water recovery in a large city, they could back up raw sewage into every home and business...have it flowing through the streets. That alone would eventually pose all sorts of issues, including health and livability of the structures affected. Cambridge would be bad enough, but Wes could imagine how unlivable a place like New York City would become overnight. Add to that: no power, water, subway, emergency response or communications.

"Oh..." his groan turned into a whimper and Wes began to curl back into a ball.

His ribs hurt from where he'd been punched, his right ankle throbbed from his fall off the fire escape, and his multitude of scrapes and bruises took him back to his early high school days when he attempted to impress his dad by trying out for football.

Wes had grown up on a working farm where they harvested both cattle and wheat, so he had the physical ability to play most any sport. And at that point, they were still young enough that the other guys weren't much bigger than he was. Except that Wes had lacked the desire. He didn't understand where the rage came from that gave some the drive to keep going down the field after being hit.

Now he understood. It was primal, and apparently all it took to bring it out was having a part in the destruction of civilization.

Wes squeezed his eyes shut and pulled his knees to his chest. No matter how his thoughts drifted, they always came back to an over-riding emotion: guilt.

Because he was guilty, and no amount of shock or denial would change that.

"I'm not running away from it," he whispered into his knees, the jeans rough against his chapped lips. "I can stop it. I have to stop it."

Whether it was his need for absolution or was simply an excuse for being a coward, Wes figured it didn't much matter. He had to get out of the city and take Helix to the only person he could think of that might be able to help.

His name was Abraham Wilson, but everyone called him Professor Abe. He reminded Wes of the actor, Morgan Freeman, due to both his appearance and deep voice, and was the man responsible for him being at MIT. He'd recruited Wes right out of the small high school in South Lawrence County, and encouraged him to apply for several scholarships. Eventually, he'd gotten a full ride, which was the only way Wes had been able to go to college, let alone MIT.

Professor Abe became a mentor and a friend, and his wife had Wes over for dinner at least once a month. Over the course of three years, that added up to a lot of conversations. Wes eventually found out that the professor had discovered him his sophomore year, through a friend at the FBI, after his hack into their database. He followed Wes's academics over the years and had a hand in some of the aptitude tests he'd been given. Though he never openly admitted it, he figured Professor Abe had something to do with the charges against him eventually being dropped for the hacking. While he'd been a minor, it still probably would have prevented him from ever getting into a good college.

"You should have let them lock me up somewhere." Wes moved a hand to press at the outline of the flash drive in his pocket, reassuring himself that it was still there. "Then Helix would have never been created."

His friend at the FBI wasn't Professor Abe's only government contact. He took on military contracts for software programming every so often, and although he wasn't able to talk about the details, Wes had no doubt the professor was involved in some high-level stuff.

Wes would get Helix to him. Professor Abe would know what to do with it. He'd be able to explain to the government how Wes had been misled and made a part of something he'd never voluntarily do. He'd make them understand that Wes could *help*.

If they could get access to the quantum computer, Wes could figure out how to reprogram Helix and shut it down. It might take years to rebuild what was already destroyed, but they could at least prevent it from going any further. Because Wes had no doubt that if left to continue executing whatever self-destruct sequence it was spiraling in, things were going to get worse.

Much worse.

Going over a plan of action helped to calm Wes's thoughts. If he succeeded, maybe...someday, he'd be able to go home. To see his family again. His parents and two younger brothers. They were tangible, and if for no other reason, he had to make things right for them.

"I have to get to the professor." Wes uncoiled his arms and reached out to drag the knife back towards him. The solid weight of it as he lifted it in his right hand felt good. It felt real. Tipping the handle, he strained to see the letters carved into it, and teared up as he read it aloud.

"Duncan."

His body aching with each movement as he held it to his chest, curled up on the ground, Wes appreciated how it meant he was still alive.

As he lay there, listening to the ebb and flow of the chaos playing out around him, Wes vaguely wondered if the landline phones would still work. Professor Abe lived over twenty miles away, outside of town, and it was going to be a long walk if he couldn't find some form of transportation. He'd give anything to make one phone call to let him know he was coming. Except even the phone system would at some point be tied into a computer system, just like every other piece of infrastructure in a big city. Even the smallest of towns now relied heavily on technology, in order to be connected with the supply chain and everything else that made the world go round.

Small towns.

As Wes's mind slowly quieted to the point that he succumbed to his deep mental and physical exhaustion, his final thought before slipping into a restless sleep was of home. The worst of the devastation would begin in the big cities but eventually, nowhere on the planet would be safe from the effects of O.N.E.

16

D AKOTA
Redemption, South Dakota

DERRIK LIFTED another pack of batteries off a storage shelf and placed it on the card table in the middle of the room. He hooked his thumbs in his police vest and stared down at the growing pile with a look of concern. "I thought I had more D cells down here. What's it say on the inventory, Dax?"

Dakota frowned as she flipped through the pages in the notebook she was clasping. It wasn't alphabetized, so she had to hunt for the entry. "Two packs of twelve."

"Humph." Her dad turned back to the supplies and moved down the wall of shelving. Stopping to rummage through a box in earnest, he made a sound of triumph. "Here we go. Knew it was here somewhere. I should have had you help me with this, inventory has never really been my thing. I'm more of an action guy."

Dakota's frown didn't fade. "I didn't know we had so much... stuff, down here." She gestured around the basement, which was one large room with unfinished walls and a cement floor. Two of the long walls were covered by floor-to-ceiling industrial shelving units, and most of them were full. Canned goods and freeze-dried food occupied a majority of one wall, but the rest of it looked like a camping supply store. Her dad had always been a sort of prepper, but he'd taken it to a whole new level.

"When did you do all of this?" she asked, wondering how she hadn't noticed. Though, it really wasn't that surprising since she avoided the basement and didn't have a reason to go down there. It was creepy, and smelled like mold.

Derrik shrugged. "Some of it we already had when we moved. You know how I feel about being prepared," he said to Dakota as he took what looked like a radio out of a black bag. "That was something hammered into me during my time in the military. Everyone should be prepared for emergencies or natural disasters. Because we are living so far out, I decided to beef up the supplies. You'd be amazed at how fast we'll burn through this stuff if provisions are cut off for even a few days."

"A few days!" Sam shrieked, dropping the power bar he'd been busy peeling open. "It's not going to be fixed in the morning?"

Sam was distraught, and Dakota's stomach clenched at the full realization of how completely their lives revolved around technology, even in Redemption. He'd typically start off his Sunday morning with some cartoons before taking off on his bike to a friend's house for a few hours. He'd be back for lunch and his two allotted hours of online time for gaming with his "other" friends. Music of some sort was always playing in the background, there was a constant stream of communication via one device or another, and the TV was always an option for entertainment.

Dakota rubbed at her stomach. Her parents had always been strict in limiting screen time and they probably went outside more than most kids their age, but it still made her physically ill to think about getting her brother through several days without all of their vices. What if they ran out of gas for the generator?

Her eyes widened and she looked around the basement again.

"Dad, do you have more gas?" She stared at the two boxes of candles he'd already put in between the batteries and flashlights and her dismay deepened.

"There's more than twenty gallons in the garage." Pushing a battery-operated lantern toward her across the table, her dad gave a curt nod. "Which isn't much, so we'll need to conserve it. That's why I went around and shut all but the two lights off. We'll leave the generator off for several hours a day. The refrigerator will stay cold enough without running twenty-four hours." Shifting his attention to Sam, he finally addressed his question. "No, bud. I don't think it's going to be fixed in the morning. You remember the big snow storm a few months ago and how the power went out for almost a week?"

Sam nodded, but wasn't satisfied. "Yeah, but that was different. We could still watch movies and play games and stuff. Dax's phone doesn't even work and the TV was *smoking*, Dad!"

Dakota reached absently for the fresh bandage on her wrist. Her dad had done a much better job of applying burn cream and a gauze wrap to the injury caused by her Fitbit. But it still hurt. It served as a constant reminder that it was so much more than a simple power outage, no matter how hard she tried to pretend otherwise.

"This is an emergency shortwave radio," Derrik explained, setting the white square box on the table near Sam. "I bought this years ago and it's the bare-bones option, so no WiFi or Bluetooth connections, which is what seems to be how everything is getting destroyed."

Sam took the radio and turned it over in his hands. "Can it play music?" he asked hopefully. He had a radio next to his bed, and couldn't fall asleep without it playing.

Plucking at the plastic wrap on the battery pack, Derrik pulled out several batteries and handed them to Sam. "Why don't you put those in it and we'll give it a try. It won't play a CD or MP3, but we should be able to find a working radio station."

Dakota watched stoically as her dad helped Sam get the cover off the back and turn the batteries the right way. "Didn't you hear anything on the radio in your car?" she asked. "About what's happening."

Looking up briefly, he squinted at her and the message was clear. He didn't want to upset Sam. He hadn't really said much during the time they'd been back at the house and she understood why, but it was driving her crazy.

Tapping her foot against the floor, Dakota studied the random supplies on the table. How much of it was going to be necessary? Would they really have to resort to burning candles and eating cans of baked beans? As the significance of that one can of food drove home how radically their lives might have changed, her foot became still.

Her dad was right. They shouldn't talk about it in front Sam. Not yet, anyway. Not until they knew more.

The hiss of static signified their success, as Sam let out a whoop. "Yes! Can I try?" He was already grabbing at the dials randomly, and Dakota couldn't help but smile. Her dad knew him so well and could always find a way to make Sam laugh or forget about whatever it was that had him worked up.

He might have been gone overseas for most of her childhood, but she always knew he was coming home. That her dad was still there for her, even if not in person. He'd been home more the last few years before Mom died, and since retiring, he'd taken on both roles seamlessly. At least, that was how he made it appear but Dakota was old enough to realize that he was just really good at protecting them from the truth. She rarely ever saw him upset and while it made him seem bulletproof and made her feel safe, the older she got, the more it also made her sad. He was always so strong for them, but who was there for him?

His own parents weren't around, and Dakota had never met them. Her mom's parents lived far away in Florida, and would visit them in California before they made the move to Redemption, but she hadn't seen them since the year before. Thinking of her grandparents made Dakota's anxiety swell again. Were they okay? Not

being able to call and check on them was gut-wrenching and she
didn't know what to do about it.

"Here, let me try," her dad was saying as he took the radio from
Sam. He pulled at the pop-up antennae to make sure it was fully
extended and then walked over to one of the two tiny windows up
near the top of the far wall. After turning the larger dial several
revolutions without any success, he flipped a switch. "We'll try the
AM frequency. I think there's only a couple of FM stations that
reach out here, anyway."

There were three. Dakota knew them all, but she figured it
wasn't worth correcting him. The static made her feel worse, for
some weird reason. Like it was an echo, or representation of the
outside world that was suddenly and incomprehensibly beyond
their grasp.

Her eyes drifted to the darkened window. The night felt so...
heavy. It was keeping secrets from them. Some cosmic plan that
they weren't privy to, and Dakota would give anything for something as simple as a smiley face sent from her best friend, to let her
know she was still there. That *anyone* was still out there.

Vague talking squelched through the speaker, and her dad tried
turning the radio and making small adjustments with the knob, but
couldn't pick it up. Giving up on it, he kept scrolling.

"*...has been a recording of the Emergency Alert System.*"

"Ha!" he exclaimed. Removing his hand from the dial, he turned
up the volume and set the radio in the window. Three long tones
were emitted, and they all looked at each other in wide-eyed anticipation.

"*This is a message from the Emergency Alert System. A national
emergency has been declared. Shelter in place until further instructed.
Repeat. This is a message from the Emergency Alert System. A national
emergency has been—*"

Derrik flipped the switch back to the FM station and then
gripped the radio while hanging his head. Dakota and Sam
exchanged a look behind his back. It was a very uncharacteristic
display of emotion and neither of them knew how to react.

"Sam, why don't you take this up to your room and get it set up?" Turning around with the radio in his hand, he appeared calm again. Holding it out to Sam, Derrik smiled encouragingly at him when he hesitated to take it. "I don't think we're going to find any music right now, but the static works as good white noise and might help you sleep."

"But I don't want to—"

"I'm not saying you have to go to bed yet," Derrik interrupted. "But I want you to get settled before I go back to work. Take this to your room and I'll be there in a minute."

As Sam silently did as he was told, Dakota suddenly wished she wasn't getting what she'd asked for. She didn't want to talk about it anymore. She didn't want to hear what her dad had to say about it without Sam in the room as a filter.

"I picked up one station out of Deadwood in my patrol car early on," Derrik said when they heard Sam's feet trod down the hallway over their heads. "The guy was basically repeating what we already know, and what other people here in Redemption saw on the news before it went down. I couldn't find it again when I got back into my car after responding to the fire. My connection to dispatch in Deadwood was also interrupted by then, as well as my phone and laptop. From what I've seen of the electronics here in the house, it seems like somehow, some of the internal wiring has been...damaged."

Dakota listened silently, absorbing what he was saying while trying not to freak out. "And the shelter in place thing?" she asked when he'd finished. "It said it's a national emergency. Does that mean this is happening like, in the whole *country*?"

Her dad stared at her grimly. "I'm afraid so. That's why I really need you to step up and help make sure we conserve everything. There's no way of knowing how long we'll be going without supplies or power. But we're going to be okay," he added quickly, when Dakota took a step back and gasped. Taking her hand, he pulled her closer, forcing her to listen. "We're going to be okay."

"Okay," she echoed. She wanted so desperately to believe that her dad would be able to take care of them the way he always did. That they'd be safe.

"*Dispatch, Romeo twenty-two.*"

Dakota jumped at the unexpected voice as her dad reached automatically for the radio clipped to his shoulder. "Romeo twenty-two."

"*I just had Howard run in here all the way from Mel's Tavern. Says someone's having a heart attack and I can't raise anyone from the fire department on the radio.*"

"I'm on my way."

Already headed for the door leading outside from the basement, her dad paused as he pulled it open and looked back at Dakota. "Tell Sam I'll be back as soon as I can, and remember what I said."

She didn't have time to respond as he ran outside, not that it mattered. Dakota would never forget what he said, only there was a visceral part of her that didn't believe it.

They weren't going to be okay.

17

JAMIE
Redemption, South Dakota

JAMIE SLAPPED at the glowing radio on the dash until the incessant tone stopped. Twice through the emergency broadcast was more than enough. He didn't need to hear it again.

The car sputtered as he shifted into fourth while coming out of a curve on the dark, high mountain road. "Come on, Grover," he muttered, eyeing the tachometer with wariness. The ancient green pinto had to have well over 300,000 miles on it, and was used as a beater car around the fracking site. Jamie had a nice truck parked outside his trailer, but given their current situation it was a little *too* nice. Since the most up-to-date technology in the Pinto was a tape deck, it was ironically the most reliable ride.

The ten-mile drive into Redemption was usually enjoyable. The heavily forested mountain was virgin territory, aside from the gravel road Marsh put in that led to the isolated, hidden oil field. It was easy to get lost in the remoteness, and pretend you were back in the pioneer days where the Lakota still hunted the land as the miners answered a primal call to their own kind of hunt. The area was rich with history and stories of triumph, and a lot of loss. It was tempting to believe the legends of ghosts and cursed land, especially when you were a part of destroying it.

Grimacing at the thought, Jamie reached for the radio again. He hadn't realized how much he relied on having a steady stream of music or chatter to keep him focused. Or distracted, depending on how you looked at it.

...Deadwood... ... ... power... ... technology. The shelter-in-place order...
... ... nationwide...but we have yet to... ... ... down everywhere... ...
... ... stay where you... ... ... until further... ... ... the... ... ...
... ...

Grunting with dissatisfaction, he turned it off again after losing the signal, and nothing but static hissed for several minutes. Since he'd already heard the emergency broadcast, the broken transmission provided more frustration than enlightenment. It was obviously the station out of Deadwood, and based on the few words he could discern, they were just as in the dark as he was.

It was the main purpose behind Jamie's trek into town. After successfully contacting the operators out in the fields and working with Carter to organize the other men into teams to help with the shut-ins, it was mutually agreed by the leads to send Jamie out for any possible information he could gather. Since Marsh hadn't returned, and there was no sign of the police, they didn't know what to do with Kacey's body. It was really freaking some of the guys out and a few insisted on at least moving him inside the trailer to show him some respect.

They were already in a highly volatile situation under extreme circumstances, and Jamie suspected it wouldn't take much to tip some of the guys over the edge. They couldn't risk a mass exodus, or else the remaining wells would become a major issue.

He wasn't sure why the radio stations wouldn't be working or have so much interference. The fact that the emergency broadcast was going out suggested the system was perhaps protected in some way against an attack. What that was, Jaimie didn't have a clue. A cyber-attack through something in the radio station that was connected to the internet? His degree wasn't in radio broadcasting or cybernetics, but environmental sciences. The whole thing was way over his head.

Approaching the edge of town, the first thing he saw through the trees was the strobing red and blue lights of a police cruiser. As Jamie rounded the last bend, Mel's Tavern came into view and he saw that the patrol car was parked out front. A group of people were milling outside the main entrance, where a light over the door illuminated them, so the building had to be on a generator.

Slowing, he debated whether or not to stop. Clearly, the cop was already dealing with something so it wouldn't be the best time to approach him. Looking up the road toward his original destination, a cluster of cars indicated the other diner was also open, so he kept going.

Olson's was always the busiest place in town, and Carter had gotten his original information there earlier, so it seemed like the best place to start. From there, he'd go to the police station and make sure Marsh had already reported Kacey's death, and try to get someone to come out and get his body.

Olson's Diner was two blocks in on Main Street, and was your typical small-town hangout. With its old western style frontage, wooden boardwalk, and even a hitch for horses taking up one of the front angled parking stalls, it was easy to imagine it being there back in the 1870s, at the birth of Redemption.

Jamie wondered how many other businesses in the town started with someone's name, as he maneuvered his rattling junk heap into a distant spot. His feet thumped along the weathered, wooden planks of the sidewalk as he made his way up the darkened road, and he paused to study the large group of people inside, through the glass windows that lined the front wall.

"Half the town must be here," he muttered, reaching for the door. He hoped it was a good sign. He'd been to the diner a few times since going to work for Marsh, during some of the rare occasions he came into Redemption. It was a local favorite, and Jamie was counting on that to make it a hub of information for the town. When word-of-mouth was suddenly the only form of communication, where you got it changed, too.

Though dimly lit, the restaurant had a cozy, inviting atmosphere and smelled of fresh coffee. A woman with a blonde ponytail scooted out from behind the bar and greeted him with a mug of it. "Come on in!" she chimed. "We've shut down the food but we've got free coffee."

Jamie recognized the woman from the only coffee stand in town, which was his usual reason for leaving the site. His one and only addiction was caffeine and the drip machine in his trailer was no competition for espresso. He gratefully accepted the cup while looking around the room. "Thanks, I'm hoping I came to the right place."

"You and everyone else," the woman answered with a shake of her head. "If it's answers you're looking for, you're welcome to join the club of the clueless, but aside from the coffee, I doubt we have much to offer."

"Lisa!" a woman shouted from behind the bar, and with a quick nod, Lisa bounced away to leave him awkwardly holding the steaming coffee.

There was an empty table in the back, so Jamie made his way there, deciding to see what he could glean while drinking the one cup before moving on to the police station. There were always baskets of peanuts set out, and he realized he'd never had his dinner. It was better than nothing.

Settling into his odd meal, Jamie quietly surveyed the room and its occupants, taking in snippets of multiple conversations.

"I'm sure this'll all blow over by morning. Everyone is overreacting."

"I saw the news before it went out. Stuff was exploding! I'm telling you; things are going to be insane in the cities."

"It's the end times. This was all prophesized by—"

"Are you doing okay?"

Jamie blinked, and then looked over at the older man who was speaking. It took a moment for it to register that the question was directed at him. Setting the coffee down, he wiped the salt from his hands and offered him a smile. "I'm fine, thanks. Just trying to determine what's going on, like everyone else it would seem."

Smiling back, he extended a hand and shook Jamie's with a strong grip. "Jack Cartwright. This is my wife, Amy. You're not local. From Marsh's set-up?"

Jamie nodded at the woman and then chuckled, looking down at his clothes. "Jamie Pratt. Is it that obvious?"

Jack gestured to Jamie's beard and greasy tactical boots. "You all have a look about you. But don't worry," he added, waving a hand dismissively. "I'm not one of the holdouts. I understand about progress and such. If it weren't for Marsh and his little project, we wouldn't have our new school going in."

Like most other communities near fracking wells, there was a lot of dissention over the pros and cons. While the sites brought in high-paying jobs and a nice tax base, the impact on the environment and some of the types of people drawn to it tended to also change the atmosphere of the cities, in addition to the land. The locals who were against it were often very passionate in their opposition, and Jamie couldn't say he blamed them.

"Anyone been to Deadwood?" Jamie asked, changing the subject to something more constructive.

"Trent Duncan tried," Jack said. He pointed at a man around Jamie's age and size, sitting on the other side of the diner. "He's one of our councilmen. The road was blocked so a group's gonna go out in the morning to clear a path. I'm sure we'll get more info then."

Nodding thoughtfully, Jamie scooped out another handful of peanuts and sipped at the coffee. "How about the police activity at the tavern? Know what that's about?"

"Horrible situation," Amy answered, leaning forward. Her greying hair was pulled back into pigtails and she was dressed in overalls. Jamie had no doubt she made a very fun grandma for some lucky kid somewhere. "It's Patty Collins. Deputy Adams had to respond because they couldn't get hold of our only ambulance crew we've got, and there's but one other deputy in town. Anyway, Patty dropped dead right in the middle of the tav. I spoke with her just a week ago and she seemed to be doing fine after getting one of those fancy pacers put in for her heart. It's a shame."

Jamie frowned. A couple of years earlier his coworker got a new pacemaker that he excitedly talked about for weeks. One of the cool features was how it stored and uploaded data for the doctor to monitor. Rubbing at his temple, he tried not to think of the implications behind the possible connection. "How about landlines?" he asked. There had to be *some* way of reaching someone outside Redemption.

"Landlines are down, too," a new voice answered.

Turning, Jamie saw that one of the waitresses was standing behind him, apparently listening to the conversation. Her long black hair was loose for once, and she wasn't holding any food or a coffee pot, but he still recognized her. She'd waited on him two of the three times he'd been in for dinner. Aside from her having striking green eyes and quick comebacks, all he knew about her was that her name badge said Sage.

"At least, the phone in my office is dead," she continued. "I'll be checking the one at city hall as soon as we close things down here, but I'm sure it'll be like all the rest."

"City hall," Jamie repeated, his brows furrowed. "Who's in charge?" It might prove even better to speak with them, instead of the police, if there were only two of them in town. The Sheriff's office was in Deadwood and the one in Redemption was just a satellite for local deputies. They wouldn't be set up to handle operating on their own.

Sage bristled, and he wondered how he'd hit a nerve. "The mayor is out of town." Glancing at Jack and Amy, she then pivoted so she could look at the council guy, Trent, before answering. "I'm the Deputy Mayor, and I'll be bringing the council together in the morning to get organized."

Shifting in his seat, Jamie tried to back the conversation up and go down a less antagonistic trail. "Have you heard the emergency broadcast?"

Sage's eyes narrowed. "What broadcast? My radio here got fried. Last person that came in about a half-hour ago couldn't get anything in their car."

"I just heard it on my way here," Jamie explained. "It's a national shelter-in-place order." It was unsettling that he was turning out to be the one with the most up-to-date information. "Does Redemption have an emergency response plan?"

Sage ran a hand through her hair and pressed her lips together before answering. "It's hard to respond appropriately when you don't know what the emergency is, but I suppose you're right. It's not a bad idea. Aren't you from Marsh's operation? How are things going out there?"

It was Jamie's turn to look uncomfortable as he debated how much to share. While he'd intended on only speaking to the police about it, Sage was the acting mayor and would therefore effectively be in charge. As that dawned on him, he decided the trip wasn't a waste of time, after all. "The outage and...interruption led to a rupture of one of the valves. Unfortunately, we lost someone. It's under control now, but we need help with..." he paused and struggled with finding the right words. "Police. Or, an ambulance. I don't suppose you have a coroner here?"

As the Cartwrights reacted with shock and condolences, Sage crossed her arms over her chest and squinted at him. "A rupture? You're telling me someone is *dead*? It's been over three hours since this all started. How come I haven't already heard about this from Bucky?"

"He was supposed to be coming to town," Jamie replied, thrown off by her reaction. Too late, he realized she must be one of the opponents to the fracking, and had an obvious issue with Marsh. "We've been a little busy trying to handle the other wells."

Her expression didn't change. "You haven't been around that

long," she said, the tone of her voice hard to interpret. "What, about a month?"

Jamie felt like he was walking into a trap. "Yeah, something like that."

Her squint deepened. "And you're already acting as Bucky's mouthpiece. You must be something special."

Snorting, he pushed the peanuts and coffee aside as he stood. It was time to go. "As a matter of fact, I doubt I'll still have a job in the morning. Look, I'll stop at the station if there's someone there and fill out a report, but could you make sure that the right people know? Ka—the guy who died deserves to be taken care of. And if you need help with anything tomorrow, like clearing the road to Deadwood, there should be plenty of us up at the site that can lend a hand by then."

Sage's scowl softened, but her arms remained crossed defensively over her chest. She was clearly on the fence about him. "I'll keep that in mind."

As Jamie watched her walk away, Jack gave him a knowing look. Offering him a mock salute as he left, Jamie let the older man think what he wanted, but he hadn't been admiring the view. He was thinking that Sage was sharp. That she was the sort of person with good intuition, if she was skeptical of Bucky Marsh.

She was also the sort of person he didn't want asking the wrong questions, and that meant he had some work to do if they were going to be friends.

18

S AGE
  Redemption, South Dakota

SAGE'S FACE burned hot as she walked away from the well operator, and she struggled to separate her personal feelings from the more pressing responsibility as Deputy Mayor. All she really knew about him was that he liked his steak medium well and paid with cash. She considered Jamie one of the "quiet and dangerous" types who kept to himself, and probably had a record. Most of the guys from the site blew off steam at the tavern, a roadhouse-style bar on the edge of town with pool tables and darts, so she didn't have to deal with them much, which was just the way she preferred it.

But hearing about the spill drummed up strong emotions that were still raw, and a bitterness that left a bad taste in her mouth. It made it extra-hard to swallow her pride and admit he'd been right, and that she'd already failed less than an hour into her new role as a leader.

"Dad, things might be even worse than we think," Sage said as she reached the bar.

Ed looked up from a deep conversation he was having with Gus and Mr. Johnson. "How so?"

"The operator that just came in, I think his name's Jamie, says he heard an emergency broadcast on the radio. That there's a national shelter-in-place order."

Old Gus leaned back from the bar and whistled. "Yup. It's a record-breaker, then. The Emergency Alert System has never been activated on the national level before."

"Really?" Mr. Johnson asked, scratching at his jaw. "Well, I'll be."

Ignoring the random fact provided by Old Gus, Sage reached across the bar to take hold of her father's arm. "I can't wait until eleven, Dad. I'm going to City Hall now so I can go through things and find a point to at least start with a plan. I have to figure out what's involved in activating our emergency response for the city. I know we have one. I should have already done it, instead of standing around here pouring coffee."

Ed placed a hand on top of hers and squeezed it. "I'll go with you. We'll take Trent with us and see about contacting the other council members. And you need to shut down the self-recrimination. You've been in charge for barely an hour and had no idea what the scope of this was."

Sage wasn't going to even try to argue with her father, it would only waste more time. "Well, now we know so we have to react appropriately."

"Emergency response plan?" Old Gus chuckled. "You mean the script handed out to every town in America by the Feds after 9/11? I'd be surprised if Irv did more than use it as a paperweight on his desk."

Sage bit back her initial response, something she'd become good at over the years after her mouth had gotten her into trouble enough times. Due to her geology background and knowledge in natural disasters, protecting the town against them happened to be one of her few interests while serving on the council. Granted, preparing for a snowstorm hardly compared to what they were experiencing, but she at least had a basic understanding of the town's emergency supplies. "Gus, don't you have one of those two-way radios? I remember you letting me play with it when I was a kid."

"My ham radio?" Gus shook his head. "Nah, I gave that piece of junk to my son going on ten years ago now." Scratching at his mop of grey hair, he turned to stare at Mr. Johnson. "You know if Harry still has his? We used to meet up and wag on about 'em every once in a while, but that was some time ago."

Mr. Johnson shrugged and was working up to a long-winded answer, so Sage quickly intervened. "Maybe one of you can check with him and get back to me tomorrow? I'll be camped out at City Hall. I doubt we have one there, but I'll still look. You never know what might be in that basement."

"I can't say that any of this comes as a surprise," Gus said as Sage moved to leave. "Ed, you of all people knew this was inevitable. Our society has been plowing this field for some time now and we're only reaping what we sowed."

Sage tugged at her dad's arm to get him moving, afraid he'd get caught up in a lengthy, philosophical discussion. Not that he'd disagree with Old Gus. He'd been cautioning anyone who would listen for years, that they were becoming too dependent on technology. As a society, a community, and individuals. It hadn't fallen on deaf ears, and Sage's lifestyle was a testimony to that. But her withdrawal from being "connected" only emphasized to her how reliant the rest of the world was.

They were caught in the perfect storm.

"Lisa!" she called, moving toward the kitchen. She found her friend sitting on top of a bar stool, staring down at the inventory notebook she'd left on the work counter. "I'm going to city hall. Can you keep the diner open? I'd like to treat it as a sort of sanctuary, at least until we can establish some sort of shelter for people to check-in at and make sure everyone's basic needs are being met."

"Sure, so long as I know Cam and the kids are okay, I'm good."

She tilted her head questioningly at Sage. "What's changed? You seem much more...decisive."

"Someone picked up an emergency broadcast. There's a national shelter-in-place order."

Lisa glanced down at the notebook like directions might magically appear on how to proceed. "So, that's it, then. We've got our confirmation that... *this*, is happening everywhere." She lifted her arms and waved them around the room for emphasis.

Sage got a thermos and began filling it with coffee as she spoke. "We have to assume we're on our own. With Irv gone, I need to start connecting the dots, Lisa. If we don't all come together now, it's going to be one hell of a catch-up game later on."

Wringing her hands nervously, Lisa busied herself with filling a small to-go bag with creamers and sugar. She knew how much coffee her friend would require for the long night ahead. "Well, we know how long it took for FEMA to respond to Katrina. I don't think we can expect them to come to our rescue way out here in little ol' Redemption anytime soon."

Sage took the paper bag and let her fingers settle over Lisa's for a moment as their eyes met. "You're probably right, but you know what? I can't think of any other place I'd rather be."

With a reassuring smile, Sage went to her office and retrieved her satchel from her desk before leaving by the back door. She didn't want to get bombarded with questions if everyone saw her go, and she had no doubt Gus would take care of informing the crowd of the updated news and what her intentions were.

Finding her dad and Trent already waiting out on the road, she hurried to join them. City Hall was less than a block away, so it made more sense to walk. With all of the street lamps out, the canopy of stars was thicker and brighter than usual and Sage had to pause to stare up at them.

"Kinda puts it all into perspective," Trent said as he stuffed his hands into his jean's pockets.

"Which one?" Sage rubbed at her eyes as she started walking. "That we can rely on the moon and sun to rise and fall regardless of what's happening down here, or that no matter what we do to ourselves with advancements and technology, the Earth will persevere and spin on?"

Trent cleared his throat and moved up to walk beside her. "I was thinking more along the lines that our world is what we make it. That—" he pointed up at the sky. "Is real. These mountains—" He lowered his arm to gesture toward the range to the west. "Are tangible. The people in this town who are experiencing the same reality as us, are the only ones who matter right now. If we worry less about what we can't control outside of it, and more about what we can do right here and now, we'll be a lot better off."

Sage glanced over at her father and saw the expected grin. "Trent, when'd you get so poetic?" she asked, giving him a gentle shove with her elbow. He'd been four years ahead of her in school, so they'd never really hung out that often, growing up. He ended up marrying his high school sweetheart, and twenty years later they had three kids and one of the more respectable farms in the community. She didn't know when he'd become so wise, but the guy had a really, really good point.

"That's the idea with getting the emergency plan rolling," Sage agreed. "Would you mind tracking down and notifying the rest of the council of what's going on? Maybe set a time to meet in the morning. Say, six?"

Headlights cast their shadows ahead of them and down the road before Trent could answer, and they all turned to see a police cruiser approaching. Waving at it to stop, Sage then went to the driver's window and saw that it was Derrik Adams at the wheel, which was a huge relief. The guy hadn't been on the job for more than a year, but he had a long military background and was someone she definitely was glad to have around.

"Derrik!" Leaning in the open window, she gave him an awkward hug. Although he'd asked her out and they had dinner a couple of times, it never progressed past a friendship. Sage wasn't sure why. He was handsome, intelligent, and pretty much everything she would say she was looking for in a guy...except for the lack of chemistry. Her dad would say it was because she sabotaged any potentially healthy relationship, which was why she never discussed it with him.

"How are you holding up?" he asked. Putting the car in park, Derrik got out and gave her a more legitimate embrace. "Ed, Trent," he said, nodding at them in turn. "You heard what happened at the tavern? I can't say for sure that Patty died because her pacemaker was somehow affected by what's happening, but—" he looked at Ed for his input.

"A pacemaker?" her dad asked, his brows furrowed. "If she had one of the newer ones that sent information online to her doctor, I suppose it might be possible that it malfunctioned like the other electronics."

Sage gasped. She hadn't even considered that, and it suddenly made it all feel more personal. Not only was their infrastructure being targeted, but also individuals. "There was another death," she blurted. "At the fracking site. One of the operators came into the diner and said a valve ruptured and they...need help with the body. He said they have the well under control, but I haven't even seen Bucky, so who knows what the hell is really happening out there, as usual."

"I'll add it to my list," Derrik said, removing his arm from her shoulders to rub at his neck. "The few fires that broke out are under control, but I'm running blind. We're cut off from the dispatch center, so Ellen is running things out of our office here the best she can. Brett's the only other deputy in the area right now and he's driving a grid, contacting people and checking for any other risks that need to be addressed."

"That's good," Sage said, feeling encouraged that someone else was already taking action. "I'm on my way to City Hall to get our emergency plan up and running. You heard about the shelter-in-place?"

"Yeah. I figure all of Redemption counts as one shelter."

"Good analogy," Ed said with a rare approval.

"I need to contact the other council members," Trent said with a nod at Derrik. "Could you help me with that, and then I'll ride out with you to the fracking site to see what the situation is?"

Derrik answered by leaning over and hitting the button to unlock the doors. "I could use another set of eyes right now. In fact," he said, turning back to Sage. "Let Irv know I could really use some volunteers. Like a block-watch on a city scale. We've got some extra hand-helds at the station, which seem to still be working for short-range communication."

Sage kicked at a rock and grimaced. "I'm the acting mayor. We don't think Irv ever made it back from his trip to Yellowstone."

Derrik surprised her by smiling. "Don't ever tell him I said it, but it makes me feel a little better knowing you'll be the one running things."

Silently accepting the compliment, Sage closed the door as Derrik got back into his cruiser. "What channel are you on? I'm pretty sure radios are part of our emergency kit, so we'll at least be able to communicate here and around town."

"Channel Two," Derrik said. "Contact me when you find them. If I don't hear from you in a couple of hours, I'll make sure to have one of ours dropped off at city hall."

As Derrik and Trent drove away, Sage held the warm thermos to her chest and avoided eye contact with her dad. Relationship advice was the absolute last thing she had the energy to get into with him.

"You know that the spill caused by a water valve on the well is different than the one that—"

Sage squeezed her eyes shut, but continued walking. She'd been wrong. It wasn't the worst thing he could bring up.

"Sage—"

"—I know!" she interrupted, swinging around to face him. "I know," Sage repeated with less vehemence. "But it still killed someone, and it's a good reminder why that place should have been shut down that first year."

"I'm the wrong person to be lecturing about that," her dad reminded her as they approached city hall. "But you're going to need to find a way to deal with Marsh without bias, when it comes to determining what takes priority over these next few days."

Her mom's breast cancer had been very rare, very aggressive, and very suspect. Because, as rare as it was, two other women in Redemption also died from it that same year, all falling ill within six months of a chemical spill at the Marsh Fields. A spill that wasn't even known about until an employee made an anonymous report. A toxic spill that wasn't looked into until months after the fact, and never fully investigated. They might not have been able to prove Marsh was directly responsible for her mother's death, but that didn't matter to Sage.

She knew.

19

KATHY
North of Flagstaff, Arizona

THE SILENCE WOULD BE the ultimate death of her. It'd been close to two hours since she left the rest stop and around ten at night. The lack of any form of music to keep her from zoning out was becoming a serious issue. Kathy was finding her imagination was limited when trying to come up with new songs to cannibalize, and Colby was likely to run away the next time they stopped and she opened the truck door.

"What?" she demanded, glancing over at the dog when he whined at a particularly off-note key from Queen's Bohemian Rhapsody. "No comments from the peanut-gallery, Colbs. It's either suffer through my serenading or find another way to keep me awake." She drove in silence for almost a mile. "What? No suggestions?"

Kathy shrugged her shoulders and tipped her head to either side in a vain attempt to stretch her neck. Even for her, she was engaging in more detailed conversations with her furry companion than was normal. But they were hardly in a normal situation.

The gaping hole in the truck's dash where the radio used to be was a mocking reminder of what the dark of night was able to hide. She was driving into the unknown, and aside from Colby, was utterly alone. Alone in a sense she'd never before experienced. Kathy was a self-made recluse. By choice, she lived deep in the woods and only ventured into town to work at the veterinarian practice on weekends, to get groceries, and occasionally a rare night out with a couple of co-workers. However, she'd always had the *option* of contacting whoever she wanted, whenever she needed. She had a phone—both a cell and landline, due to having poor cellular reception in her cabin. She had internet connection, which she used for her trivial social media interaction and entertainment.

Aside from those obvious electronics, she also had an MP3 player, a stereo system that was WiFi capable so she could stream whatever she wanted, and a security system that was connected to her phone so she could eavesdrop on Colby when she was gone. Kathy had spent the past hour making a mental list of all the technology she used and had become dependent upon over the last five years without even realizing it.

Her house was on a well and septic system, but what happened if the gas supply dried up across the country? Her well was deep and required a pump to keep the pressure up. She'd never gotten around to installing the solar panel system she wanted, and the back-up generator she had was dependent on gasoline...like so many other things, including the vehicle she was driving.

Kathy eyed the fuel gauge. She'd skirted around Flagstaff, thinking it best to avoid any larger communities. Looting would be one of the first fallouts of the blackout, and there was a good chance the congested roads wouldn't even be drivable.

Still. It might have been a mistake not to try.

She was sitting at just under three-quarters of a tank and wasn't confident it would be enough. Her plan was to drive that night for the five hours or so to Moab, Utah. Kathy was betting on its remote location and sparse population to make her odds of being able to gas up there without any issues more likely. That was, if she made it. And there was a whole lot of nothin' between her and the high-desert town.

There would be a run on gas stations, that was a given. The question was how long it would take before enough people began to panic. From Moab, it was another seven-hundred miles to get home, so she'd be forced to stop at least one more time along the way.

"We'll make it," she said out loud, presumably for Colby's benefit.

The headlights of the truck cut narrow swaths through the thick darkness, illuminating just enough of the road to cause the scrolling fog lines and dashes of yellow down the middle to have a mesmerizing effect. She could feel the vast expanse of the desert pressing in from all sides, and it gave Kathy the very uncomfortable feeling of traveling through space.

"A song, Colbs," she implored, rubbing viciously at her eyes. "Help me come up with one before I—what the!"

She didn't see where the guy came from. One moment the road was empty, and the next he was there, staggering in front of her truck with a huge backpack that came at Kathy faster than her weary mind could react.

She yanked at the wheel and slammed on the brakes at the same time, causing the truck to swerve violently, but it wasn't enough.

Thwack!

Leaving a solid line of rubber behind her, Kathy stood on the brakes until they came to a stop. Her mouth watered and she was sure she was going to vomit. Falling out of her door and dropping to her knees on the pavement, she barely registered how it was still hot from the heat of the day.

Colby barked.

Her head swam, and her vision blurred as she rose to her feet. She didn't have time to get sick, she had to go help him. Staggering sideways as she forced herself to turn and face what lay behind her, Kathy clasped at her stomach when she saw the form in the road.

"No, no, no..." she moaned, dragging her feet forward, compelling herself to move closer. Not twice in one day. A chill spread throughout her body and threatened to steal her breath, to take away her ability to think and function.

The mishappen figure on the blacktop moved.

Kathy froze. "He—hello?" she stammered, her voice cracking. It was ridiculous to be so *afraid*. But in the dim light cast by the truck's taillights and the open door of the driver's side, it was hard to discern what she was seeing. In a world turned upside-down she no longer trusted her perception of what was or wasn't real.

"Oh, man!" he moaned as he shifted around and an arm went to where his head should be. He sounded young.

Kathy crept closer. As she did so, the clamp that was squeezing her chest loosened, and she was able to inhale. What she had thought was a leg was actually a sleeping bag tied to the bottom of a large hiking backpack, knocked free and sticking out. The pack itself was canted, the weight of it making it hard for the teen to get to his legs under him. There wasn't any visible blood and he didn't look like he was in any pain.

Kathy reached out a hand. "Are you okay? I'm so sorry, I didn't see you. I—"

"No worries," he interrupted, accepting her hand and the help up. "You just clipped my bag." Once on his feet, he batted awkwardly at the sleeping bag for emphasis. "Stupid thing's way too big. I should've ditched it hours ago, but I'm already gonna be toast, and if I lose my mom's pack on top of everything else, I'll be grounded for the rest of my life."

She was trying hard to shift gears from thinking she'd killed someone, to offering a kid parental advice, but Kathy wasn't quite yet firing on all cylinders. Taking him by the upper arms, she dragged him closer to the light so she could get a better look at him. Patting at his shoulders to see if the pressure elicited any pain, she then ran her hands over his head and held them out to the light, checking for blood. Her veterinarian degree required as much schooling as an MD, and while she practiced on animals, Kathy's medical knowledge was often interchangeable.

"Seriously," the kid urged, shrugging away when she tried to press at his neck. "Other than a bruise on my butt from sitting down too hard, I'm not hurt. Promise."

Somewhat satisfied, Kathy took a step back and really saw him for the first time. He looked to be in his mid-teens, and was built like a kid who spent a lot of time outdoors. His black hair was pulled back in a ponytail, and he had bronzed skin a shade darker than the sun alone could accomplish. Based on the clipped, sing-song trait of his accent, Kathy was certain of where he was from.

"My name's Kathy Storm," she said, offering a hand again.

Taking it hesitantly at first, the boy then shook it with a firm grip when he was certain she wasn't going to try and examine him again. "Hunter Everson. I'm really sorry to freak you out like that. It was totally my fault. I guess I got a little dehydrated from walking so long with this big pack, and it made me a little unstable. I didn't even realize you were behind me until it was too late."

She waved a hand dismissively. "We're both sorry, I'm just happy you aren't hurt. I don't think my heart could take any more shocks today. You're Hawaiian?"

Hunter smiled, his teeth flashing white in the shadowy light. "Kanaka Maoli," he confirmed, using the indigenous name for native Hawaiians. "Most people aren't so good at guessing."

"I lived there for several years when I was a kid," Kathy explained. "My dad was in the Navy. My best friend is Hawaiian, and we still keep in touch. I try and go visit at least once a year." Swatting at a mosquito buzzing near her head, she became acutely aware they were having an obscenely ordinary conversation in the middle of the road, under anything but ordinary circumstances.

"How old are you?" It was the first question that popped into Kathy's head.

"Fifteen," Hunter answered, sounding a little defensive.

"And, you're out here at night in the middle of the desert by yourself walking down the freeway, because..."

Hunter unsnapped the pack, allowing it to slide off his shoulders and fall to the ground. Rubbing at his left shoulder, he let out a deep sigh. "I was on a camping trip at Sunset Crater with my friends for Spring Break. I'm going home."

Kathy looked pointedly up and down the dark highway. "Where's home? And where are you friends?"

"Home is in Aspen." Hunter squatted and began to retie the sleeping bag. "My friends are idiots and refused to take me. They think I'm making a big deal outta things. I'm sorry, but how much *bigger* does shit have to get than freaking airplanes falling out of the sky!"

Kathy squinted as Hunter attempted to lift the pack but gave up and then sat down to load it onto his back. "Don't you think your parents are going to try and come get you? Maybe it would have been better to wait there for them."

Snapping the harness into place, Hunter sighed and looked up at her. "It's just me and my mom, and no, she isn't going to come and get me because she doesn't know where I really am. I lied. As far as she knows, I'm at a Boy Scout camp with my best friend." It was hard to tell in the light, but Kathy was pretty sure he was tearing up. "I can't call her. If she drives all the way to that camp and can't find me, she's going to freak out. She'll be so worried." His voice hitched and he wiped at his nose. "I have to get home."

Kathy only hesitated for a few seconds before stepping forward. Unbuckling the pack, she ignored Hunter's confused exclamation as she lifted it off his back and tossed it into the bed of her pickup. "Come on," she ordered. "Get in."

"What, you're offering me a ride?" Hunter stood hesitantly, looking back and forth between Kathy and the idling truck. "Just like that?"

"I'm from an era where we could still bum a ride to the beach without fear of being murdered," Kathy replied as she approached her door and pressed a button to unlock the others. When she saw he hadn't moved, she tried again. "Not to imply that you should be fearful, or that I'm a murderer—because I'm not."

Still, he hesitated.

"Oh, come on already!" she said with some exasperation. "Let me at least fulfill my legal obligation to get you, a minor, safely home after nearly mowing you down. I figure it's the least I can do."

An infectious smile slowly crept across his face as Hunter came to terms with accepting her help. He was obviously relieved that he wouldn't be left to walk alone on the highway all night, even if he was still worried that she might be a psychopath.

When he opened the passenger-side door and saw Colby lying there in his dog bed, Hunter wordlessly closed it again and got into the backseat. Kathy decided she liked the kid.

"This is Colby," she said, glancing at him in the rearview mirror. "Colby, meet Hunter. He's a stray, just like you used to be, so we're going to help him find his way home."

Kathy was rewarded with another broad grin from Hunter, and she found herself smiling back. "Aspen is a long drive from here," he said, leaning forward so he could pet Colby. "Are you sure about this?"

Putting the truck in gear, she turned to give Hunter an affirmative nod. Aspen wasn't really that far out of her way. "I've always wanted to visit Aspen in the Spring."

Colby chuffed his approval.

20

DAKOTA
Redemption, South Dakota

"THANKS FOR CHECKING ON US, Mrs. Cartwright." Dakota accepted the friendly woman's hug while standing in the open doorway. Her personality had always reminded Dakota of her own grandma and the hug really did make her feel better. A little.

"You know where we are if you need anything," Mr. Cartwright said as they turned to leave. "You're always welcome in our home if your dad gets tied up."

"I'm sure he'll be home soon," Dakota reassured them as they walked away, though she wasn't sure if that was true.

Closing the door, she thought of the doorbell camera footage that had replayed earlier, and although it was now powerless, she felt a small stirring of fear. It was like the house had turned against them and as brief as it was, the invasion was enough to unsettle her. The house that had slowly been turning into a real home for the past year had lost some of its comfort and sense of safety.

That made Dakota angry. After all they'd been through, to have their hard-fought sanctuary attacked was very...personal. The anger was a welcome escape from the fear, so she clung to it. Marching into the kitchen, Dakota turned on the hot water and began throwing their dirty dishes into the sink. When she was done there, she'd go around and haul all of the ruined electronics out into the garage. She'd purge the house of any reminders and replace it with...

Replace it with what?

Dakota frowned at the negative thought. Standing in the dim glow cast by the single light left on in the main area of the house, she stared at her bandaged wrist and then at the flowing water. She probably shouldn't get it wet, and using hot water would be a drain on the generator.

Turning the water off, she stepped back from the sink and shifted to stare into the darkened living room and at the large, sixty-five-inch television mounted to the wall. "There's no way I can carry that by myself," she muttered. "Even if I manage to get it down."

She glanced over at the smaller screen attached to the wall in the kitchen, which was part of the doorbell system. She'd have to go get her dad's toolbox out in the garage, and the thought of going through all of the necessary steps just to accomplish one small part of her ambitious plan was suddenly overwhelming.

Deflated, Dakota wandered from the kitchen and down the hall. Passing Sam's room, she paused to listen to the static that was hopefully lulling him to sleep. She'd convinced him to try after suffering through three games of Life. She found the boardgame full of irony, as they went about going through college, getting careers, married, and buying houses while moving around the board. Dakota wondered if they'd now be able to do any of those things, or if they did, what it was going to look like once things were sorted out.

Sorted out.

That was a mild way of putting it. No matter how Dakota tried to rationalize what details she knew, applying it on a national or worldwide scale was beyond her comprehension. She kept coming back to the same conclusion: they were screwed.

Moving past Sam's room, she went to stand at the threshold to her own. The laptop was still sitting on her bed, the fit bit lay on the floor where she'd thrown it. In spite of her big plans, Dakota found she couldn't even bring herself to gather those small electronics up. She didn't want to touch them.

Backing away, she stood indecisively in the middle of the hall-way. She didn't know what to do with herself. It was around eleven at night, and she would normally be huddled on the couch with a snack, watching a good sci-fi.

Her face bunched up as her breath hitched and her body was wracked by a sob that she fought too hard to keep in. Would she ever watch one of her favorite movies again? Speak to her best friend, or see her grandparents?

Turning on her heel, Dakota ran through the dark house, out the back slider door, and onto the patio. It was chilly out, but compared to the suffocating weight bearing down on her inside, it was a relief. Pulling up the hood on her sweatshirt, she staggered over to one of the chaise lounges and collapsed onto it, staring up at the starlit sky.

She was exhausted, both physically and mentally, and there was a familiar, nagging voice telling her she wasn't good enough. Throughout her life, Dakota had struggled with self-doubt that only worsened after her mom's death. In the aftermath, school and other things felt trivial. She simply didn't *care* what her grades were, or that her teachers constantly told her how she wasn't living up to her potential.

Dakota despised the word. "You need to rise to your potential," had become a codeword for retreat. When getting out of bed and dressing was a battle, to be told that wasn't good enough had a way of beating you down even more.

She'd moved far beyond that phase of her mourning and depression and was finally at a place where she was comfortable with herself. Dakota had to admit that the move to Redemption had something to do with that. In spite of her complaining, there was a magic quality about the place that had a way of...absolving your burdens.

Hugging herself, she continued to concentrate on the pinpoints of light twinkling overhead. The backyard was a good half-acre of treed lawn, with the woods on one side, and distant neighbors on the other. Burning tiki torches and scattered voices were the only indication that the neighbors were home, and it smelled like they were barbecuing a late dinner.

Coyotes yipped in the distance, and a screech owl's cry made her jump. No matter how many times Dakota heard it, she was convinced it was a woman wailing. It had warmed up enough that day that the air had an earthy pine smell that lingered, and she preferred that over the cooking steaks next door.

"Dax?" Sam whispered her name from the edge of the patio.

Jumping for the second time in less than a minute, Dakota laughed at herself when she saw it was just her little brother. He had a Star Wars blanket wrapped around him, a bag of chips in one hand, and Dr. Doom in the other.

"We couldn't sleep." He held Doom up for emphasis. "He kept digging in the corner. Ya know, the way he does when he's upset about something. Watchya looking at? Can I sit with you?"

Before Dakota could answer even one of his questions, Sam ran over and jumped on the lounge with her, careful to keep Doom held out so he wouldn't get squished between them. The chips weren't so fortunate.

"I'm just looking at the stars," Dakota answered truthfully. He didn't ask why.

Reaching in for a handful of crumbs, Sam nodded like he understood some big, cosmic secret. "Yup. Dad told me that sometimes the best way to listen to what's inside your head, is to look at something so big, like the sky, that you don't have any choice but to hear it."

Dakota paused with her hand over the bag and stared at Sam.

He'd just said something really deep, and it confused the hell of out her. "What?"

Shrugging, Sam licked the salt from his fingers before digging for more pieces of chips. "I thought you'd know what it meant, 'cause I don't get it."

Chuckling, and feeling a little relieved he was still her silly little brother, Dakota wrapped an arm around him. "I don't think you were meant to. Dad was just being... you know, *Dad*. It means that as bad as things might seem sometimes, it's all in how you look at it."

Sam's face scrunched up and he absently stroked the top of Doom's little white head. "I still don't get it."

Raising her hand to ruffle his hair in a way that usually made him run away, Dakota began to finally relax. The important things, the really important things like how she loved her brother and Dad, and how they'd always take care of each other, hadn't changed. "It's okay," she told him. "You don't have to."

"Do you think we'll have school Monday if the power's still out?" he asked, settling back on the chair with the blanket, and Doom curled up against his chest.

Dakota hadn't even thought of school. "I doubt it." When she saw him frown, she did her best to put a positive spin on it. He was still at an age where he mostly liked school. It was where he saw all his friends and got to hang out with them afterwards, at the playground. "I'm sure it won't be for long, and we can make a list in the morning of all the things we can do this week."

"Like fishing?" he said, sitting back up. "Cuz you said you were going to take me to the river as soon as it was nice out."

Dakota smiled. "Sure, we'll put fishing at the top of the list. I'm not sure what's in season, but I guess it won't really matter."

Sam raised an eyebrow in one of his classic trouble-maker expressions. "Can we ride our bikes out to the Marsh Fields?"

Grimacing, Dakota thought of the long, winding dirt road up the mountain. "I told you before, it's ten miles away!"

"So?" Sam pressed. "We've gone that far before."

"When?"

"Lots of times!" Sam insisted, getting pouty. "You said we could. I've never seen a fracking well!" he giggled at his own play on words.

Dakota was certain she'd never made such a promise, but she also knew he'd be complaining by mile five and wanting to turn back. "Okay, if Dad says we can."

"Let's make smores!" he said enthusiastically, already moving on to the next topic.

"What, tonight?" Dakota balked, not wanting to go looking for the food and the means to build a fire in the pitch-dark.

"No, tomorrow—"

His voice trailed off at the same time that Dakota became aware of an odd light. It was orange, pulsating, and was coming from somewhere overhead.

Jumping to her feet, she turned to look above the trees behind their property at the same time the neighbors began talking loudly to each other. There was something in the sky. Something burning.

"A meteor!" Sam shouted excitedly, jumping up and down while clasping Dr. Doom.

"No," Dakota whispered, their faces glowing orange as it passed over. "It's moving too slow." And it was too low, much too low to be something falling from space. She thought it might be a plane, but it was a big one.

"Aliens!" Sam hooted. "Come on, we have to go see where it crashes!"

Alarmed, Dakota grabbed at Sam's arm before he could dash away. "This isn't E.T.!" she shouted, pulling him back toward her. "And that isn't a UFO." At least, she didn't *think* it was. "We can't go chasing after it, Sam. It isn't safe. And anyway, I doubt it's going to crash anywhere near—"

Her words were cut off as the ball of fire dipped just behind the trees to the west, and the unmistakable sound of an impact echoed through the mountains.

21

JAMIE
Marsh Fields,
Near Redemption, South Dakota

HE WAS UNFOLDING his body from the cramped confines of the Pinto, when Jamie noticed an odd shadow being cast out across the forest floor and onto the side of his trailer. Confused, he finished standing and then turned to look up into the sky behind him.

His brain refused to process the information at first, so he stood with his mouth hanging open for a full five seconds before even blinking. The fireball was low in the sky and while it was moving much too slow to be a meteor or even space debris, it was something big. Like...

"A plane," he said, loud enough for the other men coming out of their trailers to hear.

There wasn't time to react in any other way, as it disappeared behind the mountain ridge to the west and impacted somewhere within its miles of vast wilderness.

"What the hell!" One of the operators Jamie rarely spoke to moved out into the middle of the campground. "How's this possible?"

"Should we try and find 'em?" another guy asked. "Maybe we can... help, or something." His voice trailed off as he realized the futility of the gesture.

Carter ran up to the small group, and while Jamie was surprised that he wasn't at the site, he was happy to see him. "No way anyone could survive that."

Shaking his head, Jamie kept staring at the mountains, though there wasn't anything to see—not even a distant glow. "Commercial jets are full of computer systems now. I'll bet there's still hundreds of them in the air, flying dark or with multiple failures. I can't even imagine."

"Whatdya know?" Carter asked, focusing on Jamie. "I came down a few minutes ago to see if you'd come back. I'm glad I caught you. I'm rotating the guys here through breaks, and I can really use you, as well as any information you were able to pick up."

Grimacing, Jamie scratched at his beard, wishing he had better news. "I filed a report at the police station, but they're cut off from Deadwood and running blind with only two of their local deputies. I talked the secretary into having the doctor tracked down, so we can at least get Kacey properly...taken care of."

"Okay," Carter said evenly. He was understandably unhappy about any kind of wait. "What the hell has Marsh been up to? Didn't he already talk to 'em?"

"No." Jamie didn't try to make any guesses or excuses for the guy. "I don't know where he went, but it wasn't there. On my way into town, I picked up an emergency transmission, Carter. There's a national shelter-in-place order, so this thing? It's the real deal."

Carter was nodding. "One of the operators already caught that recording on his truck radio. We've all decided that staying here for now and sticking it out together, while keeping this place from imploding, is the best call."

"For now," one of the other men standing with them emphasized. "I got a family in Montana I need to get home to. You've got me for another day, man."

Carter didn't try and change the guy's mind as he turned to go back to his trailer, and Jamie wondered how many other operators would follow his lead. Not that he blamed them. His life at the moment was the fifth wheel at his back and the job at the fracking site. Jamie's parents moved to Arizona after selling the family farm, so with so many unknowns, the twelve-hundred-mile drive it would take to reach them wasn't a viable consideration.

Carter draped an arm over Jamie's shoulders and guided him toward his trailer, away from the few remaining operators still standing and talking while pointing up at the sky. "What else did you find out?"

"Not much, I'm afraid," Jamie admitted. "Mayor's out of town, so the dark-haired gal who seems to be running the diner is apparently in charge. I suggested they think about activating their emergency response plan."

Carter snorted. "Great. That's just great. We've got a waitress running the town, and no real police force. I may not be highly educated but I do know a lot about human nature and small town or not, when people panic, things are going to get ugly."

Jamie didn't disagree. "Only road to Deadwood is blocked, so they're going to work on clearing it in the morning. Hopefully by then, someone there will be able to fill in some of the blanks."

"Landlines are down, I take it?"

"Yeah," Jamie confirmed. "Everything but radios without WiFi connection in them. All of the electronics were fried, just like here in our trailers."

Stopping in the glow of the dim external light on Jamie's fifth wheel, Carter glanced around to make sure no one was within earshot. "The panic won't be limited to Redemption. I've already had to put out some fires and I could use your help. You've got a way with people most operators don't have."

"I'm not going anywhere," Jamie said, uncertain how long he could keep that promise.

"Great." Carter slapped him on the back. "Then do whatever you gotta do and then meet me at the Fracmaster's office when you're good to go. We've still got a long night ahead of us."

Entering the trailer, Jamie automatically checked the battery indicator. It had already dropped a bar, and he swore under his breath for not making sure everything was shut off before he left, after stopping to get changed earlier. His generator was full and they had a huge stockpile of gas at the fracking site, but they couldn't let that lull them into a false sense of security. They'd quickly burn through it without any other form of power, with no supply runs coming in to replenish things. Listening to the distant hum of other generators already running around the campground, it was an issue Jamie would bring up with Carter that night. They needed to start rationing everything.

Waiting by the door until he was sure Carter had left, Jamie then grabbed a bottle of water from the fridge and a power bar off the counter. He stopped to pull the shade over the window above the sink and then headed for the bedroom.

Tossing the bottle onto the bed, he jammed the energy bar in his mouth to free his hands. Reaching around to the waist holster hidden under his flannel shirt, Jamie removed the Glock 19. The 9mm was a nice, compact option that suited his need for concealment.

Clearing the chamber, he then set it on the bed and knelt to open the bottom drawer of the dresser in the cramped space. Under an extra set of sheets, he withdrew a yellow Pelican water-proof case and a manilla folder. Standing, he sat next to the Glock and placed the case on his lap before opening it. Inside, was a SAT phone. The case was compartmentalized so that the phone, cables, and battery pack were separated. It all looked intact, without any signs of damage.

That was what he was hoping for.

Removing the phone, Jamie held his breath as he snapped the battery into place and turned it on. The digital display lit up, glowing a dull yellow. Going through a practiced motion, he dialed the prearranged number.

While he'd expected the satellite phone to turn on, his expectations for it working weren't high. If, as they suspected, technology was being wiped out, that included satellite systems, so it would render the phone as nothing more than an electronic toy.

A short burst of tones and clicks indicated no connection. Jamie tried again, and then a third time, with the same results. Nostrils flaring as he battled to keep his emotions in check, he removed the battery and replaced the device back into the case. He'd try again in the morning.

Shoving the case onto the floor, he shifted his attention to the file folder. It was thick, and held the equivalent of a year's worth of work. Opening it, Jamie removed the top photo and stared at it, wondering how things could have gone so wrong.

He'd meant it when he told Carter he'd stick around, but that was only until he could determine his best course of action. His training dictated that when cut off or outside of communications range, he was to rely on his own experience to make the right decision. Except, no amount of training or personal experience could prepare someone for what had occurred, and was still occurring. It was so far outside the parameters, that the assignment itself may suddenly be insignificant on a personal level, if it came down to a matter of survival.

Staring at the stack of official documents, copies of reports, hand-written notes, and grainy pictures, his eyes drifted to the yellow case and the gun resting next to it. With a sharp intake of breath, Jamie caught his own reflection in the mirrored closet door along the far side of the bed. He didn't recognize the man staring back and that frightened him almost as much as the chaos raging outside.

Replacing the photo, he closed the folder and moved with more purpose as he hid it back in the drawer with the SAT phone. There might come a time when he'd have to make that call and step out of the shadows, but it wouldn't be tonight.

Retrieving the Glock, he chambered a round before reholstering it at the small of his back. Making sure all of the lights were off, Jamie stepped out into the welcoming dark of the woods.

22

SAGE
Redemption, South Dakota

"HAD to be a big commercial plane, maybe a 747," Ed said. Wiping at his forehead like he was sweating in spite of the temperature being in the forties, he turned from where he'd been staring at the mountains to face Sage. "Probably took off from the east coast just before O.N.E. went live and has been up there for the past four hours, hoping to land."

"Isn't pretty much every system on one of those jets reliant on some sort of computer?" Sage asked, horrified by the thought of what they'd just witnessed. How many people had died only miles from where they stood?

Ed shrugged. "I couldn't say, but I imagine there's any number of things that could have caused an engine to combust if there were any electronics going haywire the way they were down here, only on a much grander scale."

Sage continued to stare vacantly at the sky as it sank in. "How many thousands of people are dying just from airplane crashes alone?" she choked out, unable to swallow around the lump suddenly present in her throat. "Tens of thousands if this is worldwide."

Her dad took hold of her arm and pulled her into a forced hug as she stiffened. They were standing in the road in front of the city hall building, where they'd run out after seeing the light through an office window.

"Cruise ships," Sage gasped, twisting away from him. "The one I was on last summer had over two-thousand people on it, and *everything* was computerized." The absolute scope of what was unraveling outside of Redemption cascaded within her head. "Submarines! How many soldiers are on one of those big naval submarines? I can't imagine how—"

"Stop!" Ed shouted, moving in close again but wisely not trying to contain her. "We can't think that way. Not now. Not if we want to hold it together. Let that knowledge fuel your desire to take action, not shut down in fear. We can't afford to do that, Sage."

Biting at her lip, Sage focused on her father's face while breathing in through her nose and out through her mouth. It was the closest she'd come to a panic attack in over two years and her thoughts threatened to spiral beyond her ability to reel them back in.

"Sage." He spoke her name calmly, while holding her gaze. "Breathe with me, honey. I've got you. We're in this together and we'll get through this together. You and me, just like always."

Gritting her teeth, Sage lifted her chin and concentrated on his voice. Allowed it to soothe her and pull her back to the present. As more oxygen reached her brain, her thoughts sharpened and the greying around the edge of her vision faded so that she got a firmer grasp on where she was. She was in control.

Another, cleansing breath.

I'm in control.

"Okay," she said out loud for both of their benefit. "I'm okay."

One more breath.

I'm stronger than I think.

It was an old mantra, but an effective one, and it reminded Sage that her father was right: she had to hold it together. Whether she wanted to be or not, she was in charge of the city's response to the disaster and that meant people would be counting on her.

Take action.

That was something she excelled at, and so Sage would focus on what she *could* do, rather than what she couldn't. That entailed acting off what they knew, and the plane, as horrific as it was, provided new information. The scale of what was happening would make any outside help unlikely for several days. Possibly even weeks, or longer, if it was worldwide.

"Do you think it was shot down?" she asked her dad, eyes widening at the sudden thought.

Ed blinked and took a step back as he tried to keep up with his daughter's transition from panic to organized thoughts. "Um, no...I highly doubt there'd be missile-armed terrorists hanging out in the middle of South Dakota, waiting to shoot down commercial airliners." When Sage gave him an exasperated look, he put his hands up defensively. "I'm just being blunt. It was a reasonable question."

The radio in Ed's hand crackled and he turned up the volume.

"Romeo twenty-two to city base."

"City base," Ed replied into the handset.

"Incident command," Sage reminded her father of the proper term.

"Yeah, Trent and I are on our way out to Marsh Fields," Derrik reported. *"And it looked like that plane, if that's what it was, went down just over the ridge, but I don't think it's going to pose a threat to any part of the county."*

"Received." Ed raised his eyebrows at Sage as she took the radio from him.

"Did you have any luck with talking to the other city council members?" she asked.

"Affirmative," Derrik answered, his voice breaking up slightly. *"They'll all be there at six in the..."*

"Well," Sage said, handing the radio back to her dad as it faded into static. "I guess now we know the range of these things."

"Better than I thought they'd be." Using the thick antennae as a backscratcher, Ed looked up and down the road thoughtfully. "We may have escaped any harm from that wreckage, but who's to say something else unexpected won't crop up?"

"Which is why I'm getting the council together in the morning, and spending most of the night here preparing the incident command system as much as I can," Sage answered a little defensively.

"No, I'm talking about medical necessities," Ed said, waving his free hand at her. "I'm sure part of that plan involves coordinating with medical staff?" When Sage nodded, he clipped the radio to his belt. "Right. I'm going to make myself more useful, then, and make my way over to the clinic. If Dr. Pearlman isn't already there, I'll drive out to his house. We'll need to keep it open 24-7 until communications are back up. Treat it more like an emergency room."

"Right," Sage agreed, thankful to have her father there. "Medical care falls under logistics, I think." How many other things was she already neglecting to consider? "Are you sure you won't wear the Liaison Officer vest? I know they seem weird," she added, pointing to the Incident Commander vest she had on. "But it helps to let people know something is being done, and who to go to if they need something."

Ed grunted. "I'll put it on when I get back. Just do me a favor and pick Old Gus for something, would you? I'd pay money to see him in one."

Appreciating her father's skills with de-escalation techniques, Sage was reassured that he was the absolute best pick as a coordinator. While some of the command roles were already predetermined and most of them were either council members or city employees, she couldn't simply call them. "I need to get back inside," she said, eager to return to the inventory and reviewing the response plan.

The radio squawked with more chatter from the towns one and only fire engine and crew, clearing the scene of the house fire on the edge of town. "I'll also stop by the fire station," Ed said as he walked away, toward where he'd left his car. "Let them know you're setting up a command center so they can send whoever they want to oversee their volunteer firefighters and be their main contact."

"Operations," Sage said to herself as she waved while heading back inside. That and the logistics branch were probably the only two she'd focus on to start with.

Entering the main meeting room, she glanced at the poster taped to the far wall, beyond the large conference table. In the dim light provided by the three LED lanterns scattered around the space, she could just make out the bold-lined image. It was a map of the Incident Command System (ICS), provided in the response packet. The diagram was like a genealogy tree, only with critical roles instead of names. The Incident Commander was at the top.

She only had one other page from the packet displayed, and it was a list of the ten disciplines required to be NIMS compliant. NIMS stood for the National Incident Management System. Sage had taken some of the hour-long federal online courses a couple years back, so that she was certified and understood the basics, but that was a whole lot different than trying to implement it. The ten points were:

-Law enforcement
-Fire services
-Emergency management
-Emergency medical services
-Health care providers
-Hazardous safety communicators
-Public Health
-Public works
-Governmental administrators

SAGE STOOD in front of the wall and ran her hands through her hair while staring at the list. There were several tubs of emergency supplies spread out on the oversized table at her back, retrieved from the basement where they'd been stored for years.

Redemption was so small that the mayor was only part-time. Sage served as the fifth council member, and they all received a tiny stipend of two-hundred a month for their time at the meetings. Sage got an extra hundred as deputy mayor. They had a full-time city administrator, public works operator, and a handful of other part-time employees who really ran things.

Realistically, the ten disciplines for them could be reduced to police, fire, medical, and emergency management. She was the management, and with her dad rounding up the missing aspects they were closer to having something cohesive than Sage had realized. Although most of the initial action plan put together by Mayor Irv relied heavily upon a phone tree and text messaging, so long as they had the basic foundation in place, they'd figure the rest out as they went.

As small as it was, that first glimmer of achieving an element of control provided a huge sense of relief. Smiling as she backed away, Sage decided to pour another cup of coffee and start organizing the supplies.

"Looks like you have your hands full," Bucky said from somewhere behind her. "I came by to officially offer my services as temporary mayor in Irv's absence."

Spinning around, Sage wondered how the snake had slithered inside without her hearing him. He was leaning casually against the doorjamb, his large frame filling the space, and she understood at a basic level that his positioning was intentional. By blocking the only way out of the room, she was forced to talk to him, or admit to being intimidated by asking him to move. She refused to play his mind games.

"I'm busy," Sage snapped, pushing one of the tubs out of the way so she could move her coffee mug over. Acting like she could care less about his presence, she took her time in pouring the coffee from the thermos before saying anything further. "We're having an emergency council meeting here at six in the morning. Come to that if you want to help. Since Irv isn't back from vacation, I've already initiated the city's emergency response plan. It's... thoughtful of you to offer to step in, though I would think you've already got your hands full with your own emergencies, Bucky." While he served as one of the councilmen, and was unfortunately seen as a cornerstone in the community because of his wealth and status, Sage knew the real man behind the many masks he wore. He never did anything if it wasn't beneficial for him personally, everyone else be damned.

"Oh, that's right! Irv went through with his sentimental notion and appointed you deputy mayor, didn't he?" Bucky said with a coyness that made Sage's stomach churn.

"You might want to, oh...I don't know, go help your crew take care of the body you left lying out on your drilling pad!" Sage shouted, leaning forward on the table. "Deputy Adams and Trent should be getting there right about now." She took a twisted amount of pleasure in seeing the flicker of concern cross his moon-shaped face.

"We all know the only reason Irv strong-armed you into accepting the position was because he knew he could control your vote," Bucky said, completely ignoring the other topic. "He wanted a lap-dog, and you were it."

Sage's cheeks burned hot, but it was from humiliation as well as anger. Because as much as she wanted to call Bucky out for being the ass that he was, he wasn't completely wrong. And how she reacted was going to dictate how her new role with the council was going to play out. She might despise him, but he held a lot of sway over the council and some key townspeople. She'd just have to prove him wrong.

"I've never been anyone's lap dog," she replied, doing her best to keep her voice level. "But while I agree that he recruited me because we tend to see things the same way, you know it wasn't the only reason." The unspoken accusation hung heavily between them, and all pretenses fell away. "It's not because I'm gullible, but because I respect Irv and *most* of his actions as Mayor. You should too, Bucky, and I'm disappointed it's only taken you around what—four hours to betray him."

It was Bucky's turn to become flushed and Sage didn't feel as much satisfaction as she thought she would. His thin lips pressed together and his dark, beady eyes reflected the lantern-light in a way that reminded her of a predator stalking its prey through the woods. Bucky Marsh wasn't only selfish, but dangerous, and she was reminded of what he was capable of while trapped there in his gaze.

The moment passed, and he straightened suddenly, pushing away from the door frame while smiling broadly. "No betrayal, my dear Sage. Just concern for the well-being of our town. A concern I'm quite certain the rest of the council will share when we come together tomorrow. We'll let the people decide what's best for them."

When her only response was to lift her chin defiantly, he chuckled before disappearing into the darkened hallway behind him.

Angry that he'd succeeded in rattling her, Sage grabbed her coffee and took a moment to study the portraits of the previous mayors that adorned the walls. The building was well over a hundred-years old and filled with reminders of the past. Portraits, paintings, wooden carvings and antiques from a time long gone. Remnants of an era before technology became the primary way of life. A simpler time, when a man's word was worth something and people stood up for what was right because it was what they believed, not because social media mindlessly dictated it.

Sage wanted to have faith that the other councilmembers were beyond Bucky's reach, and would simply do what was truly best for all the people of Redemption. She was born and raised there, and it was the one constant throughout her life. Their small community would come together and help each other through whatever they had to face in the coming days. Sage *knew* the people of Redemption...

Didn't she?

PART II

SUNDAY

REDEMPTION

"I think it is possible for ordinary people to choose to be extraordinary."
-Elon Musk

23

P ETER
Tokyo Metro Fukutushin Line
Brown Line, Station 10, fifty feet below the surface
Tokyo, Japan

THE CEMENT WALL at his back was cool, but the air pressing in on Peter was stagnant and hot. It smelled of diesel, oil, and a growing putridness that had to be raw sewage. It was getting harder to breathe, and he questioned his decision again to remain underground. He pushed at his temples in a vain attempt to quell the throbbing that was making it harder to think.

What time is it? Two o'clock? Five?

His Fitbit stopped working along with all of the other electronics, and was lying deep underground on the floor of the subway he'd left behind hours ago.

"*Tasukete!*" a man yelled from somewhere further down the tunnel, his voice echoing as he begged for help in Japanese.

A woman screamed from closer-by, and her voice blended with the other less discernable sounds that had merged into a single, constant thrum within an hour of the event. While most of the six-million passengers that rode the metro at any given time had immediately made their way to the exits, others had chosen to retreat to the relative safety it provided, after seeing the chaos that raged in the streets of Tokyo.

Something moved in and out of the shadows not far from where Peter was huddled, causing him to shrink away. After the transit shut down, the darkened cars filled well beyond their capacity with panicked, screaming people quickly turned to something ripped from one of his worst nightmares. It had been nine in the morning on a pleasantly warm Sunday, above-ground in the bustling city. But eighty feet below the surface, insufficient emergency lighting plunged the six million commuters into a hellish situation.

Peter could have handled the dark. He could have even handled the uncertain trek along the tracks as they made their way to the next station during the unexpected power outage. Except, it wasn't just a power outage. Something massive and unknown was unfolding above them. It was akin to being locked in a powerless panic room without any clues on how to get out, or what would be waiting for you on the other side of your escape.

"*Kon'nichiwa?*" a woman whispered in Japanese. "*Soko ni darekaga imasu?*"

She was asking if someone was there, and Peter was ashamed that he hesitated before answering. When did he become such a coward? "I'm here." He was hoarse and pathetic sounding, but he hoped she understood English. He'd only been in Tokyo long enough to learn the very basics. The irony was that he was there teaching English as a second language, and he had ended up being the student in a lot of different ways since arriving.

"You... American?" she asked in halting English.

"Yes," Peter said right away that time, breathing a sigh of relief. Although he'd chosen to stay hidden the past couple of hours, he was incredibly happy to make contact with another person he could talk to. After his brief excursion above ground, he supposed no one would hold it against him later on.

Tokyo was the most densely populated metropolis in the world, and all thirty-seven million people in the megacity were in a state of panic.

Even though it was broad daylight, Peter hadn't been able to see very far beyond the entrance to the subway, due to the smoke and massive crowds of swarming bodies.

The sounds...

"You see—above?" the woman asked, gesturing over their heads in the dark.

"Fires," Peter said in answer. "The buildings are on fire, and—traffic isn't moving, lots of accidents. I didn't see any working lights. People were screaming, yelling..."

He wasn't sure how much she was understanding, but Peter kept talking as he took his phone out of his back pocket. "There was water everywhere."

He had an old enough style that he could remove the battery, which was what he did when the device started to go whacky earlier, before it could overheat. The battery snapped into place and as the screen glowed, his eyes adjusted to the sudden light and Peter got his first look at his companion. She was younger than he'd thought. He was twenty-seven, and he guessed she couldn't be older than thirty. "My name's Peter," he offered. After seeing each other's faces, it seemed they ought to at least acknowledge that much.

"Hinata," she said with a customary bob of her head.

Behind Hinata, Peter saw an odd sort of movement and it took a moment for him to comprehend that it was *water*. Water was flowing down the tracks of the subway like a subterranean river. He estimated that the ledge they were crouched on, positioned across the far side of the tracks from the underground entrance to the Brown Line Station, was no more than four feet high.

Peter couldn't see the tracks beneath the water, and the oily-black liquid was maybe a foot below where they were perched. That's what smelled. It had to be a combination of water and sewage, flowing freely in the streets from one of the most complex waste retrieval and water systems in the world. Gravity was pulling it down to the lowest recesses of the city.

The light glowing around them took on a different tone as the phone began cycling through stored data, the way it had done earlier. It grew hot in his hand.

Swearing, Peter almost dropped the cell as he rushed to pop the battery out. Swallowed up by the darkness once again, it felt even more complete. Hinata took hold of his arm and whimpered.

"I'm sorry," he said. It was such an insignificant thing to say under the circumstances, and Peter only wished he was saying it to his mom, instead. She'd begged him not to go to Japan, and instead take the teaching job at their local elementary school. To settle in like a good son should, so he could help take care of his father. Except Peter was a coward in that sense, too. He couldn't face watching his father's mind be eaten away by early-onset Alzheimer's, so he'd left his mom to do it alone.

"I have to get home," he muttered, unfolding his legs and pushing up onto his knees. He meant his real home, in Arkansas, but first Peter had to make his way across approximately five miles of burning city to reach his tiny apartment. In a world suddenly full of unknowns, having that one simple goal made the rest seem manageable.

"Not...safe," Hinata said, keeping a firm grasp on his arm.

"This water's going to keep rising," he tried to explain as he pulled her to her feet with him. A wave of dizziness caused him to put a hand out to brace himself against the wall. His fingers tingled, and he shook his hand to get rid of the sensation, but it didn't fade.

"Head feels...wrong." Hinata leaned against him. She was breathing rapidly.

Peter shifted to look out at the flowing water, the surface ripples barely discernible in the faint light leaking down from the station entrance across from them. "Sewage gas," he whispered. He'd heard stories of people dying from it in their homes, so it wasn't a stretch to think it could be a risk in the subway. "We have to get out of here!"

Hinata didn't resist when he helped her down into the water. It came to his waist, and he tried not to think of what he was walking in. It had a...thickness to it that added to the pull of the current, making it more substantial as it pushed against his body. Hinata clung to him, and together they crossed the putrid river as fast as possible.

The river Styx.

Peter couldn't shake the continued comparison to the underworld. The black river Styx was the border in Hades between the living and the dead, and with each bump of some unknown object against his legs, he pictured a skeletal hand of the damned clawing at his clothes to drag him down to hell.

It was so hard to *move*.

His thoughts were becoming jumbled. Time was fluid, like the putrid water lapping at his waist. The sounds ebbed and throbbed, threatening to fill his head and mind and lungs, to thrust him into a never-ending existence of torture and confusion.

"There!" Hinata shouted, tugging at his arm.

The exit.

They had reached the other side.

Peter grabbed Hinata under her armpits and lifted her up to the cement subway platform. Crawling away, she then turned and offered him a hand. In the murkiness, he could see it. Her hand. It floated in the space near his face and at first, he wasn't sure why it was there.

"Peter!" Hinata yelled, shaking her hand. "Peter, hurry!"

Blinking, he fought to maintain a cohesive thought.

I have to take her hand.

He took Hinata's hand, and hoisted himself out of the river of the dead. Nothing clung to Peter to pull him back, and he kicked at the air to make sure.

"Dad?" he called out, his voice thin and unsure. Was his dad dead, yet? Was he there in the darkness, waiting to condemn him to the underworld?

"Peter!" Hinata wasn't as forceful as before, but it was still enough to draw him back to the present.

"I have to get home," Peter muttered, squeezing Hinata's hand.

Water was running across the platform where they sat, gurgling around them to join the newly formed river. He looked up to the dual stairways ascending toward a hazy light.

They were waterfalls. The subway had been transformed, and the cement steps were converted like waterfalls leading into an underground cavern in the middle of the Amazon, fed by the surface rainfall.

Only, they were in Tokyo. And they were dying. They were being poisoned, and had to get to the surface, no matter what waited for them there.

He had to get home.

Standing, Peter hauled Hinata up with him and together they walked on weakened legs toward the nearest exit. He could see others. They weren't alone. Two...no, three people were attempting to climb the stairs above them.

Reaching blindly to take hold of the metal bannister that he knew was there, Peter coughed and sputtered as the torrent of foul water splashed in his face. Turning his head, he tried to avoid it while mounting the first three cement steps. It was an impossible task. He couldn't breathe, and was forced to open his mouth, only to have it filled with an unimaginable foulness.

Hinata slid from his grasp.

"No!" his plea was sucked into the darkness; swallowed up by the floodwaters.

He clung to the bannister with both hands.

One more step.

I have to get home.

His mom needed him. His father needed them both. There were things that he had to say, and love he had to show. It couldn't be left that way... not like that.

One more...

Peter slipped.

With a grunt that was indiscernible among the cries of so many other lost souls, he hit the platform and rolled.

As the edges of his vision—his reality, became one with the blackness of the subway, far below the raging streets of Tokyo, Peter saw the shadows moving. He saw them coming, and knew they wouldn't let him leave.

Peter was never going home.

24

K ATHY
Moab, Utah

"YOU REALIZE this is the very definition of highway robbery and price gouging." Kathy tapped her foot against the pavement as the old, haggard-looking gas station owner stared back at her in the pre-dawn light, unblinking. "And you'll probably answer for it in the after-life with a sadistic demon poking at your feet for all of eternity," she continued, trying again.

That at least got a confused grimace in response and the guy scratched at his weather-beaten face. "Look, I told you, five gallons for a hundred. That's all you get and that's what it'll cost ya. You want the gas or not?"

Kathy muttered expletives under her breath as she counted out five twenties from her emergency travel cash. He snatched it from her fingers without comment, and then stomped away to leave the gas canister sitting where he'd left it.

"So much for small-town charity," she said to his back. Moab,

Utah was indeed a small town, with a population of around five thousand, according to the dusty sign on the edge of the city limits. Thanks to its multitude of tourist traps, there were plenty of gas stations. Unfortunately, none of the pumps were operational and only a couple were still selling any, and even then, only in small quantities.

Kathy supposed she ought to be grateful she got any at all. After rolling into Moab around three in the morning, she'd been the third in line when the old coot flipped the open sign around before the sun came up.

Carrying the large plastic gas can back to the truck, she smiled apologetically at the next vehicle. More were already rapidly falling in behind them, and Kathy wouldn't be surprised if the same was happening at every other gas station in Moab. Any larger cities would be in a state of unrest before the end of the day, if they weren't already.

She'd probably waste too much gas by driving around trying to find another station that didn't already have an extra-long line. They'd be better off leaving and hoping the next small stop along the way would be more generous. The more remote the town, the better the chances, and they were certainly heading into an isolated stretch of mountainous highway.

After carefully pouring in every last drop, Kathy tossed the container into the back. At least she had a cannister, so that was another positive spin. Settling into the driver's seat, she wrinkled her nose at the smell of gas. Wiping her hand off on her jeans, Kathy then automatically reached to pet Colby and almost shouted when she saw the face in the rearview mirror.

Turning to look into the murkiness of the backseat, she smiled at the half-awake teen. "Good morning, sunshine."

Hunter rubbed at his eyes and then squinted as he stared out the front window. "It's still dark out."

"Close enough," Kathy said, starting the truck. "There's a glow to the east, so I'm guessing it has to be after five. Maybe closer to six."

"We don't even know what time it is," Hunter said, his demeanor

changing as he became fully awake and remembered the circumstances that led to him being in a stranger's vehicle. "Where
are we?"

"Moab." Kathy was headed for the other side of the town, and
the entrance to the freeway, but slowed when she saw that one of
the stores on Main Street looked open. There was a police cruiser
slowly patrolling the road and several people were already out
walking around. One of them looked like they were armed with a
rifle.

Deciding that stopping was worth the risk, she pulled in front of
the unremarkable building with its glowing windows. They stood
out on the otherwise dark street, and Kathy took it as an open
invitation.

Hunter yawned and scooted forward so he could pet Colby. "Did
you get any sleep?"

"An hour or so," Kathy said, watching as Colby licked the offered
hand. Another uncharacteristic move on the part of her canine
friend. "I'm good. I'm a pro at power naps."

Shrugging an acceptance to her answer, Hunter gestured to the
store. "Why are we stopping here? Aspen's only four hours away. I'll
give you all the food and water you need when we get to my house.
And dog food," he added, speaking to Colby. "I'm sure Nala won't
mind sharing with a handsome guy like you."

Kathy raised her eyebrows at him.

"Don't judge me," Hunter quipped. "I was ten when we got her,
obsessed with The Lion King, and she's a Golden Retriever."

Chuckling, Kathy let it go, in spite of several quick comebacks
that sprang to her lips. "I'm stopping because while it might only be
a four-hour drive to Aspen, I don't have four hours' worth of gas in
this truck," she explained, patting the steering wheel for emphasis.
"Even if I did, there's a whole lot of unknowns right now, and I think
it's prudent to stock-up on at least some water and snacks while we
can."

Considering her explanation, Hunter nodded and then tugged

at his backpack. "I've got a bunch of trail mix and some granola bars in here. I mean, it's not much but it's something."

Relieved that the kid seemed to get it, Kathy smiled at him. "I salvaged a bag of food from my trailer so I've got a small stash, too." When he looked at her questioningly, Kathy waved off the unasked question. "I was in an accident yesterday and lost my travel trailer. We've both had bad days, just like I suspect millions of other people did."

"*Millions*?" Hunter sat back in the seat, scowling. "I guess I hadn't really thought about it that way. You think this program thing is really causing shi—stuff, to whack-out all over the place?"

"I don't know much of anything," Kathy admitted, amused he'd try and curb his language around her. "Except for what I heard from some truckers yesterday with working radios, which is that this is at least a nationwide thing we're dealing with. Considering how much our society relies upon technology to function, as we're already seeing with the gas, then I think whacked is a pretty good descriptor. Stay here," she ordered, opening the door. "Keep an eye on Colby for me."

The sky was indeed warming to the east with a tell-tale glow as Kathy headed into the small mercantile. Two people were at the front counter making purchases, and at least two more were visible in the nearest aisle.

Good. It was indeed open for business.

Making a beeline for a stack of cases of water, Kathy balked when she saw the handwritten sign next to it. "Ten dollars," she muttered as she hauled one up and tucked it under an arm. The sign also said there was a limit of one per person.

Turning, she found the snack aisle and grabbed a handful of pepperoni sticks, peanut-butter crackers, and nuts. High fat and protein was in order, and at least the rogue marker hadn't made its way to that aisle yet, so she could still afford it. But not anything else. Her emergency cash had its limits and they still needed to find and purchase more gas. The way things were going, one gallon might be a hundred dollars instead of twenty by the end of the day.

After waiting her turn in line, Kathy drudged up the best smile she could manage for the woman behind the counter as she dropped her items.

"Cash only," she said, before Kathy had a chance to say anything.

Her smile faltered but she kept it in place. "Not a problem. Hey, I was wondering if you know of any places around here selling gas."

The middle-aged woman tucked some stray hair behind an ear and then pointed outside, before she started writing down the tally for the goods. "Only place I know for sure is Burt's. Been directing folks his way."

Kathy's hopes wavered. "Is Burt an ornery old— "

"Yup!" the woman confirmed. "That's him. Never misses an opportunity to make a buck."

Kathy looked down at the total amount scrawled on the paper the woman was shoving toward her, and then tipped her head toward the handwritten sign as she pulled out her cash. "Is that right?"

The woman shrugged, taking the money. "Seems like a fair price for water right now."

Kathy collected her goods. "You have a point. I guess it's at least cheaper than a gallon of gas."

"It is?" the woman blurted. Frowning, she grabbed her black marker and hurried out from behind the counter.

Stepping outside, Kathy was overcome by the "normalness" of it. The tidy shops, inviting sidewalks with old-style lamp posts that stood dark behind quaint benches. The sky was brightening and birds were heralding in a new day. It all felt like a lie, and if she stood there long enough, Kathy was certain she'd begin to notice other things, too. Like the suspicious glances from the man with the rifle across the street, the lack of any mechanical sounds or electricity, and the woman at her back who was rushing to mark-up the price of something as easily attainable as water. Only, given another day or two, would it still be available? Or would everyone be fighting each other to snatch it up no matter what the cost?

Kathy's interpretation of the scene suddenly shifted from charming to menacing. The police car drove by again, and the woman behind the wheel didn't smile at her. The tap of brake lights was the push Kathy needed.

Moving with purpose, she set the water in the bed of the truck and took the bag of food with her into the front seat. It was time to go.

"Scored?" Hunter asked as she started the engine. "Find somewhere to get more gas?"

Pulling out onto the road after the cruiser passed, Kathy concentrated on spotting the sign that announced the way to the freeway. "We'll come across something along the way."

"And if we don't?" Hunter leaned forward, a half-eaten pepperoni stick hanging from his mouth. Colby whined and tried to lick it.

Her emotions once again conflicted, Kathy smiled and grimaced at the same time. She was glad to have the company, but the weight of responsibility she felt for the boy in her backseat went beyond that of a stranger. She was suffering from an increasing surety that their paths crossing wasn't entirely coincidental. That fate was testing her and she was meant to protect him. It was a role Kathy didn't necessarily trust herself with. She'd failed at it before, and it wasn't something she could ever go through again.

Turning onto the next street, they were soon on the freeway, heading deeper into the mountains and an unknown future. After several minutes, Kathy realized she hadn't answered Hunter's question.

Perhaps it was because there wasn't an answer either of them wanted to hear. It was over two-hundred miles to Aspen, and they had about a hundred miles worth of gas.

Glancing in the rearview mirror, Hunter surprised Kathy by meeting her gaze and smiling broadly. "Good thing I've got my mega backpack, then. Mai hopohopo."

The Hawaiian term took Kathy back to her carefree days as a

child and the relative safety she felt on the islands, with her parents. "Mai hopohopo," she repeated.

Looking back to the road, she clung desperately to the unburdened phrase, and that she wasn't alone.

No worries.

25

Wes
Cambridge, Massachusetts

Wes caught himself touching the cut on his forehead again, probing it in a way that elicited enough pain to keep him focused. It reminded him how close he'd come to death.

He stepped over an outstretched leg and then skirted around another partially covered body.

Because there was a lot of death.

"Now what?" a man was asking a woman dressed in identical emergency fire gear, as they set another victim down amongst the others. "What are we supposed to do with them? We can't even reach dispatch anymore."

"Someone will come," the woman said with a hollowness that betrayed her outer calm. "Someone has to come."

It had been a mistake to go to the square.

Wes backpedaled away from the firefighters, unsure of how he'd managed to end up in the maze of bodies being laid out in the open space around the Harvard Transit Station. It had seemed liked a reasonable idea, to make sure the subway system wasn't still running, or that he might even be able to walk the tracks and avoid the streets and unrest unfolding aboveground.

It was a short walk there from the park, where he'd woken at dawn, and he wasn't sure what else to do. Every face Wes saw was a potential enemy, every sideways glance a possible prelude to them pulling a gun. Entangled had to be looking for him, and he wasn't far enough away from the dorm, where Carrie and Steve were—

Wes gasped and quickened his step. He broke out into a jog as soon as his feet hit the sidewalk, and he didn't look back. Back at the thick smoke rolling out of the entrance to the subway, where multiple cars had jumped the tracks and turned the tunnels into a subterranean funeral pyre.

The smell—

Tugging at the hood of his sweatshirt as he slowed, Wes hunched over and tried to cover all of his hair and make himself as small of a target as possible. It made it harder to see where he was going, but also narrowed his field of vision which was a small relief.

It was a grey, overcast day with a fine mist coming down that only added to the bleakness. In addition to the fire, EMS, and police scattered throughout the streets, there were also a lot of people. Where they all came from, Wes couldn't even guess, but it appeared that the blackout and absence of technology was forcing everyone outside.

They weren't all friendly.

Even in the upscale neighborhood, panic and fear were driving people to behave in ways that social media would have you think only occurred in certain subsets. Apparently, once death and chaos reigned supreme, it was everyone for themselves, regardless of class.

A gunshot popped off somewhere to his left, and Wes threw himself to the ground. Cries of alarm and the stampede of feet masked his own grunt as he rolled into a crouch and looked back the way it'd come from.

"Drop it!" a man shouted. "We're not doing this!"

Three car lengths away, across the street, a cop stood next to his cruiser, in front of one of the many shops that lined John F Kennedy Street. The old-style brick buildings and cobbled sidewalks gave it a vintage appeal, but at the moment, it might have been any other ghetto portrayed on the evening news.

The storefront had been broken out, and there was a group of people advancing on it, as yet others ran from inside, arms laden with goods. The officer was clearly distraught, swinging his weapon from side-to-side, uncertain who to direct his orders to. He'd probably been up all night and was just as scared as the looters. Another cop ran to his side, pushing her way through the crowd. As she reached him, she grabbed at his gun arm and yelled something that Wes couldn't hear.

Blinking rapidly, the gun-wielding officer slowly lowered his arm while nodding. Shoulders dropping, he and the second cop moved cautiously together back through the mob. "Remember what you've done!" he yelled with less vigor as they reached his patrol car.

Shaking from the rush of adrenaline, Wes staggered back to his feet, but didn't walk away. Not only was he witness to two murders, and his own attempted assassination, but he *knew* what was happening. He knew what had caused it, and how to possibly stop O.N.E. All his life, he'd been taught to trust the police, and a part of him was compelled to run over to the two cops and confess it all. To beg for their help and to take him someplace safe.

Wes even took a step in their direction before a stronger voice of reason made him freeze. He envisioned himself: a shaggy-haired, twenty-something college type in a black hoodie with wounds all over his face, randomly approaching them to confess. He'd be admitting to taking part in the worldwide destruction of all technology that put those bodies on the ground and the looters in the store, all while begging *them* for help.

They'd think I'm crazy.

Wes admitted the thought might not be too far from the truth. Regardless, he was still the best hope to stop the ongoing destruction, and being put in either a cell or loony bin wouldn't accomplish more than maybe keeping him safe for a little while.

The coward in him perked up.

Safe.

A woman in a cashmere sweater ran past him, her arms full of random items from the store. A bottle of brand name water fell near his feet and Wes bent to pick it up as he watched her run away. How quickly they all abandoned social norms and accepted a new standard of survival of the fittest. He thought of how he'd sat with Carrie while she gasped her last breaths. He unscrewed the water bottle and took a long drink before walking away from the police.

No. Without any way to communicate, the local police couldn't confirm any aspects of his story. Professor Abe. He was Wes's best bet to be heard, and to get Helix to the authorities. His hand dropped automatically to the flash drive in his pocket, to make sure he hadn't dreamed or imagined the whole scene from the night before.

Confirming it was still there was both reassuring as well as terrifying.

Wes rubbed at his ribs before tugging at the hood again as he walked. His upper lip was swollen from where he'd been punched, and he kept running his tongue over it. He wished the beating made him feel like he'd at least made up for something. That his ordeal was all part of a series of punishments in a trial for absolution. The miserable realization that that was something unattainable put him at risk of lacking motivation.

Hesitating at the next cross street, Wes pivoted to look back the way he'd come. While the bodies were no longer visible, he knew they were there. "There's your motivation," he whispered. Not for the dead, but the living. He had to believe his family was still alive.

His pace quickened. It was now well beyond sunrise and he estimated that it was at least twenty miles to the professor's house, maybe more. It was normally close to a half-hour drive to the nice suburb on the edge of town, near a private country club.

As he passed one of the last college buildings before reaching the park he'd left less than two hours earlier, Wes saw a bike rack. Approaching it, it was obvious not all of them were locked up. He doubted bike theft was rampant on the ivy-league campus. Except it wasn't anywhere near a normal day, and Wes was desperately in need of transportation. Given the condition of the roads, a bike was likely to get him farther than a car would.

He'd never stolen anything in his life, and if he had a way of tracking down the owner to get permission, he would. As Wes hauled his choice of bikes off the rack, he almost laughed at the irony of his guilt. Almost.

His intelligence afforded him the unfortunate insight to the futility of his moral compass. And while his role in the massive death toll in only the first twelve hours couldn't be ignored, he refused to let it snuff out the rest of his conscience.

So he allowed himself to feel guilty about stealing the bike.

On the far side of the John F Kennedy park was one of several bridges that crossed the Charles River. The Great Bridge was known for its historical significance as the first to be built over the river, back in the 1600's. Made of brick like most of the other structures from that era, it sat as a monument and seemed timeless. As Wes peddled out onto the structure, he immediately saw that even giants crumbled.

It was still standing, though vehicles weren't able to cross. A large boat had collided with one of the three grand arches, and must have caught fire. Its charred remains were mixed in with the rubble from a portion of the collapsed bridge, where a second boat had also become lodged in the wreckage scattered around its base.

Several other boats were dead in the water, pressing up against other sections of the bridge, along the shore, or set adrift in the swift currents. Wes hadn't even considered what would happen with the waterway, and it was yet another reminder of how far-reaching the impact of the computer virus was. Most of the disabled boats he could see were newer, high-end yachts that relied heavily upon advanced computerized systems to operate.

Wes was forced to carry the bike over the worst of the sections of cracked and separated pavement, and was relieved to see the rest of the way was clear of debris. Jumping onto the mountain bike, he took only a moment to orient himself with what was the best and most direct route to take to the professor's.

As he began pedaling, he ignored the Harvard Business Campus directly in front of him, where students were throwing things out windows billowing black smoke. Or the stores further down the street, where active looting was going on as sirens wailed and people screamed.

The stench of sewage was overwhelming there, underscored by the smoke and other chemicals that Wes couldn't identify. Even if he were an innocent bystander, he'd still be taking the same action to get out of the city, in any way possible. It was what everyone should have been doing, and he didn't understand why they weren't.

Twenty miles.

Wes should be able to easily reach the professor's house before sundown. If he could hang onto his sanity for just a little while longer, and avoid being found and shot by the assassins sent by Entangled, he'd be okay. He'd make Professor Abe believe him. He'd make him understand, and then he'd *want* to help him.

As much as Wes clung to the thought of not being alone in such a frightening world, his stomach clenched as he tried to envision how he'd tell his mentor and close friend what he'd done. That he was partly responsible for O.N.E.'s rogue behavior.

What if Professor Abe threw him out, or refused to help, or even threatened to—

Wes shook his head.

It didn't matter. Whatever the professor did, Wes would deserve it. All of it.

The cut on his forehead throbbed and his ribs ached as Wes leaned into the bike and pedaled harder.

He deserved it all.

26

D AKOTA
Redemption, South Dakota

Groaning, Dakota rolled over to avoid the sunlight falling across her face. She'd been so tired, and her room had been so dark when she'd finally gone to sleep, that she didn't think to close the curtains.

With her eyes still shut, she buried her face into the pillow and started to pull the covers up, when the sound of a closing door from somewhere deep in the house made her pause. When it wasn't followed by footsteps coming down the hall, she sighed and finished the motion, snuggling the blanket under her chin. It must have been her dad leaving.

He'd gotten home sometime in the middle of the night, but Dakota had been half asleep when he poked his head into her room and told her goodnight. Tensing, her fingers curled into the thick blanket. Thinking about her father's late-night appearance reminded her that something was very, very wrong.

The cobwebs of sleep were slow to fade, but as they did and

Dakota became more aware, they were replaced with a shadow of fear. Squeezing her eyes more tightly, she pulled the blanket all the way over her head.

She didn't want to face the new day. Not if it wasn't any different than the one before. Or worse...

Would it be possible to simply stay in bed all day? To hide away and pretend like it had all been a nightmare. Becky would text her good morning after sleeping in, the sound of Sunday morning cartoons would drift down the hall in an hour or so, and she'd slowly start her day off with a long hot shower followed by her dad's famous eggs and bacon breakfast before going to church.

Maybe those things *could* happen. Maybe the glitch, or whatever it was, had been fixed during the night and they'd at least get the power back and the electronics that didn't go crazy would still work. Dakota decided to test her theory and cautiously lowered the blanket to below her nose.

The alarm clock/radio combo next to her bed was dark, as was her room, aside from the narrow beam of sunlight that split it down the middle. She could see the light switch on the wall was flipped up, a reminder of how suddenly their lives had been interrupted. It was an automatic gesture to swat at it when she came into her room, as she'd done the night before, forgetting her dad had tripped all but a select few breakers.

The house was too quiet, even for that extreme, and she suspected her dad turned the generator off during the night to conserve the gas. That wasn't a good sign of what his outlook was. Dakota made a habit out of complaining about Sam's need to have a radio playing at all times, but she would have given anything to hear it at that moment. In fact, she couldn't even hear the static of the emergency radio. Was it possible the batteries died already?

Well, at least they had plenty more of those in the basement.

The basement.

Grunting in defeat, Dakota pushed the covers all the way down and sat up. There was no turning her brain off now, not after conjuring up the images of prepper central, and the conversation she'd had with her dad down there the night before.

Her left wrist throbbed, another reminder that it was all too real, and she gingerly pressed at the bandage wrapped around it. She'd need to change the dressing and put some more antibiotic ointment on the burn. The last thing she needed was for it to get infected.

Swinging her feet over the side of the bed, Dakota stared accusingly at the laptop sitting on top of her dresser, where she'd moved it before getting into bed. In the weak glare of the flashlight, she'd been able to confirm the plastic on the bottom was charred and warped from whatever had burnt up inside of it, and there was no salvaging the computer. Or her phone, Fitbit, the TV, doorbell monitor, Xbox, tablet, Switch, radios, voice-activated speakers and lights, air purifier, and probably a whole list of other things she hadn't thought of yet.

Those were just the fried electronics that wouldn't work if they managed to get the power restored. Without power, the list was a lot longer, and the generator would only work for as long as they had gas for it. That made Dakota consider the stockpile in the basement again, and the gas that her dad said was stored out in the garage. She wanted to know how much was there, and then try and estimate how long it and the other stuff would last. Making out the lists and planning for the next couple of weeks would help to occupy both the time and her brain.

She'd have to get creative and think up a way to get Sam involved so that he thought it was like a game. Otherwise, he'd be nagging her every minute of the day to play with him. Entertaining her brother during the apocalypse was going to end up being what killed her.

"Now who's being dramatic?" Dakota said to her dark and tooquiet room. Snagging her headband from the nightstand, she attempted to contain her wild fray of black curls and then rubbed at her face, trying to think more clearly.

She had no idea what time it was. Twisting on the bed, she squinted at the window and decided it was definitely early-morning light. The orangish kind that starts out dark and misty before burning a brighter yellow after it finished cresting the mountains. The upper sky was a midnight blue, and still absorbing the light, so that she could easily envision the ball of fire—

The plane!

Dakota blinked and sat up straighter. Her hand started to move for where her phone would normally be, and there was a physical pain in her chest as it hung in the air and then stopped. She couldn't do a search of the news to find out what they'd seen burning over the mountains. There was no Facebook news group to jump on, no CNN website to browse, no Google to type 'plane crash South Dakota' into, or a friend to text about it. She couldn't go switch on the television for the latest updates, or call her dad at the office to check in.

Dakota suddenly felt lost: cut-off, stranded, and even...claustrophobic.

Jumping up from the bed, she ran from her room and toward the kitchen, intent on doing the one thing she could still salvage from a normal Sunday. She'd turn the generator on and make Dad's breakfast for her and Sam. Then, they'd go around and collect the burnt-up electronics like she'd thought of doing the night before. The two of them together should be able to handle it, and it would be a lot easier in the daylight. When all of the reminders were gone, they'd go down to the basement and she'd go over the inventory again before bringing up some of the stuff they'd need over the next few days.

With her hand on the door to the silent fridge, Dakota suffered another wave of fear from the lack of information. Like what happened to that plane last night, if the power was coming back on anywhere, or if anything else had come up while she'd been asleep. Would Becky be okay? Her apartment building was on a busy street in San Francisco. What if people panicked and freaked out in the big cities, like her dad predicted they would? Becky's mom was a kindergarten teacher and her dad was a banker. It wasn't like they were prepared for that sort of thing. They ate out several times a week and had their drinking water delivered. She doubted they had more than the very basic emergency supplies.

Dwelling on the fate of her best friend only made her feel worse.

The Cartwrights were right across the street, and Dakota knew they'd be happy to talk to her. Even if it was only to confirm they didn't know anything more than she did, making some useless small talk and not feeling so alone would be a relief. *Then*, she'd make breakfast.

As she went to leave the kitchen, Dakota noticed the hand-written note left on the counter. It was still dim inside without the lights on, and would be until the sun came up all the way, but it was enough so that she recognized her dad's bold handwriting.

I HAVE *an early meeting at City Hall.*
  Generator is full. You can turn it on after you get up.
  Be back as soon as I can.
  Love-
  Dad

AT FIRST, Dakota didn't register the other, messier words scrawled at the bottom, and assumed her dad had grabbed something that already had writing on it. But as she dropped it back onto the counter, one word stood out: SHIP.

Frowning, she snatched the paper back up and moved closer to the window by the sink. As Dakota read it, her feeling of dread deepened and any hope of a calm morning evaporated. Her little brother's blocky penmanship was unmistakable:

WENT TO FIND THE SHIP
  SAM

. . .

BELOW IT, in smaller letters:

P.S. DON'T TELL DAD!

BALLING HER HAND INTO A FIST, she crumbled the paper and stomped from the kitchen, back down the hall. At the door to Sam's room, she hesitated as her anger turned to a fresh upswelling of fear. She was suddenly afraid to look. She couldn't handle anything else. If she could only conjure up the radio blaring and Sam sitting with his Xbox and a half-eaten bag of chips, she'd never complain about him and his normalness ever again.

Dakota half-heartedly pushed at the partially opened door so that it swung slowly inward. Dr. Doom startled and bolted across his cage, making her jump, and she cussed out loud.

It wasn't only directed at the rat, but also Sam's empty bed. Taking a step into the room, she saw that the emergency radio was gone, as well as his school backpack that was always on the floor by his bed.

Went to find the ship.

E.T. was one of Sam's favorite shows, and all Dakota could conjure up was one of the scenes that had always scared her as a child, where Elliot was running through the dark, misty woods. Sam had been talking half the night about going fishing and camping, and after they saw the plane—

That he was convinced was a UFO...

Backing out of the room, Dakota ran to get dressed. She instantly forgot about breakfast, Becky, the power outage, and the spreading devastation.

All she cared about was finding her little brother.

27

J AMIE
Marsh Fracking Site
Near Redemption, South Dakota

JAMIE USED the hike through the woods up to the office to try and organize his thoughts. He'd only managed to get a couple hours of sleep before several generators kicking on woke him up, but it was enough to help him see things more clearly in the daylight. Disappointed that everything was still disabled, he decided to ditch trying to get any more sleep. Besides, Carter had been up all night and would need a break.

The sun hadn't risen high enough yet to crest the mountains, and a mist pooled beneath the trees. That high up, it sometimes took until noon before the fog was burned off, and Jamie enjoyed the fresh crisp air it provided in the mornings.

Breathing in the pine-laden scent, he paused to close his eyes for a moment while he was in the thick of the evergreens. With most of the big rigs and pumps shut down, the whole atmosphere of the place had changed drastically overnight. There, in the hollow between the camp and the well pad, it was easy for Jamie to forget where he was. He could just as well have been at his grandpa's hunting cabin high in the Rocky Mountains, or on one of the many trails in the woods not far from his own home in western Montana. He'd bought the house a few years back, and though small, it was perfect. The trailer he'd been living in at the site wasn't his, and he wanted nothing more than to return it on his way home.

Jamie opened his eyes and took another breath before continuing down the trail. Running both hands over his head, he then scratched at his beard to remind himself of who he was portraying. He was still Jamie Pratt, Site Operator and nomad with a big chip on his shoulder. Although he was feeling more grounded and less likely to lose his temper since the sun was up, he still lacked enough information to make any decisions. He was hoping Carter might be able to provide some, though it probably wouldn't be until later in the day when someone came back from Deadwood or another, larger city.

If things were winding down with the shut-ins on the wells, he'd go to Deadwood himself, regardless of what it took to get there. One thing Jamie was *not* good at, was sitting around. He needed to take action, one way or the other, and he was ready to go in whatever direction the conditions dictated. There wasn't exactly a protocol in place for what he was facing, but he was also good at improvising. That was one of the many reasons he was there.

As he emerged from the tree line, the first thing Jamie noticed that had been hidden earlier by the dark was the large, washed-out area surrounding the damaged sections of piping. Under normal circumstances, there would have been an immediate containment and clean-up procedure implemented. But with the lack of any emergency response, and then the power outage and subsequent failures, it was impossible to follow the regular safety regs. Hell, they were lucky no one else ended up getting killed, or that a much larger and more dangerous spill didn't happen. As it was, the slick-water was only mildly toxic, in comparison to the more dangerous wastewater regurgitated from the ground. At least that was what Bucky insisted, although Jamie had no clue as to what was really in the proprietary blend.

Rubbing at an itchy spot on his arm, he frowned. He wanted to laugh at the irony of him finding himself doused in that crap, but he couldn't muster up any humor. Nothing about the situation was funny, no matter how he spun it.

Under the brightening sky, more evidence of the damage became visible and he stopped next to one of the large light-stands to study the back casing. They were fortunate there hadn't been a fire on top of everything else. The bottom half of the housing was melted and scorched. There had to have been a massive surge from the power center, which explained why most of their lighting and some equipment had gone down. They'd already hauled up a few of their small gas generators from the campsite to run the fracmaster office and supply trailer, as well as the other lights that weren't connected to the burned-up power center. It was a good thing they were essentially shut down, because they literally didn't have the power to run things, and based on what Jamie heard and saw in the campground that morning, they were soon going to run out of hired hands, too.

The door to the office opened as Jamie was approaching, and Bucky came barreling out, moving with what Jamie was coming to understand as a characteristic brusqueness. The man walked like a bull, and it was either because he had incredibly poor situational awareness, or else he simply didn't care about anything other than himself. Jamie was leaning toward the latter analogy.

"Pratt!" he growled when he narrowly avoided shouldering Jamie on his way to his truck. "Don't you have something to do somewhere else? Why is it I'm always running into you at this office?"

Jamie scowled, but considered his words. "I'm just checking in to see where I'm needed...Sir."

Bucky squinted, trying to decide if he was being serious or mocking him. Huffing, he stared at Jamie with his arms crossed.

"I'm surprised you're still here. Sounds like half the crew is already packing up."

Jamie shrugged. "I don't have anywhere else to go. Figured I may as well stick around and see what pans out."

"What's panning out is the annihilation of my oil company!" Bucky spat. "We all know the odds of getting these wells back at a hundred percent after capping 'em, if at all. That's assuming whatever...*this*," he waved a hand around dramatically in the air, "whatever the hell caused it all, is rectified. I need answers."

"We all need answers," Jamie corrected him, unmoved.

"Right." Bucky leveled him with his steely gaze again and they stood staring at each other, unflinching. "If you're intent on sticking around, I just informed Carter that as of now, I can offer you room and board."

Jamie scoffed. "Room and board?"

"You're lucky I'm doing that much!" Bucky pointed a finger at his chest, and it was all Jamie could do not to bat it away. What he really wanted to do was take it and shove it down the bastard's throat.

Instead, he stuffed his hands in his pockets and averted his eyes to the mountains behind Marsh. "Right."

Shaking his head, Bucky put his sunglasses on as he stomped off to where his truck was parked. It wasn't the same flashy one he normally drove around, but a much older model with a lot of life etched into it. It had fresh mud splashed up its sides, much like the old cowboy boots Jamie noticed Bucky was wearing.

It reminded him how the site owner also had a working farm, one of four in his family. His parents split up the remaining five-thousand acres from the homestead amongst Marsh and his four other siblings, and all of them still worked the land. What wasn't common knowledge was the dispute between him and his father over what Bucky decided to do with the majority of his.

The truck kicked up gravel as it sped off down the road, and Jamie wondered where he was really off to. When he'd finally shown up back at the site around midnight, he'd stormed into the office where Jamie and Carter had been talking with the deputy and councilman about arrangements for Kacey, and the shut-in timeline and risks. Bucky claimed to have been tied up with his family and securing the farms, but of course, Jamie had reason to suspect he was lying. The man was a pro at it.

When Jamie entered the trailer, Carter looked up from the desk with a surprised look on his face. "Back already?"

"Couldn't sleep. Thought I'd give you a chance to get some rest."

Carter shook his head and lifted the mug sitting in front of him. "Nah, I'm good. I'm used to pulling all-nighters, and I'm on my second pot of coffee. I won't be able to shake off this rush until later this afternoon. Help yourself," he added, gesturing to the coffee pot on the other side of the room.

"I ran into Marsh outside," Jamie said as he poured a cup, grimacing at the burnt-coffee smell.

"Lucky you."

"Offered me room and board," Jamie chuckled. He took a sip, and then added several more teaspoons of sugar.

Carter lowered the notepad he'd been writing on and grinned at Jamie. "Shows you how desperate he is."

Jamie wanted to smile back at the small jab, but it would have been futile. There was no sugar-coating anything, just like the foul coffee. "Did they—" he turned to look at the closed door to the bedroom at the back of the trailer.

Carter looked down at the pen he was rolling between his fingers. "Yeah. Firefighters came around four and got Kacey. Said the doctor would...take care of things. Whatever that means. It's not like we can notify his family."

"I'm surprised such a small fire department has an ambulance," Jamie said, changing the subject.

"It's an old one. And they don't have a paramedic or anything," Carter explained. "They're all volunteers and just have basic training, but at least Redemption has a way of transporting people. Ya know, in case things drag out and they end up... needing one."

"Too bad the radios don't reach this far." Jamie glanced at what Carter was jotting down. "Three wells left to cap?"

With a sleep-deprived and caffeine-induced startle, Carter flinched and tapped at the pad of paper with his pen. "Um, yeah. No issues so far. They're moving the shut-in rig now. We're lucky it wasn't affected enough to keep it from working."

"Want me to head out and give 'em a hand?" Jamie offered.

"No." Carter was quick to answer, and he'd clearly been thinking about it. "Like you said, the radios don't reach out here, and Bucky was useless in providing any information, except that he's on his way now to some emergency city council meeting. We're dead in the water, man, and I don't know how long we can float. We're losing guys left and right, and I don't blame them.

"I need you to get into Redemption and find out anything you can, Jamie. If that means crashing the meeting, then do it. If it means driving to Deadwood, or even Sturgis, we have to find out what's happening out there."

"Agreed," Jamie stated simply. He was relieved the other man was thinking the same as himself. He felt a small pang of guilt over misleading Carter. He was a good, hardworking man that as far as Jamie had been able to tell, was honest. He didn't deserve to get caught up in things.

Carter set the pen down and stood. "If things are as drastic out there as we think they are, Redemption, and even this fracking site are going to look real inviting once the true shit hits the fan. If overnight, the stock market has been wiped out, our ability to communicate, get and spend money, and everything else that's connected to that is just... gone?"

Jamie blinked, stunned by the broader impact he'd failed to consider. Carter was right. A strike against the stock market alone would cause an economic collapse and anarchy in the streets. As only one layer in a thick multitude of others, they were looking at a complete country-wide infrastructure failure. Perhaps worldwide. There would already be riots and looting in the cities.

"Can I count on you?" Carter was saying.

Jamie looked at him, and saw that Carter was holding his hand out. "Because even if I did have anywhere else to go, I don't think it would be safe to get there." Carter lifted his outstretched hand for emphasis. "If we stick together, I think we'll be okay. Can I *count* on you?"

Taking his hand firmly in his own, Jamie shook it. "Always."

He sincerely wished he had more confidence in his own word.

28

S AGE
City Hall
Redemption, South Dakota

"I'M IMPRESSED with how much you've already accomplished," Javi said as he looked over the combination of federal handouts and the hand-drawn Incident Command System (ICS) structure Sage was recommending. Javier Perez was a retired entrepreneur who owned several local businesses, and had sat on the city council for two terms. He was charismatic, generous, well-liked by anyone who'd ever met him, and insisted on people using his nickname at their first introduction.

Sage couldn't help but feel that the overly-friendly guy was just being nice. She'd gotten a few hours of sleep on a cot she'd dragged up from the basement, and wasn't feeling at all accomplished at the moment. She kept glancing at the door to the meeting room, hoping that Irv would walk through it and simplify her life. She'd even sent her dad out to his house earlier, before the meeting, to make sure the mayor hadn't returned during the night.

"Um, thanks," Sage said, clearing her throat. "But most of these papers came in the pre-arranged packets with the disaster kit Irv got from the government. I've simplified our response by focusing on what I consider our primary concerns at this point: medical, fire, police, and setting up a shelter here at City Hall as a resource for people."

Sage looked at each person associated with the branches as she named them, and found it satisfying to have them all coming together to work as a team. Aside from herself and her dad, Derrik had shown up to represent the police, a woman from the fire department, their local doctor, and three of the other council members. The only person missing was Bucky, which didn't surprise or worry Sage. They'd be better off without him, in her opinion.

The light from the two windows on the outside wall of the room didn't offer quite enough light to see by, so they'd been forced to turn some lights on. Sage was finding that most of them had burned out when the power surged, but two table lamps still worked. With the dark oak trim, antique wooden furniture, original wood floors and portrait-adorned walls, the dim lighting added to the overall atmosphere of being thrown back in time to a shadowy collaboration during the days of the old west. Except, their most pressing issues were very modern.

"Our greatest challenge is going to be communication," Sage continued. "Most of the recommended action plans require the ability to have a call center, an emergency phone tree, and texting. You know, all the things we can't do right now. Honestly, I spent most of the night going through our inventory in the basement and bringing some of the more important stuff upstairs, so we can get the shelter and information center open."

"And you want to put it in the front lobby of this building?" Dr. Pearlman asked, sounding skeptical.

Sage didn't know the doctor very well. He'd moved to Redemption with his wife a few years back to run their small clinic, and the one time she'd been in, his only nurse treated her for a sinus infection. Looking at him now, she took in his well-groomed greying hair and astute features. He reminded her of their high school principal, which only made her shrink a little more under his cynicism. "Just for now," she answered with a small smile. "Unless anyone has a better idea. I thought that since this is most likely where residents will go for information, it's a good place to start. Plus, it's centralized and will help keep our range of communication more consistent. There are eight of the hand-held radios in the kit, and we've determined their range is somewhere around four miles."

"Ours and the fire departments go a few miles further," Derrik added. He'd opted not to sit at the table with the rest of the council and other guests, and was instead leaning against the wall at the back of the room. Everyone shifted to look at him, and Sage noticed the attention had no effect on his body language as his arms remained casually crossed. He was also well-groomed, but his wavy brown hair and intelligent blue eyes projected a sense of power rather than arrogance. The guy was cool under fire. "Higher wattage and bigger antenna," he continued. "We've got five, fire's got what...eight?"

His question was directed at Callie Ramirez, a long-time volunteer firefighter/EMT, who had been sent as their representative. The thirty-three-year-old was also working as a waitress at Sage's diner while she relentlessly applied for paid firefighter positions with the surrounding, larger departments. Sage had known Callie off and on since they were teens, and considered her one of her few real friends.

"That's right," Callie confirmed. She looked tired as she scratched at her short, black hair before holding up the ICS diagram.

COMMAND (Sage)
    (Trent) SAFETY LIASON (Ed)

. . .

(Derrik) <u>OPERATIONS</u> <u>LOGISTICS</u> (Erica)
  Fire Medical
  Police Shelter
  Diner

"I THINK KEEPING things small like this is a smart way to go, and I like having Derrik as Operations," Callie added, looking at the deputy. "I'm sure all your military background and training will come in handy with coordinating stuff between our departments. The Chief has too much to look after at his farm to get that involved."

"That's what I thought," Sage said, appreciating her support. "At this point, I want to focus on making sure emergency services are available and that the people of Redemption have someplace to go, whether it's just for someone to talk to, or to sleep and eat, which is why I added our diner to the list. I'll be continuing to keep it open and we can coordinate its use however needed, including food preparation."

"Is this all really necessary?" Erica West was the oldest council member, and was another Redemption "lifer". A retired real-estate agent, she was now the City Manager, which was one of the few paid city employees, and a close friend of Irv's. Gesturing to the supplies spread around the room and the people gathered at the table, she appeared flustered and weary. "I mean, really, Sage. We don't even know what's happened. Our power could come back on this afternoon and we'll all look like fools."

"With all due respect, Erica," Ed said, leaning forward on the table across from her. "I don't know how much you've seen or heard, but I'm afraid this is much more serious than a simple power outage. Even *if*, and that's a big if, this were limited to the power grid, those transformers have all been destroyed. In addition to that, some of the internal wiring and electronics have been damaged and aren't functioning in most of the buildings and homes, so our power availability is still only partial with the generators. No," he sat back in his chair, shaking his head. "This goes much deeper. It'll be days, perhaps weeks, before we can even hope to see any line repairs being done. That's if the damage is isolated to the grid, which I very much doubt."

"Which is why I've organized a group I'm meeting in..." Trent glanced up at the old-style clock mounted above the door. "In less than a half-hour, over at the diner. We're going to go clear the road and get to Deadwood. We hope to have some answers by this afternoon, but meanwhile I support implementing this plan."

"Plan for the worst and hope for the best," Callie said with a wink at Sage. "Emergency response, 101. Better to over-react than find ourselves scrambling a few days from now."

"I'm going with you," Derrik said to Trent. Sage noticed it wasn't a request, though Trent didn't appear to be put off by it. Derrik pushed away from the wall and went to stand near the windows so he could look outside. "I suspect we'll have to go a lot further to find what we want. The Sheriff's office is in Deadwood, so I need to check in and get some standing orders, but they're probably in the dark as much as we are. Deadwood's got barely more than what...a thousand for population?"

Trent nodded. "Yup. Sturgis is another fifteen miles to the east, but they're still considered a small town at less than seven thousand. I suspect we'll have to go to Rapid City, unless we can find someone closer who's already been there. That's another thirty miles to the south."

"I'm sorry, Deputy Adams," Erica interrupted, tapping impatiently at the table with her fingers. "No disrespect, but doesn't Deputy Johns have seniority? May I ask why he isn't the one making these decisions for our police department?"

"Brett Johns was camped out at my store for several hours late last night," Javi said, before Derrik could answer. "We haven't had any attempted looting, but I put a limit on how much can be bought and I've already had some pushback, so I appreciated his presence."

"I knew you'd be busy with The Corner Store and other shops," Sage said, feeling a need to explain his lack of an assignment on the

ICS. "If this goes on for any longer than a week or so, the supplies at several of your stores will become critical assets, and we'll need to expand our chart to include you for managing that." She turned to Erica. "I hope we don't get to that point, and I know this might seem like an overreaction, but we need people with the most experience and knowledge coordinating it."

"Once it became apparent that we were cut off and on our own in an unknown and evolving situation, Brett asked me to lead our response," Derrik explained. "While he's been a sworn police officer for two years longer than myself, we're both the same rank within the department, Mrs. West, and he felt more comfortable deferring to my twenty plus years' experience as a commanding officer in the Air Force."

When the councilwoman accepted his explanation with a silent nod, he moved away from the window and placed his hands on the table, narrowing his eyes as he stared at each person in turn. "The point I'd like to emphasize this morning, is that until we know more and can determine what our situation is, we have to consider the fact that we've got miles of vacant mountains to the west, and the next nearest town large enough in size to have any sort of formidable infrastructure is close to fifty miles to the southeast of here. Redemption is already isolated geographically, which ironically, if things deteriorate to the point I suspect they might, could end up being beneficial, but only if we respond appropriately from the beginning. Which is why I fully support what Sage is suggesting for an action plan. Odds are, this will change...perhaps daily, but for now I think we need to go with a plan and do it quickly."

"Agreed," Ed said enthusiastically, as he and everyone but Erica nodded in agreement. "I say we move ahead and reconvene this evening after we've returned. I'd like to go with you," he said, looking over at Trent. "I've got some specific information I'd like to look into."

"I can work on handing out radios," Callie offered, obviously on board with the plan.

"I still need one for the clinic," Dr. Pearlman said, already putting her to work. "And if this does go on for much longer than a couple of days, we'll need to look into finding people with the right qualifications to help me. I can't keep the doors open 24/7 with only myself and one nurse."

"Right," Derrik answered with a glance at Sage. "We'll be facing the same problem with our department, and probably Fire, as well. That's when we'll need to expand our response."

Feeling somewhat overwhelmed, and thankful for Derrik's insight, Sage started collecting her papers and then stood. "Why don't we meet later at the restaurant? I'll provide dinner and we can go back over everything. If you'd rather have someone else organize the shelter, I'm sure I can find a volunteer," she said to Erica. Sage had always gotten along well enough with the older woman, and while she understood her reservations, it was still hard not to take some of it personally.

Erica waved a heavily-ringed hand, looking chagrined. "Don't be silly. As City Manager, you're correct that I'm the most qualified. Besides, it'll give me something to do and take my mind off all of this other nonsense."

Nonsense. Taken aback by the reference, Sage struggled to accept that Erica's reaction would probably closely reflect the response from a large portion of the population. Refusing to accept the seriousness of what was happening and narrowing her view was a weak coping mechanism. Sage was concerned that society in general had regressed in its ability to cope. It was an existence that demanded instant satisfaction, and when that didn't happen, blame was placed anywhere but on the one demanding it.

It was going to be challenging enough to work around that type of mindset in a small community, and she couldn't imagine what that might translate to in the big cities.

For the moment, it meant Sage's coping skills had to expand to include accepting others' limitations. Smiling at Erica, she pointed to a particular tub on the floor. "72-hour emergency kits are in there, along with notebooks and pens, to get you started. I'll help carry out the supplies and maybe we can recruit a few others to get the cots."

"Cots?" Erica frowned. "Where are we—"

The door to the conference room banged open and Sage looked up with a surge of excitement that her wish for the mayor to return at the eleventh hour had come true. But her hope turned to disappointment when Bucky Marsh barged inside instead.

"Nice of you to show up," Sage muttered with a scowl.

"My apologies," he said, not even attempting to sound genuine. "But as I'm sure you're all aware, my first priority was to the safety of my oil fields, which ultimately includes the safety of this town."

Ed scoffed, and Bucky shot him a dirty look.

"But what's important is that I'm here now," he continued, walking to the front of the room and opening his arms as if to address his royal court. "And I'm happy to inform everyone that with my time freed up by the shut-in of the wells, as of now, I'm able to take over the role of Mayor of Redemption."

29

B UCKY
City Hall
Redemption, South Dakota

THE MIXED RESPONSE from the people in the room wasn't unexpected, but it still irritated Bucky so that he was cursing Sage Olson and her pest of a father as he outwardly smiled.

"I'm Deputy Mayor," Sage said evenly. "It's my obligation to step in during Irv's absence."

It tickled him to see her squirm. "And it was sweet of you to accept Irv's appointment, but really?" Bucky tipped his head at her and tsked. "You might have the qualifications to run a diner, but not a town."

As Sage's face burned a satisfactory crimson, the deputy spoke up before she found her voice. "She seems to be doing a pretty good job of it so far."

The police officer hadn't been in Redemption for long, but he'd still managed to be a thorn in Bucky's side. At least the other deputy, Brett, was a local guy and knew his place in the food chain. But

Derrik had too much confidence. He asked too many questions and stuck his nose in places where it didn't belong. Irv had been able to keep a leash on the bulldog, but Sage? Well, with things already unraveling, the last thing he needed was the Olsons at the helm of Redemption. No, the only option was for him to seize control where and when he could.

Derrik coming to her defense only seemed to deepen Sage's humiliation and her hand was shaking as she pointed at him. "You can showboat all you want, Bucky, but the people in this room know you well enough to call you on your bullshit. If you want to actually step up and act like a councilmember for once...great. I'm sure we could use your help in some areas. But that's where it ends."

"How quickly history forgets its origins." Bucky pivoted to peer at the painting of his great-great grandfather. "Charles Marsh founded this town and I simply want to help protect it." The Marsh's political reign had ended with Bucky's father, when he'd lost in what was likely the first unbiased vote from the town's growing population.

Erica cleared her throat. "Perhaps we shouldn't be so hasty to dismiss the idea."

Bucky had counted on her backing, and with some persuasion he thought Javi might be swayed. "Thank you, Erica. I'm only suggesting that the council consider who has the greater management experience here, as well as having worked closely with our mayor on some key projects."

"This isn't a job interview!" Sage interjected.

"Bucky runs a multi-million-dollar corporation," Erica persisted.

Ed chortled. "Yeah, and we all know how he does it."

Bucky turned on the one man who'd come the closest in the past to upsetting his growing empire. "You shouldn't even be in this meeting!" He turned to the rest of the council, focusing on Erica and Javi. "Ed dragged half this town through a messy protest over my water rights and almost cost the taxpayers several amenities most of you have enjoyed in the years since."

Sage slammed her hands down on the table, cutting him off. "Enough!"

Bucky resisted the urge to chuckle. She was so easy to trigger that it almost took the fun out of it.

Addressing the other council members, she held a small stack of papers to her chest and stepped away from the table. "Unless you want to throw me out on a no-confidence vote, then I am and will remain the acting mayor."

There was a long, drawn-out silence before Trent threw a hand up. "No one's asking for a no-confidence vote," he said, sounding irritated. "We've all got work to do and I'm more concerned at the moment with going and finding out what the hell is going on, than I am with arguing about who's in charge."

His comment was directed at Bucky, but it was clear that the undercurrent of hostility between the Olsons and the Marshes wasn't a welcome element. Satisfied he'd caused enough disruption for the time being, Bucky nodded complacently at Trent. "You're absolutely right. I just wanted to make it clear that I'm here to offer my support, however it might be needed."

There would be other opportunities for him to insert himself where necessary, so long as he didn't ostracize himself from the group. He'd always been a patient man, and one of his strengths was knowing when to strike. There were plenty of others who would support him when the time came.

Grunting in obvious disbelief, Sage moved for the exit. "I have to go check in at the diner. Erica, it looks like you found your help."

"Where are the rest of you off to?" Bucky asked, ignoring Erica's flustered expression at being tasked with him.

"Deadwood," Trent answered. "Further, if we have to."

"Could you stop in at my place later and let my kids know I might not be back for a while?" Derrik asked Sage before she reached the door. Unclipping a radio from his belt, he held it out to her. "And give this to Dakota. If I'm going to be on call at all hours, I need a way to contact them."

It didn't surprise Bucky that the two of them were chummy. All the more reason to keep everyone in check. "I thought there was a national shelter-in-place order in effect," he said with a tip of his head. Eyeing the deputy and Ed skeptically, he then turned his gaze on Trent. "Do you think it wise to be driving around to other towns right now? Seems like we should be using our time to advise everyone to stay in their homes, like we've been told to."

"Oh pipe down, Buck," Old Gus blurted from the open doorway.

Bucky stiffened at the nickname and all of the dreaded memories it elicited.

Shuffling into the room, the old codger sat down next to Erica and began leafing through her handouts while he spoke. "Since the message hasn't been followed up by any more information or directions, I think it's safe to assume our wayward government has once again failed us and we're left to take our own initiative. Something I'd think you would understand," he added coyly while looking up at Bucky.

"Is there a reason you're here?" Bucky retorted, not caring if anyone thought he was overstepping again. He'd suffered more disrespect in the past twelve hours than the previous two years and was reaching his limit.

"Flashlights," Old Gus said bluntly. Putting the papers down, he scratched at his gullet and stood again. "People aren't coming to the diner asking for coffee, or water, or even beer. They want flashlights."

Erica pointed at the large plastic tub on the floor, and Bucky noticed for the first time how much crap was spread out around the room. Grunting at it, he wondered if maybe Sage *was* better suited for all the mindless tasks, leaving him to do more of the...heavy lifting.

"We've got kits in there," Erica was saying. "Bucky and I are getting ready to get the shelter set up, if you want to lend a hand."

Appalled at the proposal of how his time would be allotted that morning, Bucky quickly conjured up a more appealing itinerary for himself. "I'm sure my father is already at his hardware store. Why don't I head over there and see what he's willing to donate to the city as far as emergency supplies go? Or, what he won't donate, I'm certain we can come to a fair price."

Gus snickered. "Oh, I'm sure Stewart Marsh would be happy to come to a *fair* price. He's never one to miss out on an opportunity."

Bucky wasn't going to bother trying to deny the accusation. Gus was absolutely right. He'd been a teenager when his father gave up on farming and turned to running the hardware store and renovating some old cabin properties into vacation rentals. His childish optimism that the change might make the man more caring was quickly snuffed out when the business side of things only brought out the miser in him.

Where his mother was soft, his dad was hard. He was made of sharp angles and hard planes, and Bucky couldn't remember a time his father ever hugged him or told him he loved him. He'd vowed to do better by his own kids. A lot better.

Disturbed by the memories and the reminder of how he'd recently been losing touch with his family, Bucky decided to include some time in his schedule that afternoon to check in on them.

"We have an emergency fund and the ability to vote on its use," Erica said, always the peacemaker.

"I'll leave that to your discretion," Sage said on her way out. "Not that we have a way to even pay for anything. Money is worthless now."

While the others all filed out of the room, Bucky considered her comment as his stomach knotted. He understood better than most about the stock market and global economy. How fast it could all come crumbling down and leave their society in ruins.

Entering the hallway, he didn't follow the others but instead turned right and headed for Irv's office. What should have been *his* office.

It was dark inside with the shades drawn, and Bucky was relieved when a couple of lights responded when he flipped the switch. It was enough to see by, and he didn't want to open the windows.

Crossing to the antique desk, he paused to admire the original painting of Redemption that hung on the wall behind it. It was dated 1901 and showed a bustling Main Street, full of horse-drawn wagons and hardened pioneers. Charles Marsh started out with ten-thousand acres of pristine Black Hills Mountains. Over the years, Bucky's relatives had broken off widening chunks of land to sell to the expanding town, after the rights were given over so it could be officially declared as a city, with all of the associated benefits.

"I don't think you ever expected the Marshes to lose control," Bucky said to whatever ghosts might linger in the room.

Pulling open the top drawer, he dug out a small key from its hiding place in the back and used it to unlock the bottom drawer. He didn't think Irv was stupid enough to keep anything in the office, but the guy also wasn't the brightest and he'd been acting weird the past couple of weeks. To the point that Bucky sent Kacey out to have a "talk" with him before he left on his vacation, to make sure things were in order.

When he didn't hear from Irv on Friday like they'd arranged, he was already on edge before the other crap rained down.

Bucky scowled at a file-folder labeled 'Marsh'. "Really?" he muttered. "How about something like 'Criminal Activity', instead. You know, keep it less obvious." Yanking it from the drawer, he threw it onto the desk and quickly thumbed through the rest of the files before sitting down.

Opening the folder, Bucky only needed to see the top page to confirm his suspicions. "Idiot." He doubted Sage had seen it, but she would eventually break into the locked drawer. What else did Irv leave lying around?

Drumming his fingers on the paper, he then clawed at it viciously and crumpled it into a ball. It was time to circle the wagons. If the others suspicions were accurate about the event, then they were about to find themselves thrown back into a time that would resemble the original pioneer town where everyday life was a hardship. A time where control wasn't about who had the most digital reach and technological advancement.

Charles Marsh had understood the laws of nature and man, and how to use the power of isolation and fear to control them. Pivoting in the chair, Bucky stared up at the painting again, seeing it in a new light.

Grinning as he studied the fine details, he folded his hands in his lap and leaned back against the worn leather. "Welcome to Redemption."

30

K ATHY
75 miles west of Aspen, Colorado

"THERE!" Hunter was pointing out the front windshield eagerly, his nose scrunched up as he scooted forward to the edge of the seat. Colby whined in protest from where he'd been curled up on the boy's lap. Hunter had graduated from the back to sharing the front seat with the dog but they were still working out the details of the arrangement.

"There's a farm," he insisted. "I'm sure they've got to have *some* gas."

Kathy spotted the top of the house and a barn in the distance, as she considered his proposal. "And what—we're just supposed to go take it?" she said with some skepticism. "I don't think people are going to be feeling very charitable, certainly not any more than all of the gas stations we've tried hitting up."

They'd just passed through a town slightly larger than Moab, but all three stations they found were closed up. In a matter of hours, the gas was either already gone or shut down. Why they'd choose to stop selling it, Kathy wasn't entirely sure. Even if the pumps failed, she knew they'd have hand-powered ones they could use to siphon from the main tanks. She suspected it had more to do with the owners wanting to hold on to what they had for either their own use, or to wait until the demand was greater so they could get more out of it.

Either way, it meant the same thing for her and Hunter. They were driving on empty and didn't have much longer before they'd end up on the side of the road. She slowed as they approached the farm.

"I've got ten bucks," Hunter offered. "We'll just ask to buy it from them. The worst they can say is no."

Kathy thought of the man with the rifle patrolling the streets that morning, and how quick people would be to panic. However, considering where they were, they had a better chance of running into someone that wasn't too wary of strangers.

The state highway they were on followed a small valley between the Rocky Mountains of Colorado, and they'd just started to climb into the higher elevations. The scattered patches of civilization were getting smaller and further apart and she wasn't too keen on the idea of being stranded out there, so far away from home.

With a grunt of dissatisfaction, Kathy pulled off onto the long gravel driveway. "I've got money, that isn't what I meant. I'm more concerned with how people tend to react when in crisis mode. The sweet grandma willing to take in a stranger can quickly turn when it comes down to protecting her family.

"We're experiencing something totally unprecedented," she said with a sideways glance at Hunter. She hoped he was getting it. She needed him to understand how serious things were. "Someone in fight-or-flight mode might not wait long enough to find out what our question is."

He frowned while thinking about what she'd said as they slowly rolled down the gravel road. It was further off the narrow two-way highway than Kathy liked, and she was already looking for areas to turn around in, if it came to that.

"So, stop a ways out and honk the horn," Hunter suggested. "You know, so we don't look sneaky."

It wasn't a bad idea. "You stay in the truck," she ordered as they came to a stop. "Do you know how to drive?"

Hunter nodded, grinning. "Sure do! My grandpa taught me last summer when I went to visit." His smile fading, he ran his hands over his hair and into the ponytail hanging down his back. Kathy had noticed it was a sort of nervous gesture for the boy.

He looked up to meet her gaze. "That's the last thing I said to my mom before I left for the weekend."

"What was?" Kathy asked, troubled by his obvious remorse. The kid wore his heart on his sleeve, and it made it more difficult for her to keep up her normal level of indifference.

"That I wanted to move back to Hawaii and stay with my grandparents again this summer. They'd already said yes." Hunter turned to stare out the window at the quaint white clapboard house with its broad porch and stone walkway. "Mom got pretty upset and said she wouldn't let me go. So I— I said some stuff I shouldn't have, and when she finds out I'm not at the camp, she might think I ran away or something. I don't want her to think that."

His voice faded with the final words and he started rubbing at Colby's head. His explanation for the urgent need to get home had a greater impact on Kathy than he could have ever imagined. The reminder of how special a mother-son relationship was, partially because of the strong interplay of stubbornness and intense love, was something she'd allowed to fade. She understood why he was so desperate to get the gas. Why he had to get home to his mom.

"Wait here," Kathy repeated, pushing her door open. She didn't trust her voice to say anything more.

Going to the back of the truck she retrieved the gas can. Assuming calling out would be less likely to cause a strong reaction, she only took a few steps toward the house before stopping. "Hello!"

No answer, but she thought she saw movement behind the

curtains of the front window. Taking several more steps, she held the gas can out and gave it a shake. "Hello! We're about out of gas and I'm hoping I might be able to buy some from you. I have money."

Since Kathy was focused on the front door and window, she didn't see the man at first as he came stomping around the side of the house. It was Colby barking that alerted her, and when she saw him, she cursed and stumbled back away from him and the shotgun he was holding. It wasn't pointed at her, but that was a small consolation.

"Whoa!" Kathy held out one hand while clasping the bright red can protectively in front of herself with the other. Not that the plastic container would do much if he decided to shoot her. "Did you hear me? I said we just want to buy some gas!"

The middle-aged man would have looked normal on any other day. His nicely styled brown hair matched his clean flannel shirt and jeans, and he wore the leather gloves of a rancher. "You need to get off my property," he snapped, looking around nervously like they were engaged in a high-risk drug deal and SWAT could sweep in at any second. He partially raised the shotgun for emphasis.

"I'm not trying to rob you!" Kathy yelled as she backpedaled toward the truck. "I'm holding a *gas* can, not a gun! I'll leave, just calm down."

"Patrick O'Day, what in the *hell* are you doing?" an older woman shouted from the porch. "Put that gun down!"

"Get back inside, Mom," Patrick retorted. "I'm handling this."

The woman marched down the steps and walking straight up to the man, wrenched the weapon out of his hands. Kathy flinched, expecting it to accidentally go off with the violent motion.

"Handling what, exactly?" she said as Patrick reacted by moving away from her and crossing his arms over his chest while glaring at Kathy. "What, you think this lady with the gas can and a boy clutching that poor dog to death on the front seat of their truck is here to burn our house down? I told you, people aren't going to go all crazy like you think they will. Only one I see acting irrational is you!

"I'm sorry," she continued, turning to address Kathy. "You running outta gas? I heard they were shutting the stations down already. Earl from the next farm over heard on his ham radio that much worse is happening in the bigger cities. But *we* aren't like that out here." She glared at her son again.

Kathy did her best to settle her rattled nerves enough to answer the question. "Yes, we're on fumes already and we're trying to get to Aspen. I've got money and I'd be happy to pay you as much as I can. I'm trying to get this boy here home to his mom."

The woman followed to where Kathy was pointing, and smiled at Hunter. "I've got a can of gas in the barn for the lawnmower. You're welcome to whatever's in it, though I'm afraid it isn't likely more than a few gallons."

"That might be enough," Kathy said, relieved to have the situation turned around so dramatically. "We'd be thankful for whatever amount it is."

"Go get it, Patrick." When the man started to protest, she stuck a hand out at him. "It's just the lawnmower gas. If we can't scratch up enough compassion for that, then we're already defeated before the rest of the collapse reaches us."

"Collapse?" Kathy didn't like the sound of that.

Tilting her head at Kathy, the farmer moved closer and raised her eyebrows. "Honey, you've been driving since this all started? You don't even know what's happening?"

"Just that the power outage and some other weird...technology failure is throughout the whole country," Kathy said. "And I heard the emergency broadcast for sheltering in place."

Patrick jogged back with the gas and went to pour it in the truck himself. Kathy refrained from saying anything to him, not wanting to set the man off.

"It's everything."

Kathy looked back at the woman, frowning. "Everything?"

She nodded, gripping the shotgun tighter. "Reports being

passed around via the radio operators is that the whole grid, both power and computer, is just...gone. Shut down. Destroyed. Same as anything else dependent on it. No one can say for sure how, why, or who—but honey, the whole infrastructure of our country was erased overnight. We're on our own."

Patrick stepped back from the truck and joined them, still looking around nervously. "It was about three gallons. It'd be best if you keep moving now."

Kathy reached into her back pocket and removed the last of her cash.

"No." Stepping forward, the woman placed her hand over Kathy's and shook her head once. "If we're going to maintain our humanity and civility, it needs to start now. From the beginning."

The beginning.

The beginning of what? Kathy felt the weight of the woman's hand like it was some sort of gavel hammering down. She stared at it for a moment before clearing her throat. "Thank you."

Nothing further was said as Kathy returned to the truck and once again put her empty gas can in the back. Hunter remained silent as she started the truck and then got them turned around.

It wasn't until they were back on the highway and she looked down to see where the gas peg was at that either of them spoke. "Not even a quarter of a tank," she said. "It probably isn't going to be enough, but it'll at least get us closer."

"Thank you," Hunter said quietly.

Kathy glanced over and without thinking about it, put a hand on his shoulder and gave it a squeeze. The poor kid must have been terrified when he saw that shotgun, and now he was blaming himself for pushing her into the whole situation. "I'm glad that we stopped," she offered. When he gave her a look that indicated he wasn't buying it, she raised her brows at him. "We got free gas, *and* information. Information that confirms getting you home asap is at the top of our agenda."

When his muscles relaxed under her hand, Kathy removed it and then had to stop herself from reaching for the non-existent radio. Instead, she punched Hunter's arm good-naturedly, and then laughed when he dramatically fell sideways, rubbing at his shoulder. "You a good singer?" she asked. "Because I need some tunes and if you can sing, I guarantee you'll be Colby's new best bud."

As he immediately began to belt out a song Kathy had never heard before, she was grateful for the distraction. She didn't want to keep thinking about what they were at the beginning of. She didn't want to contemplate what might very well be the final act of kindness she was going to experience in a world that had drastically, and irreversibly, changed with the literal touch of a button.

31

W ES
Cambridge, Massachusetts

WES HAD BEEN WRONG. It didn't take long for him to come to that determination, as he tried to get onto the freeway, only to discover that everyone really *was* trying to get out of the city. He suspected the mass exodus clogging Interstate 90 wasn't so much Cambridge as it was from nearby Boston. Over four-million people lived in the mega city, a city that was now without power, water, and a rapidly failing system without any support. With the ocean to the east, the network of highways looked like a widening spiderweb without that many options running west. The result was a bottleneck, and that would have been bad enough on its own.

He'd managed to navigate through several miles of stopped cars, and as he rode away from the exit ramp and into the suburb of Newton, Wes breathed a sigh of relief. Because it *wasn't* just a massive traffic jam. People were *fleeing* the city in a panic that was palpable, and when it was underscored by all of the accidents and a prime view of the burning cities, there was no escaping being caught up in it.

Heading into the handsome, tree-lined residential area, Wes glanced up at the overpass where he could see an ambulance. Its lights were off, and he suspected they had run out of gas like a majority of the other vehicles stuck in the hours-long gridlock. It was going on thirteen hours since O.N.E. went live, and in an area that was so densely populated, gas was already gone. Most of the stations would have been rendered inoperable simply from the outage, and without the current supply being replenished it wouldn't last long in the rush, regardless.

How quickly it all fell apart.

Like dominos set in an intricate pattern, one falling piece led to another until there was nothing left. No emergency response, no functioning hospitals, no amenities, and no way to even call for help. That morning, people woke up to a new existence where your wealth or stature didn't matter. It wouldn't move the dead vehicles out of your way or bring you fresh water. You couldn't buy your way out of it.

There's no way out.

Wes's heart raced at the thought and he struggled to control his breathing as he became lightheaded. Stopping at an intersection surrounded by stately homes with gorgeous lawns and pristine side-walks, he put his feet down and hung his head. Closing his eyes, Wes tried to block out the sirens that were becoming more distant and instead focus on the light birdsong coming from the trees that were partially sheltering him from a gentle rain.

The expensive suburb was drastically different from the cities, and the people there would be wise to follow the shelter-in-place order. If they were prepared to stay holed-up for a few weeks before having to venture out for food and water, they might have a chance of coming through it okay.

"Are you alright?" a woman called out from somewhere behind him.

Twisting on the bike seat, Wes saw a middle-aged woman

standing out on her lawn, holding something that might have been a newspaper. Had she come outside to collect it like any other Sunday morning? How had it even gotten there? It struck him as so odd, that he couldn't stop staring at her hands.

"Do...do you need some help? Are you injured?" She took a step closer and brought the object to her chest.

Wes lifted a hand to his face and as his fingers brushed over the scabs and welts, he was reminded as to how he must look. Blinking, he finally met her eyes. They were kind, though properly wary. "I'm okay," he lied. "Just catching my breath. I have a long ride ahead of me." After two hours, Wes thought he'd already be at the professor's, and it was disheartening to consider that he was only halfway there.

The woman nodded, her head darting one way and then the other as she looked up and down the street. It was mostly vacant, though some people were out gathering together on their front lawns, seemingly oblivious to the fact that they were getting wet. Most of them would be in a state of shock or denial and would be slow to accept what was transpiring. Of course, Wes was at an advantage in that respect. He knew more than anyone, though it wasn't necessarily the sort of advantage he wanted.

Dark smoke hung above the treetops, and he could see evidence of more than one housefire on that single block alone. The upscale district wasn't left unscathed, and once people from the city were forced out on foot to seek a safe shelter; the atmosphere would change more drastically.

"Have you come from Boston?" she asked with a hopeful air.

"No."

She frowned, lowered her arms, and unrolled the item she'd been holding. It wasn't a newspaper, but a large portrait of her and a man. "My husband was in Boston yesterday. He hasn't come home yet."

A gunshot from a few blocks over made them both jump, and a group of neighbors down the street quickly dispersed to run for their houses. The cawing crow that moments before seemed so ordinary, suddenly sounded like a harbinger of misery. The peaceful façade might dissipate faster than Wes had guessed. He needed to keep moving.

"He'll know what to do...when he gets home," the woman stammered. She rolled the photo up and rung it between her hands in a way that Wes suspected she'd been doing for hours. "Do you need help?" she blurted when he lifted one foot back onto the peddle, as if she was greeting him for the first time again.

"No, I—I don't need anything from you. I have to go." He wanted to tell her that he didn't deserve her help. That her concern was misplaced because he was the reason her husband might never come home. The reason she'd been left to survive on her own. Wes didn't give her very good odds, and as he rode away, he couldn't look back.

He didn't want to think about it.

Unfortunately, he'd always found his time on a bike to be cathartic in the sense that it promoted free thought and introspection. And in the midst of such a traumatic situation, his mind automatically began to wander as a way to avoid acknowledging the things around him that were outside of his control.

Wes thought about home. He pictured what his parents and brothers would be doing in the wake of it all. How the basic chores around the farm would carry on pretty much the same as any other day, which is what would give them a better chance of persevering where others would fall far short.

If Entangled hadn't gotten to them first.

Wes's jaw clenched and he gripped the handles tight enough to turn his knuckles white. "It would be pointless," he muttered, hoping the sound of his own voice would somehow make the statement more convincing. Eliminating the people who created the original worm to cover their tracks made sense. That much he got. But his family who lived two-thousand miles away and he saw a few times a year? It wouldn't be worth it. He sat up a little straighter on the bike, and his legs slowed in their pumping motion. "It would draw way too much attention."

Entangled might be able to come up with some believable reason to make Wes and his friends disappear, but if both he and his family were killed? It would bring down all sorts of questions and investigations, which would be exactly what Entangled would want to avoid.

He began peddling harder, but was still thoughtful. "Why bother at all, if you're going to wipe everything out?" he asked the passing trees and parked cars. Because if they had intended for all forms of technology to be rendered useless, which would obviously lead to a complete societal collapse, there would be no need to cover up the cause. Other than perhaps to silence one of the few people in the world capable of coming up with a way of stopping it, or preventing it from continuing when attempts were made to turn things back on.

Wes shook his head as he became more confused, instead of gaining any clarity by his contemplation. He didn't even know how he'd come to be so vulnerable to the manipulation. When had he gotten so *dumb*?

Wes tried to pinpoint when the first shift in his behavior had happened. When his hacking evolved from a bored kid looking for something to challenge him, to being a key component in an urban terrorist attack.

In high school it was for fun. The greatest immoral act he'd ever done was to drop the chemistry grade of a kid that bullied him in the tenth grade. After his run-in with the feds, Wes was scared shitless, so when he was given the opportunity to go to MIT and use the talent as a career, he jumped at it.

He'd been "clean" for over three years when Entangled first reached out. In a way, he wished he could claim they'd brainwashed him into believing he was a part of something that was for the betterment of mankind. That he'd been led astray by some sort of cult-leader and was as much a victim as everyone else. But that would be a lie.

His stomach began to ache again, but Wes refused to shut down his line of reasoning. He knew it was wrong. The purpose behind the program he believed Entangled wanted him to write was morally and ethically wrong, but he'd done it anyway. Regardless of what he thought he was a part of, Wes understood that the worm he created was ultimately going to destroy a company. Everyone from the C.E.O. of O.N.E., to the stockholders was going to suffer financially.

He'd done it for the money, and to take advantage of the vacancy the downfall of the company would leave in the tech world.

Wes couldn't pretend to be a victim, which meant getting the thumb drive to Professor Abe at any cost.

One more block and he'd attempt to get back onto the freeway. He'd have to cross over the Charles River again, and if he was unable to use the turnpike, it meant a huge detour.

A large mushroom cloud of black smoke hovered to the east and Wes was pretty sure it was coming from some sort of warehouse and the Greenline rapid transit station. He'd seen it enough times driving by on the freeway to know the general location.

The damage he was seeing evidence of seemed more malevolent than simple malfunctions or meltdowns. Though he supposed it might all be explained by failures, he couldn't help but wonder if his initial concern was gaining more validity: that the quantum computer, with the self-destruct order from O.N.E., had turned into something more...precise.

Battlestar Galactica.

Wes frowned as he reached the onramp, standing on the pedals as he climbed up the slope while trying to determine why he'd chosen to think about his favorite television show.

The ship.

While they certainly weren't battling killer robots that had advanced to the point of taking on an indistinguishable human form, the concept of the initial attacks was still similar. In the show, the Battlestar Galactica survived because it was one of the oldest ships in the fleet, and still hardened against a virus attack. While it had computers, they weren't networked or tied into external sensors or communication.

That was ultimately going to be the only way to come back and eventually fight back against O.N.E. Because the genie was out of the bottle. The quantum computer was so fast that to the human perception, it performed tasks instantaneously what would have taken any other modern computer months, or even years to complete. Anything it gained access to via the internet would have its own version of the virus downloaded. Essentially, all of their tech was infested. It was now programmed to destroy itself once it was turned back on.

Unless Wes could come up with a way to prevent it, and if the process wasn't interrupted fast enough, their society might devolve to the point that it wouldn't matter anymore.

A rumbling on the overpass brought Wes out of his own head, and he stopped in between two cars to evaluate the situation. Most of the traffic was at a standstill, and people had taken to walking while trying to avoid the numerous car fires and accidents that dotted the freeway. He couldn't see a source for the lower noise and vibration that was similar to a heavy rush-hour.

"The train!" someone screamed.

There were two sets of tracks that paralleled the turnpike and Wes could clearly see them some twenty feet below. There was a passenger train running, and although that should have been seen as encouraging, it was immediately obvious to him that it was going way too fast. It wasn't going to make the curve.

Sparks were shooting from the tracks, and the cars were already threatening to derail and crash into the supports of the elevated freeway, as people trapped on the overpass started to run. Wes should have run too, but he was fixated by the faces he could just make out in the windows. Whether it was real or his guilt-ridden imagination, he could have sworn he saw them screaming as it slammed into the cement structure, and flames rolled up to block his view of the sky.

32

D AKOTA
The foothills of Redemption, South Dakota

DAKOTA WAS TRYING NOT to panic. The tires of her bike crunched over the uneven, dirt trail that wound its way through the massive Ponderosa Pines that gave the Black Hills their name. It was well-used and led to the fishing hole that was popular with the locals. She'd debated leaving her bike back on the gravel road and going on foot, but time was going by fast enough to make her head spin and she couldn't afford to lose another minute. She'd already wasted too many of them.

The first place Dakota went after confirming Sam's bike was gone, was the police station. She should have stopped at the Cartwrights. She should have gone straight to City Hall, but all she could think of was to get to the police station. No one was there. The door was locked and a hand-written sign said '*back in a half-hour*', but of course Dakota had no idea when the sign went up.

She'd waited for ten minutes before sweating through her t-shirt and then racing to City Hall.

There, an older lady who introduced herself as Mrs. West told Dakota she'd just missed her dad. That he'd gone to Deadwood, and then offered her a survival kit and bottle of water.

Those items were now tucked away into Dakota's backpack, alongside a sweatshirt, another water bottle, and two of the power bars from their basement stash.

The time she'd spent running uselessly around town had at least given her an opportunity to calm down and think more rationally. She knew her brother. He would start out with these grand schemes, like biking all the way to the fracking wells, and then ditch them almost immediately after attempting it.

Sam had been to the fishing hole on the river with their dad a couple of times before, late in the summer after they'd moved there the previous year. The gravel road that wound up the steep mountain started out in the woods just behind their house, and most of the hiking trails they used also branched off of it. That's where he would have gone to start out whatever adventure he had in his head; Dakota was sure of it.

Whether he ditched his original quest after the half-hour uphill ride and decided to go fishing instead, she had no way of knowing, so it was a gamble to take the detour. She prayed it paid off.

It took another thirty minutes of peddling before she saw the end of the trail, where it opened up to a grassy clearing alongside a picturesque, slow-moving bend in the high-mountain river. The sun wasn't quite full enough to have burned off the last of the fog from the tops of the trees, but the early morning light was dazzling as it created a halo effect in the haze and reflected off the water.

Dakota gasped in surprise and dropped her feet to stop her forward motion. There wasn't another bike there. Instead, there was a horse. A gorgeous white horse with a long mane and tail that were intricately braided. He nickered in greeting and bobbed his bead before going back to snacking on the long green grass growing around the base of the trees.

Before Dakota had a chance to even get off her bike, a young girl with blonde braids ran up from the water, pole in hand. "Hey!" she called out cheerfully. "You come to fish? Nothin biting right now, but I've got a good feeling about it, even though I saw some dead ones. We'll just have to be patient. I found some good worms. Dug them up myself from right over there." She pointed to the base of a nearby tree. "You're welcome to use one. I don't mind sharing. Did you bring a lunch? My mom sent a ton of food with me. We can have a picnic."

Dakota paused, taking it all in, and then got off her bike, letting it fall to the ground. "Um, I'm not here to fish. I—"

"I'm sorry!" the girl interrupted. Wiping her hand off on her jeans first, she rushed forward and stuck it out at Dakota. "Hi! I'm Maggie."

Not sure what to make of Maggie, Dakota shook her hand and took note of the girl's strong grip. She'd seen her around town, but didn't know who she was. While there was a K-8 school in Redemption, the high schoolers were bussed to the county school near Deadwood.

"I'm Dakota. I—" that time it wasn't Maggie's words that cut her off, but the girl's inquisitive blue eyes. She was staring so intensely at Dakota that she thought for sure she must have had something crawling on her face. "What?"

Maggie's smile broadened and she pointed at Dakota's head. "Your hair. I like how it's different. How'd you get it to curl like that? Is it natural? Mine's boring." She tugged at one of her long braids. "Flat as a Sunday morning pancake."

Dakota chortled and patted at her mass of hair barely held in check by the headband. She was unable to stop herself from getting caught up in the young girl's positive energy. "It's natural. My grandmother is black. Trust me, after trying to tame these curls for a week you'd be changing your mind. I'm sorry," she rushed to say before she could be interrupted again. "But I can't stay. I'm looking for my brother."

"Your brother?" Maggie's expressive face registered the proper amount of concern. "Why, is he lost? Oh! What's he look like? I met a kid on my way here."

Dakota took a step toward Maggie and placed a hand on her arm. "Yes! I mean, no...he's not really lost, just kind of missing. He's too young to be up here by himself. He's only nine, and he's about this tall." She held her hand up to the proper height. "He's got black hair, tan-looking skin like mine, and a stupid purple backpack."

Maggie was already bobbing her head eagerly. "Yup! That's him, alright. My mom wouldn't let me come here alone when I was nine, either. I'm twelve now, so Dad said it's okay to go as far as the watering hole. We were supposed to go to Rapid City this morning for a 4-H show. I got up at five to get ready, even though Mom said last night it would probably be cancelled because of the whole stupid power thing. No way I could've gone back to sleep. I mean... who can sleep with everything going on, right? I thought Felix should get to do something since his plans got ruined, too. Oh! Your brother. He asked if he could pet Felix. Said his name was Sam. He seemed like a nice enough kid, but he didn't want to come fishing with me."

"Felix," Dakota muttered as her hopes swelled.

"My horse!" Maggie rubbed absently at Felix's neck. Maggie was tall for her age, and wiry, and spoke so fast that it was hard to keep up.

"How long ago do you think that was? Where was he?" Dakota knew she was sounding more like the twelve-year-old, but didn't care.

"Umm," Maggie's face screwed up and she pursed her lips. "About an hour ago, I'd say. Real close to the trail, on the road."

"An hour." Dakota's optimism plummeted. It would take a half-hour to get back to where he'd been, so he'd have a good hour-and-a-half head start up the road. There were other county roads, logging roads, and trails further up, and she'd have no way of knowing which way he might have gone.

"Maybe he already went home," Maggie suggested. "My little

brother is ten, and he'd be getting hungry by now. Kids are easy to predict like that. Why's he up here by himself, anyway?"

Dakota was already turning her bike around, but she stopped to grin at Maggie. "You talk pretty big for a twelve-year-old."

Shrugging, she circled around Dakota so that they were still facing each other. "My mom says it's because of all the books I read. Dad doesn't like it, though. Thinks I daydream too much and that the stories 'fill my head with nonsense'. What do *you* think?"

Dakota was drawn in by the girl's charm, despite the worry for her brother. "I think a good imagination will take you places that others don't see."

Maggie cocked her head conspiratorially and nodded slowly. "That's really deep."

Laughing, Dakota put her foot on the peddle, eager to leave. "It's something my mom used to say."

"She sounds smart."

Dakota's smile faltered. "She, um—she died a couple of years ago."

"Oh." Maggie was uncharacteristically quiet, and she kicked at a clump of dirt. The silence only lasted for all of five seconds before she looked earnestly at Dakota with a new kind of enthusiastic energy. "Can I help you look for Sam? No one knows this area better than me! I grew up here," she added. "My dad owns most of the land, but leases it out and stuff. I can help!"

Thankful the girl didn't apologize or try to pretend to relate to her losing her mom, like other people usually did, Dakota seriously considered the offer. If she biked back to town, Sam would then have a two-hour head start. But she could get either her dad or the Cartwrights to drive up and look, so they could catch up to him in no time.

If she tried to go after him on her bike, by herself, she might never catch up and she'd keep making the situation worse. She'd been making the wrong decisions all morning. It started with not checking his room as soon as she heard the door closing that morning, and going to town first instead of going after him right away.

Then, choosing to take the trail to the fishing hole instead of continuing up the road. At any one of those points, if she'd acted differently, she would have probably run right into him.

As a result, Dakota was doubting her decision-making even more than she normally did. Her anxiety increasing, she pivoted on the seat to look at Maggie. She might be a tad annoying but she was also a welcome distraction and incredibly genuine. It was so much better than being alone, and besides, the girl had a good point. She knew the area a lot better than Dakota, who was likely to get lost if she got too far off the road on her own.

"My dad's a deputy here," Dakota explained, making up her mind. "If you could check up the road while I go back to the station to get him or someone else to drive up, that would be great."

Maggie was already gathering her things and working to untether her horse. "You betcha! You know, it gets a lot steeper a couple miles up, so he'd probably either turn around there, or take one of the other roads. I doubt he's that far. Like I said: he'll be hungry. You can always count on boys to come home for food!"

Dakota clung to that positive thought.

As impatient as she was to get moving, she waited for Maggie to finish and mount her horse before she started off down the trail. The companionship made her feel stronger, and more confident in her actions. And while Maggie might be several years younger than her, Dakota felt an odd sort of kinship with her. She understood being a little different, and she had a feeling the charismatic girl didn't fit in very well with the other kids her age in Redemption.

As the last of the fog lifted and she felt the full force of the sun breaking through the canopy of trees they were moving through, Dakota was reminded of how the truly vital things in life were being revealed, pulled from the darkness of the blackout.

She'd already been through enough trauma to appreciate the importance of her family, but Dakota had no idea how critical the *connections* to other people were. Regardless of anything else, of who you were or what was happening, the one element many wouldn't consider in a survival situation was the impact of being by yourself.

Something as seemingly insignificant as a young girl with a horse in the middle of the woods could be just what she needed. Dakota glanced back at Maggie, astride a trotting Felix with his magnificent braids, and smiled.

She wasn't alone.

33

J AMIE
Deadwood, South Dakota

DOWNTOWN DEADWOOD DIDN'T NORMALLY LOOK ALL that different from Redemption. The extra population was generally confined to the surrounding urban growth, while Main Street maintained its famous wild west historic flair. Wild Bill Hickock and Calamity Jane rested in the town cemetery and the place was rife with museums, old-style bars, and countless gift shops.

They were lucky it was still too early in the year to attract the summer-rush of vacationers, or else things would be even more difficult than they already were.

When Jamie arrived at the diner and saw the group gathered out front, he recognized Trent from the night before and immediately invited himself to be a part of the excursion. Several other vehicles were already in line and Jamie found out later, as he worked along-side the others in clearing power poles and a couple of trees, that they were tourists. Someone had gotten the word out that the only road out of Redemption would be cleared in the morning, and they were understandably eager to try and get back home.

Jamie envied them to a certain degree. His trip into Deadwood would be his determining factor, as to whether he'd be sticking around or making the same pilgrimage.

"I'd like to start at the Sheriff's Office," Derrik said from where he sat in the front passenger seat. "I need to check in."

"It's likely to be the best place to get the most up-to-date info," Ed said. He shifted in the back seat next to Jamie and leaned forward toward Trent. "The dispatch center is in the same building. They'll have a short wave and ham radio."

Trent nodded in agreement while Derrik looked back at Jamie inquisitively. "I'm just along for the ride," Jamie said. "I'm fine with that plan."

Derrik held his gaze a fraction longer than necessary, enough to confirm the wariness Jamie had already picked up on from the other man. Staring at the back of Derrik's head, he assessed the deputy in comparison to himself. They were around the same age and height, but that was where most of their similarities ended. Derrik had more of an endurance athlete build, while Jamie resembled a lineman. The deputy was clean-shaven, and by the way he stood and handled himself, it was obvious to Jamie that the guy was career military.

He ran a hand over his head, contemplating his own appearance, and it was hard for Jamie to refrain from checking in the rearview mirror. He wasn't used to looking like the sort of dangerous backwoods character that a deputy like Derrik Adams would be arresting for fighting at a local bar. He was limiting his interaction with the guy intentionally, because it wouldn't take much to tip him off to that disconnect in his own behavior. However, he was beginning to think his plan was backfiring.

Assess and act. One thing at a time, Pratt.

Jamie took his own advice and stared out the passenger window. He didn't have any expectations as to what they'd see once they arrived, but he was still shocked. They were forced to slow down, and then stop only after having gone a few blocks, due to the amount of people milling about openly in the streets. It was smokey, and in addition to the obvious buildings still smoldering along Main Street, there looked to be an active fire not far up ahead.

Several store-fronts were broken out, there were abandoned cars strewn about down the narrow lanes, and a deputy on horseback was waving at them as he made his way in their direction.

Ed grunted. "This is worse than I thought it'd be."

Trent rolled his window down and motioned for the rest of their group that was travelling in another truck behind them, to stay put. "I've got this," Derrik said, opening his door.

After a couple of minutes of animated conversation with the man on horseback, Derrik jogged back to the truck. "Come on," he said, both his voice and demeanor curt. "Leave the truck here. I talked him into allowing you three to come with me, but he wants the other vehicle to go back."

Trent scowled. "That seems pretty extreme. You can't just close down a town."

"They're trying to enforce the shelter-in-place order," Derrik explained, gesturing for them to get out. "Look, Trent. Their main gas station blew up last night and they're trying to keep half the town from burning down. They've had looting and some civil unrest and I don't blame them for not wanting to add more people to the mix. Let's just go to the station and get what we came here for. We have our own problems without trying to handle Deadwood's, too."

Jamie was the first to open his door. "He's right. Let's keep this simple."

As they all filed out and began working their way through the scattered crowd of people, Jamie took in as much as he could. Most of them were clearly just worried residents looking for answers, companionship, or even something to do. Most looked lost and confused, scared to be a part of something unknown that was still unfolding. Others were angry...their fear already turning to the uglier side of fight-or-flight. It was that undertone of hostility that concerned Jamie. It was a match waiting to be struck, and there appeared to be plenty of fire both figuratively and literally.

Similar to Redemption and several other smaller communities in the region, there were very few roads leading in or out. While the larger cities might be a short half-hour to an hour drive away, without gas or other means of transportation, traveling through the mountains that surrounded them had suddenly became a much more daunting task.

That aspect of isolation would fuel the fear and ultimately speed up the timeline for when supplies wouldn't meet demand. "This place is about twice the size of Redemption?" Jamie asked Ed as he came alongside the older man.

"Roughly," Ed agreed. "Though they have a much larger commercial base, and being closer to Sturgis and Spearfish, they'll have a lot more outsiders. I'd imagine as people try to get home from other places, they'll also be trying to pass through. The two main routes going in both directions converge right here through town. I'm sure people are already desperately looking for gas in order to get home."

That information painted things in a more troublesome light and based on the crowd's behavior, Jamie was worried it also confirmed they were in fact dealing with a large-scale event. He'd still been holding onto some hope that they'd get to Deadwood and discover it wasn't nearly as bad as they had all thought. From the expressions of the other three men he was with, he wasn't the only one.

Derrik led them across the road and down another block before they reached their destination. The three-story brick building was also the location of the county jail, and as they entered the structure, Jamie realized the potential ethical and moral conflict behind what to do with the prisoners housed there.

Another deputy was tromping down the dusky hall, a two-way radio clutched in his hand. Obviously, the guy on horseback must have radioed ahead. "You here to lend a hand?" he asked, speaking directly to Derrik, who was in uniform.

"I don't think we've met," Derrik said as he stepped forward. "I'm Deputy Adams, Romeo twenty-two out at Redemption. I'm also with one of the council members from the town. I'm sorry that I can't offer to stay, but I'm only here to check in and hopefully get some information. Is the sheriff around?"

"Deputy Swift," the other man replied, but didn't offer a hand. "Sorry, but the sheriff isn't here. He got called to Sturgis last night to help with getting things there back under control. Only a couple of us live here in town, and I couldn't tell ya where anyone else is. Local police department is handling what they can and have their ICS set-up next door in the dispatch center, but I'm sure you noticed that things aren't going so well out there."

"How much infrastructure has been impacted?" Ed asked, moving closer. "Does it involve the whole country? The *world*?"

Deputy Swift looked from Ed and then back to Derrik in disbelief. "Wait, you said you're here to check in? Didn't you already do that via the radio? Don't you *know*?"

"The ham radio we had was hooked up at our office and shorted out during the...event," Derrik said. His hands clenched into fists at his sides and his back went rigid as he ran out of patience. "We obviously wouldn't be here asking if we didn't have to."

Swift scowled and shook his head. "You're telling me no one in the town of Redemption has a ham radio?"

"I'm sure they do," Trent offered. "And we're actively looking for one, but meanwhile coming here was a lot faster than a door-to-door search."

"If talking with us is too much trouble, maybe you can direct us to someone who can be more helpful." Jamie moved up next to Derrik and it wasn't much of a stretch to play into the more menacing persona.

Swift appeared genuinely taken aback and then seemed to comprehend how he was coming across. Sighing, he adjusted his gun belt and then rubbed at his face. Hard. "I'm sorry. It's been a long night. I saw my kid for about five minutes this morning and I haven't eaten since sometime yesterday afternoon. It's—overwhelming. For everyone."

"*What's* overwhelming," Ed urged, clearly not as interested in his apology as he was in the information.

"It's worldwide," Swift said without any more preamble. "We're trying to stick with the proper command structure but even with the ham radio, it's getting harder to follow and disseminate everything that's going on."

Jamie took a step back. He knew it was a possibility. From not only what happened with their phones and the power, but especially with how the downhole communication program malfunctioned. Something that could impact...literally *hijack* the satellite feed and piggyback into all of their systems was something so colossal that he'd known it had to be worldwide. But in that moment, Jamie realized he'd still been in denial. He was still holding out for that reality to be proven wrong, and to have the ability to go pick up his life where he'd left it and carry on.

"It was the O.N.E. program," the deputy was saying. "Or, the quantum computer. I don't know how the damn thing works, but they're saying it's somehow set out to destroy... *everything.*"

"What do you mean, everything?" Derrik demanded. He sounded rattled and it surprised Jamie.

"Everything that's connected to, or has the ability to be networked and ultimately connected to the internet," Ed explained. He was rubbing his hands together in a manner that may have represented either anticipation, or extreme nervousness. "The IoT, the Internet of Things. Anything embedded with the software, sensors, or other technologies needed to achieve that connectivity. O.N.E. used the quantum computer to execute some kind of destruction protocol on a scale we quite possibly will never comprehend."

Deputy Swift was nodding. "That, uh—that's how it looks. There's some report now, I think in New York or some other bigger city, stuff that was off when it happened? When it's turned back on, even though it seems like there's no way for it to be connected or get fried, it's still being...activated, or self-destructing, or whatever you want to call it."

"It's all infected," Ed murmured.

"Infected?" Jamie repeated, thinking of the SAT phone he'd been turning on.

"O.N.E. was the trojan horse," Ed said, sounding sure of himself. "The perfect delivery system using an unfathomably advanced quantum computer capable of doing things we don't even know yet."

"Oh, that's great." Trent turned and began to pace up and down the short hallway. "So, we can forget about the power being restored or gas, food, and other supplies being delivered anytime soon."

Swift hung his head. "It's so much worse than that."

Jamie exchanged a look with Derrik and he decided in that moment that it was time to accept things and shift his focus to staying alive, versus saving a job.

"It's everything," Ed said. "No stock market means no economy, which in turn means no money or commerce. No communication means a very limited ability to coordinate a response at the government level, so we'll be facing famine and—" he stopped and abruptly walked away from them.

Trent hesitated before following the older man outside, and Swift disappeared back the way he'd come, leaving Jamie alone with Derrik who was watching him, eyes narrowed.

Clearing his throat, Jamie didn't waver under his gaze. "You and I need to talk."

34

S AGE
Redemption, South Dakota

SAGE CLOSED the door to her cabin with a sense of purpose she
hadn't felt in...well, she couldn't remember when. It was strange,
how calm she was in the face of everything that was happening.
The hour or so she'd given herself to run home to check on things,
change, and simply sit and do nothing for a few minutes somewhere she felt normal, was the rejuvenation she'd needed.

Lisa was back at the diner and overseeing things there, Erica
had a surprisingly solid grip on organizing the shelter, and the
clinic was getting some extra help from another nurse who lived in
town. The only item Sage hadn't been able to check off her list yet
was to let Dakota know that her dad had gone to Deadwood.

Neither the teen nor her younger brother had been home when
she stopped by their house, which she found odd. It was barely
eight in the morning and she'd been expecting to find them still in

bed. After knocking several times, she decided to swing back after making the run up to her house.

A nudge against her calf was followed by a purr, and Sage smiled as she knelt down to pet her cat. "There you are, Sumatra," she cooed. Her dad gave her a hard time for naming the black cat after her favorite dark roast coffee, but she thought it suited the feline perfectly. He was warm, comforting, and full of energy. "Catch any good mice while I was gone?"

Sumatra was an indoor-outdoor cat who came and went as he pleased. The back porch was enclosed and she'd already put out fresh food and water for him. "I'll be back tonight." Picking him up, she held him to her chest for a moment and buried her face in the soft fur of his back. Wishing she could stay and cuddle with him as she set him back down, Sage ran her hands down his sides one more time and laughed when he stretched under her touch before springing away after a bird that caught his eye.

Standing, she adjusted the backpack on her shoulder and hoped she could keep her promise to return. While she planned on sleeping in her own bed that night, she'd also packed some essentials just in case. Erica insisted she was already getting all sorts of volunteers lined up to man the shelter at city hall, but as the incident commander, Sage felt like she needed to be there. At least until they had a better understanding of what was happening.

The thought made her heart race slightly and she lost some of her Zen, feeling a greater urge to get back to town to meet her dad when he returned. Sage's hand slid down to the radio clipped onto the strap of the backpack. She was just inside the working range of the handheld, so dispatch would let her know when the group showed up.

Since they were such a small community and were implementing only a few elements of the ICS, it was decided before parting that morning that it would be best to have the police station dispatcher route all of the radio traffic, in order to keep things clear and organized. Her father was going to recruit some candidates to round out the twenty-four-hour coverage, as soon as he was done with the trip to Deadwood.

Sage had *really* wanted to go with them, but in addition to being the acting mayor and incident commander and needing to stay available, she had the diner to oversee. She trusted her dad and Trent, and Derrik would be the best one to make contact with law enforcement and communications.

It was going to be another beautiful day, and standing there on her front lawn, it was hard to imagine that anything residing beyond the trees surrounding her had changed. That particular section of the mountainside had been her home—her solitude, for the past three years. It was about as close to off the grid as she could handle, and the only thing she lacked to being completely self-contained were enough solar panels and batteries to store the energy. As it was, she could run all of the lights and some of the smaller appliances, including the pump that brought the water up from a deep well, which was typical for the area.

Her dad was in the family home she'd grown up in, closer to town. Her current cabin was one of four rustic lodges that had been in the Olson family for several generations. Three of them had been renovated and rented out during the summers, but her dad didn't want to deal with them after her mother's death and decided to sell them. Sage had jumped at the opportunity to live in her favorite cabin, a small two-bedroom that sat on ten acres backed up to the national forest. While Sage wasn't quite ten percent Lakota Indian from her mother's side, she believed part of the intense connection she felt with the land came from her Native American heritage.

She'd slowly made improvements and some renovations over the past few years, and now had a small orchard, moderately impressive garden space, and an area cleared to eventually house chickens and maybe a goat or pig. Sage still spent most of her time at the diner so it was easier to buy fresh eggs and meat from local farmers, rather than struggle to raise her own. She knew what sort of work it took to do it right, which was also why she didn't have a horse. As much as she wanted one, growing up in Redemption,

Sage had a clear understanding that having a horse was like having a relationship. To do it right, it wasn't a matter of throwing some food out and cleaning a stall once a week. It took a daily commitment that she wasn't capable of yet.

She paused halfway down the walkway and pivoted to look at the acre of open grassland with a partially constructed split-rail fence. It might become her reality a whole lot sooner than she'd expected. Sage's property was a three-mile drive up the mountain, outside of town. She had less than half a tank of gas in her truck. A more economic vehicle hadn't been feasible for driving up her road during the harsh winter months.

She was one of the fortunate ones who even still had a working vehicle, but how much longer before that didn't matter because the gas was gone?

Sage mentally added that to her list of things to go over at their meeting that evening. The two gas stations in town were currently shut down. They'd need to contact the owners and find out exactly how much they had and then discuss how they'd use or distribute it. *If* it came to that.

Sage clung to the possibility of having good news out of Deadwood. Perhaps it was all just more of a "reset", rather than a crash. Standing beside her truck, she pondered her choice of words, thinking it a fairly accurate analogy, based on what her father was saying.

Reaching inside the loose flannel she'd chosen to wear over a plain t-shirt, Sage removed her Kimber 1911 from the shoulder holster. The weight of the 45-caliber felt good in her hand, and she gripped the wooden stock before leaning in to place it on the passenger side floor. The weapon was another choice her father liked to tease her about. She was the first to admit that the full-sized handgun wasn't the most practical for her to carry. However, she'd spent a lot of time on the range and it was what felt best. It didn't buck in her hands and packed one hell of a punch.

Sage usually kept the weapon locked up, and only took it out for shooting practice or the occasional time she got spooked by a sound during the night. Getting into the truck, she eyed it warily. Not because she was at all uncomfortable in her abilities to safely handle the gun, but because of the looming danger that its need represented.

Sage wasn't naïve. She'd lived in a larger city, gone to college, worked for a big corporation, and been involved in enough things to understand how the world worked. How the human psyche worked. On the chance that it was bad news her father brought back, the need for self-protection could come a lot faster than most would expect.

She wouldn't get caught unprepared.

Driving through the woods down her long gravel driveway, Sage went over different scenarios in her head. Secluding and protecting herself would be much easier than protecting the town of Redemption, a role she'd never anticipated finding herself in. It reminded her that she still needed to swing by the Adams's house.

Derrik wasn't going to be happy if he got back to find out his kids were gone. Even on a regular Sunday it would be extremely unusual to not have tabs on each other. It used to be a normal thing for kids to take off and play for the day, to not be seen or spoken to by their parents until they got home for dinner. Nowadays, the ability to instantly chat was a driving force behind most relationships, including between parents and kids. She was glad she'd avoided that era. Sage didn't know if she would have survived unscathed by the constant scrutiny and oversight of her father.

Taking the first road on the outskirts of town, she reached the Adams's rambler in only a few minutes. She'd never been there before that morning, but Sage had known the Cartwright's for most of her life, and they'd told her which house the "new deputy" moved into on the day it happened.

The house was quiet as she approached the front door, but that didn't necessarily mean anything. With the power out, everything was overlaid with an unnatural silence. Knocking, Sage glanced up and down the street, hoping to possibly spot them out on the front lawn of a neighbor.

No answer. She knocked again, harder. "Hello!" she yelled, leaning in close to the door. "Dakota?"

No answer.

Her frustration growing with the situation and the additional layer of stress she didn't want or need, Sage decided to walk around to the backyard. Maybe they were just playing outside, since the power was out.

The immaculate yard and large patio were empty. A blanket and bag of chips were strewn on one of the lounges, so they'd been there recently.

Going to the back glass slider, she pressed her face to the glass and peered inside. It looked empty. Trying the door, Sage found it was unlocked. Feeling like an intruder, she stuck her head inside and called out loudly. "Dakota! Sam! Is anyone here?"

The silence dragged out until Sage closed the door and took a few steps back and looked around the property with a heavy skepticism. Where would they be?

Behind the house and opposite the patio was a large detached garage. The side door was standing open, which was all the invitation Sage needed. "Hello!" she yelled as she approached, hoping it would prove to be something that simple.

Stepping into the dusky interior, Sage already knew it was going to be empty. They would have answered her. Sure enough, the large space was unoccupied, and two of the three bike racks mounted to the far wall were also empty. "An early morning bike ride," she muttered with a shake of her head.

Taking another step inside toward the racks, Sage's eye was drawn to the back of the garage, and a broad wooden counter that spanned the wall. But it wasn't the counter that caught her attention, but the bright red gas cans stored under it. A *lot* of them.

Crossing the dingy interior of the garage, Sage estimated there were at least twenty of the five-gallon cans. Bending over, she lifted the first in the front row. "Full. Why would someone need—"

"Hey!" a young girl's voice interrupted her musings. Sage jumped and spun around. "Sage!" Dakota shouted, sounding both alarmed and hopeful. "What are you doing here? Have you seen Sam? Did he come back home?"

"Sam?" Sage asked, confused by the question. Taking in the teen's demeanor, it was immediately obvious that things were *not* okay. Hurrying across the room, she took Dakota by the hand and looked at her earnestly, searching her face for answers. "What's happened? Where's your brother?"

Sagging against a workbench, Dakota's breath hitched and she began to cry. "I don't know."

35

K ATHY
Aspen, Colorado

THEY'D BEEN WALKING along the freeway for over an hour, but were thankfully already beyond the outskirts of town. The truck ran out of gas near an airport, but when Kathy suggested going there in search of fuel, Hunter insisted it would be better to just walk to his house and bring it back.

"How much further?" Kathy asked, trying her best not to sound like an impatient child in the backseat of a car. "I think Colby is getting tired."

Hunter laughed as he looked over at the dog, and then pointed to a sign they were approaching. "This exit," he stated. "I told you we were close. I wasn't lying."

Kathy wouldn't normally be so opposed to a nice walk on a mild Spring morning, high in the Rocky Mountains, if it weren't for the increasing signs of devastation. The airport had obviously suffered some sort of catastrophic accident involving a plane, and one of the craggy mountains nearby had what could have been the remnants of another one.

Traffic was still sporadically moving along Colorado Highway 82, although they weren't the first and definitely wouldn't be the last to run out of gas. The closer they got to Aspen, the more abandoned vehicles they passed. The town itself was just as small as Moab but four-thousand feet higher in elevation. Snow still capped the surrounding Rockies and the air, though around fifty, was crisp that early in the morning. There was a distinct underscore of smoke that got thicker as they walked down the exit ramp and more of the town came into view through a narrow valley pass.

"Only a few more blocks," Hunter said, speeding up.

Kathy struggled to keep pace with him but was determined not to complain. She'd probably be running if she were that close to her own home. The boy had been uncharacteristically quiet since leaving the farmhouse, and she suspected his anxiety about reaching his mom was at an all-time high. The inability to call or text loved ones created an almost physical reaction. She was used to being isolated. She lived that way by choice. It was the loss of control, and feeling of utter helplessness it invoked that was the most difficult aspect to cope with.

Hunter must have had that safety-line there for most of his life. Certainly, for all of his teens, and the fact that he was able to remain as calm as he was stood as a testament to his fortitude. Kathy had no doubt she was going to like his mom. She'd raised a good kid.

The first street they passed led to a row of businesses, and even though it was still relatively early in the morning, Kathy could see signs of active looting.

In Aspen.

There was *looting* less then twenty-four hours after losing power in a small, remote, high-mountain vacation town.

"What the hell," Kathy muttered, scooting to catch up with Hunter and get across the intersection as fast as possible. Colby pulled at his leash and began to bark at two men who were shoving each other less than fifty-feet down a cobbled sidewalk.

"Come on, Colbs," she urged with an extra tug on his leash. She reached back to pat at the bulge at her waist under her sweatshirt. Kathy took comfort knowing she could protect them, if it ever came to that. Hunter's eyes had widened when she pulled the gun out of the glovebox earlier, but she saw him glancing back at her now and thought he might be thinking the same thing. The world was a different place, even in scenic Aspen, Colorado.

Two more blocks took them to a residential side street, and she was relieved when Hunter jogged down it. She let him go without comment. They'd catch up.

Five houses of evenly-spaced manicured lawns in, he sprinted up the driveway of a cute two-story craftsman-style home. There was a Toyota parked out front and the shades were open in the large, front picture window.

By the time Kathy climbed the porch, Hunter was already inside calling for his mom. She entered the murky interior with some hesitation, suddenly feeling like she was a party to something very wrong. It felt—off. It wasn't her house yet her immediate impression was that no one was there.

"Mom!" Hunter's voice echoed through the back hallway as he ran down it.

A golden retriever came bounding from that direction and shot past Kathy and Colby, making a frantic dash for the door. "Nala?" Kathy called, turning to follow her.

Nala was already squatting on the front lawn, visibly shaking and clearly stressed. Poor thing must have been stuck in there for at least fourteen hours. Hunter said his mom went to work earlier in the day on Saturday's, so it could have been much longer.

"Here, Nala," Kathy prompted, kneeling down after the dog had finished her business. "Colby, behave!" she reminded him as the larger retriever approached. Kathy allowed the two of them to sniff it out before she got into the mix and offered a hand. Nala was as friendly as Hunter professed her to be and was soon quivering in Kathy's arms as she hugged and consoled the dog.

"She isn't here," Hunter said a couple minutes later, from behind her on the porch.

Kathy rose as Nala bounded up the steps and nearly knocked Hunter off his feet. "That's her car, isn't it?" she asked, pointing to the Camry.

"She commutes on Saturday's," he explained. "And her work shoes are gone. I don't think she came home from work last night. Why wouldn't she come home?" he asked, looking at Kathy with such a deep concern that it was hard for her to come up with a suitable answer.

"You said she's in charge of the resort up there, right?" When he nodded in affirmation, she smiled at him encouragingly. "With the power out and nothing working, I'll bet she had to stay and oversee things. That's all."

Hunter seemed to buy into it at first, but then frowned again as he stared at Nala. "She wouldn't have done that to Nala." He gestured over his shoulder. "She had an accident in the front room. That never happens, and Mom wouldn't have left her alone that long. Something's wrong."

Kathy refrained from pointing out the obvious, that everything was wrong, because she got what he meant. Something was extra-wrong, and she was afraid he might be right.

Moving up to the doorway, she could see a framed portrait of him and his mom on the foyer wall. They were standing on a beach that had to be somewhere in the islands of Hawaii. Hunter looked to be a year or two younger and he was holding on tightly to his mother's arm as they both laughed at each other. She was a beautiful Hawaiian woman with sun-kissed skin and long, black silky hair.

Hunter stepped inside and grabbed a set of keys off a side table by the door. Tossing them at Kathy, he slammed the door and was already jumping down the steps as she caught them. "We'll take the car to the resort. I'll show you where to go."

When Kathy hesitated, he scowled at her. "I promise we have

gas in the garage. We'll take all of it back to your truck, *after* I find my mom."

"Hunter!" she gasped, horrified he'd think she would be that selfish. "I don't care about my truck or the gas right now. I'm worried that it isn't safe. Why don't you just tell me how to get there. You can stay here with Nala while I go and find her."

"No way!" Hunter shook his head emphatically and opened the back door to the car. "Come on, Nala! Come, Colby!"

When her dog followed his new friend's command better than usual on a *good* doggie-behavior day, Kathy felt slightly betrayed. On the other hand, all of the thrillers she could ever remember watching had an element of bad things happening when people didn't stick together. Maybe the dog knew best. "Okay," she begrudgingly agreed. "But if we end up somewhere that looks like we're getting into the middle of some wild-west shootout scene, we come back and I go it alone. Deal?"

Hunter took a moment to think about it before smiling briefly. "Deal."

It wasn't a long drive to the ski resort, and the spring weather meant the roads were clear of snow, but it still took longer than it should have. Several streets were blocked by either downed power poles or disabled cars, and one had a group of rowdy people in front of a storefront. Kathy almost turned around at that point, but Hunter was able to redirect them so that they managed to avoid the worst of it.

"It won't be long before people are attacking you or hijacking your car if it's still running," Kathy said as they turned up the final road to the resort.

The street was windy and heavily treed, but a dense, black smoke was still clearly visible directly ahead. A siren grew louder and Kathy had to pull over to allow a firetruck to pass.

Hunter went rigid in his seat and never took his eyes off the road as he replied. "You think it'll get that bad? People would really do that to each other?"

"That, and a lot worse," she answered before thinking enough to apply a filter. Wincing at her own insensitivity, Kathy's sense of foreboding increased as she followed the signs for the hotel lodge area of the resort. Hunter's mom worked as the General Manager, so that was their best bet for finding her.

When they emerged from the trees and pulled into the back end of a huge parking lot, Kathy sucked in a loud breath as Hunter moaned.

Most of it was gone.

What was obviously once a huge structure had been reduced by fire to the bottom two floors, and a corner that had collapsed in on itself. Three fire trucks, two ambulances, and a police car took up a good portion of the lot and Kathy could see several firefighters spaced out around what remained of the building. They were holding hoses that were showering the smoldering rubble as other firefighters closer in moved about in full fire gear.

Hunter leapt from the car before they'd come to a complete stop, and Nala ran out after him. Jamming on the brakes, Kathy started to follow, but didn't know what she was going to do. It was his *mom*. She wanted to protect him from both physical and emotional harm, but he had the right to know what had happened to her, and if she was okay.

Bending to gather Colby up in her arms, Kathy followed after Hunter at a slower pace. He was old enough to handle himself and by all rights, she was a stranger. She meant nothing in the scheme of things and it wasn't her place to intervene.

Another woman had spotted Hunter and obviously recognized him, because she moved in his direction. Hesitantly at first, until she was running. He put his arms out to stop her from hugging him. "Where is she?" he demanded, his voice cracking as he looked frantically at the ruined resort. "Where's my mom?"

The younger woman's face screwed up in a chasm of guttural pain and her eyes darted despairingly from Hunter to Kathy and back again. "I—" she stammered, sobbing. Her resort uniform was wet and covered in soot, and there was a dark smudge of black under her nose. "We tried. She, she went inside to save them..."

Hunter reeled back from the woman and flung her arms away. "Where is she!" he wailed.

The lady hugged herself and cried, shaking her head at Hunter. "I'm...sorry."

Kathy set Colby down and rushed to grab at Hunter before he could run away. Taking hold of his arms, she held on as the woman finished saying what he had to hear.

The woman sat down hard on the ground, one foot clad in a white work shoe, the other one bare. Looking over her shoulder toward the streams of water and charred remains, she finally met Hunter's eyes and let out a wretched moan. "She's dead."

He didn't run away, or yell, or try to get into what remained of his mother's smoldering tomb. Instead, he turned into Kathy's arms and she found herself embracing the young boy she'd only met the night before, as he sobbed for the loss of his mom.

Stranger or not, their lives were now intertwined in a way that couldn't be explained. Fate had led her to him. In a world that didn't make sense, that one thing was clear.

And so, Kathy held him.

36

W ES
Cambridge, Massachusetts

WES COULDN'T STOP TOUCHING his face. He knew no matter how many times he ran his fingers over the cuts, swelling and burns, it would still be there. Reminders of the hell he'd been trapped in since nine o'clock the night before.

What time is it?

He'd been forced to abandon the damaged bike on the overpass after running from the train fire, and he hadn't seen a clock anywhere since before then. Looking up at the sky, Wes guessed it had to be around noon. That shouldn't be possible.

How could everything change so drastically in such a short period of time? It was a brutal wake-up call: the discovery that the foundation of their lives was nothing more than a house of cards. When you existed in a society that relied upon imaginary currency, friends you'd never actually met, and the ability to have the most basic elements of survival delivered to your door at the swipe of a button, it was nearly impossible to have a firm grip on what was real.

The world had just been woken up from the matrix and reality was a bitch.

"We've all taken the red pill and wish we could go back to sleep," Wes muttered as he approached a row of stately maple trees. They marked a sort of demarcation along the border of the country club and pricey homes that went with it.

He'd finally reached the professor's neighborhood. One block away from the larger estates, the houses leading up to them were impressive, but situated much closer together and with smaller yards. The fires and obvious damage or evidence of looting decreased the further away he got from downtown Cambridge, but the upscale district hadn't gone unscathed.

The smell of natural gas was enough to give him a headache in places, water flowed down the street from failed water mains, and apparently their sewage was just as foul as the rest of the town. Like a spreading plague, the air of desperation was already reaching the outer limits and would only worsen in the coming days.

In several of the driveways Wes could see along the cobbled road, cars of various makes and models stood with their doors open. People were running back and forth from the vehicles to their homes, arms loaded with various and sometimes the most random of items. Clothes, a box of food, sleeping bags... a painting. One man had a large statue of a dog that he was trying desperately to cram into his trunk while a woman stood watching.

"Leave it! What are you doing?" she yelled. "We need to bring food!"

Wes didn't hear his reply, and he didn't look back as he walked past them; the grey-haired man in a fine suit, the lady in a matching jogging outfit. Normal people forced into extraordinary circumstances they weren't equipped to handle.

Based on some of the other conversations he overheard, it sounded like most of them were in a mad rush to get to either extended family or vacation homes that were situated further out in the countryside.

Smart.

The professor would probably do okay on his several acres of fenced, private property. His was an older estate on a well and septic, but anything less was at risk of becoming uninhabitable. It wouldn't take much.

The closer Wes got, the more paranoid he became. Snugging the sweatshirt hood further down his face, he was glad for once that the weather was still miserable. It was cold. Colder than normal, and the rain hadn't let up. He was soaked and if he stopped walking for more than a minute or two, he began to shiver.

Although he wanted nothing more than to reach the professor and be welcomed into what he was sure would be a warm house running off a large generator and roaring fire in the river stone fireplace; he hesitated.

He'd been existing on adrenaline and instinct, and his inner voice was currently screaming at him to be careful. His step faltered, and Wes made a quick decision to turn down an alley that would take him to the back of the property, instead of the front entrance. It was the road the garbage truck and other delivery services used. Wes had seen it when he'd taken the garbage out for Mrs. Abe.

The last time had been on Christmas eve. There was an unexpected snow storm that hit a few days before the holidays that prevented Wes from making his normal trek home. Mrs. Abe wouldn't hear of him spending Christmas alone and insisted he come over for dinner.

The experience of the formal, four-course meal under a crystal chandelier had been vastly different from the cozy family farm, but he'd enjoyed it. While the professor maintained a more professional air in his role as mentor and academic advisor, Mrs. Abe doted on him and called him dear. She was like a grandmother figure and always went out of her way to make sure he felt welcome.

A new upswelling of guilt made Wes slow as he moved through the back gate. He hated to bring them into it, but it was for all of the same reasons that he felt he didn't have much of a choice. He had no doubt that Mrs. Abe would agree.

Turning, he crouched behind a row of evergreens that provided further privacy at the back of the property and then followed an ornate brick wall that ran the full length of the grounds. Scattered trees amongst manicured grass provided a parklike setting and led to a garden area.

The gardens were Mrs. Abe's passion and from what Wes could gather, where she spent most of her time. They covered at least an acre and were broken into different segments of vegetation, interspersed with ponds and greenhouses.

Wes wound his way through the roses at the back corner and worked his way over to what she referred to as her 'grove' of mature rhododendron bushes that looked more like trees. Easing his way in between them, he stopped short of emerging from the other side to take a minute and evaluate the house.

The three-story Victorian had lights on in several windows and smoke coming from one of its three chimneys, just as Wes thought it would. To the right of it, he could see both of their cars in the driveway, and the garage door was standing open. French doors faced the patio and he saw Mrs. Abe walking past them, holding a cluster of flowers in her hands. She was headed for the kitchen, and he could imagine her getting a vase out and filling it with water, wanting to make the room less depressing in the midst of a miserable situation.

His eyes darting off to both sides of the house, Wes hesitated. Now that he was there, he had no idea how to do it. How to approach two people he respected and confess his involvement in the downfall of civilization as they knew it.

Jamming his hand into his jeans pocket, he withdrew the flash drive. Standing there in the rain, a suspicious-looking man hunched over in a hoody and watching the house, Wes felt like the criminal he'd become. He was holding the possible salvation of their future tech in his hand, only feet away from someone who could do something with it...and still, he hesitated.

Coward.

Crouching down, Wes hung his head in defeat at his own personal assessment. It was true, and so long as he was being honest with himself, he may as well face the fact he'd always taken the easier path. He was supposedly smarter than a large percentage of the human population, yet he chose not to apply himself. He had barely adequate grades through high school, he almost flunked out of MIT—twice—because he couldn't be bothered to do the homework. Even after being given another chance and the opportunity of a lifetime, he was constantly letting himself and those he cared about down.

That was how Entangled was able to recruit him. They didn't even have to try very hard. All they had to do was dangle the cash in front of him, and Wes leapt at the chance to get the money without having to do what he considered any *real* work. If he'd cared enough about anyone other than himself, he might have paid more attention to the propaganda behind the group and suspected they were up to more than what they were telling him. Any idiot could have seen that.

It's not too late to leave.

Wes pushed the hoodie off his head with an angry gesture and gritted his teeth. His dad would be so disappointed with him. Grimacing, he clutched the flash drive more tightly. He'd been raised better, with a strong work-ethic and clear morals. He didn't know where or how he'd gone so far off-track, but he wanted nothing more than to set things right.

Wes stood. He could see Mrs. Abe again, now holding a vase and leaning over to set it on the table situated on the other side of the French doors. A table at which he'd eaten several meals, and had good conversations with two people he cared about. He didn't see the professor, but he had to be there.

It was time.

Taking a breath, Wes noticed the intense smell of natural gas at the same time as he began to move. Mrs. Abe dropped the vase and reached out for the door—when the room filled with a brilliant flash of blinding light that engulfed everything before blowing out the windows.

The blast wave from the explosion knocked Wes off his feet and onto his back, his vision dimming as the heat rolled over him. Bits of debris rained down, a larger piece of something unknown striking him painfully in the shoulder.

His ears rang, and his eyes watered as he stared up, confused, at the grey skies suddenly burning brighter.

Moaning, Wes rolled over onto his stomach and twisted around, trying desperately to form a cohesive thought.

An explosion.

Where was he? The ringing began to fade and he coughed as he wiped at his eyes, lying there in the mulch that surrounded the rhododendrons. Wes looked up at the nearest bush and blinked slowly.

Mrs. Abe. The professor. I have to help them.

Shoving up onto his hands and knees, he stared open-mouthed at what remained of their home. Of what was left of *them.*

There was no one to save. There was nothing left to salvage.

"No," Wes choked on the word. On the inadequacy of it.

They deserved better.

He shuffled backward, into the depths of the gardens, where he could hide and cower and fade away until he no longer existed.

37

D AKOTA
Redemption Police Station, South Dakota

"I SURE AM sorry I wasn't here when you stopped by earlier," Ellen said, looking distressed. "I had to step out real quick to go get some breakfast. I'd been up all night and hadn't had a thing."

Ellen Evans was the local police dispatcher and secretary, and Dakota had met her several times over the past year. She usually worked days, during the normal business hours, since all of the emergency calls were handled at the 911 center in Deadwood.

Ellen was typically very put together and quick-witted, but the older woman appeared haggard and had dark bags under her eyes. Dakota immediately regretted making her feel like she'd somehow done something wrong. "You can't be here all the time," she said, doing her best to sound okay. Except, she really wasn't okay. She was freaking out on the inside and the longer they went without finding Sam, the worse it got.

Sage had driven her around for the past hour, looking everywhere they could think of in town, in case he slipped back down the mountain while she'd been at the fishing hole. They checked the park, the school, the diner, his two closest friends' houses, and then finally the police station for the second time after driving several miles back up the mountain road until they'd run into Maggie.

"Maggie's doing a pretty thorough job of checking the sideroads," Sage said to Ellen, getting right to the point. Dakota appreciated that about her. Sage wasn't one for much small talk. "I'd still like to inform everyone out doing the house checks that we're looking for him, if you wouldn't mind making an announcement and asking that everyone keep an eye out for a young boy on a bike."

Ellen was nodding, and grabbed a pen and pad of paper. She looked earnestly at Dakota. "What was he wearing this morning, dear?"

Dakota flinched, feeling more and more like a failure as a big sister. "I, um—I'm not sure. He left before I got up, but he's probably wearing his grey hoodie and has a purple backpack."

Still nodding, Ellen jotted the details down. "Excellent. That'll help. Now, don't you worry. My boys did stuff like this all the time when they were little. It's a sort of prerogative for them to scare the livin' daylights out of the women in their lives as much as humanly possible. I'm sure he'll come traipsing home anytime now, wondering what all the fuss is about."

The pep talk actually helped to ease some of Dakota's apprehension, and she smiled sincerely at Ellen. "I sure hope so. I mean, he *has* taken off on his bike before without permission, but he only went to his friend's house and back. He got in so much trouble that I didn't think he'd ever do it again."

Ellen harrumphed. "Don't let the little devil fool ya. It's just a set-up to scare you more the next time."

Dakota almost laughed.

The front door of the small station opened before Ellen had a chance to queue up her radio, and Deputy Brett Johns came barreling inside. He was a younger guy that was cute enough to make Dakota blush whenever he was around, to her horror. He looked rougher than Ellen did and he didn't acknowledge her, but went straight for Sage.

"I thought that was your truck out front, I'm glad you're here. I didn't want to broadcast what I've got to say over the radio." He finally looked over at Dakota, but it was with skepticism, not pleasantry.

"It's okay," Sage said with a wave of her hand. "Dakota's practically an adult. I'm sure she can handle whatever it is."

He didn't wait for any further encouragement. Hooking his thumbs on his gun belt, he pursed his lips and gave his head a wary shake. "We're only a few hours into our door-to-door, to check on people and locate a working ham radio, and we've already found—" he paused and glanced at Dakota again before clearing his throat. "We've discovered four more fatalities."

Dakota did her best not to react and prove Sage wrong in her assessment of her maturity level, but a small gasp escaped anyway. She'd heard the chatter over the radio Sage was carrying with her, while they'd been driving around. There'd been a couple of dispatches for the fire department, and then one request for the doctor to go to an address. Obviously, Sage hadn't been concerned about it at the time, because she didn't ask what was going on.

"I was wondering about those medical requests," Sage said absently, pulling her hair back from her face and giving a loud sigh. "Any idea what they died from?"

Brett scratched at his head and his brows creased as he thought about it. "Doc already figures Patty died on account of her new fancy pacemaker. There were two more deaths reported overnight by family, and one of them also had a pacemaker, the other an insulin pump that apparently dumped it's whole reserve all at once."

Sage cringed at that, and Dakota knew enough about diabetes to understand, too. She had a friend at her last high school who was on a pump and so she knew the basics of how they worked. She was pretty sure someone could go into what her friend called a diabetic coma and die really fast from a massive dose of insulin like that.

Brett wasn't done yet, and Dakota found herself wishing Sage had gone ahead and embarrassed her by sending her out of the room. She didn't think she wanted to hear any more.

"One of the ladies we found also had a pump, and a guy is...um, *was* a patient of Doctor Pearlman's. Said he had one of those implants in his brain to help with tremors from Parkinson's. He didn't know the other two and they lived alone, so they're more of a mystery, but they're checking the old paper files at the clinic to see if they can find anything."

"Well, mercy be in heaven," Ellen muttered. "That's...seven people we know of now who's died since last night?"

"Eight," Sage corrected. When Dakota looked at her questioningly, she appeared slightly frustrated. "There was an accident at the well site last night and one of the operators died."

Dakota had a better understanding as to why her dad had been gone most of the night. It was so much more than a power outage, or inconvenience. People were dying *there*, in Redemption, not just in the big cities. Afraid again, she needed to keep looking for Sam. She had to find him.

Several radios in the room all crackled at once. *"Romeo twenty-two to dispatch, we're back in town. Enroute."*

At the sound of her father's voice, Dakota almost started crying again. The only thing preventing it was her confidence that he'd know exactly what to do. There'd be no hesitation. He'd see it all clearly for what it was, and make it okay. Dakota felt like a little girl again, clinging to that adolescent hope, but it was what she had to do in that moment to keep it together.

"We should get more people to help with the door-to-door," Sage said. "I'll stop in at City Hall and talk with Erica. She claims to have a big list of volunteers already, so I'll have her coordinate with you and get more teams out there."

Brett gave a curt nod and then hesitated, looking even more uncomfortable than before. "About the bodies? The doc doesn't know what...um, what to do with them. We don't have a morgue here," he added for clarification. "He's concerned that it could become a health hazard."

Cringing at the imagery the statement conjured up, Dakota looked away, closing her eyes and wishing that none of it was real. How many more people were dead inside their houses, waiting to be found? How long would it take before they started to rot and—

The door banged open again, but that time it was her father who stepped inside. He was already frowning when he saw that Dakota was there, and deep lines of worry were etched into his face. "What's going on?" he demanded, looking somewhat accusingly at Sage. "Why's my daughter here?"

"I lost Sam!" Dakota blurted, stepping forward so he'd be forced to address her instead of Sage. "He left right before I got up, to go look for that stupid plane that crashed last night. He insisted it was a UFO!"

The words all came tumbling out in a rush and Dakota couldn't stop them. "He took his bike, and I tried to find him because you weren't here, and I didn't know what else to do. But I missed him, Dad, and now he's alone up there somewhere!"

Derrik turned from a somewhat flustered Sage and took hold of Dakota's arm. "Slow down. Take a breath. What time do you think he left?"

"Not long after the sun rose. I think around six."

Glancing at a battery-operated clock on the office wall, he offered her a small smile. "That means he's only been gone four hours, at the most. You know your brother. He gets these big ideas in his head and then regrets it later on. We'll just drive up there and get him."

"We already did that," Sage said, sounding a little put-off. "I took her around to his local haunts here in town, and then we drove up Canyon Road a good ten miles before heading back."

Frowning, Derrik unclipped his radio but paused with it halfway to his mouth. "How do you know he's even on that road?"

"Maggie Marsh is up there on her horse," Sage said. Dakota was impressed that she wasn't backing down or losing her confidence at all under the obvious scrutiny of her dad. Most people would. "The girl saw him on the road near the trailhead for the fishing hole, about an hour before Dakota got there. She even talked to him, let him pet her horse. He was fine then, and I suspect he's fine now and probably getting hungry."

"Agreed," Derrik said. "Incident Command and all EMS, this is Deputy Adams," he spoke into the radio. "Please be on the lookout for my son, Sam, who hasn't returned from a bike ride up Canyon Road this morning. He'll be on a black mountain bike, with a purple backpack." He raised his eyes questioningly at Dakota.

"Yeah, he had his backpack, and probably his grey sweatshirt." She looked sheepishly at Sage. "I didn't think to ask Maggie what else he was wearing."

"A purple backpack and probably a grey sweatshirt." Derrik finished with his broadcast, and then reattached the radio to his belt, moving with jerking motions that Dakota recognized as a sure sign of his agitation.

"I'm sorry, dad."

Raising his eyebrows at her, he rubbed at his forehead before answering. "You don't need to be sorry. This is on your brother, not you. He knows better. Especially now—" he looked over at Sage. "I'm the one that needs to apologize. Thank you for helping her. This isn't your problem."

Sage smiled at him and jammed her hands into the pockets of her jeans. "I get it. Kids will make you crazy. How'd it go in Deadwood?"

Becoming guarded again, Derrik glanced at Brett. "Why don't you go with Sage to the diner? I'd rather as many people hear this at once as possible." He turned to Sage. "I'll handle this. Your dad and the others are already at the diner. You need to call a meeting. Now."

When Sage hesitated, he put a hand on her arm. "You should go. We'll be there in a few minutes."

When the door closed behind Sage and Brett, her dad turned to

Ellen, who'd been silently taking it all in. "We're on our own for the time being. We can't count on Deadwood or the county for anything, but I'm working on finding someone to relieve you."

Ellen shrugged and waved at the door. "Go ahead. Go do what you gotta do, I'm fine for a few more hours."

"Sam might show up here."

"Right," Ellen answered. "I'll be sure to hide him away and let you worry as long as possible if that occurs."

Scowling at her sarcasm, Derrik led Dakota outside and then looked up and down the street like he was considering what to do with her.

"I want to go with you," she said. "I want to know what's happening, and then I'll go look for Sam again. I'm not going to stop until he comes home."

Her dad was taken aback. "Of course not. Neither of us will, Dakota, but we have to start living differently. *Now*. Whether we like it or not, our lives have drastically changed. And your brother's selfish stunt of taking off like this isn't going to get him the same amount of attention that it would have a day ago. Come on."

He started walking, and Dakota hurried to catch up, trying to process the information and influx of confused emotions all at the same time. She'd been prepared for her father's anger at Sam and disappointment in her for allowing it to happen.

What she wasn't prepared for was his indifference.

38

JAMIE
Redemption, South Dakota

JAMIE STOOD in the middle of Main Street debating which way to go, both physically and philosophically. After dropping Derrik off, Ed and Trent had immediately gone into the diner to "circle the wagons", as they put it. Jamie wasn't exactly on any wagon, and that was where his conflict lay.

He wanted nothing more than to go back to the site, pack up, and do his damnedest to get home. But he had some unfinished business, and the one character trait Jamie's superiors described as both a benefit and a flaw, was the inability to let things go. It made him like a dog on a bone: determined to the end, but also sometimes blind to the repercussions.

It wasn't a matter of being right or wrong. He was very clear on that front. It was about priorities and seeing the bigger picture. In light of things and what they now knew, the problems of Redemption were technically no longer his.

He should just walk away.

Except, lives could be at stake. And that wasn't a bone Jamie could let go.

"You're Jamie, right?" a woman asked, interrupting his deliberations.

Turning, he saw it was the same blonde waitress from the night before: Lisa, the coffee gal. Her hair was up in a messy bun that adequately reflected the rest of her composure. Jamie was guessing she'd been up most of the night, like the rest of them. She was holding a large silver coffee urn in her arms, the commercial kind that served a lot of people. He simply nodded in answer.

Gesturing with her head at a truck parked next to her with its back doors open, she smiled at him. "I've got another one of these in there, filled with my best brew. There's a free cup in it for you if you could give me a hand carrying it inside."

Contrary to what most people might think of him, Jamie was a firm believer in fate. Coincidences were rarely what they seemed, and the woman's intervention was telling in several different ways. So long as he could help, Jamie couldn't—wouldn't, walk away. "Sure," he said with little hesitation, concealing his internal dialogue. "I could never turn down your coffee, free or not."

Laughing lightly, she adjusted the urn as Jamie collected the other one from the truck and then opened the door to the diner for them both. "My name's Lisa, by the way. My, uh—*husband* and I own the stand in town, but I also work for Sage. I'm helping to keep the diner running since things are so crazy and I don't have enough gas to keep my stand open."

Following her inside, Jamie raised his brows at her not-so-subtle mention of a husband. He figured the attractive woman was used to being hit on and found it easier to cut off any passes before they were ever attempted. "Well, it seems I'm at a disadvantage since you already know who I am. Is Sage at City Hall?" He'd noticed the small crowd milling in front of the building when they drove past it. It would be his next stop.

It was Lisa's turn to look questioningly at him as she set the coffee down on the counter in the back kitchen. "Nope. Last I heard, she was escorting some teen around to look for her little brother who wandered off. You know, the duties of Mayor Sage and all that. What's your interest?"

Jamie chortled at her directness. He liked her, and it made him relax more than he had since it all started unraveling the night before. He decided to toss it back at her and crossed his arms with a crooked grin. "I don't know if it's the beard or charming personality, but my only "interest" here is of an official sort. I need to talk to her."

Eyes narrowed, Lisa tapped on the coffee pot, the stainless steel making a sound similar to a ticking clock. "It's not so much the beard as it is the profession. We're used to the operators around here and I have to say that you don't quite fit the mold."

So, Lisa fell on the same side of the fence as Sage did when it came to her opinion of the fracking business. Again, he didn't hold it against her. "I think it's safe to say I no longer work for the Marsh Fracking Corporation, and given the current situation, I think we can toss prior employment and preconceived conceptions aside. For instance, how your coffee honestly stacks up against my favorite stand near my house in Montana. It's an incredible, locally grown and roasted brew."

Lisa's mouth hung open and she gasped in mock horror while slapping a hand to her chest. "Jamie, I've underestimated you. Attacking my coffee is hitting below the belt." Growing serious, she grabbed a mug and began pouring a cup. "Is it really that bad? Are we already to the point of erasing past crimes and settling for mediocre coffee?" She held the full cup out to him.

Taking it, Jamie glanced out front, where he could partially see the filling tables in the diner through the service opening where plates of food were normally put up. "They're going to hold a sort of town hall meeting," he explained, taking a sip of the coffee. He'd lied, of course. It was the best coffee he'd ever had. "Trent and Ed will give all the details, but yeah. What's happened here? It's going on worldwide, and the repercussions are a lot further reaching than you can imagine."

"Oh, I've got a very wild imagination," Lisa said, also pouring herself a cup. She glanced sideways at him. "You sticking around? In Redemption, I mean. Might be a little tough getting home when the gas runs out."

"It's already running out," Jamie said. Setting the cup down, his face was grim. "You'll want to go out and listen in. I've got some other things I have to take care of. Thanks for the coffee."

She didn't bother with trying to make small-talk or parting pleasantries as he walked away, another confirmation she was someone refreshing to be around. Sage had good taste in friends, which didn't surprise him now that he knew her dad. Ed was certainly one-of-a-kind, and after spending several hours with the incredibly intelligent man that morning, he was someone else on Jamie's "people I want on my wagon" list.

He grimaced and shook his head at himself as he left the diner. Getting caught up in the town's social workings and politics would be a mistake. He was there for one reason, and once he was done seeing that through, he'd be gone.

"Gone," he muttered. Distracted, he nearly collided with someone going in through the door as he tried to go out, and he put his arms out to stop them from barreling into him.

"Oh!" Sage gasped as she danced around him on the wooden boardwalk. "I'm sorry, I wasn't watching where I was—oh. It's you." She scowled at him, stepping back and removing herself from his grip. "You're still here?"

Here's to chance encounters.

Rubbing at his beard to hide his grin, Jamie then hooked his thumb toward the group already inside the diner. "I rode into Deadwood with them this morning. Did you talk with Derrik?"

Sage eyed him suspiciously. "Sort of. But not much about

anything other than his son, who decided to go for a joyride on his bike and hasn't come back."

"Ah, the missing kid. Lisa told me about it."

"Lisa?" Sage repeated, sounding rather annoyed that he was on first-name basis with at least two of her friends behind her back. Wait until she found out he was buds with her dad.

Trent opened the door and stuck his head out. "Sage? We're waiting for you. Erica's on her way over."

It would have to wait. "Are you going to be in town later? I need to fill you in on some things," he asked before she could walk away.

Frowning, Sage stuck her hands on her hips and sighed, looking up at him. Even without makeup and her hair pulled back in a pony, she was striking in a natural sort of way. "I'll be going over to City Hall after this to help coordinate whatever needs to be done."

With her flannel parted, Jamie noticed she was wearing a leather shoulder-holster, another aspect of the new mayor to take note of. Like he'd suspected, Sage was very observant, and when she caught him looking at her chest her frown deepened. Pointing, he commented before she could finish jumping to any conclusions. "What are you carrying?"

Instead of answering or removing the weapon, she chose to pull her outer shirt aside to reveal a striking 1911. It was an impressive gun, if not very practical. He smiled appreciatively. "Somehow, that just doesn't surprise me."

When the remark caused a look of confusion to play across her face, Jamie decided it was a good time to take his leave. "Later, then," he said, scooting abruptly around her before she could recover.

Leaving Grover, the old Pinto, to bake in the sun further down the street, Jamie decided to walk to his next destination and save the gas, which was already a precious commodity. In another day or two it would be worth more than gold. Another week, and he predicted people would be killing each other over it. Probably not in Redemption, but in other areas where their survival would depend on getting out or away from the cities, things would be much different.

The office that Marsh Industries kept in town wasn't far, and Jamie was standing outside the door in less than five minutes. He wasn't surprised to find it locked, since the one engineer and two office employees that Marsh had worked only when needed. He didn't expect them to stay in Redemption. However, the old pickup Jamie saw Marsh driving earlier was parked out front.

Jumping off the porch, Jamie walked around the side of the independent, single-story building and peered in through a street-level window. It was dark inside and from what he could tell, it was empty.

He was on one of the short side streets that ran east-to-west through town, intersecting with Main Street which ran down the middle. To the north, a row of newer buildings similar to the one where he was at went to the end of the street. The small bungalows had been built by Marsh and used for the office as well as five independent housing units for the top operators on the crew—one of the perks of being a senior employee.

As Jamie went to walk back around to the front, he heard the door from a couple of units down open, and the distinct sound of a heated conversation between two men. One of them was Marsh.

Stopping, Jamie turned and walked around the backside of the next bungalow over, edging up to the far corner until he could hear what was being said.

"What are you still doing here?" Bucky hissed. "I'm not paying you to sit around on your ass. I need you up there taking care of things. *Now.*"

The sound of a boot skidding along the wooden deck. Probably tamping out the cigarette Jamie could smell.

"I don't know how else I can say this to you, Mr. Marsh, so that you understand it."

Jamie recognized the voice. The man talking was Kevin Carpenter, one of the more dangerous men on the crew with a dicey criminal background. He'd done his research on all of the regular crew, in addition to Bucky and his family.

"I've done all I can," Kevin growled. "Power isn't the issue anymore; I took care of that already. It's the whole system. It's opened up wide and I can't override it, not without a manual shutoff I can get to." There was a long pause. "It's too late."

Heavy footfalls, followed by a solid thud. "What do you mean, *too late!*"

"It's draining. All of it." The sound of a short scuffle. More footsteps, and then a grunt. "I *told* you last night that this was going to happen!" Carpenter shouted. "I'm leaving. I'm done!" The door slammed.

"To hell with you!" Bucky bellowed as he tromped down the steps and out into the road. "I'll take care of this myself."

Jamie ducked back behind the bungalow and out of view. That was when he saw the motorcycle, stored in the back alley with the keys in the ignition. It was barely street-legal, and absolutely perfect for where they'd be going.

It was the chance he'd been waiting for; to follow Marsh. Because he wasn't talking about the fracking site. Carpenter never showed up to help the night before, and Marsh had reported him as being one of the operators who'd already left.

"We're long overdue to bring this full-circle," Jamie said as he listened to the old truck start up.

It was time to do some chewing on that bone.

39

S AGE
Olson's Diner
Redemption, South Dakota

"YOU WANT US TO LIE?" Sage blurted.

They were all gathered in her back office, and she could hear the din of the crowd growing out in the diner. Her father had just finished briefing her and Lisa, along with the rest of the council and IC team as Derrik and Dakota joined them.

"Not so much lie as filter what information we share," Derrik corrected. It wasn't said in a way as to garner her support, but rather stating a fact.

Sage's frustration continued to grow. She should have gone to Deadwood with them. Not getting the information first-hand was already contributing to her feeling of isolation, but Derrik's behavior was making it worse. She chalked-up his dismissiveness at the police station to concern for his son, but now she was beginning to think it was part of his nature to order people around. Especially those he felt had inferior knowledge to himself.

She appreciated the insight from others who had more experience than herself in critical areas, because acting logistically wasn't what being Mayor was about. But at the same time, while she may have found herself in her current role due to being seen as a cute figurehead that would be easily manipulated, Sage was intent on doing right by the people of Redemption.

The reality was that a mayor had no more legislative power than any other council member and the title was mostly ceremonial. Aside from administrative duties, the main role was to provide leadership. Especially in a town as small as Redemption. Her friends, family, and neighbors would expect her to at least be honest with them and to act in their best interest. As Incident Commander, she would help to organize those with the proper knowledge to provide critical care, such as fire and police, but not control them. Just like it wasn't her job to control the public, and that included deciding what they should or shouldn't know about things that would have a direct impact on their lives.

"Derrik makes a valid point," Trent spoke up from where he was leaning in the doorway. "They're already losing control in Deadwood. Once people begin to panic it'll be near-impossible to reign them back in."

"We aren't Deadwood," Sage countered. She glanced at Derrik. "And this isn't a military operation. As the mayor and council, we're supposed to represent the people of this town, and we promised to get information. We don't have the right to lie and then claim it's to protect them from the truth. That's manipulation, not management."

"I agree." Everyone turned to look at Bucky as he walked up to stand behind Trent.

Sage's nostril's flared as her anger intensified. Of all the people in the room to agree with her. He probably did it just to piss her off.

"Did you hear all of that?" Ed asked. "You understand what we're facing."

"I heard enough," Bucky said. "While I believe your intentions are noble, it's guaranteed to backfire. Once the rest of our neighbors out there find out you withheld info so you could go stockpile your own goodies while they obligingly waited for the power to come back on, you're guaranteed to have anarchy."

Erica looked aghast. "But we wouldn't—"

"It doesn't matter what your reasons are," Bucky interrupted. "It's life or death, people. Fight or flight. Give 'em something to fight for, together, or else they *will* turn on you first, and then each other. If you want to actually control their behavior, fear is a much greater motivator than complacency. There's plenty out there to be scared of, so now adequately explain why they need to listen to us to keep them safe."

Sage was always the first to acknowledge when someone was better at something, and there was no denying that Bucky was a great politician. He was a master at twisting things around to suit whatever narrative benefited him, and he'd just managed to act like he was agreeing with her while making her look weak and establishing himself as a stronger leader, all at the same time.

He wanted her to be defensive, which would only solidify his position. Sage couldn't believe she was being forced to play such juvenile games in the midst of a real crisis, and what made it worse was that he could succeed at it if she wasn't careful.

"That's an...interesting take on things," she said instead.

Looking disappointed at the lack of argument, Bucky waved a hand dismissively. "Gotta run. I still have obligations to handle with my wells, but I'll be back in town later."

"Oh, Joy," Lisa said glibly from where she sat, perched on the edge of Sage's desk.

Trent ran a hand over his head and looked fleetingly at Derrik and Dakota before turning to Ed. "We both know the people of this town. I think if we have a solid approach, we can avoid any widespread panic."

"Maybe it'd be better to discuss this over at City Hall," Sage suggested, growing more nervous about the size of the crowd. The diner had a capacity of eighty-five, and it was already standing-room only when she'd arrived.

"I think a townhall style meeting is the best way," Erica said, surprising Sage. "People are already here, so let's keep it real. Give them an opportunity to be a part of the plan and pool our resources. We can meet later tonight at the command center to organize a more formal response, based on their suggestions."

Sage wasn't the only one nodding in agreement. What would set them apart from other towns, other than their isolation, would be their ability to come together as a community. They'd done it before, several times, during more localized emergencies that typically involved the weather. It would be a matter of deploying the same kind of approach and mindset, only long-term.

"Why don't you start things off, Dad," Sage suggested. "We tell them the truth, but also what we're going to do about it and how they can be a part of it. They already trust you and I think you're the one with the best understanding of what's happened, anyway."

When no one objected, he gave a curt nod and headed out to the front of the diner, with Erica and Trent following close behind. As Trent passed by, Sage put out a hand to stop him.

He couldn't have been back to his farm for more than a few hours during the night. In addition to the daily operation of the ranch, he also had two younger children and an older son away in college. He had more at stake than most of them. "Do you need to go home?" she asked.

Trent sucked air in around his clenched teeth and then let it out forcefully. "I need a lot of things, but I'll stay through this before I go. I'll see you later tonight at command."

"We're going to take off," Derrik said once Trent was gone and it was only the three of them left in the room. Dakota had been silent throughout the conversation, though it was clear by her expressions that she was taking it all in. "Brett's out front. He's going to stay until you're done with this meeting, to make sure things remain under control."

"Thank you," Sage said, having a hard time reading him. "I can find some people to come help look, once we—"

"No!" Derrik snapped, cutting her off. "I can't justify using limited resources and eating up our gas by running around on those logging roads up there. Not for something that most likely isn't an emergency. It's not even lunchtime, and I have a feeling he'll be showing up sooner than later. If he isn't home by this afternoon, I'll organize a formal search party well before dark."

Dakota was wringing her hands together and watching her dad nervously. "If we run into Maggie, she can help me search the trails while you drive further up, so we can cover more ground." Sage didn't know the girl very well, but she didn't seem as convinced as her dad that her little brother was simply being careless.

Several people began shouting questions from out front, indicating the beginning of her father's announcement, and it was Sage's signal to go join them. "Call me on the radio if you need anything," she insisted with a parting smile at Derrik as the three of them moved through the back of the diner.

Watching Derrik and Dakota leave, she noticed Bucky driving by in his hilarious new ride. Sage was contemplating the irony of seeing him in the beater, when a moment later a man she could have sworn was Jamie went past on a motorcycle.

"What the...?" she muttered. The guy was a mystery, and Sage wasn't a fan of mysteries, especially when it came to people. He confused her, which didn't happen very often. Typically, she was good at reading people and heavily relied on first-impressions, but there was something about the guy that didn't add up.

Wondering what it was he had to talk to her about, she turned her attention back to her dad, who was finishing up with his short but traumatic news update.

"Why are the gas stations shut down?" Mr. Cartwright posed the first question, after a few seconds of silence followed the final revelation that the apparent destruction of their technology was worldwide. "Can't you siphon out enough to sell us a few gallons? My generator is about to run dry."

"Mine too!" a woman shouted from somewhere deeper in the room so that Sage couldn't see who it was. "Why is the diner still running, if the rest of us are gonna be in the dark by tonight?"

Sage winced, hoping the decision to be honest was the right one. She understood the concept behind keeping people ignorantly calm for as long as possible, but since they were facing months of being cut off from any resources, there was no way to keep up any sort of charade.

"Because I have a natural gas generator," Sage answered for her father, as she moved up to where he was standing on a raised platform in the back corner, in between the dart boards. It was a small stage normally reserved for a live, local band that sometimes played on Friday or Saturday nights.

Stepping up next to her dad, Sage rubbed her sweaty hands on her jeans as he faced a larger group than she'd expected. "I spent a bunch of money on it this past winter after that snowstorm had us without power for a week. It's got enough gas to keep minimal stuff running for several days, and it's adaptable to portable tanks, which gives me even more options. I'm keeping the diner open for the benefit of everyone," she added when there were still a few negative comments. "I'm sure you noticed I'm not charging anyone for the drinks and snacks I've been putting out. We're all in this together."

At the risk of sounding too sappy by offering simple platitudes, Sage decided to change tactics. "The rumors are true: Irv hasn't made it back from his vacation and I'm acting mayor. The city council and I have initiated the emergency response plan, which includes a shelter at City Hall that's being run in conjunction with the diner, to provide shelter and basic supplies to whoever needs it."

"What about my medication?" an older woman asked from a table close to the stage. "I'll run out of insulin in a week."

Dr. Pearlman stood, and Sage was glad to see him there. Callie was sitting at the same table and smiled encouragingly at Sage.

"If you have any immediate needs, come to the clinic," the doctor directed. "Another nurse who lives in town has graciously volunteered to help us keep the doors open, and we're currently taking down information for anyone who's going to be needing a refill in the near future. We've got a limited supply in our small in-clinic pharmacy, but I'll be working on getting more from Deadwood, or other towns."

Erica stood as Dr. Pearlman sat down. "For those who haven't already been by, the front lobby of City Hall is now serving as an emergency shelter and information center. Please stop in and register with me. We'll be tracking all residents, their welfare, and needs. If your well pump has stopped and you need water...I'm the one to tell. If you're going to run out of food in two days, then come see me and we'll make sure you're taken care of. We also need more volunteers," she added. "We can all contribute."

Sage looked out at the mix of young and old, scared faces belonging to people she'd spent most of her life with. "Communication is going to be one of our greatest challenges, starting out. We'll be relying on you to share this information with your neighbors, when you check in on them, because I'm asking you to do that. Please. Take care of each other, the same way our grandparents did back before they knew any other way of living. That's what we'll have to do to get through this."

Okay, that sounded sappy.

Sage fought against the negative voice in her head, and the encouraging smiles she got from the room helped to silence it. Except, she wondered how long the sentiment would last. Two weeks? A month? Maybe even less. How long would it take for them to turn on each other, like Bucky predicted? Because as much as she hated to admit it, the reason why politicians were so good at manipulating was because they understood human nature. They had the ability to tap into the primal workings of a person's subconscious that was hardwired to do whatever it took to stay alive.

"I haven't got it yet, but I've tracked down a ham radio and it'll be operational by tonight," Old Gus was saying.

That was good news, so Sage didn't understand why he sounded and looked so defeated. Gus was working his way through the crowd, stopping now and again to touch a shoulder or shake a hand of an old friend. Tucked under one of his arms was an old-style looking radio with a red band across the back.

"This here is a shortwave radio," he explained when he finally reached the stage. "I keep one as part of my emergency supply, and fortunately it's almost as old as I am so it still works."

That brought on some much-needed laughter and Gus let it run its course before he continued, his ability to work a crowd more prevalent than ever. "The reason why I'm sharing it with you all, is to emphasize how important it is that we listen to Sage and the council. I'm telling ya now to forget about your cars, and turn to your horses for transportation. Forget about fighting with your friends over what's left of the gas to keep those lights lit for a couple of more days, because you know what? It ain't worth it. We'll all be better off if we accept these conditions for what they are, instead of wasting time by putting off the inevitable."

Turning with a grunt, he handed the radio to Sage. Not sure what she was expected to do with it, or where Old Gus was going with his speech, she simply held it up. Apparently, that was what he wanted, because he turned on the power and then dialed up the volume so that the room was filled with the sharp hiss of static.

"This is the station the Emergency Alert System was broadcasting on," Gus shouted, taking his time to look around the room and make eye contact with anyone willing. "Up until about fifteen minutes ago, when it went off the air." Taking the radio back, he flipped the switch, plunging the room into a dramatic vacuum of silence.

With a forlorn look at Sage, he shook his head at the people of Redemption. "We're on our own."

40

K ATHY
Aspen, Colorado

HUNTER HAD BEEN SITTING with his mother for over an hour. Watching from a respectable distance, Kathy's heart ached with such an intensity that she was starting to become concerned. It'd been a while since she had her cholesterol checked and she'd certainly been through one hell of a stress test in the past fifteen or so hours.

Nala was sprawled protectively across the boy's lap, and Colby had taken up a spot next to them both, head on paws like he was in it for the long-haul. The bodies had been laid out on a patch of grass a safe distance from where they were still working the structure fire. Kathy counted eight of them, and based on the handful of others also mourning their loss, it was a mix of guests and employees.

Rubbing at her chest, she stopped a passing firefighter. He stared at her with glassy eyes, his face smeared with soot, and uniform soaked. "Do you, um—know what's going to happen with them?" She gestured to the corpses.

The question seemed to elicit a pain response, as his face contorted and he looked away for a moment before answering. It was hard to tell his age through the weariness and grime, but he couldn't be more than thirty. "A few more hours and we'll be out of gas for our trucks, let alone a place to properly store...them." He rubbed at his chin, revealing the source of the streaks on his face. He was oblivious to the patchwork being created on his skin.

"I heard no one can even find the coroner." He looked around briefly at the limited personnel and then back at the bodies. "The chief was talking with the city manager about moving them soon and getting them buried in the morning, so we don't end up with a —you know, public health issue. They aren't the only fatalities since last night."

Kathy frowned, wondering what else could have gone wrong in such a small town. "What sort of fatalities?"

The man shrugged. "A couple of bad car accidents on the freeway, one other house fire we couldn't even respond to before it'd burned to the ground. Our new engine isn't working," he explained. "Computer system that controls the pump is all screwed up. All we've got is our old one, and this ancient tanker." He hooked a thumb toward the yellow truck in the middle of the parking lot.

Taking his helmet off, he scratched at his head and stared up at the snow-kissed mountain range that rose up behind the resort. "Then, there's the weird ones. People dropping dead for no apparent reason, other than that they all seem to have some sort of implant." He looked at her then and his eyes were haunted. With a nod, he put his helmet back and started to walk away. "Cemetery is on the east edge of town."

He didn't wait for a response, which was fine. There wasn't much else to be said. It was what it was, and they were all just along for the ride at that point.

Although the news wasn't good, Kathy was still encouraged by her success in learning anything at all, so she decided to seek out the nearest uniformed police officer. There weren't many, so she went for the closest who happened to be a woman who'd just finished speaking with another family.

"Excuse me," Kathy said, side-stepping to get in front of her. "I know you're busy, but I've been traveling and haven't really heard much."

"There's not a lot to say," the woman replied. According to her nametag, she was Officer Hanson. "We're all in the dark, literally and figuratively. Our dispatch has a broadband radio set up and we are getting bits and pieces, but you know the old telephone game, where information is lost and changed as it goes down the line?" When Kathy nodded, Hanson grunted. "Yeah. And now, the emergency broadcast has cut out, so we don't even know at what capacity the US government is functioning. I was in the Army for eight years, and I can tell you that with most of our communications, and all of our technology wiped out, it's going to be a real slow roll to get things moving in the right direction."

"What direction would that be?" Kathy asked.

Hanson stared at her blankly for a moment. "Well, I guess that'll be the big question in the coming weeks, won't it? Because it isn't just us. We've heard it repeated enough times to believe that this is worldwide."

Kathy closed her eyes.

So. There it was.

"The collapse," Kathy muttered, remembering the choice of words used by the woman at the farm.

"Collapse is a good way of looking at it," Hanson agreed. "The world economy is gone. Our realm of existence has been reduced to what's in front of us, and for most, that doesn't include what's necessary to survive for very long, so..." she looked around, the first hint of fear creeping into her demeanor. "I'd get to where you want to be for the long haul as quickly as you can. And then stay there."

As Hanson moved away, Hunter and his canine entourage came back into view, reminding Kathy that it wasn't going to be as simple as all that. Gathering herself, she finally approached him.

Crouching down, she reached out and set a hand on Colby's head until Hunter shifted slightly in acknowledgement.

"They're going to be moving her soon," she said as gently as possible. "They've decided to go ahead and, um—bury them in the morning. I know it's fast, but—"

"That's good." Hunter surprised her with his quick response, though he wouldn't look at her. "I don't want her to stay out here like this."

They sat in silence for several minutes, until the pump on the tanker shut down, leaving a vacuum that needed to be filled by something. Kathy cleared her throat as she tried to think of something meaningful to say, but Hunter beat her to it.

"I don't know how I'm supposed to feel."

Kathy glanced over at him; a teen boy forced to say goodbye to the single most important person in his life. "I don't think there's a right or wrong emotion."

He finally shifted to face her, disturbing Nala from his lap. "I don't feel much of anything."

"That's okay," Kathy replied, remembering the numbness. The cold that had spread from her heart and through her body as she'd sat holding the body of a loved one not so many years ago. Unfortunately, it was something Hunter was never going to be able to forget.

"The firefighter said she didn't burn." He tugged at the flimsy sheet that hid her morbidity from him. "That she suffocated, which is good, I guess. It's good that she just fell asleep and wasn't in pain. But I still can't look at her." His lips quivered as their eyes met. "Is that okay? That I don't look at her?"

Barely maintaining control of her own emotions, Kathy took his nearest hand and held it. Tightly. "Of course, it's okay. You remember her how you need to. Remember her on the beach, with her hair blowing in the wind, like in the picture of you hanging in the foyer. I think that's what she would want. I know it's what I would have wanted."

The woman who'd told them of her death was his mother's closest friend, and the woman she commuted to work with. She'd already made the positive identification, so there was no reason to put Hunter through the extra trauma, unless he needed it for closure. That was something Kathy understood as being a very personal decision that was different for everyone, and she was relieved he'd chosen not to mar his young and fragile memory of his mom.

A large, nondescript white van pulled up and after speaking with the driver, Officer Hanson came over to them. "We're going to move them now." She looked pointedly at Hunter. "I promise she'll be shown respect, and my understanding is that there'll be someone at the cemetery tomorrow to help with identifying the gravesites."

Still holding Kathy's hand, Hunter simply nodded and then stood. As awful a situation as it was, Kathy was grateful that his mother's body was being taken care of. If things were as dire as Hanson made it out to be, the luxury of a dignified burial wasn't something a lot of people were going to get. Especially not after the next few days.

"Come on." She gave Hunter's hand a small tug. "I'll take you home. We'll go to the cemetery tomorrow. I promise."

Nala and Colby followed obediently as they made their way back to the car, sensing the heaviness of the atmosphere and Hunter's intense sorrow. Kathy had no doubt the two would have been chasing each other around and going through all the normal doggy antics of getting to know each other, if it weren't for their ability to comprehend human emotions. She was already aware of Colby's capacity to be an emotional support dog, and was impressed by the same temperament in Nala.

They rode most of the way back to the house in silence. It wasn't the sort of trip you tried to fill with small talk.

"You don't have to stay," Hunter said as they turned down his street. "You've already done more than most people would."

Kathy waited until the car was parked and she turned it off, before shifting on her seat. Pointing at the golden retriever glued to his lap, she shook her head. "You really think Colby is going to let me abandon Nala?"

Hunter wound his fingers into the long hair of the dog's neck and raised an eyebrow. "Well, she *is* pretty amazing." His voice was barely more than a whisper, but it was still enough to give Kathy permission to follow him inside. She wasn't about to leave him, but would ultimately have to respect his wishes.

Kathy went around and opened windows while Hunter went to the fridge. It was still cool inside, and he pulled out water and a collection of snacks, which he then spread out on the counter. Neither of them spoke as they ate and drank, and Colby found Nala's dishes on his own.

He was in shock, and it would be some time before Hunter was able to process his loss, but he wasn't going to be able to take the normal time to grieve. Decisions had to be made quickly, and Kathy would have to help guide him through it. She only hoped she'd be able to make him understand.

"You need to get going," he said, surprising her.

She probably wasn't doing a good job at hiding her edginess, but there was no getting around it. "One of the cops back there told me this is happening all over the world."

Straight to the point.

Hunter took a long swallow of water and then stared at her. "The world?"

"Yes. The world. That means no world market, no money, no travel, no phone, no gas, which equates to no supplies moving around." Kathy hated to throw more at the poor kid, but he had to know. She watched his face as he took it all in, though there wasn't much change. Numb.

"I'll be okay." He took another drink of water.

She already knew he didn't have any other family in Aspen. "You said you have a best friend who lives here?"

Hunter sat the empty bottle down on the counter. "He'd still be at the boy scout camp his family took him to in California. How long do you think it'll take for them to get back? I'm sure they'd help me."

Kathy rubbed at her face.

"I'll be okay," he said again. "Once things are fixed, I'll go live with my grandparents in Hawaii. They already said it would be okay, remember?"

Kathy peeked through her fingers at him, her anxiety increasing. No, he wasn't getting it. Of course, he wasn't. "Hunter," she said, moving around the counter to stand in front of him. "I don't know if or when your friend is going to make it back here from as far away as California, and your grandparents—" she rubbed at her face again, desperate to choose the right words. "It's going to be a while before anyone will be flying to Hawaii. Too long for you to be by yourself."

Hunter turned to look at the picture of him and his mom, and then around at the dim and powerless house. Nala nudged against his leg and sat, gazing up at him, and the direness of the situation finally seemed to sink in. Kneeling down, he grasped the dog by her face and touched his nose to hers. "How am I supposed to take care of Nala? There's only half a bag of dog food in the garage."

His voice hitched on the last word, and Kathy moved quickly to squat down on the other side of the retriever. "You'll come with me." When it looked like he was going to try and argue with her, she rushed to finish the offer as it formed in her head. "We'll leave a note at your friend's house, telling him where you are, and when the planes are up and running again, I promise to personally take you to the Big Island myself. I have family there, too, that I'll want to see."

His shoulders sagging, Hunter slowly nodded in agreement. "I don't know what else to do."

Kathy put a hand on his shoulder. "I know you don't, and that's okay. We'll take care of each other. I promise you that."

When Hunter sighed and stood again, he wiped once at his face before getting his bearings. "I don't want to go until—until I can say goodbye."

"Absolutely," Kathy agreed, also standing. "We'll stop at the cemetery in the morning, on our way out." She thought about whether they should just take the more fuel-economic sedan, or go back for the truck. Having the ability to go off-road might end up being critical. "Do you have bikes?"

Hunter tilted his head at her. "In case we run out of gas again?"

"We have over five-hundred miles to travel," she explained. "We can siphon off the gas in the Camry, but there's no way of knowing what we'll find between here and there."

"Mom got us matching mountain bikes for Christmas," he said with a small smile. "To use this summer on the trails around here. We've got lots of camping stuff, too," he added, becoming thought-ful. "It's all out in the garage."

"Good," Kathy said, feeling more optimism again now that they had a solid plan. "That's good. We'll go through it all and get packed up by tonight."

"Where are we going?" Hunter asked, sounding so young and lost.

Clapping her hands together, Kathy pursed her lips and then broke out in a genuine smile, because she truly believed her home to be the one place she'd want to retreat to.

"Someplace safe," Kathy assured him. "You're going to love Redemption."

41

W^{ES} *Cambridge, Massachusetts*

TIME DIDN'T HAVE the same meaning anymore. Now that most people wouldn't have a way of checking...their phones, and smartwatches reduced to useless plastic. It would be measured by the shadows on the ground and the hue of the sky, instead of by the seconds, and endless messages and notifications.

Wes wasn't sure how long he'd been hiding. Hours, at least. It was still light out, but with the dark rainclouds and heavy smoke it may as well have been twilight.

The ringing in his ears had faded enough so that he could hear the fire as it ate away at what was left of the house. It wasn't much. Easing his eyes open, Wes was mesmerized by the flickering light. It was easy to get lost in the dancing patterns and ignore the splintered remains of what used to be a solid structure.

"It was a gas leak," he muttered. "That's all."

But was it? Could he really accept the coincidence that another person he was close to had just died? He had no way of knowing. There'd been no emergency response. No way to call for help and probably not anyone left to give it. There were no fire trucks, or police, or ambulances. A few curious neighbors wandered through the front lawn sporadically, but even that had diminished so that Wes had been alone for over an hour.

Not that any of them had seen him, and he didn't come out to speak with anyone. Because it seemed like a heavy dose of paranoia was absolutely appropriate in his given situation, and so he was going to assume the explosion wasn't random.

"Entangled." Saying the word out loud caused a fresh wave of fear, and Wes pulled his hoodie down more tightly and nervously glanced around the yard, checking one more time for any kind of movement.

How? How, in a world that was cut-off could they be organizing and carrying out the on-going attacks?

They would have been prepared.

"Of course," Wes whispered, growing more than a little concerned for his sanity. They would have taken measures to harden their own tech, to isolate it the same way they did on Battlestar. Just like certain government bunkers and types of equipment would be.

There would still be a functioning government to a certain degree. Martial law was probably already declared, and the National Guard deployed. But how much of their resources would be limited, and how effective could they be? They might have been able to protect some of their more sensitive systems, and still have intra-net set up in some of their federal buildings, but how much good would that do them when the power grid was down and there wasn't any more oil being produced? They would eventually fall victim to the same shortfalls as the rest of their society, it would just take longer.

The race was already on. It was a ticking bomb, and there was no way of knowing what other kinds of issues were going to spring up to get in the way of any sort of relief, or patchy repairs. Especially if it was worldwide. If it were just in the states, they might get back on their feet in a matter of months. However, most countries had even more fragile and vulnerable infrastructures in place and much less of a military geared to respond with aid. There wouldn't be any outside help, and the likelihood of any export materials being available in the foreseeable future were...

Wes dropped his head into his hands. He couldn't shut his brain off. His thoughts had been tumbling around with the fallout potential in a way that paralyzed him. It rendered him helpless, and unable to move. He went back to staring at the fire.

The fire, that was the result of a massive explosion that no one could have possibly survived. No one.

Wes gasped and tore his gaze away. The professor was dead. Mrs. Abe was dead. They were both gone and he could add the guilt of their deaths to his growing list of shame.

A new thought tickled at the edges of his subconscious mind, and he fought back against it.

"No!" he hissed. "No..."

Is my family already dead?

He slapped his hands to his face and turned away from the rubble. "No."

He wanted to go home.

Maybe it was yet another selfish act, but Wes didn't know what else to do. If they'd already been killed, then it wouldn't matter, either way.

He staggered to his feet and stumbled away from the leveled house. Blown from the inside out, pieces of various sizes lay strewn across the yard, much like his life. Like the world.

His dad would know what to do. Wes needed his dad.

With that single thought replaying through his head, over and over again, he finally began to move. Slowly at first, as he crept cautiously through the gardens with the hood pulled tight. Faster, when he reached the alley, dodging behind garbage bins. And then running, when he hit the first sidewalk that led away from the end of the long alley.

He remembered the motorcycle.

He'd spotted it in the open garage, behind the man in the driveway who was trying to shove the dog statue into his car trunk. Wes was sure he'd seen a motorcycle.

He had a long way to go. Close to eighteen hundred miles across six states, and a different time zone. He normally split it up into three, ten-hour days of driving, but with a fast motorcycle and a lot of adrenaline, so long as he was able to find some gas and make it around any blockades, he could make it in two.

Occupying his weary mind with a plan instead of morbid thoughts of doom, helped to ease his panic. Wes began to think more clearly as he approached the house. It appeared to be closed up without any signs of anyone moving around, the same as the immediate houses around it. He walked around to the back as if he belonged there, in case anyone *was* watching.

The doors were locked, so he selected a paving stone from the back patio and used it to break a small pane of glass on the door leading to the garage. Sticking his hand through, Wes was troubled by how easily he fell into a mindset where breaking and entering was acceptable.

That was the problem with an emergency such as the one they were facing: everyone would have different boundaries as to what sort of actions were acceptable. It would eventually come down to the old debate of killing another person to take their water in order to save your own child.

"We aren't there yet," Wes told himself, as he stepped into the shadowy interior.

He'd been right, there was indeed a motorcycle. Fortunately, it wasn't a big Harley or some other gas-guzzler, but a Honda Rebel 300.

Wes smiled. He knew his bikes, and had an old Honda back home. The one he was looking at could get close to eighty miles to the gallon, and was lightweight and easy to maneuver. Plus, the keys were in the ignition. Checking the gas gauge to confirm it was full, he then used bungie cords to strap down a three-gallon gas can that was stored conveniently on a back shelf.

Feeling like his luck was finally changing, Wes used the connecting door to the house to let himself in. "Hello!" he waited a moment to make sure no one answered before entering. He'd just grab some water and snacks to toss into his backpack.

Add burglary to the list.

As he began pillaging through the kitchen, Wes thought more about his family, and what he was going to say to his dad. He was excited to get home, but already dreading the reunion. He had to believe they were okay. There was no other way for him to function.

But, what then? His dad would have good advice, he always did, but he was a farmer. When it came to computer programming and the knowledge that was necessary to know where locally to go and try to get the right people to listen, his dad would be clueless.

There was only one man in town who would. He was another anomaly, such as himself. Wes had him as a teacher his senior year, for computer sciences. The guy was a retired programmer—brilliant, really. Not at the same level as Wes, of course, because few in the world were, but brilliant nonetheless.

With a full backpack and a much better attitude, Wes went back to the garage. Looking out the broken window of the door, he could see that the rain had finally let up and the sun was even poking through in places. He prayed it was a sign that things might get easier.

He touched the array of injuries on his face, and grimaced at the pain in his ribs as he straddled the bike. Thinking about his classmates back at the dorm, and the professor and his wife still burning down the street, he felt ashamed again. He didn't deserve easy.

Lifting the helmet from where it hung on the motorcycle's handle, Wes put it on with a sense of relief. It would be night soon, and in the dark with the full-faced helmet, he'd be completely anonymous... a shadow amongst shadows.

A sense of calm stole over him as he reached out to press the garage-door opener.

I'm going home.

Wes would confess to his dad, and seek out Mr. Olson. Together, they'd figure out how to make a difference.

He was going home to Redemption.

42

B UCKY
Mountains near Redemption, South Dakota

BUCKY KEPT GLANCING at the watch that wasn't on his wrist anymore, and tapped his fingers against the steering wheel in agitation. He'd spent much more time at home than he intended, but what was he supposed to say to his wife? Laura was a smart woman. There were only so many excuses he could come up with, and she knew him well enough to read right through a blatant lie.

He made the decision early on in the creation of his company to not involve her in some of his...questionable business choices. Not only because she was an honest woman, but because he never wanted her to look at him with disappointment or shame. She was the one person in his life who had shown him respect, and loved him flaws and all.

Bucky figured Laura suspected some of his business dealings were on the shady side, but there were some grey areas when it came to the fracking industry, especially when you were mining your own property. It made it easier for her to turn a blind eye, but there were enough glances and backhanded comments to make it clear that she simply accepted not knowing the details.

That was how it started for him: turning a blind eye. Kacey had proven to be quite persuasive in selling Bucky on some of his endeavors for saving money. One of the reasons he went along with it was because most of the time, all it required from him was to not interfere. All Bucky had to do was allow Kacey to make it happen and then reap the benefit of the bottom line.

There were a few occasions where he had to intervene with the locals in order to help sway things in the right direction, but otherwise, it was the same as the rest of the operation. He was aware of the mechanisms and how it all worked, but didn't get his hands dirty.

What had seemed a perfect arrangement was now backfiring, and it wasn't going to matter how much Bucky scrambled. According to Kevin, he was screwed, and without Kacey there to handle things, he didn't know what to do. It was a feeling he wasn't accustomed to, and his only saving grace was that the rest of the world was essentially at a stand-still. If he didn't lose his cool and played his cards right, he might still walk away from it without anyone being the wiser.

I'll know. I'll know when they start getting sick. If I don't say anything...

Bucky wiped at his forehead and then rolled down the window, cursing at the sticky handle. There hadn't been any rain for over a week so the gravel and dirt roads were dusty, but he'd take the grit over not being able to breathe.

He was on a network of roads that spanned the mountainside above Redemption, a combination of forestry, logging, and private roads owned by the Marsh's. Most of them weren't on any maps, and you could drive for hours without getting anywhere.

It hadn't been hard to connect the patchwork in a few spots, enabling the water trucks to travel directly and discreetly from the fracking site and onto the backroads that wound deep into the woods of his father's upper property. It had to be on his, because that was where the river ran through. Some called it a river, others a creek, and it depended on the time of year as to how much volume flowed down it from the snow melt higher up in the mountains. All that mattered to Bucky was that according to Kacey, it was adequate for what they needed.

The trucks front tire hit a particularly large pothole, and Bucky thought the old rust bucket was going to fall apart. Easing off the gas, he squinted into the sunlight that managed to break through the canopy of evergreens that lined the winding road. He glanced in the rearview mirror—a nervous habit without any merit. The only people that ever came up there were hunters, hikers, and wayward tourists, which was another reason why the location was chosen.

Slowing further as he eased around a particularly sharp curve, he almost missed the turn. Its only distinction were the deep ruts left in the road by heavy trucks. A quarter-mile in, he came to a locked, tubular metal gate. Getting out, he paused when he thought he heard something cut out. It may have been either a small motor, or a chainsaw. Illegal cutting of firewood was a thing in their area, so it wouldn't be a surprise, especially with the power out. With his hand on the padlock, he gave it another ten seconds of continued silence before being satisfied. Unlocking it, he glanced around once more before swinging the gate outward.

After driving through he took the extra measure of resecuring it, another indicator of his growing paranoia that he chose not to address. It was a by-product of a guilty conscience. That's what Laura would tell him, and she would probably be right.

Another half-mile in brought Bucky to a second gate that stood open. He wondered how often Kevin bothered to lock everything up. The guy was an idiot and he never understood why Kacey trusted him, but one thing he wouldn't budge on was control. It was made clear early on, that if Bucky wanted Kacey's help to cut corners and get him the extra cash, he had to be willing to give him full control of the "projects".

They started out small, and then over the past two years had grown in size and value...and risk. To the point that Bucky was convinced the other operators would say something to the wrong people and get the plug pulled on his whole empire.

Driving into the large parking and pull-out area, he sat with the truck idling while gripping the steering wheel. "The plug's been pulled," he muttered, staring out the window at the retention pond that occupied a large, cleared area in front of him. "In more ways than one."

It was basically empty. More cold sweat collected on his brow, but Bucky didn't bother to wipe at it. There was nothing he could do to reduce the burn in his stomach or the tightening vice around his chest. He'd been hoping Kevin was exaggerating and looking for an excuse to bail and run. Who knew if the guy had even come up like he said he did?

Bucky continued to stare.

A slight wind rustled the ponderosas and made its way in through his open window, but instead of carrying a warm pine smell with it, there was an obvious chemical odor. The sort that burned your eyes and made you wonder if it was safe to breathe.

Was it safe to breathe?

Jumping out of the truck, Bucky moved with a sudden purpose to the edge of the pond. It was identical to the other official ones at the site, and held around 400,000 gallons of water. However, unlike the legal pools of heavily toxic wastewater, this one had a couple of special adaptations made to it.

Engineered and built by Kacey, the intake and outtake, as explained by him over a steak dinner two summers ago, was pretty straight-forward. Once enough river-water was added to properly dilute the soup of toxins, it was then slowly released into the river over a long enough course of time that it was deemed harmless.

That was the concept, and Kacey insisted that he knew what he was doing. That there would be no negative ecological impact. That no one would ever know. Since the operation began, it had saved Bucky millions. Money, he now told himself, that was given back to the community.

Well, at least some of it.

What little was left in the bottom of the pond was still and murky. There should have been enough remaining to swim laps in, but instead, the foot or so of water had the consistency of watery pudding. And it was probably still draining. All of it, without any dilution, straight into the river.

Turning, Bucky jogged to a nearby metal shed that housed a generator, pump, and the computer system that controlled it. It only took a couple of minutes to determine that the generator was fried. Running back to the truck, he hauled a smaller replacement generator down from the bed and lugged it inside. At least he'd thought ahead enough to think to bring it, and it wouldn't have been unusual to claim it was needed at the drilling site, if Laura had asked. Which, she didn't.

Distracted, Bucky wiped the sweat away from his eyes and wondered briefly if the chemicals were starting to get to him. Either that, or the stress. Probably both.

It didn't take long before he had the generator running and plugged into the power supply, but when he attempted to start-up the pump it wasn't nearly as straight-forward.

He'd been out there with Kacey three times: once to survey the area, a second time to see the completed project, and then once the summer before to see it all in action. Granted, he wasn't paying attention to the technical jargon when Kacey showed him the system's set-up, but he *did* remember him saying that he could monitor it remotely. It didn't run off cell reception all the way out there, obviously, but Bucky thought it was something similar to the system used in Garmin, or other remote tracking systems. So... a satellite, probably.

Shrugging, Bucky slapped at the dead display. It didn't matter how, only that it wasn't working, and just like Kevin reported, it somehow got frozen with the outlet wide open. He had no idea how to close it. Everything was buried, which was why Kacey had the system set up the way it was.

Grunting in frustration, Bucky leaned forward to get a closer look at the pump. Obviously, it was for the intake since the outtake was gravity-fed. It sounded like it was grinding and smelled hot. Going back to the door, he stared out at the retention pond. A small trickle of water was flowing in from the far side.

Perhaps it was best to leave it alone. If he kept filling it with water, that might make things worse. Once it got low enough, the sludge would likely become too thick to move through on its own. Problem solved. It might have already stopped.

Making up his mind, Bucky returned to the generator and cut the power. In the sudden silence, the sound of approaching footsteps was unmistakable.

Confused, his first reaction was to look for somewhere to hide. Realizing how ridiculous that was, he tugged at his shirt and gathered his bearings. It had to be Kevin. The guy realized he'd be better off staying in Redemption and changed his mind. Good, he could get his opinion on things.

Stepping outside, Bucky was stunned to see the mouthy operator rapidly approaching him. Jamie. Jamie Pratt was his name, and he looked particularly *pissed*.

"What have you done?" Jamie bellowed, stopping close enough for spittle to fly onto Bucky's face. "What have you done!"

Blinking, Bucky took a step back and tried to piece it together. "Who are you?"

Jamie pointed at the retention pond. "How much?"

Clearly, he wasn't just an operator.

"How *much*?"

"At least 200,000 gallons," Bucky replied automatically, feeling nauseous. "Everything that was in there."

Scowling, Jamie spun away from him and walked to the edge of the pond. Cursing, he looked back at Bucky. "Was it treated at all? Please tell me you aren't stupid enough to be dumping it without *any* treatment."

No, not an operator.

Bucky considered his options, his mind racing through various scenarios that all ended the same way. He'd spent many sleepless nights thinking about what he'd do...how he'd handle an exposure.

Plausible deniability. The ability for senior officials in a chain of command to deny knowledge or responsibility for the criminal actions of others. "I didn't know!" he blurted.

Jamie's scowl deepened and he moved so quickly that Bucky didn't have a chance to react before he found himself slammed up against the side of the shed. "I'm not interested in hearing any of your cowardice bullshit! What I want from you right now is whether or not that water was treated!"

Bucky shook his head, a small gasp escaping him as Jamie removed the weight from his chest. "I didn't know," he repeated, already starting to believe his own lie. It felt so much better than the crushing guilt. "Kacey put this together. I just found out about it and was trying to stop it! But it's too late!"

Jamie quickly surveyed the clearing: the pond, the shed, the pump. He followed the piping from where it came out of the shed and disappeared into the ground. Walking a short distance into the trees, toward the river, he then came back with an incredulous look of utter horror. "Straight into the river?"

"Kevin," Bucky stammered. "Kevin Carpenter. I knew I shouldn't have let Kacey hire him, but he was in on this. He told me about it all this morning when I confronted him." It was another blatant lie, but he was warming up to it.

Clearly not believing a word of it, Jamie pointed a finger at him, a dangerous look in his eyes. "I should have moved on you weeks ago, to hell with the bureaucracy. Now—" he shook his head, looking again toward the river.

His adrenaline fading, Bucky began to think more clearly. Considering the situation, he had to do more than simple damage control. They were in a situation where he couldn't afford to lose the support of the council. The welfare of his family depended on his ability to maintain control and provide for them.

"You're trespassing on private property," Bucky said, already scheming how he'd proceed over the course of the next several hours.

It was the wrong approach. Reaching behind him, Jamie started to withdraw a weapon while pointing at Bucky with the other hand. "Uh-uh. You don't get to do that. I'm going to—"

"Hey!" a young voice called out, making both men freeze.

Pivoting, Bucky couldn't quite believe what he was seeing. Pushing his bike and looking very tired and dirty, was Sam Adams. "Sam!" he called out, walking away from Jamie. He was counting on the guy's inability to scare or harm a child to come to his aid. "I'm Mr. Marsh. Remember me? I came and spoke to your class last week for career day. I'm a friend of your father's."

"Hey, Mr. Marsh," Sam said casually, though he was looking back and forth hesitantly between the two men. He had to have heard them arguing.

Bucky knelt down so that he was at eye-level with the child. "You know, your dad is very, very worried about you. He's been out looking for you all afternoon."

Sam's eyes widened and he gulped audibly. "Oh...well, I, uh kinda got turned around."

Nodding, Bucky glanced over his shoulder at Jamie and then back at Sam. "That's easy to do up here on the mountain. My radio won't work this far away, but I'd be happy to give you a ride home. How does that sound?"

Smiling, Sam let the bike fall and gave Bucky a hug.

I'll know when they start getting sick.

Bucky pushed the thought away, already denying to himself that he'd ever been tempted not to report the polluted water. He wouldn't have done that. He wasn't that sort of man.

Taking Sam's hand, he then picked the bike up in the other and walked with him over to the truck. Jamie stared at him the whole way, leaving no doubt that the conversation ... or the consequences, weren't over.

43

D AKOTA
Mountains near Redemption, South Dakota

"WHERE EXACTLY ARE WE?" Dakota asked as she scrunched up her nose and stared at the azure sky. The sun had passed overhead a couple hours ago, meaning it was heading into late afternoon. Her dad would be getting ready to gather a formal search party. For all she knew, he could already be doing it.

Maggie had taken them beyond the range of the radio a few miles back, so they weren't hearing any updates and had missed a check-in. It took some convincing to get her dad to agree to the two of them pairing up in the first place, and Dakota could already hear the lecture she'd be getting from him later on. But she'd gone way past the point of caring about that sort of stuff. Getting in trouble was the least of her concerns.

They had to keep going, after finding a power bar wrapper next to what looked like fresh bike tracks in the dirt that turned onto a random side road. She'd be adding littering to the growing list of reasons to ground her brother.

"It's Grandpa's property," Maggie said. She was still seated on Felix's tall back, looking down at her, even though Dakota had been sitting on the ground for a good ten minutes. "Are you rested enough yet?" Maggie asked without bothering to hide her growing impatience.

Dakota moaned. She couldn't remember the last time she'd ever ridden a bike as far. Probably never, and especially not so many steep miles on something that barely qualified as a road. But aside from her Jell-O legs, there was another reason she was hesitating. "Are you *sure* you know where we are?" Dakota insisted. "Because I feel sorta like we might be lost. I've lost track of how many times we've turned, doubled back, and turned again. It all looks the same out here."

Maggie crossed her arms over her chest and huffed, clearly offended. "Of *course* I'm sure. I mean, yeah…it's been a while since I've been this far into what Grandpa calls the back-forty, and I was always with someone else, but I know where we are. It wouldn't make any sense to stay on Canyon Road, since your dad is already driving all the way to the top and back." She waved a hand around at the trees that surrounded them. "It was logged up here like, a hundred years ago or something. Grandpa told me this super cool story about it once, and showed me this really old saw and some other tools that were left behind. Only reason anyone comes up here now is for hunting and camping and stuff."

Not sure if she felt any better, Dakota slowly stood on trembling legs and looked around. She was at a sort of crossroads again: either keep going in the same direction as the possible bike track, or go back to town and let her dad know about it. She stared up at the sky again. It was going to take at least a half-hour just to get far enough to use the radio, even with going mostly downhill. If they went much further, they'd get stuck out there in the dark and the search would probably expand to include them, too.

Maggie might be the local, and related to the guy who owned the property they were on, but that didn't make Dakota feel any less responsible for her. It was easy to forget the girl was only twelve-years-old. If Maggie didn't get back home soon, her parents were going to be worried sick.

"We need to go back," Dakota finally said, having made up her mind. When Maggie huffed again, she put a hand out to stop her complaint. "Seriously, it's getting too late. We have to go. Doesn't Felix need more water or something?"

Maggie shifted in the saddle and frowned, looking down at her hands in defeat. "I guess you're right. If I'm not home by dinner my mom will probably never let me take Felix out here again." She reached out and stroked the horse's muscular neck. "That would suck."

Dakota grinned in spite of her discomfort as she got back on the bike. She'd have to remember that the way to reason with the bull-headed girl was through her horse. "Thank you," she said, and meant it. "Thank you for helping me."

"You betcha!" Maggie quipped, whipping Felix around. "This was tons better than spending the rest of the day with my brothers. They drive me insane. I mean, you know how it is, right? Nag, nag, nag. They never leave you alone! One time, I was..."

Dakota began to tune her out, and instead focused on the crunch of her tires as she dodged some impressive potholes. She noticed that there were also some deep ruts and wondered what had caused them. There had to have been some big trucks driving through somewhat recently to—

Her head snapped up at the sound of an approaching vehicle. They'd heard distant engines a couple of times but hadn't seen anyone else the whole day, not since her dad passed them before they turned off the main road. Her first thought was that maybe that's who it was. But it was coming from the wrong direction, and her dad would be in Redemption by then, gathering help for a more thorough search.

"Uh-oh," Maggie muttered, as an old pickup came into view. "I'm toast. That's my dad."

Dakota's immediate flash of guilt over dragging Maggie into her problems turned to elation, when she saw a familiar face in the passenger seat. "Sam!"

Letting the bike drop, she ran to the truck when it came to a stop and threw open the door. "Sam! You're okay!"

Sam blinked at her with such a casual expression that Dakota wanted to throttle him. "Geeze, I'm okay!" he gasped, squirming away from her on the seat so she couldn't properly hug him. "Do you think Dad's gonna be mad?"

Laughing evilly, Dakota leaned back and placed her hands on her hips. "Oh, little man, you have *no* idea." Feeling satisfied by the appropriately terrified look on her brother's face, she shifted her focus to Mr. Marsh. "Thank you!"

But Mr. Marsh was ignoring her, and leaning out his window to stare at his daughter. "Maggie-May, what on *Earth* are you doing out here? And on Felix! If your mother knew she'd never allow you on that horse again!" He glanced behind the truck then, and back at Maggie. "Go. Now. Get yourself home and we'll pray she doesn't ask too many specific questions."

Dakota remained standing awkwardly in the open door, unsure of what to say. The guy was sweating so much that his shirt was soaked through, and he didn't look like he felt very well. He looked behind them again.

"Dad?" Maggie said, edging closer on Felix. "Are you okay?"

"Of course, I'm okay!" he spat, wiping at his face and then rubbing his hands on his thighs before replacing them on the steering-wheel. "I'd just like to get this boy back home, and there's too many things going on right now to have to deal with more needless drama, including you and your blatant disregard for our agreed-upon rules."

The whine of a smaller engine revving echoed through the trees, causing Mr. Marsh's head to jerk around. Licking his lips, he finally acknowledged Dakota. "Throw your bike in the back. I'll take you both home."

Maggie waved goodbye half-heartedly as she turned Felix and started back down the road the way they'd come. As Dakota grunted with the effort to lift the bike, she was oddly disappointed by how she felt. What should have been a massive relief was instead confused by her brother's lack of remorse and the older man's odd behavior. Getting into the truck, she was especially bothered that she'd gotten Maggie into so much trouble.

"It really isn't Maggie's fault," she said somewhat timidly as Mr. Marsh started driving without uttering another word. "She was just trying to help me, and I take full responsibility."

"Well, that's very noble of you," Marsh said evenly. He glanced in the rearview mirror, his hands spasmodically clasping at the steering wheel.

Dakota twisted in the seat, and spotted a plume of dust rising on the road behind them as the sound of the approaching engine got louder. She frowned at Mr. Marsh until he briefly met her eyes. "Is everything okay?"

A man on a motorcycle passed them, going much too fast for the road. Marsh muttered something under his breath and then rolled up his window as the dirt that was kicked up began to seep inside. "It's fine."

Sam surprised Dakota by taking her hand. "He was there," he whispered.

Her frown deepening, she looked at her brother and then at Marsh again. "Who was where?"

His fingers spasmed again, and Marsh shifted on the seat nervously. "No one. Just an employee of mine up at...a remote site. It's nothing that concerns you, I'm just glad I happened to find your brother." He looked pointedly at Sam. "Wandering around on private property this big is a dangerous thing to do, son. You could have gotten lost if I hadn't been there."

Sam sank further into the seat and squeezed at Dakota's hand.

Confused by the whole situation, she decided the best thing to do was to shift the conversation to something the guy was comfortable with. She didn't know much about him, except that he ran the fracking company, was really rich, and according to her dad, thought a lot about himself. "You're right. Sam was *very* lucky. We'll never be able to thank you enough."

His posture relaxing, Marsh gave a curt nod and even managed a small smile. "No thanks are necessary. We look out for each other around here. That's what Redemption has always been about." He was silent for a moment, staring intently at the road. "Remember that."

Dakota didn't know what to say, so remained silent. Pulling her backpack up into her lap, she pulled out the radio. Turning it on, she was relieved to hear voices after driving for only a few more minutes.

"May I?" Mr. Marsh asked, holding out a hand.

After he reported in and notified dispatch that both Sam and Dakota were safe, her father requested they meet at their house. The three of them rode the rest of the way into town in silence, and Dakota was so relieved when they pulled into the driveway, that she was opening the door before they'd even come to a complete stop. She didn't care anymore if she got into trouble. She'd much rather face her father's wrath than spend another minute in the hot, stuffy truck with the rancid-smelling man.

Her dad was waiting, standing in the driveway with an air that was hard to interpret. Like herself, he appeared to have a mix of emotions. Though smiling, his body was tense, and he was standing in a way he normally reserved for the workplace. It certainly wasn't the warm welcome for Sam she'd been expecting.

Sam didn't seem to notice, and he ran to their dad, throwing himself at him. At some point during the drive home, he must have come to terms with the fact that maybe he hadn't been as okay as he'd been pretending to be.

Dakota quietly retrieved her bike and walked with it around the truck and to the front of the garage. She couldn't hear what her father was saying to Sam, but her little brother was nodding his head eagerly while pressed up against his chest.

"Okay." Standing, Derrik patted at Sam's shoulders and then shooed him toward the house. "Inside. Go get a bath running, listen to your sister, and we'll talk more when I get back."

"Back?" Dakota asked, abandoning the bike. How could her dad be leaving again after what happened?

Mr. Marsh had exited the truck but was unusually quiet. Instead of acting the hero and rushing in to get his thanks, he was hanging back and staring questioningly at her dad.

Derrik was returning his stare, his body tense, hands at his sides. "Go help your brother," he said without looking away. "I'll explain later ... I'm glad you're okay," he added, with a sideward glance at her. "Now, go inside."

Her confusion growing, Dakota did as she was told. She found her brother standing in the middle of the bathroom, staring at the tub. "Here," she said, moving around him to turn on the water. "I got it. Go find a towel and whatever else you want. We can keep the light on in here while you're in the bath."

"I thought I found it," he whispered, without moving from his spot. "It sounded just like...*then*."

Twisting around on her knees to look at Sam, Dakota's irritation turned to concern when she saw the genuine sorrow in his deep-brown eyes. "Found what? What are you talking about? Dad said earlier that the plane crashed on the other side of the mountain."

Sam shook his head and sighed. His face screwed up and a tear slid down his left cheek. "I don't know...I, it just—" He turned away. "It sounded like when they...when they took— Mom."

She was so tired. Dakota didn't know if she'd ever been so tired, both physically and emotionally, and it was making it hard for her to concentrate. To make sense of what her brother was talking about. How had it turned into a discussion about their mom?"

"Sam, I don't understand." She figured the best response was an honest one. "You heard something in the woods that reminded you of—the accident?" He'd never...*never* spoken of the accident before. All Dakota knew about it was what she'd heard that night and read in the papers. Sam was taken to the hospital from the scene, and their dad identified their mom while she was still trapped in the car. It took a while to get her body out.

Sam nodded. When he looked back at her, his eyes were wide and he appeared more confident. "It sounded just like the engines. The engines from...the *ship*. The one that took her."

Dakota reeled away from him, standing abruptly while reaching out for the wall to steady herself. Was her little brother losing it again? Maybe everything that happened the night before had pushed him back over the edge and he was having some sort of breakdown. He'd retreated into a fantasy world before, where he insisted their mom was still alive, and it had taken over a year of professional therapy to bring him out of it.

She felt sick to her stomach.

"But it wasn't." Sam's shoulders slumped and he sighed. "It was just some pump thingy those guys were arguing about. Kinda weird, having a swimming pool in the woods."

Dakota blinked. She couldn't keep up. At least he understood he'd been wrong. But, wrong about what? Maybe there was a helicopter at the accident all those years ago, and he was confused about it. Sometimes the easiest approach was none. She'd let it go, and not push him about it. At least for now.

Turning the water off, she instead chose to comment on the part that didn't necessarily involve them. "I'm sure Mr. Marsh has a lot to deal with. He said the guy was an employee so I wouldn't worry about it. Just get your bath, okay?"

With Sam situated, Dakota's curiosity was at an all-time high. What had her brother stumbled into the middle of? Because her dad was seriously acting weird, too. She went to her bedroom since her window overlooked the front of the house.

The curtains were still open, so she approached cautiously from the side and then peered out slowly. Her dad had moved to within a

couple of feet of Mr. Marsh and the other man was talking animatedly, throwing his hands around in obvious agitation.

To Dakota's shock, her dad casually reached around to remove
the cuffs from his utility belt, and in the midst of all the unex-
plained craziness, they fell a little further down the rabbit hole as
he arrested the most powerful man in Redemption.

44

J AMIE
City Hall
Redemption, South Dakota

JAMIE SLAPPED his hand onto the desk, the metallic emblem in his palm clacking against the wood. "We haven't been properly introduced."

As he stepped back, Sage looked down at the gold-colored badge with the eagle at the top and the words 'Environmental Protection Agency' written under it in blue. Below that was the department insignia and 'Special Agent' at the bottom.

There was a moment of silence so complete that Jamie could hear a child calling to another from below the City Hall office, out on Main Street. "The EPA?" she finally asked, the shock clearly discernable in her voice.

Jamie stuck out his hand. "Special Agent Jamie Pratt. I've been here as part of an undercover investigation of the Marsh Fracking Site for the past month."

Sage didn't respond with a smile or even try to look impressed. While she leaned forward to shake his hand, it was with an obvious lack of enthusiasm. "For *months* I tried to get you guys to do something. Marsh should have been closed down years ago; you know— right about the time their *first* spill sickened three people and killed my mom."

Jamie shifted his weight and squinted at her as he cautiously chose his words. "That, um...incident, was the year before I was hired as a special agent." He'd read the files, of course, but since that case was closed and the current investigation was unrelated, it had been nothing more than background research. He glanced out the window behind the desk and to where people were milling down in front of the diner.

Olson's Diner. Olson.

Jamie flinched. He felt like a fool for not making the connection sooner. She wasn't just a waitress at the restaurant, but the owner. "Your mother must have been Carol Olson. She died of a rare form of leukemia four years ago, one year after the fracking started."

"A very rare form of leukemia," Sage said quietly, sliding her arms forward to either side of the badge. "The kind you can get from benzine exposure, which you and I both know came from the unreported spill at the site. A spill that was never fully investigated because no one was willing to come forward about it officially."

"Your mom settled out of court," Jamie reminded her. "Just like the other alleged victims. Without any proof, witnesses, or victims, there was no longer a case." He immediately regretted being so blunt when she jerked back and jumped up, pointing a finger at him.

"The only reason my mom did that was so Dad and I would be forced to let it go!" Sage yelled, her face growing red. "I was consumed by it, and putting together my own investigation since the EPA refused to, was the only way I could keep my sanity while my mom died in front of us."

Jamie didn't try to argue with her. There was nothing to be gained by it, and it wasn't his fight. While he'd rather take the time to handle the situation with more tact, he wasn't in the right frame of mind. The whole town was at risk, and hashing over past EPA failures would get them nowhere.

Sage turned her back to him and walked closer to the large window. It offered a great view of downtown from the second floor of the building, and was framed with a rich wood trim that likely dated back to the early years of the town. Much like all of the other antique furniture in the Mayor's office, it leant an air of the old west and a time when oil lamps and horse-driven carts were considered luxuries. Something that might once again become a normal part of life in Redemption before too long.

"Mom wanted a nice funeral without bankrupting us, and to pay off the second mortgage on the diner before giving it to me," she said with less anger, without turning around. "She took the settlement for *me*. Except what she couldn't understand, was that instead of freeing me, it buried me along with her. It was murder. My *mom's* murder, and there wasn't a thing I could do about it."

It was rare for Jamie to find himself so indecisive. They were in the middle of several different disasters, any of which on their own would warrant a full emergency response. It was hard to see clearly through it all, while still wanting to deal with the emotional confrontation he'd unknowingly stepped into. Before he'd navigated his way through his internal debate, Sage squared her shoulders and turned to face him.

The fight was gone from her eyes, replaced with a mixture of embarrassment and sadness. When he opened his mouth to say something likely inadequate, she put a hand out to stop him. "I owe you an apology."

Jamie shook his head. "No, I'm the one who needs to apologize. I blindsided you with this, and if I'd done my job better, I would have known who you were before walking in here. You're entitled to an emotional response, considering what you've been through."

Sage chortled. "An emotional response is exactly what I *can't* afford right now, but a lack of sleep and this overwhelming feeling that the world is crashing down around us is making that harder to control." She pressed her fingers to her temples. When Jamie eyed her questioningly, she let out a long breath. "I'm running on pure caffeine at this point. I love Lisa's coffee, but it's going to be the death of me if I don't collapse in my own bed soon."

Jamie grimaced. "You might want to pour another cup."

Sitting back down very slowly, Sage stared intensely at him with her intriguing green eyes. "Since I'm done unloading my personal baggage against the agency you work for, I suppose we need to get to the real reason why you're here. I don't think it's just to show off your shiny badge and impressive ability to blend in with the operators."

Joking. That's a sign of good coping skills. She'll need that if she's going to stay behind that desk.

Jamie chose one of the two leather chairs facing the desk, and sat on the edge with his fingers interlaced, taking on a less confrontational posture. "I just came from an illegal dumping site up the mountain. I suspected that one existed, but hadn't been able to locate it before following Bucky up there today."

Squinting at him, Sage tilted her head. "Why now? Because your timing sucks." She spread her arms out, palms up. "We're in the middle of a crisis here, and you choose now to make your move? You're a federal agent. I could have really used your help last night when we were struggling to figure out the best way to respond to all of this. You do remember that our civilization appears to be under some sort of attack?"

"Every point you've made is valid." Jamie shifted in the chair, once again having to think through how to explain things as precisely as possible. "Until this morning, I didn't have enough information to make the decision to break cover. The investigation has been on-going for months, and involves a whole team of investigators. We failed your town once already and I didn't want that to happen again, if it could be avoided."

When Sage only gave a small, accepting nod in response, he continued. "I talked to Derrik while we were in Deadwood, as soon as the full depth and breadth of the failures were confirmed."

"And you tried to talk to me when you got back this morning," she said with a small smile. "I just thought you were making a very poor attempt at flirting with me." Sage patted the gun under her shirt.

Hanging his head, Jamie appreciated her attempt to lighten the mood. He needed it. He normally relied heavily on his first, or sometimes second impressions of people, but Sage Olson was proving to be an anomaly. He didn't quite have her figured out yet, but he was feeling more confident that she could handle the coming storm.

"I'm on board with anything that involves sticking it to Marsh," Sage continued, moving around to sit on the edge of the desk a couple of feet away from him. "But you still haven't told me why any of this matters right now. The fracking site is shut down, and I don't see how some remote illegal dump up the mountain trumps our other concerns at the moment."

"I stopped and talked to Derrik first, before coming here," Jamie said. "He should be arresting Marsh right about now."

Sage froze, processing the information before slowly smiling. But as she continued to stare at Jamie and observed his body language, along with the implications behind his actions, the smile faded. She stood. "Why? What did he do?"

"You need to move up the council meeting for tonight," Jamie replied, encouraged by her ability to properly interpret things. "Because Redemption has a serious water issue, and you need to take action soon. Very soon."

Her shoulders sagging, Sage stood and grabbed at the radio that was sitting on the desk. With her other hand, she picked up a massively large ceramic coffee mug painted with a woodsy scene. "You're right. I'm going to need more coffee."

45

S AGE
City Hall
Redemption, South Dakota

"I DEMAND that you remove these, immediately!" Bucky shouted, holding his cuffed hands up for everyone in the council meeting to see. "You have no proof of my involvement and no legal grounds for any of this!"

"I think they look good on you," Ed said with a wry grin. "Should have been in 'em a long time ago."

Javi stood, while shooting Ed a disapproving frown. "Is it true there's no proof?" he asked Sage. "I apologize for being absent this morning, but I had to attend to my stores. Food is already starting to spoil due to the generators running out of gas, and I had to personally chase off some potential looters."

Shifting his focus to Derrik, Javi gestured toward Bucky. "Proof or not of something illegal, I'm afraid I don't understand how this can take priority over these other, more urgent matters. Unless you caught Bucky breaking into the freezer at the diner?"

Bucky scoffed, playing perfectly into the opening Javi had given him, and Sage realized she needed to take control of the meeting. "Sit down!" she shouted, slapping her hands on the table. When Javi flinched, she looked to where he was standing across the table from her. "Please. Allow us to explain and then we'll address everyone's concerns."

Derrik was already standing at the front of the room, where he and Jamie were flanking Bucky. Once Javi sat down without further comment, Derrik raised a hand to get everyone's attention. "Agent Pratt here is with the EPA," he explained with a nod at Jamie.

Bucky's face darkened, and Sage got a small amount of satisfaction at witnessing his initial understanding of how utterly screwed he was. She could see the wheels turning as his face twitched while he thought back over the past month, and everything Jamie might have been witness to.

Jamie stepped forward. "I work in the Criminal Investigation Division, where we investigate and prosecute offenses of the environmental statutes. I requested that Deputy Adams assist me in arresting Mr. Marsh for violation of the Resource, Conservation and Recovery Act, involving the improper disposal of hazardous waste."

"I didn't know!" Bucky retorted, shaking his hands again. "Not the specifics, not until today. This was all Kacey's doing, and Carpenter was the one helping him, which is how I found out after confronting him this morning."

Sage frowned as she looked up at the man she'd come to despise over the years. He was pathological, and already believing his own lies. The problem was that it made him very convincing, and if she hadn't already known better, it would be tempting to believe him.

Trent ran a hand over his head as he leaned back in his seat and whistled. "I can't say I'm necessarily shocked by any of these accusations, but I'm having a hard time grasping why you all are acting on this information now."

"Because part of my investigation this past month was testing the water supply from the local spring," Jamie said without any hesitation. "Trace amounts of several fracking toxins were detected."

Sage carefully gauged the reactions of all the people gathered in the room. Aside from the council were Derrik, Jamie, her dad, and then the doctor and Callie. The two of them were seated together at the other end of the table and had been quiet up until that point.

Dr. Pearlman looked appalled. "You had evidence of contamination and didn't notify the town? You have to know what sort of health effects that could have!"

"It wasn't enough." Jamie glanced at Sage, looking apologetic. "The trace elements were well below the FDA cut-offs for what's considered safe, though along with the other evidence I submitted, I was able to get a search warrant. It was going to be executed next week."

"What that all really means," Sage added, standing for emphasis. "Is that we know that the shit Bucky's been dumping is making its way into our water supply." Bucky opened his mouth to interrupt her but she cut him off. "200,000 gallons of untreated fracking wastewater were dumped directly into the river above town over the past twenty-four hours, and there's a good chance it's already seeped into the springs."

"Kevin Carpenter," Bucky muttered, repeating the name with less vigor. "It was him and Kacey that did it. I didn't know. The system they set up failed like everything else, and released it before I could stop it."

Trent looked at Derrik. "You know where this Carpenter guy is?"

"He was seen leaving town this afternoon," Derrik said, his jaw clenching. "So, he's conveniently blaming this all on a dead man and one who's disappeared."

"It doesn't matter who we blame it on!" Dr. Pearlman yelled. "We've got to take action now, before we start seeing symptoms. Even if there's only a remote chance of contamination, we can't risk it."

"What are the symptoms?" Erica asked, wringing her hands together nervously.

"Nausea, fever...probably vomiting and diarrhea." The doctor looked at Jamie for confirmation.

Jamie nodded. "Yeah, all of that and then potentially delirium, convulsions and eventually coma, depending on the level of toxicity."

Callie spoke for the first time, looking pale and afraid. "Do you have a way to test the water? You said you tested it before."

"No," Jamie said. "I had to send the samples in to our lab. We have to assume that the spring, as well as any wells on the south end of town, might already be contaminated."

"What a mess." Trent crossed his arms and confronted Bucky. "The way you have your finger on the pulse of every aspect of that fracking site? I find it hard to believe you didn't know about this."

"You're right," Bucky gushed, leaning toward him. "You're absolutely right, Trent. There are no excuses. Not when it's something as serious as this. I'm learning the full scope of it right now, right along with the rest of you and it's making me sick to my stomach. All I want to focus on is how to make this right. I'll do whatever is needed to make sure the people of Redemption have safe drinking water."

Sage cringed, finding to her surprise that she preferred the obnoxious arrogance to whatever act Bucky was trying to pull off. She was concerned that it might work, because she understood that in spite of however complicit he was, given the current situation, there were no rules to play by. It was about enduring the long-haul, and that meant having resources, some of which were only available through the very man responsible for their most pressing issue.

"We'll have to truck it into town down from the reservoir," Sage said before anyone could play into his martyr ploy. The reservoir was a natural body of water high up on the mountain, above where the wastewater was dumped. It was normally pulled from for farming irrigation and fed directly into the river, eventually making its way through the water table and partially feeding the towns spring.

It was also the source of a hotly-contested agreement between the town and Marsh industries, where Bucky was granted permission to draw a million gallons a year from it, at a cost that was beneficial to Redemption but a huge savings to Marsh.

Bucky was quick to take advantage of her announcement, just like Sage knew he would. "You're going to need water trucks for that."

Jamie scowled at him. "I'm sure you have a proposal."

"Well," Bucky said, feigning meekness. "Given your lack of evidence proving *any* of the allegations you've made against me, I'm willing to overlook the way I've been treated in the spirit of community, to do whatever I can to atone for what my employees have done without my knowledge."

Sage was pretty sure she'd ground away half of her back molars, but managed to hold herself in check. Reaching out, she grabbed at her dad's arm in an attempt to silence him. He was an incredibly intelligent man, but sometimes failed to recognize the interconnected workings of politics and the people involved.

"You have no proof?" Javi asked, looking quickly from Bucky to Jamie, and then to Derrik.

"Obviously, most of my reports and findings aren't accessible at the moment," Jamie explained. "But you have my eyewitness account of numerous violations of various natures at the site, as well as a conversation between Marsh and Carpenter I overheard, and then what I saw today."

"Eyewitness account," Javi repeated, glancing over at Erica. "From a man I've never met before."

"From a federal agent," Derrik corrected.

"Does it matter?" Dr. Pearlman challenged. "We're wasting time. It's senseless for us to sit here, arguing over whether to throw Bucky into a jail we don't even have, instead of taking action *right now* to keep our water supply safe. That's all that's important."

Bucky was nodding. "I'm afraid the freshwater trucks I have on site are privately owned, so if you're hoping to get cooperation from the drivers, and access to the large store of diesel I have, you're going to need me."

Sage couldn't tell if he was lying, and looked hopefully at Jamie, who shrugged. "I don't know."

"He doesn't know because he's only been there for a *month*," Bucky said, jumping at the opportunity to prove his point, whatever that might be. "Some of those men have been on my payroll for five years. They're loyal to me. Just like my family is, and we control the majority of the beef and lumber rights in the valley. My family also has the largest horse ranch, wheat farm, and let's not forget The Mercantile. All resources that are going to come in handy over the coming months...maybe even years."

"And there it is," Sage said, her voice dangerously low.

"*Are* the handcuffs really necessary?" Erica questioned while staring wide-eyed at Bucky, and Sage actually felt bad for her. The normally poised older woman looked a mess. The stress over the past twenty-four hours was catching up with all of them. Dr. Pearlman was right; they had to keep focused.

"Take the cuffs off," Sage said with a resolution that made it clear she was giving an order, not submitting to a demand.

Jamie was the first to react, and Sage found herself appreciating his quick show of support. "She's right." He gave Bucky a disgusted look. "He's more useful to us out there, with his clearly proclaimed resources, than he is in a jail cell."

Ed leaped up from his seat, sending his chair clattering backwards onto the wooden floor. "He has to pay for what he's done!"

"Stop it, Dad!" Sage put an arm out to prevent him from moving away from the table, and there was a tense moment where she thought he was going to push back.

One breath, two, and then his face relaxed as his hands balled into fists. Slowly, methodically, he retrieved the chair, set it upright and sat back down.

His silence weighed on her more than his outburst, and Sage took his hands in hers. "This isn't about us. It isn't even about what's right or wrong, but what has to be done in order for the people of Redemption to survive."

He nodded then, and unclenched his hands to hold hers. "Spoken like a true mayor."

As Derrik removed the cuffs from Bucky's wrists, Sage held Jamie's approving gaze briefly before looking around at the rest of the people gathered in the room. Some of them she'd grown up with, was friends with, and had buried loved ones with. They would all have to do their part if they were going to make it.

Clearing her throat, Sage stood, still holding one of her father's hands. "We're going to do whatever's necessary. We're going to survive."

46

WATCHTOWER
Undisclosed Location

THE HINGES on the Faraday cage creaked as Watchtower opened it and removed the encrypted radio from inside. The unique encryption key generated by the NSA (National Security Agency), ensured no one outside of Entangled could intercept the communications.

Convinced it wasn't going to work in spite of the protective box, Watchtower was surprised when after hooking everything up, the power button resulted in the device springing to life.

"Halfway there," Watchtower muttered, their anxiety rising. Power was one thing, having someone respond on the other end of the prototype radio was another. Enough of what had unfolded over the past thirty hours was a surprise, so that Watchtower was second guessing pretty much everything.

"Watchtower to Command." The act of speaking the words into the microphone was a relief, and helped soften some of their doubts. Watchtower was a part of something bigger than any movement in history, and there was likely a plausible explanation as to why the event had been so comprehensive. It was an accident. A malfunction of O.N.E., instead of an intentional act. Certainly, Watchtower would have been included in planning such a massive attack, after all the sacrifices that had been made.

Impatient, they keyed the mic up again. "Watchtower to Command."

"This is Command. Verify."

Their breath partially stolen, it was hard to form the words. "What happened? How did this—"

"Verify!"

Watchtower flinched, recoiling slightly from the glowing box. Such a small, unobtrusive device that somehow managed to represent all that had been lost. "Authentication: Alpha Sierra Hotel zero zero zero niner zero zero one."

A pause, followed by a couple of clicks.

"Good evening, Watchtower. Authentication accepted. Status?"

Good evening?

Blinking once, Watchtower stared with a mix of irritation and disbelief at the radio. "My status?" they repeated, incredulous. "My status is I'd like to know what the hell is going on!"

"You missed your initial check-in window by six hours. Your status?"

Tilting their head back, Watchtower tried and failed to get a better grip on their rage. "I missed the check-in because I've been scrambling to pick up the pieces of my op. In spite of all that, my status is green. What's yours?"

Another pause. More clicks.

"Command's status is green. Is Helix secure?"

Helix.

"You've lost him." Watchtower spoke into the room with disdain. Leaning toward the microphone, they stripped their voice of any obvious emotion before responding. "No, Helix is not secure from my position. He hasn't shown up, but his family is secure."

Radio silence.

"Request to speak with Oversight."

An extra long pause. *"Request granted. Stand by."*

Their agitation growing, Watchtower stood from the small, nondescript desk and began pacing the room. Noises drifted in from another part of the house, confirming that they weren't alone. They may as well have been, and unless they could get some direct answers, they'd have to take extraordinary measures to fortify their position.

"Watchtower! It's a relief to hear that you're okay, though I never had a doubt." The rich, baritone voice was unmistakably Oversight. He had a way of lulling anyone into complacency with it, including Watchtower.

"What happened?" There was no point to wasting time with pleasantries. It was all an act.

There was no pause. *"Clearly, the unpredictability of the quantum computer has taken us all by surprise. Though, I must say that while the extent to which some of our additional modifications were carried out has caused us some unexpected challenges, in the end, it's all beneficial to our goals. Entangled couldn't have hoped for a better outcome. Wouldn't you agree?"*

Watchtower stopped in their pacing and stared at the radio. No. They wouldn't agree that the end of civilization as they knew it was a good thing. The attacks were supposed to be specific. Targeted at key holdings, information caches, and some choice industries. Watchtower knew that power and communication would likely suffer some major blows, and the resulting chaos from the masses would threaten to collapse the market and lead to scores of deaths, but that was a far cry from what they were currently facing.

Watchtower methodically pressed the button on the microphone. "Of course, I agree. Do I need to hit the kill switch on the kid's family?" Watchtower had been a part of the urban terrorist network long enough to understand their place. They were the clean-up crew that handled the jobs no one else had the stomach for. Collapse or not, Oversight's reach would be far, so they'd have to tread carefully. If Watchtower played it right, the situation might still be salvageable, to where it was beneficial on a personal level.

"Not yet. You might need to use them to help...persuade Helix to cooperate. In order to ensure no one is allowed to rise from the ashes, we must make certain Helix is destroyed. That includes all traces or connections to it," Oversight directed. *"Can I count on you?"*

Watchtower grinned. If Oversight was counting on them, then perhaps the reach wasn't as far as it once used to be. "I've been in direct contact with the father, and will continue to monitor. I'll clean things up at the first sign of Helix."

"Excellent," the deep voice boomed. *"Oversight out."*

Watchtower set the speaker down and stepped back from the radio. Crossing to the window, they looked out at the thick, dark woods and listened to the rush of the wind blowing through the eaves of the cabin. They'd always been good at landing on their feet, and the more they thought about it, Oversight wasn't so far from the truth. It was all going to work out just fine.

Watchtower smiled. "Helix isn't in Redemption, but I am."

Made in the USA
Columbia, SC
06 July 2022

62836602R00192